MAIN

AMERICA LOVES ALESIA HOLLIDAY AND *AMERICAN IDLE*!

"I loved this book! It's laugh-out-loud funny
with characters that win your heart."
—SUZANNE BROCKMANN, *New York Times*
bestselling author

"*American Idle* is even more fun and much
smarter than reality TV."
—SUSAN WIGGS, author of *The Ocean Between Us*

"Turn off your TV and read this book!
I laughed my way through *American Idle*—much
more entertaining than any reality TV show."
—LYDIA FUNNEMAN, *Writers Unlimited*

American Idle

ALESIA HOLLIDAY

Making it

MAKING IT®

August 2004

Published by

Dorchester Publishing Co., Inc.
200 Madison Avenue
New York, NY 10016

ISBN 0-8439-5370-5

The name "Making It" and its logo are trademarks of Dorchester Publishing Co., Inc.

Printed in the United States of America.

Visit us on the web at www.dorchesterpub.com.

To three American women who are never idle:

My fabulous editor, Kate Seaver, who loved
my voice enough to launch a line.
Thank you for your enthusiasm and insight.

My talented agent, Michelle Grajkowski, who is
as hardworking as she is gracious. You're a star!

My wonderful friend, Beverly Brandt,
who said, "Just sit down and write the thing!"
So I did.

To D. S., the Deep Throat of reality TV:
Thanks for dishing!

ACKNOWLEDGMENTS

Thank you to everyone at Dorchester Publishing for this fabulous opportunity. I'm so glad to be part of the team. Tim DeYoung, Brooke Borneman, and Leah Hultenschmidt worked so hard behind the scenes to make *American Idle* a success. I'm forever grateful.

Thank you to Suz Brockmann for being a gracious mentor and kind friend. May you never have to eat processed meat food again! Thanks to Ed Gaffney and Eric Ruben for more fun than seemed possible during a week in a minivan!

Thank you to Susan Wiggs for your encouragement and support. You are amazing!

Thank you to Deanna Carlyle and the amazing writers and members of the Chicklit loop. Your support, encouragement, and senses of humor helped so much during this process. I'll never forget "Is it *gum*?"

Thank you to my awesome kids, Connor and Lauren, who love me and understand the "no new toys until Mommy sells another book" rule. You are my life.

Most of all, and always, thank you to my wonderful husband (and research department), Judd, who asked me what the heck a kitten-heeled Miu Miu was, and why did a woman need more than one pair of black shoes, anyway? You gave me the courage to take this leap into the unknown. You are forever my hero.

American
Idle

Prologue

POP STAR LIVE! And the winner is . . .

It doesn't matter who wins. It doesn't matter who wins.

I say it, but I know I'm kidding myself. Twenty-four million votes say it matters. A big, fat contract at KCM Records to the winner—worth a million bucks, minimum—says it matters. Lurking backstage, I split my attention between the only two men who've seen me naked in the past two years. Well, with the lights on, anyway.

One onstage, one in the front row.

I'm as caught up in the drama as anyone else in the country. More, maybe. I'm part of it. Me. Jules Vernon. *People* magazine's "Face Behind Reality TV."

What a joke.

"And, finally, the name we've waited all these long weeks to hear. America's new *Pop Star Live!* is . . ."

Chapter One

Concussion by Sauté Pan

How it all started:

"I need SEA SALT, you moron. Not salt with a freaking UMBRELLA on the box. SEA SALT! I am a chef, an *artiste*. Not a short-order cook at your local diner. Is my publisher hiring the mentally challenged, now?"

"Er, your list didn't specify . . ."

"Of course it didn't *specify*. What kind of idiot would have to be told that you cook asparagus quiche with sea salt? You, Julia, are a media escort. Your job is to make my life easier. I don't ask for Evian water. I don't ask for Belgian chocolate or white roses. I'm not some freaking prima donna. I must have the right ingredients to do this demonstration on live television. I don't want all of Dallas to think I'm the kind of peasant who cooks with TABLE SALT."

[NOTE TO SELF: Bet she didn't learn to use the word *peasant* when she was growing up in New Jersey.]

"It's, um, Jules, not Julia. And I'll try to find sea

salt. But if you have to, could you make do? We only have seven minutes until your demo, and . . ."

When I woke up in the hospital, they said she'd smashed her sauté pan into my head. And then (like this fact was in any way important to my concussed brain), she'd gone on to do the segment. *Isn't that great? What a trooper!* Even with the stress of braining her media escort with a cast-iron instrument of death, she'd made quiche on live TV. *And look, she even sent flowers.*

Bitch.

I decide that this is the end of my media escort career, even before I press charges. Two years are up; time to move on. So I call Jerry. Again.

"Oh, God, has it been two years already?" At least he recognizes my voice this time. The last time I called, he started yelling at me about missing my first day at Chuck E. Cheese's. Now *there's* a job. The constant headache of screaming, obnoxious two-year-olds. OK, so it wouldn't be that different from media escorting. Except nobody at the pizza place would expect me to have hot monkey sex with them.

Anyway, Jerry apologized by saying I have the same "little-girl phone voice" as pizza chick. *Little girl?* I was seriously ticked off at him for at least six minutes. But it's impossible to stay mad at Jerry, or J.B. as he's calling himself now. He reinvents my life every two years.

"I thought this one would stick, Jules. I mean, what the hell could be wrong with this position? All you've ever wanted to do is write a book. As a media escort you get to hang out with all these famous authors and even get paid for it. What is it with you and job hopping? Why can't you see a shrink, or screw a younger guy, or get liposuction, like everybody else your age?"

My age is *his* age, too, but Jerry likes to play the wise mentor in spite of his mere thirty-two years. He wears Armani suits with Seattle Mariners ball caps, and it somehow works for him. It's probably the tall, dark, and handsome thing he's got going on. We met when he was in law school, going through the mandatory phase of lusting after obscure Latin words and the idea of suing people. He used to whisper *res ipsa loquitur* to his girlfriend to get her in the mood. I wonder if he still does it with his current arm-candy of the week.

Back then, we couldn't go anywhere for lunch, because he was always threatening to sue. "This rug is raised up off the floor at least one-half inch. What if I tripped from your expository carpet-induced tortfeasance and sued for intentional affliction of emotional distress?"

If you think it's tough to get thrown out of McDonald's, try taking a law student to lunch.

I try again. "I did see a shrink, and she made me itch. The only younger guy I know is seven years old, and I'm not having someone vacuum fat out of my ass unless you go first. Besides, I'm tired of playing therapist to neurotic authors. Did I mention the concussion that Chef Francesca gave me?"

"I *love* her." He makes some noise he must think is a wolf whistle, but it sounds like an asthmatic walrus with sinus problems. "She makes the best Fusion tiramisu in the world, and she rocks in that red dress. Total wet dream. What part of Italy is she from?"

I sigh. Loudly. "Trenton. Look, Jerry, I need a job. You run the biggest job-hopping service on the west coast. You *owe* me." There's the little matter of how I covered for him back in school. The dean of his law school still doesn't know what happened to the bronze bust of Socrates. "What have you got?"

"It's career placement, Jules, and I'm running out of ideas for you. You wanted to run the fundraiser for that community college—you could learn golf at the same time. What happened to that?" Jerry's big on rhetorical questions.

"Golf is a stupid sport played by fat people in bad clothes. Besides, it wasn't *my* fault that she almost drowned. She should have said she didn't know how to swim."

"You don't usually expect to have to know how to *swim* to go *golfing*. Only *you* could turn a simple water hazard into the Whirling Fountain of Doom and almost drown the college president."

"It was Halloween. We had a haunted course theme." I was tired of defending myself over this one. When I raised $25,000 more than they'd ever made before, nobody was complaining. One teeny little near-fatality, and everybody gets their panties in a twist.

"Anyway, you're changing the subject, Jerry. I need a job and I need it fast. I took two weeks off last month to heal up from the concussion, so my funds are kind of low." Kind of low is an understatement. I'm reduced to hiding in the laundry room of my apartment building to keep from getting evicted. My skin smells like bleach and fabric softener. Trust me, Chanel isn't going to bottle the scent anytime soon.

"Heal up, Jules? Does that translate to hanging out in your mother's pool and getting tuna fish casserole brought to you on a tray? You escaped to the Midwest, didn't you? Whenever you go to Ohio, I know you're getting ready to bail on your latest job."

"Who else would go to Ohio for a life-changing cat-alyst? It's like Walden Pond, but with pot roast. Besides, you'd be bored without me. I'm a challenge, admit it."

He sighs, quite theatrically for someone with zero acting ability. Only Jerry can make a Serious Dramatic Production out of expelling wind. He probably does it when he farts, too.

"Oh, all right. You may be in luck. I've got something bizarre that just came up. One of those reality TV shows is in town auditioning people, and they called me in a panic about five minutes ago. One of their production coordinators got run over on Pike Street, evidently. Tried to cross the road against the light. Ha! They think *New York* traffic is tough." Jerry is taking an unseemly amount of pride in the hometown Seattle assault-by-car statistics, I think, but keep quiet. I *am* asking another favor, after all, and even best friends have their limits. I can't milk that Socrates thing forever.

"Anyway, they need another body fast. And it has to be someone who knows her way around a TV set and won't drool on the celebrities, yada yada. You'd be perfect for it."

"What kind of reality TV?" I am a closet *Survivor* and *American Idol* fan, but like to pretend that populist television is beneath me. I usually tell the authors I escort that I wouldn't even own a TV, except to watch the news. *Ha!* I get the travel trivia right on Regis and Kelly every day. And how the *hell* does she look so good five days after having a baby? But, whatever, I'm wandering. "It's not one of those things where they lock them up with rats and make them eat bugs, is it? Because I don't do bugs. Or vermin."

"Yeah, right, tell it to someone who hasn't met your boyfriend. How *is* Robert, by the way?" He says this in that snide little voice that all lawyers perfect. I think it's part of the bar exam. *"Applicant 1607B, you didn't sneer convincingly enough to pass. You'll have to do something worthwhile with your life, instead. We're terribly sorry."*

"Robert who?" No way I'm getting into the subject of Robert and his food fetishes. Licking whipped cream off my nipples, OK. Chocolate sauce on my neck, fine, although I felt like a mud wrestler taking *those* sheets to the laundry room. But sucking ranch dip out of my armpits was *way* beyond where I was going to let anybody go.

I still can't look at a salad bar without flinching.

"OK, back to the job?" I don't want to admit that I'm excited by the idea of doing TV. Not to either of us.

"Well, they need somebody fast and are a little desperate, so we'll puff up the excitement of your last job and they'll be happy as shit." Not that I think shit is ever happy, but Jerry uses lots of these inane expressions; slick as a pig in shit; does a bear shit in the woods?; shit happens. If I were a Freudian, I'd wonder about his early toilet training.

"Be at the convention center at ten A.M. And, Jules?"

"Yes?"

"This could *make* me in Hollywood job placement. You know how long I've wanted to break into the L.A. market. Don't screw this one up."

Chapter Two

Jules Vernon

That's me. Jules Vernon. Yes, I've heard all the jokes and, no, I'm not taking anybody around the world in eighty days. My parents met in college when Mom was going through her literature-is-my-life phase, and I was conceived on the floor in the back of the Lit 101 classroom. Dad's name is Tom Vernon, so you can figure out the rest.

I know, I know, tacky, but the tackiest part is that they actually *told* people this story. In front of me. My mom was pretty much as close to being a hippie as you could get, while still being hygienic. The whole free love thing left her cold; "all those *germs*," she'd say and shudder.

Dad and Mom got divorced about five years ago for no reason. I mean, *they* apparently thought they had a reason, but "grown apart" still doesn't make sense to me. There was no bimbo waiting in the wings, no big drama or tragedy. They decided they didn't have enough passion. I'm all for "P" words—piña coladas, Prozac, and Prada, for example—but I can't quite handle parents and passion in the same sentence.

It's sick and wrong.

The shrink—"call me your therapist, Jules, not shrink"—that I saw briefly a few years ago, before I discovered I was allergic to her, said that at twenty-nine I was too old to still be mourning my parents' marriage. She also said I confuse pain, anguish, and drama with love.

Which is *so* not true. I think you have to have euphoria, too.

We had this conversation about the time the itching started. Not that it was related. I read in a medical journal somewhere that you can be allergic to other people. Some women are allergic to their husbands' sperm, even. Not that Shrink and I were exchanging body fluids or anything. But you see my point.

And she refused to believe that my Sunday solution was a good answer for stress. It's pretty simple. I write down every stressful thought I have during the week and save them to freak out about on Sunday afternoon from one till three P.M. I think it's more efficient that way, but Shrink evidently hadn't read the chapter in the psychotherapy handbook about "thinking outside the box."

Plus, she kept harping about "moving on." Why is movement so important? How many of life's truths would we miss if we were always speeding past them instead of standing still with our minds and hearts open to the possibilities? So I quit seeing her before we ever got to the part about my impostor hang-ups. But we got a lot worked out during the time we were together. I mean, it was a thought-provoking three weeks.

The Job Interview

There must be 3,000 people lined up outside the convention center. The line stretches all the way down to Fifth Avenue. Starbucks has a cart with a couple of baristas ringing up big bucks for portable caffeine. I'm staring in a bug-eyed, open-mouthed sort of way at the most sequins, hairspray, and makeup the Seattle Convention Center has ever seen at ten A.M. I mean, it makes me feel about a hundred years old to say this, but some of these kids *must* be under the age-eighteen minimum for the show. (Yes, I did some research online; they've already held auditions in Omaha. That's right, Omaha. This is not exactly the top tier of television we're talking about here.)

As I thread my way past dozens of singers, hummers, sleeping bags, discarded shoes, and a pup tent to get to the front door, a lot of under-dressed teenagers who think I'm cutting in line blast me with the evil eye. The security guards keeping hopeful contestants from stampeding the door roll their eyes at each other. "Go to the back of the line, miss."

No way I've sunk so low as to be considered a fifteen-minutes-of-fame wanna-be, pending eviction or not. "I'm Jules Vernon; here to meet with Nellie Castano and Roger Scowl."

"Yeah, aren't they all. You got a number, that's your place in line. You'll get your turn soon enough." He hitches up the sides of his gray-blue pants, which are losing the battle with his enormous stomach. It takes everything I have not to watch as the belt slides slowly down his bulk. *Will his pants fall completely off? Will his belt somehow catch on his non-existent hips? Film at 11.* I tear my gaze away from his belly and find his nametag.

"Officer Sharp, if you'll check your information or call somebody, you'll find out that I'm here for the Production Coordinator job, and not as a contestant. Do I *look* like a contestant?" I gesture at my dove-gray power suit (Nordstrom's spring sale, $399; worn to all interviews) and then wave my hand grandly to encompass the Britney Spears look-alikes, boy-band clones, and Springsteen acolytes in line. "Plus, I couldn't sing if my life depended on it. Please check for me."

Sharp isn't living up to his name, but his partner flips through crumpled pages on a clipboard. "Here she is. Let her in, and I'll radio up that she's on the way."

Pantyhose

The women on the escalator look doomed. What is it about nine-to-fivers that makes them all look like they're heading off to the guillotine? Dead Women Walking in Pantyhose.

Maybe wearing pantyhose causes the bleak expressions. I tried to wear pantyhose today; I really did. But, the girdle-panty thingy got twisted up so badly when I put it on that the left leg was cutting off my circulation. I had to hop around with my leg hiked up at an unnatural angle, since it wouldn't bend in a normal fashion. Then I hopped the wrong way when I was reaching for my nail scissors on top of the plant stand, and I tripped over the toilet and got my knee wedged between the toilet and the wall, facing the wrong way.

This would have been bad enough, but the "I'm on the toilet, now I can pee" urge kicked in, and I was desperately trying to hold it, since I still had the stupid pantyhose on, and there's no way in hell that *that* weave was going to let anything through, let alone the gallon of coffee I drank this morning. Finally I got the edge of the nail scissors wedged under the waistband and cut them off, in the nick of time.

So I reach the fourth floor of the convention center, already wondering how somebody who's not smarter than her underwear is going to make it in the Fast-Paced World of Reality Television. But I figure I'll fake it, like I always do. How hard can it be, right?

Barracudas and Cholera

Nellie Castano looks about ten years younger now than she did in the late eighties, when she was a three-hit wonder. It's amazing what South Beach Dieting, laser teeth whitening, a personal trainer, and twenty or thirty thousand dollars' worth of plastic surgery can do for a girl. The *reality* part of reality TV doesn't apply to the hosts.

She doesn't look up when I enter the conference room, but continues tapping her long acrylic fingernails on the faux wooden tabletop, and reaming various new orifices in the brittle-looking woman standing across from her. "I distinctly remember that we put all of this in my contract. I don't have to listen to all the dreck, because I am the star. I am the judge. *Who* is the star?"

The ream-ee flinches, but answers so quickly I get the feeling that this is an established pattern with them. "You are the star, Nellie. You are the judge."

Nellie smiles, showing a lot of teeth. It's like watching an alligator stalk an unusually tasty heron. Except this reptile has blindingly white teeth. No laugh lines anywhere, either. "Then why am I lined up to listen to more than twenty auditions? Do you think I want to hear a hundred crappy variations on the same Norah Jones song? DO YOU? Do you *realize* that I had a migraine after those triplets in Nebraska sang their rap version of 'Somewhere Over the Damn Rainbow'? DO YOU??"

The assistant is trembling now and pushes the sleeves of her shapeless brown dress farther up on her sticklike arms. "No, Nellie, I don't. I mean, I do. I mean, I'll take care of it. No more than twenty auditions and those will all be the Seattle finalists. Is that all?"

Nellie leans back in her chair, satisfied to the depths of her black and orange troll soul. She turns her attention to me, and I suddenly know what barracuda bait must feel like in its final moments. Nellie doesn't look at her hapless victim again, but makes a flicking motion with her hand, like she's swatting a particularly annoying gnat. As the poor woman scurries out of the room, I walk forward and plaster what I hope is a friendly smile on my face. "I'm Jules Vernon. Jerry Blaine at JB Employment sent me over for the production . . ."

"I know who you are, for God's sake. Do you think I'd have let some stranger hear how stupid one of my staff is? Sit down and I'll call and find out where the *hell* Roger is." She tosses her perfectly cut, perfectly colored blond hair over one shoulder and pulls a tiny cell phone out of her purse. Even *I* know that, in cell phones and status, Size Does Matter, but this one is so small I don't have a clue how she's going to dial. Suddenly she stops with one perfect fingernail poised over the phone and narrows her eyes. "Jules Vernon? I know that name. Were you on the *Island Temptresses* pilot?"

I get this a lot. I bet people named Charlotte Dickens or Ernestine Hemingway do, too. (OK, Ernestine Hemingway is pushing it, but it's the best I can do on short notice.) The name is vaguely familiar, so they think they must know us. Er, me. Know *me*, I mean.

"No, this is my first . . ."

"I know." She smiles triumphantly, which is as scary as the other smile, to be honest. "You worked the shoot of *Can Your Marriage Survive This?* in Barbados, didn't you? I remember those hideous shoes."

Now, I can put up with a lot, but insulting my Manolos is over the line. *Way* over. Just as I'm getting ready to tell her off, the door opens again and one of the most gorgeous men I've ever seen strides in. Actually *strides*. No mere walking here. This guy is sex on the hoof, as my best friend Kirby would say. Sheer drama with big blue eyes.

I think Oh, God, *please* let this be Roger Scowl, and I'll donate all my pay to the church. After taxes, of course. And rent. And expenses. And I'll have to find a church, which may take a while. You have to be careful about charitable donations, considering what huge frauds some of these so-called charities turn out to be. Well, I'll give five bucks to the homeless guy standing outside the Cheesecake Factory.

Oh, scritchy sounds and Nellie's mouth is moving. She's talking again. ". . . is Jules Herman, Roger. Be gentle with her, she's fresh off the *Can Your Marriage Survive This?* shoot. Did you hear about the one wife going nuts after her husband was filmed in the hot tub with three of the Seductive Singles and one of the camerawomen? *Too* funny."

OK, revise "troll soul" to "demon spawn." Finding humor in the destruction of a marriage on national TV merits an instant promotion.

I'm deciding between keeping Jules Vernon and changing it to Jules Scowl after the wedding, when Roger drops the hand he'd been raising to shake mine and backs away. "The Barbados shoot? Did you come down with cholera? I heard there was a bad case of cholera running amok amongst the camera crew and staff down there. Were you one of them?

Did they quarantine you? Have you been checked out in hospital?"

The British accent doesn't sound so sexy when it's hysterical, in case you're wondering.

Before I can take a breath to answer, he pounces on Nellie, "Did you know about this? Do we have any quinine on the set? I won't have this. I won't!"

Nellie rolls her eyes. "Relax, Roger. There was no cholera. It was Barbados, not . . . not . . ." Naming a geographic location likely to have cholera running amok is obviously beyond her. "Well, it was Barbados. You Brits practically own that place, don't you? Don't you have the sense to keep diseases out? Anyway, calm down and meet our new production coordinator."

I'm the new . . . ? When did the interview happen? Was that it? Was I hired? As much as I hate to start talking and potentially ruin this, what with Jerry's final words still ringing in my ears, I have to straighten out the misimpression about my prior TV experience. It's only ethical, after all. "I didn't . . ."

"Have cholera. Yes, we know. We're not *all* moronic hypochondriacs around here. My assistant will show you around. This is your big chance, welcome to reality TV, blah blah blah. Don't screw it up."

It's like an omen that she would use Jerry's exact words, right? Omens trump ethical standards in all gray areas. It's practically a rule. So I shake Nellie's limp hand and thank her, then thank Roger, pretending not to notice when he cringes and puts a white silk handkerchief over his nose and mouth.

Jules the Con Artist strikes again. It's time to meet the contestants. *This will be fun.*

* * *

Seattle Auditions

My brain cells are melting. I have listened to more than four hundred of the worst singers in the state. No, the country. No, make that the known universe. There must be a pre-evolutionary worm on Pluto who sings better than this. If I were God, I'd be thinking about hurling a plague of frogs upon Seattle after hearing so many people butcher "God Bless The U.S.A."

Bless?? BLESS?? *MOSES, GET THE FROGS!*

The burning question in my brain, besides who has the Tylenol, is this: How are these kids so confident? These are mostly people who should never, ever sing outside of their own showers. Maybe not even then, if the bathrooms aren't soundproofed. And yet, they have the confidence and courage to come here and audition for total strangers for the chance to be on national TV. Whereas I, on the other hand, can work at a job for two whole years and still feel like I'm not good enough to do it. Posturing and impostoring my way through my days, waiting for the Aha moment I know is coming any minute.

Aha, you're not really a: production coordinator, media escort, fundraiser, writer.

Aha, you've been faking it all this time.

Aha, you're fired, we finally found you out, you're nothing.

But these kids, many of whom *deserve* an Aha, stood fearlessly before us, in their glittering approxima-tions of what they think pop stars wear. Belly-button jewelry and hope shining; cleavages and song lyrics polished. Nerves, yes. Jitters, stage fright, even anx-ious anticipation. But no real fear. No lack of confi-dence. How do they *do* it? We should answer *that* question, if we want to make reality TV that matters.

* * *

Lisette

Oh. Dear. Lord.

This girl can sing.

Her name is Lisette, and she has a good fifty pounds on the majority of the wanna-bees, or bees, as we're all calling them now. All I can figure is that every ounce of the extra weight must be used to support that voice. She's singing a jazzed-up remix of a Patsy Cline song, "Crazy," and Joe and Norman (my fellow PCs) and I are all holding our breath. As the last silvery notes of "crazy for lo-oving you" feather through the air, we all stare at her in disbelief.

It's like finding a gold mine in your garbage disposal. After two days, we're resigned to the musical equivalent of week-old spaghetti fragments and coffee grounds that had started to stink, and suddenly, Hallelujah, there it is. Or, rather, there *she* is. A powerhouse voice like a freight train wrapped in velvet.

We must have been staring at her for too long in utter silence, because she freaks out and starts twisting a few of the dozens of long, orange-tinted braids that reach nearly to her waist around her pudgy fingers. "Well, um, was that OK? Do you want to hear something else?"

"Dude!! No way!! That rocked!! That was totally a Luke-finding-the-Force-and-destroying-the-Death-Star moment!"

I may not have mentioned that Norman is the exec producer's little brother and has the brains of a flea. A flea that's been trapped in a *Star Wars* video for most of his twenty-something years. But he's Marshall's brother, and Marshall is God. And, I have to admit, it *was* kind of a destroying-the-Death-Star moment.

Lisette stares at us, hope battling confusion on her

round face. I jump in with the human translation of Norman. "We *loved* it. You're fantastic! What an amazing voice. You're definitely going in to Roger and Nellie for the finals."

Between you and me, Lisette is a shoo-in for one of the Seattle slots to go to Hollywood, but I can't tell her. No authority. We're the lowly PCs, ranking somewhere above the guy who delivers lunch, but below Nellie's makeup artist. Admittedly, on salmon Caesar salad day, we drop down a little.

To be fair, I have precisely zero musical ability, talent, or background. So Nellie, a former singer who cut at least one record, and Roger, a record producer, are better qualified than I am to decide who the finalists are. The simple truth about listening to four hundred singers audition in a row, though, is that even a rock could tell that this girl has a huge talent. I mean, she literally gave me chills.

I walk her through to our version of a green room, where Lisette can wait with the other twelve people we've picked so far to move up to Roger and Nellie. Seven of them have talent, though nowhere near as much as Lisette. The other five are the comic relief for the B roll. The ones who will get humiliated in person, and then over and over and over on commercials, and on the show, when the taped proof of their destruction will run again and again.

I warned one of the girls that we were setting her up, when I walked her in here. She was so hopeful and eager during her audition, it was painful to watch. A puppy panting for praise. I couldn't let her get eviscerated and live with myself.

That was in the morning on Day One. I can probably pull the wings off butterflies now.

Anyway, she refused my offer to bow out gracefully. She thanked me in an oddly dignified way for someone wearing a crop top that had NASTY spelled out in sequins across her chest and a SpongeBob SquarePants tattoo on her ankle. "I don't care. Maybe you're wrong, maybe not. Thank you for caring about me and trying to be nice or whatever. But *everybody's* on TV. Three hundred and fifty channels. If I can't get on one of them, even in a bad way, what kind of loser am I?"

It's not *reality TV* that matters. It's that our only reality that *matters* is TV. Our collective cultural consciousness has been reduced to the interstitial spaces between commercials for household cleaning products and Viagra.

Derek

Derek swaggers across the room like the guy in high school you secretly wanted to have sex with under the bleachers. You knew it was hopeless; he would only be taking the panties off of cheerleaders. So you pretended that your skinny co-chair on the debate team was hotter, because the Mind is an Aphrodisiac and all that lofty crap. But when you practiced kissing on your pillow at night, it was the fantasy of a Derek, sweaty after football practice, grabbing you and declaring his overpowering love and lust for you, that made your baby-doll PJs a little damp.

The thing is, we've heard a lot of Dereks in the past couple of days, and none of them can sing. Buoyed by unshakeable confidence and way too much . . . *is that* Old Spice*?? Do they still* make *that stuff??* . . . way too much arrogance, a couple of them blink at us when we say, "Thank you. Next." It never crosses a Derek's mind that he might not win the award, throw the touch down pass, hit a home run with bases loaded, or become the next *POP STAR LIVE!* Even when confronted with the evidence, rejection is unreal to somebody who's never faced it before. We had to let one of the Dereks sing three different songs before security finally led him out of the room.

This Derek, though, is different. This one can actually sing. He's a bizarre cross between Frank Sinatra and Justin Timberlake, but he can belt it out. And he is so hot in his black jeans and white shirt, with his golden-brown hair casually tousled in the style you know most guys would need five minutes in front of a mirror to achieve, but comes effortlessly to Derek. You can visualize the CD cover as you listen.

Derek's on his way to Hollywood, and *POP STAR LIVE!* is on its way to Reno.

Chapter Three

Reno

The next stop on our *POP STAR LIVE!* world tour is glamorous Reno, Nevada, which consists entirely of slums and casinos. Plus, the air is so dry I woke up with a nosebleed and the feeling that my skin had been mummified during the night. The auditions are in the enormous casino that takes up most of the square footage of the Dancing Nugget Hotel and, even though it's nine in the morning, there are dozens of dedicated gamblers already feeding change into slot machines with the kind of feverish intensity I reserve for wall-banging sex or shoe shopping.

We whittle the field of more than 2,000 hopefuls down to twenty in a two-day blur of hideous singing, oversized belt buckles, and cowboy hats, until we finally seat Nellie and Roger at the table, evaluating which two of the finalists we will rescue from casino hell. Our third judge, a very popular rap star who calls himself Infamous IQ, or Q for short, has yet to make an appearance. The *Star* and the *National Enquirer* keep running stories on a feud between Q and Nellie, so maybe he wants to spend as little time with her as possible. If this is true, I like him already.

Norman and I pegged the two we're sure will go to Hollywood. Amanda sings like Whitney Houston and looks like Christina Aguilera, so she's a sure thing. We're a little less positive on the guy side of the coin, but bet on Lucas. He's one of the dozens of country-star bees that Reno breeds like rabbits wearing imitation leather, but he's a great singer. He has that whole Garth Brooks thing going on, except he isn't bald. I don't know why he isn't trying out for one of the Nashville reality shows, but whatever. There's a boy who looks twelve, but isn't (we checked), who can belt out Broadway show tunes, but it's not the sound we're going for here, so our money's on Lucas. Norman says he has as good a chance as Anakin had to win the race on Tattoine in Episode I. I have no idea what that means, but it must be good. [NOTE TO SELF: Buy complete *Star Wars* DVD set, so I can translate Norman-speak.]

Notice that I said Norman and I. Joe won't actually speak to us. He's been in the business for about nineteen years, but never made it past production coordinator, and is morally outraged that I walked in off the street and have the same job. I probably get paid a lot less, but that doesn't matter. He tried to get me fired by telling everyone that I lied about having previous TV experience. I went to Nellie and tried to explain about the whole misunderstanding, but she brushed me off. I think she actually likes me a little, now that she thinks I'm deceitful and conniving. Joe doesn't actively mess with Norman, since he's Marshall's baby brother and Joe has a healthy sense of self-preservation, but he mutters snide comments whenever Norman pops out with a *Star Wars* reference.

* * *

Bingo on the contestants. Roger and Nellie pick Amanda and Lucas, after some almost desultory viciousness about the sacrificial lambs we sent up for the finals. We're *all* getting tired.

Oh, and the viciousness is all on *Roger's* part, too. Like every other reality show out there, *POP STAR LIVE!* decided it needed its own evil judge and picked Roger for the part. If ever there were a case of casting against type, this is it. Not only does Roger have to play Bad Judge, but—get this—Nellie plays Good Judge! To give the blow-dried devil her due, Nellie is an Oscar-caliber actress. Whenever the contestants are around or a camera switches on, she turns into Miss Sweetness and Light 2004.

After the second contestant runs crying from the room, Roger gets a tiny paper cut, which is a disaster, because in Roger's world, there are enormous, terminal-disease-bearing germs lying in wait everywhere for the chance to attack him. But, since the minute he freaked out about cholera and quinine, I know how to handle him. I have an uncle Herbert who once stayed in bed for six weeks after he got a mosquito bite and was convinced he had both typhoid *and* malaria. In Michigan.

Roger is a mere amateur in the hypochondria game, in comparison.

I rush up to the table and open my tote bag, newly stocked with Neosporin; antibacterial spray, wipe, and lotion; sanitized and sealed bandages; and, in fact, the entire contents of the first-aid kit from my car. Roger takes one look and decides I'm a goddess. He presents his wounded finger to me in supplication. I spray his whole hand with Bactine, liberally slather ointment everywhere and bandage it up till he looks like he barely escaped hand amputation by a meat grinder. This makes him deliriously happy, of course. When people participate in our delusions instead of mocking them, we believe they're on our side.

After Roger's Serious Medical Emergency, we get back to work, break down the mini-set, and give Amanda and Lucas their information packets. During this whole process, I try to ignore the death glares I'm getting from Joe. Now he probably thinks I'm sucking up to Roger. It's stupid and paranoid, but I'm starting to feel like the Storm Troopers are after me.

Oh, God. Norman is rubbing off on me.

Testicle Fungus and What Rhymes with Penis

The crew is going out for dinner, but I don't think I can stand another minute of Reno. I opt for room service and splurging on a pay-per-view movie. I'm up for a good romantic comedy; my life is all black humor and no romance right now.

After a bubble bath, which goes a long way toward draining the stress of this week out of my body, I'm waiting for my dinner and flipping channels, when my cell phone rings. It's Kirby, thank goodness. I don't think I'm up for talking to Mom or Dad right now. Maybe after a few more weeks, when I'm a Major Name in Television.

"Jules, thank God. I have to *rhyme* now. RHYME! After three years of writing perfectly good box copy about electric nipple clamps and vibrators named after movie stars, I have to *rhyme*." Kirby sounds like she could chew glass. "W&L hired some new marketing director who thinks he's the next Steve honkin' Forbes or something, and now I have to rhyme. Have *you* ever tried to find words that rhyme with penis? I challenge you. Name one. ONE."

Kirby has been my best friend since we were twelve years old and got detention together for starting a *Pass Your Algebra Test Now! Results Guaranteed!* class on school property. We claimed we were forward-thinking entrepreneurs trying to raise the level of academic excellence in the school, but Principal Gattley made us give everybody back their five dollars. Which was *so* unfair, because everybody passed algebra, even Wilbur the Weasel, and he never passed *anything* the first go-around.

I hear he's a retired dot-com millionaire now.

Anyway, Kirby's a copywriter, and her biggest account is Whips and Lace Manufacturing, Inc. (motto: *Your Pain is Our Pleasure*), a company that recently added retail shops around the country and is planning its IPO. The Internet seriously boosted sales of marital aids, if you know what I mean. The W&L account is worth a half million in annual revenue to her agency and made Kirby into a senior account exec. I like to tease her that dildoes paid for her new Mercedes, but she doesn't think it's funny.

"Jules! Are you listening to me or daydreaming again? If you're checking your e-mail when I'm having a crisis, I'm going to fly to Vegas and *kill* you!" Kirby is not a patient woman.

"It's Reno. The low-rent Vegas. And, yes, I'm listening to you. What about *Venus*? I just got out of the shower and am waiting on the room service guy. Hold on while I throw on shorts and a T-shirt." I grab my clothes and finish pulling my *Doesn't Play Well With Others* T-shirt over my head, when there's a knock. I put my earpiece in and head for the door. "Hang on Kirby, it's my food." As I open the door, I catch sight of my discarded panties on the floor and snatch them up. "You can put the tray . . . Roger?

What are you doing here?"

He strides into my room, looking like a darker-haired Hugh Grant. It's too bad that knowing what somebody's personality is like can ruin the fantasy. All that *striding* is so hot. But the constant haze of Lysol surrounding him totally dissolved my nuptial fantasies. He stops dead in the middle of my room and wheels around to face me. "Jules, I think I'm going to die."

With anybody else, I might be worried—he's white-knuckled, digging his nails into his palms, and his eyes are almost rolling around in his head. But this is Roger.

I close the door. "You're not going to die, Roger."

"Who is that? Who's Roger? Are you having a fling? Is it that sexy British guy? Oooh, I love British accents. Maybe I can use a British theme. Quick, ask him what the British word for penis is?" Kirby is practically shouting in my ear.

"I'm not asking him about British penises," I hiss.

Roger's mouth falls open. "How did you know? Does it show? Oh, my God, does *everybody* know?"

My head is hurting. "Does everybody know *what*, Roger? I'm talking to a friend of mine on the phone, and it's important. Perhaps I could meet you some-where later?"

Kirby pipes up again. She's not what you'd call quiet, either. "You're damn right it's important. I'm going to be up all night working on the copy for this new line of products. What the hell rhymes with humongous?"

Roger isn't budging. "Jules, I'm dying. I know it. I've got a fungus."

"You don't have a fungus, Roger. And if you did, people don't die from fungus. It's like, like athlete's foot or something. You get a spray."

"Fungus? FUNGUS? I can't rhyme humongous with fungus! I'm writing about a vibrator here, Jules! Nothing says Buy Me like crotch fungus. Are you *nuts*?"

Holy cow. I've got paranoia near tears in my hotel room and sarcasm shrieking in my ear. Luckily, another knock sounds on the door. Saved by room service.

"Jules, we—um, sorry, didn't know you were, um, entertaining, um—" Great. It's Norman. And I'm standing in my hotel room with Roger behind me and my panties still clutched in my hand. This is all I need. Now he'll tell everybody that I'm screwing the boss. Norman's not malicious, but he couldn't keep a secret if Princess Leia and the future of the Rebellion depended on it.

Oh, God, he *is* rubbing off on me. That's two *Star Wars* references in one day.

"No, no, Roger stopped by for, um, well," I see Roger out of the corner of my eye, frantically gesturing for me to make Norman go away.

Kirby is still on the line. "Who the hell is that? *Another* man?? You go on the road and turn into a total slut, after you haven't gotten laid in more than a year? I can't *wait* to hear about this. Let me talk to the British guy about penises."

"No, you are *not* talking to him about penises!" I am practically shouting now, which scares the room service guy who picked now to finally show up. He better not think he's getting a tip. Norman starts backing away.

"No, Norman, I wasn't talking to you. My friend is on the phone and she has to rhyme something with humongous, but the British word for penis . . . I mean, British is still English, right? So the word is probably the same, and anyway, Roger stopped by for, um, for, for something out of my first-aid kit! That's it!" I am triumphant to find a plausible story, but not even the room-service guy looks convinced. By now, Norman is halfway down the hall, almost running. "Norman, NORMAN!" He doesn't even look back. Great. Tomorrow's staff meeting should be perfect.

"Leave the tray on the table. You don't have to pour the water. Go, please. Thank you, thank you." I am practically pushing him out the door before Roger breaks down totally. I shut the door and collapse back against it in relief.

"Jules, I have testicle fungus. I'm sure it's the precursor to some hideous form of cancer, and I'm dying. I wanted you to be the first to know." Roger looks somber and yet resigned. This must be his patented Serenity in the Face of Despair expression.

"Oh, my God, your boyfriend is DYING? That's so sad and romantic. Jules, tell me everything. No, wait, I have to talk to him." Kirby is panting in my ear.

"NO!" Now I *am* shouting. "No, no, no. No, Kirby, you're not talking to Roger. And I'm hanging up. We'll rhyme body parts later." I push the off button on my cell and whip the earpiece out.

"And, no, Roger, you're not dying. Tell me what's going on, and we'll get you to a doctor." I'm sure I don't want to hear this, but I can't think of any other way to get rid of him.

"Well, there's actually *chafing*." He sits down, quite gingerly, on the edge of the bed. The delicious aroma of grilled chicken alfredo from the tray reaches my nose and my stomach growls, but I have a feeling dinner is going to be a cold, congealed mess by the time I get around to eating it. And the whole fungus thing is kind of ruining my appetite, anyway.

"Chafing. OK. What else?" I can't believe I'm having this conversation. Mom would be so proud. Sigh.

"Burning. And redness." He is almost whispering now, head down, staring at the hideous purple carpet in my forty-nine-dollar-a-night hotel room. Nothing but the best for the *POP STAR LIVE!* crew.

"Roger, it's probably heat rash. It *is* about a hundred degrees here, and you *have* been wearing tight pants every day. It's air-conditioned inside, but you've been going out to lunch with the crew every day. And walking. In the heat. In. Tight. Pants." I say this slowly, in case I'm not getting through his preoccupation with his imminent genitalia-induced demise.

He looks at me, the first glimmer of hope stirring. "You think so? I mean, is it possible?"

"I'm sure of it, Roger. And we'll get you in to a doctor first thing in the morning, or you could even go to the ER tonight, if it will make you feel better." I'm starting to think I may get to eat my dinner after all.

Roger stands up, lifting his chin. Is this what they mean by stiff upper lip? I don't care, if he'll get out of my hotel room. I turn toward my tote bag that I'd tossed on the floor behind the door. "Roger, let's call it a night. I have some medicated powder you can have. Take a cool shower and use some of it on the, um, affected area. I'm sure you'll be much better." I turn back around, holding the powder up in triumph, and my mouth falls back open. Roger is standing exactly where he was, with one rather glaring difference.

His pants are down around his ankles. All of his pants. And he's clutching his parts with both hands.

"Jules, if you'd have a quick look, I'd feel quite a lot better. There's a bit right here that—"

"No! I'm not going to look at your testicles! That is way above and beyond the call of duty. In fact, this is probably some kind of sexual harassment. For God's sake, Roger, you're my boss, and you're standing here practically naked in my hotel room, trying to show me your testicles! Don't you think that's a teensy bit *OVER THE TOP?*"

I can't believe this is happening. Normal people live their whole lives without being attacked by insane chefs or having their boss demonstrate testicle fungus. Why is it that this kind of thing always happens to me?

Roger looks startled at my outburst, and then he regains some semblance of sanity and starts to chuckle. "Well, erm, quite right, then. I am standing here a bit starkers. I've gotten carried away with this one. A man doesn't want to face death in quite such an embarrassing manner. And you understood, and, well. Right, then." He's fastening his pants, thankfully. He laughs again, which makes him nearly as attractive as I first thought he was, before I knew about the rampant hypochondria. Maybe there's a normal person under all those phobias. Maybe even a nice guy.

"I'll retire now and let you enjoy your dinner. So sorry to have intruded. Erm, I'll take that powder with me, if you don't mind." He's kind of embarrassed now, which makes me like him a little.

/ I open the door again. "And no more tight pants, Roger. See you tomorrow." As I close the door behind him and fasten every lock, bolt, and chain, I resolve not to open it again until morning.

Maybe not even then.

The Staff Meeting

It's as bad as I expected. Everybody stops talking when I walk in the door. Norman looks guilty and won't meet my eyes. Joe can't decide if he's outraged (his usual state) or gleeful. "So, Jules, get any *sleep* last night?"

I guess we're going with gleeful.

I ignore him and go to my seat. At least Marshall doesn't pick up on the undertones. He moves right into the agenda: travel plans, what we have in front of us in San Diego, meetings scheduled for everyone with the head of the set design company who's flying in from L.A., and all the other details that keep a travelling TV show running. It's hard for me to pay attention, though, with all the snide looks coming my way. When Marshall is done and leaves the room, I take a deep breath and get on with it. It's better to face the gossip head-on, right?

I stand up and look straight at Norman, but I'm talking to the whole crew. "I did *not* sleep with Roger. Or have sex with him. Or anything else with him. He stopped by my room to get the first-aid kit, so he could feel safer sleeping in a 'germ-infested hotel room.'"

I can tell by their expressions that I'm winning them over; we all know Roger. "Norman stopped by when Roger was telling me that he felt ill, and I was on the phone with a friend who's having a crisis at work. So everything got jumbled, but I am not sleeping with Roger. I mean, does he let people get their germs close enough to even *have* sex?"

Everybody starts laughing and Joe looks pissed off, which is his normal expression, so I know I'm home free. We're breaking up the meeting and everyone's chatting when the door bangs open and Roger rushes in. (In loose cotton pants, so at least he listened.)

He hurries over and leans down to speak into my ear, in a loud whisper that carries across the whole room, naturally.

"I'm sorry about knocking you up last night, Jules, but my testicles feel much better."

I'm doomed.

Chapter Four

LBP v. HBP

About a year ago, after my ranch-dip-armpit boyfriend fiasco, Kirby and I went out for a restorative cosmopolitan or seven and came up with a new rating system for men.

Kirby eyed the bartender in a moderately blurry kind of way. Full-on blurry came later. "Do you think it's a job requirement?" She sucked on an olive with ladylike slurping noises.

"Is what a job req . . . req . . . thing?" I was closer to full-on blurry, myself.

She looked around the dim afternoon gloom of the bar, unpopulated as yet by the Loud and Brittles—the freshly off work happy-hours-ers who competed for who was busier and, thus, more important. Puffer fish in a goldfish bowl. At three o'clock, they hadn't ridden their laptops into the bar.

"The teeny little ponytail, suitably covered in goo. Looks like Vaseline to me, but it's probably some twenty-five-dollar a tube crap they get at Gene Juarez when they go in for combover class." She drained the rest of her unfashionable vodka martini and waved it in the air for another.

I looked at the bartender and had an epiphany. Right there in The Seattle Grill. Probably the first time *that's* ever happened. "I had an epiphany," I announced, banging my glass on the bar and sloshing a little.

"I thought it was a cosmopolitan. I can't keep up with these stupid drink names. Daniel keeps trying to get me to try apple martinis. Excuse me. Appletinis. Damn stupid idea. Apples are for pies, especially those fried ones at McDonald's—two for a buck, by the way. Wanna go?"

I didn't want to hear about apple pies. Or Daniel. *Especially* not Daniel, who is the greatest lay on the planet, according to Kirby, but who hasn't had a job in three years.

"No, no, no. Not the drink. The epiphany. The entire way we understand men is totally off. We need to be objective in our rankings. Get the data." I grabbed her by the shoulders and made her look at me.

"We need to use blood pressure."

Kirby's eyebrows shot up. I noticed that her eyes were a weird shade of purple that matched her dress and it threw me off track. "Nice purple eyes."

She batted her eyelashes at me. "It's Vision in Violet, not purple. The latest fashion in contacts."

I propped my head up with my hand to make the room quit spinning. "You still have the hots for your eye doctor? In spite of Daniel, the Orgasm King? I can't keep up with you."

Kirby tossed her head and all that glossy straight black hair sent twinges flaming into the Dockers of at least four guys in the bar. Sometimes I hate having a beautiful friend.

"I didn't *do* him, Jules, I got an eye exam. Proper

eye health is very important to . . ."

"Health, that's right. Health. We were talking about blood pressure. Can you forget about your overactive sex life for a minute and listen to this plan?" I glared at her when she started to open her mouth to defend herself. Kirby gets more sex than any three Democratic congressmen but spends her life selling vibrators to lonely singles. It's bizarre.

I waved ponytail boy down for more drinks. "OK, listen. What is the single most important characteristic of any man?"

Kirby laughed. "Is this a trick question? His dick, of course."

Her picture is next to One-Track Mind in Webster's. "No, no, no. Characteristic, not body part. Your job has frazzled your brain, Kirbs. What do we need more than anything else in a man?"

I answered my own question, before she could start talking about tongue agility. *"Energy."*

"Energy?"

"Energy," I affirmed, with a decisive nod. "What have you had to deal with in the past?" I started counting them off on my fingers. "Henry, who lived in his mother's basement and always wanted to split the check. To which he conveniently forgot to add the tax or tip, so you always had to make up the difference. What was he like in bed?"

Kirby made a face like she'd stepped on a hairball. "He wanted to lie there and do nothing. He said he was 'letting me get in touch with my Amazon side,' which was a load of horse shit meaning he wanted me to do all the work. And forget any south of the border action, unless it was all on *my* side. That scumbag . . ."

"OK, OK, I get it," I cut in before we had a ten-minute diatribe on Henry. "But you see, that proves my point. Henry's a classic LBP. His blood pressure is so low he can't even get up off the couch."

Kirby snickered. "And sometimes he couldn't get *it* up, either. Definite LPB."

"L*BP*, Kirby. Low Blood Pressure. Now what about Rex?" Rex was the investment banker she dated whenever she threw Daniel out. He was a millionaire at thirty-five and had bought a house a few months earlier on Queen Anne Hill for a cool three million.

"Rex fucked like the Dow Jones depended on it. He was a marathoner." Kirby sighed and a goofy grin spread over her face. "I *miss* Rex. Whatever happened to him?"

"He overbooked dates one night, and you caught him in the hot tub with the *Seattle Times* business reporter. But that's the down side of HBPs—they have so much energy, they don't want to confine it to one woman. What we need, therefore," I took a long sip of my seventh or eighth cosmopolitan—hey, I know how to build a dramatic pause—and said, "What we need is a man who's weighted toward the high end of the BP scale but not clear off the chart. He has to have enough LBP in him to enjoy picnics and walks in the park without bringing along his cell phone, his laptop, and his Blackberry." I slid off the bar stool into a rather wobbly standing position and gave a bow. Wow. Head rush.

"Kirby, I present to you, the perfect man-o-meter."

Kirby was clapping. "Bravo, Jules. Bravo. I only have one question. When we meet a hot guy, how do we get that inflatable cuff thingy on him?" Kirby's eyes sparkled.

Well, tiny flaws can always be worked out.

Hangovers and E Coli

San Diego is a big improvement over Reno, but it

kind of feels like the geriatric L.A. I mean, the parking lot at auditions is filled with Lincoln Continentals, for Pete's sake. I thought only my grandmother still drove those.

Also, you'd think I'd have learned by now that *POP STAR LIVE!* is not the high-class TV production it pretends to be. But, no. Gullible Jules. Case in point: When I heard we were going to stay at the Del, I thought Nellie meant the Hotel Del Coronado, which is one of the most perfect places to watch the sunset on the west coast. I tagged along to one of Jerry's conventions there, when he was in between girlfriends. (Strictly platonic, of course. Jerry's like a brother to me.) But anyway, it's a gorgeous place and the rooms are serious luxe.

Which means I should have known better. No luxury for us. In fact, no private bathrooms, either, at Del's Bar, Grill, and Motel. My room shares a bathroom with Norman's. At least it's not Joe. He'd probably try to throw a radio in my bathtub and electrocute me or something. Not that I'm paranoid, but he's getting weirder by the day. At lunch yesterday, I caught him asking the caterer if any of the sandwiches had been left out in the heat for a long time, right after he'd offered to bring me a ham, cheese, and mayo. I don't know if food poisoning can kill a person, and I don't want to find out. Or even get diarrhea.

Especially when I'm sharing a bathroom with somebody who has a Luke Skywalker towel.

To continue on with my disgusting bodily functions theme, I am so hungover from last night's festivities that I'm trying not to puke. My head is literally ringing. Oh, wait. That's the phone.

"This better be good, I'm dying here." I ease myself back down against my pillows, wondering who was evil enough to set a nine A.M. call for auditions.

Kirby is chirping in my ear. I hate perky people.

"Jules, guess what? I did such a great job on the W&L new product line, they've asked me to join the company as senior vice president of marketing. Jules, I'd get *stock options*."

Wincing from her enthusiasm, which is reverberating through my skull by way of my eardrum, I briefly consider what kind of stock options this would mean. A lifetime supply of nipple clamps? Ouch.

"That's great, Kirby. I know you've been wanting to get out of that ad agency for a while. But is this the opportunity you want? I mean, you'll have Whips and Lace on your business cards. How will that play at the chamber of commerce meetings?" I am speaking as softly as I can, because there is a direct correlation between the sound of my own voice and my need to toss my cookies all over the rug. Which is puke-green, by the way, so the maid probably wouldn't even notice if I did. But, yuck.

"I know, isn't it great? I mean, senior vice president, Jules. Come on! And the IPO took off. W&L has nowhere to go but up."

"That's a good thing, considering the company makes vibrators." I'm pretty funny, even in my near-death state, I think.

"Ha, ha, ha. Don't quit your day job. By the way, what's up with you? Why do you sound so bad? Are you getting a migraine or is this hangover-ville?"

"It's total hangover-ville, Kirbs. We found one— count 'em—*one* good singer—Kayley—out of the four hundred and seventy-three who auditioned yesterday. And we almost didn't take *her*, because her dad started trying to bribe crew members before she even got in the door." I think Joe took the hundred bucks, too, but I sure wasn't going to be the one to say anything.

"So we went to the bar and got karaoke drunk. Then we all ended up here in my room, somehow." I look at the Hefty bag listing precariously in the corner. The smell of stale beer from the overflowing bag is enough to make me lose it. I have no idea how I'm going to get it to the Dumpster before the maid gets here.

"You need to give up this nun thing, Jules. It's turning you into an alcoholic. And please tell me it wasn't "Margaritaville." You suck at that song." Kirby clearly hasn't read the Supportive Friend Manual.

"If you're going to do tequila shooters, it has to be Buffett. It's a rule." I may be a hopeless drunk who hasn't had sex in a year and can't keep a job, but even I have standards. "I have to go, Kirby. Great news on the job offer. Have you decided to take it?"

"I think so, but I told them I'd let them know in a day or two. It's going to be a big change and I want to think about it. Plus the new CEO is totally hot and, if I go to work for him, won't I be sexually harassing him if I ask him out?"

"Not if *you* work for *him*, Kirby. Wait, is this the guy who thinks he's 'Steve honking Forbes'? He's hot?" I can't keep up, sometimes. Especially with jackhammers pounding in my brain.

"You know, Jules, this habit you have of throwing people's words back at them is not attractive." I can hear her grinning through the phone. Of course, I can also hear mold growing in the walls right now, so I'm not sure what that says about me.

"Good bye, Kirby. I have to go to auditions. With a hangover. Please say nice things at my funeral."

"When you die, can I have your Stuart Weitzman pumps?" she says, as I hang up on her. She's definitely out of my will.

I can't put it off any longer. I have to get that Hefty bag to the Dumpster. I don't know why I can't let the maid deal with it, but it's probably the same reason I pre-cleaned my apartment during the two months I actually had a housekeeper. My mother's genes battling to come through.

I spend a couple of minutes fighting vertigo when I stand up. I wonder if Roger has ever been this hungover? He'd be sure he had a brain tumor. Maybe I have a brain tumor. Or an ulcer. I'm getting an ugly feeling in my stomach that has nothing to do with today's hangover, but a lot to do with the number of hangovers I've faced recently. As they say, Denial ain't just a river in Egypt. I may sometimes substitute cosmopolitans for cuddling and beer for sex, but at least I never spend whole days wondering if a bottle of Bacardi is going to call me and ask me out for Saturday night.

If I drag the bag along, it's going to make a Big Ugly Noise, so I tie it closed while holding my breath. This is not as easy as you might think. Then I lift it and go in search of the Dumpster I know I saw last night before the Jell-O Shots Championship Volleyball match. I lost, in case you haven't guessed. There is tequila-flavored Jell-O in my system, yet I wonder why I'm dying. In spite of all that, I'm wobbling down the sidewalk, quite proud of myself for carrying on in the face of adversity and all that vaguely British-sounding crap. I'm even thinking I might survive the day after all.

Right up until I throw up on the guy's shoes.

Chapter Five

LBPs and Tool Belts

I may have to shoot myself now. I've spent a year on my self-proclaimed Abstinence World Tour, and the first man other than my deranged hypochondriac boss who shows promise for the grand finale is wearing the steaming remains of my Jell-O shots on his Nikes. In my defense, it *was* his fault.

I saw him out of the corner of one bloodshot eye as I dragged the evidence of last night's bad judgment down the sidewalk toward the Dumpster. Plastic bag plus uneven sidewalk equals big hole in bag's side and empty beer cans tumbling out all over the place.

Loudly.

As I scrambled around muttering blisteringly bad words and picking up cans, the stench of stale beer overwhelmed my shredded control over my gag reflex. In mid-retch, I heard a beautifully deep male voice ask, "Can I help?" I didn't even try to answer by then; I waved frantically for him to get out of the way.

He didn't.

Oh, God, strike me dead.

So now I'm wiping my face off with the hem of my T-shirt and talking to the knees of a pair of faded jeans. Well-filled-out faded jeans, I can't help but noticing, even in my near-death state. This may be the most humiliated any person has ever been in the history of the world, and there's no way I'm looking up at his face. "I'm so sorry. I'm so very sick and so very sorry and so very embarrassed. I'll buy you a new pair of shoes. And socks. And jeans, even." There was splatter. Oh, please God, let this be a bad dream.

Oh, no. Now he's kneeling down. He must be a lunatic. What sane person would bring his face closer in proximity to somebody else's barf? I clench my eyes closed. "I'm so sorry. I'm in room 102. I'm Jules Vernon, and I'll pay for everything. Please go away and leave me to die of humiliation in peace."

I feel the touch of a hand under my chin, and my eyes fly open. I mean, this *is* Del's Bar and Grill. This guy could be some kind of perverted drug dealer who sees throwing up as foreplay.

I'm looking into the warmest brown eyes I've ever seen outside of a pet shop. This man could give sit up and beg a whole new meaning. I can't believe I'm having amorous thoughts about the guy I yarked on. He looks concerned, though. Probably not a drug dealer.

"Miss, are you . . . I mean, clearly you're ill. Why don't you let me help you to your room? Do you need a doctor?" His tool is brushing against the ground. No, I actually do mean his *tool*. He's wearing a tool belt with a long hammer on one side. OK, he's a carpenter. Definite LBP to have enough patience to build things. No laptop anywhere in sight, either. But he does have a job. He must be the motel carpenter or something. His next words confirm it.

"I'll get somebody to clean up this trash. Please let me help you up. You look pale."

His hands are gentle on my wrists, but the strength in his arms is clear from the muscles filling out his white T-shirt. As he pulls me up to stand, I see that he's taller than me, too. By a good three or four inches. I'm five eleven barefoot, so this is unusual.

As he kicks his shoes off by scraping the heels against the edge of the sidewalk (and leaves them in the gutter), I try for a calm, I-wasn't-gaping-at-your-body-right-after-I-puked-on-you voice. "I'm fine, a little too much to drink last night. I'm not used to drinking and the, um, atmospheric pressure here kind of got to me."

He raises one elegant eyebrow. "The atmospheric pressure."

"Exactly. There's too much oxygen. I mean, not enough oxygen. I'm used to Seattle, and, um, the thin air makes beer metabolize faster."

Great. Now I've irrefutably proven I'm a drunken airhead, judging by the grin that spreads slowly across his face. Add that grin to the wavy dark-Godiva-chocolate hair, and this carpenter has revived my will to live. We walk toward my room, and I try not to stumble too much.

Heaven knows I wouldn't want to make a bad impression.

I need to get a grip here. I threw up on his shoes. It's not like he's going to ask me out. And, anyway, what kind of story would *that* be to tell our grandkids?

I fumble with the key and finally get the door open, while he supports my elbow with a warm hand. "Well, thank you. Again, I'm so sorry. And please give me a bill for the replacement. I'll be here until tomorrow. Room 102. Jules Vernon. Thank you."

He smiles and turns to walk away. I don't even know

his name. "Wait! What's your name? I mean, you didn't, er, well . . ."

He looks back at me over his shoulder as he moves away. "Call me Phileas. I hope you feel better soon. In spite of the oxygen problem."

I hurled on a drop-dead gorgeous man who works with his hands and has actually read Jules Verne. Please kill me now.

After four Tylenol, two Diet Cokes, and a long, hot shower, I'm almost human again. I head over to the auditions, which are being held on the beach volley-ball court. Where else? The hammering starts up in my head again as I get closer, until I round the cor-ner and see that actual hammering is going on.

The temporary stage Nellie demanded is being put in place, and the butt leaning over the front edge is the same one I watched walk away from my door less than an hour ago. Different jeans, though. I should have known the motel would loan him to us to work on the set. Now the story of my morning's humilia-tion can be fodder for this week's staff meeting. I should call Jerry now, since I probably won't have this job long. This time it won't be because I quit, though. I'm not sure if getting fired is all that much of an improvement.

Nellie is leaning over the stage next to him as if she wants to get her hands on his hammer. Her outfit has enough fabric to dress the average five-year-old child, if transparent zebra stripes are the going thing in the kindergarten set these days.

I don't understand why I care what Nellie does with or to the carpenter, but I recognize the ugly wrench in my gut for what it is. Either I'm feeling a twinge of jealousy about somebody who didn't even give me his real name, or Joe finally succeeded in poisoning me.

The two hundred or so hopeful auditioners being held back by the security team are an ominous reminder that I have to face bad singing on an empty stomach. A very, very empty stomach. I yell for Sharp and Johnson (yes, the Bobbsey twins of security travel with us, too) to send the first contestant in and move to my place at the table. As I'm sitting down, my gaze is drawn back to my carpenter, er, I mean *the* carpenter, who has straightened up and is ignoring Nellie and looking straight into my eyes with a hint of a smile playing on his lips. I can feel my face turning brick red and quickly look down at my nonexistent notes and line up my pens exactly at right angles.

Norman's already seated at my left and turns to me slowly. "Are you OK?" he asks hoarsely. I look up at Norman; his hangover must be even worse than mine. His skin looks faintly green. I'm not kidding. His eyes are sunken about three inches into his skull and a scary grimace which I can only guess is supposed to be a smile is pasted on his face. "Dude, my mouth tastes like I swallowed half the swamp water on Dagobah. And I already brushed my teeth like a hundred times. Don't even get me started on my head, either. I'm never drinking again."

I nod, feeling sorry for the hopeful contestants. The *real* Norah Jones could walk in here this morning, and we'd eliminate her. This is going to be a long, ugly day.

Suddenly, I feel something cold next to my arm and somebody hot next to my chair. It's him. Phileas.

"I thought you looked like you could use this." He's crouched down next to me, his voice pitched low. The husky timbre sends a little shiver straight to my La Perla thong. He brought me a Diet Coke and a large bottle of water.

"I, um, thank you. I'm actually feeling a little better, but this is, um, great. Thanks so much. I, well, you, um, you can add this to my tab, I guess," I say, trying to be The Funny Girl Who Can Laugh at Herself.

He smiles. He has to quit doing that. Smiling, I mean. The man's got a beautiful mouth. White teeth and firm lips that make me think about all the places on my body that haven't had any lips on them in almost a year now. Any teeth, either, to be honest. A little nipping never hurt anybody.

I'm staring at his mouth like a crazed dentist contemplating a root canal; I drag my gaze back to his eyes. "Thanks, really. Thanks for the soda and water. And, um, thanks for not saying anything to anybody about, um, before." Because it's clear he hasn't. If he had, Joe would be dancing on the tabletop, laughing at me. "I'm glad you had extra clothes with you."

He grins and stands up. "No problem. Although when a beautiful woman makes me take my pants off, I usually like it if she's in the room with me. And it's Sam. Sam Blake." He holds his hand out to shake mine, with the kind of firm grip that is perfect in a handshake. I can't stand men who give you that limp-handed grip, like they can't decide whether you should shake their hand or kiss their ring. Nothing limp here.

I'm so hungover I don't even realize I'm thinking in cheesy double entendres until he's walking away, and contestant number one starts singing "God Bless the U.S.A."

Here come the frogs.

Chapter Six

Emotions and Other Scary Subjects

OK, here's the deal. My shrink may have had a point about that commitment issue. I don't know how to commit to anybody, when I can't figure out who the perfect man might be. And I can't choose the perfect man, when I don't even know who *I'm* going to be if I ever grow up. Which version of me is the real one? I usually start dating a new guy within a month or two of starting a new career, and they always match. I've never seen an article in *Cosmopolitan* about accessorizing your man to your job. Maybe I should write one.

It's so bad, my mother even noticed, and she doesn't notice anything. I took her out to lunch when I was hiding out, er, recharging my batteries in Ohio, and our conversation wasn't all that much fun for me. We usually discuss an eclectic mix of topics, like the weather in Ohio vs. Seattle (I should move home; too much rain in the Pacific Northwest), how her favorites the Cleveland Indians are doing (I should move home; we could get season tickets together); and what parallels we can draw between fundamental Christianity and Proustian secular humanism (I

should move home and get a Ph.D. in comparative
something-ology or -osophy).

But this lunch was like the failed pilot of a '50s sit-
com: *Leave it to Mother who Knows Best*. It was all
about Mom telling me what I was doing wrong in my
life, and especially my love life. She never liked
Robert, but she'd been a huge fan of the professor I
dated during my brief foray into college fundraising.

"Jules, you know I don't like to interfere." These are
words that send ice stabbing through the heart of the
most courageous daughter, whoever *she* might be.
I'm a wimp. I downed the rest of my chardonnay in
two gulps.

"But?" I asked.

"But, I've noticed a recurring theme in your dating
adventures, or misadventures. Every time you get a
new job, you get a new man. And the man always
matches the job, instead of being a match for you."

"Mom, it's only natural to meet people through
your job. Most women work so much these days,
that's the only way we can meet guys. Do you want
me to start hanging out in bars again? I'm not in my
twenties anymore." Feint and parry. I learned my
defenses well when I was a teenager.

"Jules, of course I'm not saying that I want you to
pick men up in bars. And I'm on to your defense-by-
attack tricks, by the way. Listen to me for one minute.
You think that a relationship is something you try on
for size like a pair of shoes. You're trying to match
men to your job, like that Gucci bag with your suede
miniskirt. You can't switch men like you change outfits. Love is not a shopping spree." She stopped to
take a breath, leaving me staring at her in disbelief.

I didn't know she could recognize a Gucci bag.

"Mom, I can't believe you said that."

"I know, I'm sorry to interfere, but . . ."

I shook my head. "No, I can't believe you said *that*. A woman who was short-listed for the National Book Award comes out with dialogue like 'love is not a shopping spree'? Are you going to be writing for *The National Enquirer* next?"

That was the end of the topic, at least for that day. Insulting her writing has always been the one surefire way to distract my mother. Even with her stunning literary success and critical acclaim, it was hard for Sylvia DuPree to always be known as Tom Vernon's wife.

Dad writes unapologetically commercial fiction. He says he's only a storyteller, and his favorite fan letters are the ones where people curse at him for making them stay up all night reading his latest Professor Maxwell archaeologist mystery. He did the number thing, like Janet Evanovich's Stephanie Plum series, because he said he might want to write more than twenty-six of them and look at the pickle Sue Grafton will be in after Kinsey Milhone gets to Z.

Professor Maxwell and the First Pharaoh surprised everybody by hitting the *USA Today* bestseller list and, by the time he got to *Professor Maxwell and the Eight Treasures of Mesopotamia*, he debuted at number two on the *New York Times* bestseller list. He's up to the thirteen tombs of Tutankhamen next, I think.

Anyway, he's rolling in money, and there are over nine million copies of his books in print in about sixteen different languages. Mom, on the other hand, writes gritty, elegiac laments about the historical role female sexuality plays in the subjugation of our entire gender. Mom's books make *The Vagina Monologues* look tame. (Imagine having *Conquered by the Clitoris* sitting on the coffee table when you're twelve years old.)

When my parents divorced, I always thought "lack of passion" for my mother might have something to do with the disparity between Dad's success and her university-press print runs of ten thousand or so. Not that Mom has a petty bone in her body. But that has to be hard to live with.

Trust me, I know. As the only child of Mr. *New York Times* list and Ms. Darling of the literati set, people have been expecting me to write the Great American Novel since I was about three years old. I reacted to the pressure by refusing to learn to read until I was almost eight. Only the fact that the remedial reading teacher my parents hired smelled like moth balls and stale armpit brought me around. I was reading within a week (OK, I had been faking a little) and writing putrid poetry within a month.

I fall on my knees on the hard, cold gym floor
Are scabs a metaphor for life?

I think Mom still had that one up on the refrigerator when I turned sixteen. I'd be embarrassed to admit it, if I hadn't already confessed to throwing up on a guy. That makes bad poetry look pretty mundane.

Kirby, who likes to analyze other people in spite of the fact that she writes about sex toys for a living and keeps her very own boy toy in her condo, thinks my whole impostor syndrome stems from my parents and their spectacular success. I think it's a load of crap. I never bought into the popular victimology theory, where everything that goes wrong in your life is somebody else's fault. I'm honestly not good at anything. It's nobody's fault but mine.

So, until I find something that I *am* good at—something I have a passion for doing—I keep my distance from men. I don't want to find the perfect guy for Charity Golf Organizer Jules and then have to go through the pain of discovering we don't work when I'm Important Reality TV Producer Jules. For me, safe sex is about putting condoms on my emotions.

Chapter Seven

Infamous IQ Arrives

This guy takes the concept of entourage way too seriously. Our third judge is finally Making His Entrance, surrounded by twenty or so hangers-on. It's seventy degrees and sunny in San Diego, and he's wearing a fur coat. It looks like roadkill to me, but I don't know much about fur. If conspicuous ostentation is a sign of insecurity, Infamous IQ must have a penis about an inch long. He's cute, though, in a grunge-meets-bling-bling kind of way.

We're getting ready to start the finals, so it's perfect timing. Norman rushes up to him.

"Oh, dude, you, like, totally rocked on the *Swing a Dead Cat With Your Bitch* CD. Totally amazing musical talent. The sensitive emotions in your monologue version of *Trailer Trash Ghetto* blew me away. It's an honor to meet you, Mr. Q."

Nobody's laughing, so these must be actual album titles. And this guy is judging *POP STAR LIVE!* why? From the sneer on Q's face as he looks at the stage setup, he's wondering the same thing.

He ditches the dead-animal coat with one of his

minions and swaggers over to Nellie. (Nobody on this show *walks* anywhere; it's all attitude by ambulation.)

"Hey, Nellie. Long time, no see. They roll you out of retirement for this gig?" He reaches out and touches the side of her face. "Whoa, careful, babe. I think the stitches from your last lift are showing."

Nellie is, for the first time since I've known her, speechless. Unfortunately, it doesn't last long. "Look, you no-talent Eminem-wannabe, don't start your shit with me."

The finalists are still waiting inside Del's bar, or Nellie would never use the S-word. She rises to her full five foot, four inch height (including three-inch heels), and points her finger at him. "I am the star of this show, you moron. You can be replaced. Don't mess with me, or it will happen sooner rather than later." I've never seen actual death rays shoot out of somebody's eyes before. Q should have huge holes in the middle of his forehead by now.

Q laughs and grabs her head with one hand and plants a smacking kiss on her lips. "That's not what Marshall said. They like the friction, babe. Good for ratings. Get used to it."

He grabs the chair next to hers and swings it around to straddle it. "OK, let's get on with it. Do we have any singers here or what?"

Nellie looks like her head may explode any second. I would enjoy watching it, but am not sure my weakened stomach could take the whole brain-spatter thing, so I ask Norman to go find Roger and call in the first contestant.

Perfect. A guy in nothing but a trench coat, cowboy boots, and yellow G-string walks on to the stage. Nausea, the sequel. Did I mention that this is going to be a long day?

* * *

When we finally get to Anton, he sings with the power and grace of a young Barry White. Plus, he's beautiful. I know it's trite, but there's no other word that fits. Anton has skin like polished mahogany over a body that is sculpted to total deliciousness. I sneak a peek at his entry forms while he's singing for the judges, and he works as a personal trainer part-time while enrolled at U.C. I bet there are a lot of women in that gym who seriously concentrate on their thigh work.

For a change, though, we have a close decision on the guy we're sending to Hollywood. It's an unwritten rule that we take one of each gender from each location. Equal numbers of male and female contestants will spice up the ratings, natch. Kayley of the hundred-dollar-bill Dad has no real competition in this bunch, so she's pretty much a sure thing. But there's a young Latino who sang a salsa-inspired number yesterday that was so hot it made my nipples hard. He's up next, I think.

"Next contestant, please," Roger says primly. He keeps darting sideways glances at Q and curling his lip. I'm guessing proper British record producers aren't all that fond of American rap stars.

The contestant leaps on the stage with the grace of a born dancer. I could learn to tango for this guy. Nothing like a dose of healthy lust for guys ten years younger to perk a person right up.

I was right. This is going to be a tough choice. Almost before he's done singing, the judges are at it.

"Anton is clearly the only choice," Roger says.

"There's nothin' clear about it. This guy brings the heat; the little girls will be stealing Mommy's MasterCard to buy his tunes," Q says.

"There's more to this competition than the fantasies

of prepubescent females. We are, actually, looking for talent," Roger says.

"You wouldn't know talent if it bit you on the *arse*, Rog. Whatever happened to Latent Earwax?" Q is smirking. Latent was a punk band Roger's record label touted as the biggest thing to hit London since the Sex Pistols. When the band's first CD belly-flopped its way to the bottom, and audiences stayed away from their concerts in droves, Roger's reputation suffered a little. OK, let's be honest. The London tabloids crucified him. Evidently Q keeps current on his music industry news.

Nellie can't stand not being the center of attention for longer than thirty seconds. "I vote for Anton," she says. "They're both fabulous, but he has that extra quality of liquid meaningfulness of expression in his tone."

If Roger is the intellectual, and Q is the edgy one, then Nellie is the comic book of music criticism. Nobody ever understands what the hell she's talking about. I'm getting a little cranky here, because I have nothing in my stomach but a gallon of battery acid. I sip some more water and try to avoid looking at Joe, who is sneering at me from the other side of the stage. He refused to participate in last night's drunkenness, of course. Probably had his weekly online meeting of Nutjobs Dot Com to attend.

Anyway, it's not like logical reasoning is a prereq for this job, so Nellie breaks the tie vote and Anton wins. I'm so glad we're done I could cry in relief, until Joe announces that the plans have changed. We're going to Tampa Bay today, so we can get an earlier start tomorrow. Flying should be fun. Nothing says happiness like adding turbulence to a hangover.

Kayley's dad breaks out the case of Cristal he had chilling in his limo when he hears the news that she's going to Hollywood. I wonder if he was *that* confident in her singing, or if he always drives around with a case of two-hundred-dollar-a-bottle champagne. There's no way I'm drinking alcohol this morning, not even Cristal, so I slink away to my room.

I'm not really a drunk, I just play one on TV.

I have to walk past Sam to get in my room, since he's leaning on the door. My door. Somehow, I think this isn't coincidence. He must have heard we're leaving, and he wants his money. I hope I have enough cash to pay for jeans and shoes. The socks I can afford. *PSL!* doesn't exactly pay a fortune, and I haven't hit an ATM lately.

"Hi, Phil—er, Sam. How much do I owe you?" The man is scrumptious. Almost a year without ice cream, and suddenly I'm surrounded by thirty-one flavors. Sam's gourmet praline pecan; all long, lean muscle relaxed into a pose of understated power. I have an insane urge to lick him.

This is the kind of guy who has a Harley and a black leather jacket at home. I've never gone out with a bad boy, unless you count the painter I dated during my starving artist phase, who had a shoplifting habit.

Sam waves his hand, unaware that I'm mentally categorizing all the places he may have tattoos. "Don't worry about it. I came to see if you're all right." He's searching my face, as if to look for signs of dissolution. His next words tell me I'm not far off.

"Be sure to drink lots of water. It'll help with the dehydration. Especially on the plane. And stay away from the booze for a while, if you can." He's not smiling, either, but still has that look of concern on his face. Does he think I'm an alcoholic, crossing the country one Hefty bag at a time?

"Look, I appreciate the concern, but staying away from the booze, as you put it, is not really an issue," I say. I root around in my purse for cash. "Here's two hundred bucks. I hope that covers it. It's all I've got till payday. Again, I'm so sorry about this morning. I'm sure you're busy, so I won't keep you." He may be a total hot fudge sundae, but I'm not interested in breaking my sexual fast with somebody who has such a low opinion of me. Talk about self sabotage.

Sam ignores the cash I'm holding out. "No, I don't want your money. The housekeeping staff threw my jeans in the wash, and those shoes were older than some of your singers, anyway. Take care of yourself. I'll see you around." He walks off, after flashing that ought-to-be-outlawed smile again. I almost wish he *would* be seeing me around, but this is one first impression I probably can't overcome. It's better this way. Besides, what future would Important TV Personality Jules have with a motel carpenter who lives in San Diego?

The upside of all these free-floating hormones is that I haven't thought once all day about how unqualified I am for this job.

Until now. Damn.

Chapter Eight
A Goldfish Named Spot

Roger is creating an international incident at the San Diego airport. A perky man at the Northwest Airlines counter is explaining why Roger cannot take his goldfish on the plane. The perkiness is getting a little frazzled around the edges, though.

"Sir, as I've explained again and again, a goldfish cannot be carried on board a Northwest Airlines airplane. Not even as carry-on luggage. Not in the baggage compartment, either. No, we do not consider this to be illegal discrimination against fish, even though cats and dogs are allowed. There are different requirements for fish."

"What about in first class? For God's sake, I sat next to a woman who had her smelly little rat dog in a carry-on bag in first class last week. I pay good money to fly first class on your airline; why do I have fewer rights than a woman with a rat dog?" Roger has a desperate look in his eyes and his British accent is getting thicker by the minute.

The customer service guy looks pretty desperate himself.

"Sir, as I've said at least five times, you cannot take a goldfish in first class, either. That still falls into the category of carry-on luggage. I'll be glad to let you talk to my supervisor, and he can tell you about our Priority Pet Program." He looks like he's wondering what the Customer Service Manual says about tossing customers over the railing into the baggage claim area.

Roger's breathing faster and faster. I'm afraid he's going to hyperventilate. Could this day get any better, really? Almost in spite of myself, I step in to help.

"Roger, step away from the counter." I gently grasp his arm. "No, no, shhh. Step away and let the nice man do his job. We can't take your fish on board, so we'll have to figure out something else." We're backing away from the counter, step by step.

"Now, tell me about this fish." I'm trying not to be obvious about searching the concourse for Joe. After all, he *is* the senior production coordinator on this show, as he delights in rubbing in my face. It's past time for him to step up and take charge of this situation. That's what they pay him the big bucks for, right? Of course, Joe is nowhere in sight. Probably comfortably ensconced in Starbucks, guzzling lattes, the prick.

"Jules, I can't leave Spot behind. He, well, he helps me calm down." Roger has a death grip on my hand. I'm going to lose circulation any minute.

"Well, we—Spot? Your goldfish is named *Spot?*"

"It's a long story, but I'd already had a hamster named Hermione, and of course Flavius was out. Jules, what are we going to do?" He's looking at me as if I have magical answers to the goldfish dilemma. No such luck.

"Roger, here's the deal. First, we can't get that fish on the plane. I'm sorry, but that's the bottom line.

The airlines are much more strict with all the terrorism worries these days. Not that goldfish are known consorts of terrorists, but you know what I mean. Second, we don't have time to rent a car and drive to Tampa Bay with Spot. Finally, there's no way the show will pay for a charter flight, and who knows what the cabin pressure would do to Spot, anyway. Wouldn't you rather that he be safe than face what might be a hideous death at thirty thousand feet?"

We're both silent for a moment, contemplating Spot exploding all over the first-class cabin.

Roger takes a deep breath. "You're right, Jules. I couldn't face causing him harm like that. I'll carry on without him, and you can help me with my relaxation exercises instead. I'll have your seat moved up to first class." He thrusts a small leather case at me. "I'll trust you to do the honors."

I open the bag and, sure enough, Spot is inside, swimming around in his specially-designed carrying case. He's pretty nonchalant for a creature who barely escaped explosive death. Roger starts to walk toward the lines for the security checkpoint, shoulders slumped. Suddenly, he turns and looks at me.

"Jules, I don't know what we'd do without you. You always know what to do and have been an amazing asset to the show since you joined us. Even Nellie said she was glad our other PC was struck by that car."

As I stand there, fish in hand, with Roger's words echoing in my abused head, my mouth falls open. It's not what he said that shocks me, but my reaction to it. No, not the part about Nellie enjoying somebody's bodily injury. That's pure Nellie. The part about my being an asset to the show.

I'm used to comments like this in the early days of a new career. You can fool some of the people some of the time, and all that. I shine with overachieving excellence in a big way each time I start a new job. But this is the first time I've ever felt a small glimmer of hope that a compliment on my competence might, in fact, be true.

"What do you think, Spot? Is it possible for a thirty-two-year-old to finally grow up right here in front of the Northwest Airlines counter?"

Maybe not. I am talking to a fish, after all.

First Class and Lamaze Breathing

True to his word, Roger moved me up to first class. I have mixed feelings about this. I enjoy boarding early and the extra leg room. On the other hand, I have to sit next to Roger who—big surprise—is afraid of flying. As the coach passengers start trooping in, Joe walks by and gives me a dirty look. I can't help it, I turn and stick my tongue out at his back. Mid-tongue extension, I look right into the eyes of the man sitting directly behind me.

The warm, brown eyes.

My tongue shoots back into my mouth so fast I almost choke. "Sam? What are *you* doing here?" If I were auditioning for Loser of the Year with this guy, I'd be a sure bet. Oh, no, there's that smile again. I can't stand it.

"Nice tongue, Jules. You've recovered pretty well."

Great, now he's mocking me. But I notice he avoided my question. What's a carpenter who works for Del's Bar, Grill, and Motel doing flying first class? Unless . . . "Are you working for the show now?"

"Yes, I am. We have the contract for all set design for *POP STAR LIVE!* I'm overseeing the temporary stages as a sort of side benefit while I interview the principals to see what they envision for the set we'll use for the weekly TV show." He leans forward.

"This will be great, Jules. You and I can talk on the flight, so I can get a head start. I've heard you're a big part of this production."

Oh, oh. Hormone Overload. I can feel his breath and his words are shimmering in the air, heard but somehow untranslatable. The sound of his voice converts the words into hieroglyphics, and the wrappings are starting to unravel from my mummified emotions. The same magic makes my brain a little hazy. I try to form a semi-coherent response, then I hear a loud throat-clearing noise beside me.

"Umhmmm. Sam, that's very admirable of you to wish to begin your work in such an expedient fashion, but Jules and I have a great deal to discuss on the flight. I'm sure Joe or Norman can fill you in quite well." I may be imagining it, but Roger's voice sounds a tad icy. I wrench my gaze away from Sam's to look at him. Oh, boy. Those blue eyes are suddenly as cold as a blueberry slushee and a little intense. And a *lot* possessive. I think I'm in trouble.

Roger's finally asleep. I taught him the Lamaze breathing techniques one of my friends showed us when she was rhapsodizing about the natural childbirth she planned with her first child. (She wound up going for the epidural and naming her son after the anesthesiologist, but still.)

He deep-breathed his way to sleep, finally letting go of the vise-grip he had on my hand. I'm trying to rub circulation back into my fingers when the flight attendant stops by.

"The gentleman behind you thought you'd like this," she says, beaming a coffee, tea, or come-do-me-in-the-galley smile over the back of my seat at Sam. She places a Diet Coke and another bottle of water on my tray table and sways her hips off toward the front.

Can't anybody just freaking *walk* anywhere anymore?

I look at the drinks and sigh. Sam must be working toward his Help a Twelve-Stepper Boy Scout badge. I turn and lean around my seat to talk to him. "You really need to quit taking care of me."

He's sprawled back in his seat, completely relaxed. A grin twitches at the edge of his lips. "I thought you might need it, after two hours of hypochondria boy clutching at you." He gestures at the empty seat next to him. "If you're up for it, I'd still like to talk about the set design with you."

This feels like leaping out of the frying pan into the extra large George Foreman grill, but I notice I'm unbuckling my seat belt. Sam doesn't move over to the window seat, or even move his legs much, but instead reaches up to hold my hands and steady me while I climb over him. For an instant in mid-straddle, I meet his eyes and the heat blazing in them nearly buckles my knees. I know I should laugh or make a joke, but the humor has dried up in my throat.

I've got to get out of here, I think, even as I sink down into the seat, trapped between the window on one side and the probable destruction of my vow of celibacy on the other.

He's still holding one of my hands, and brings it to his lips. "I'm glad you're feeling better," he murmurs, then kisses my palm gently. I can literally feel my jeans catch on fire. How am I going to explain this to the sky marshal? *It wasn't my fault I torched the plane. My panties ignited.*

Sam lets go of my hand, and I'm momentarily bereft. His smile flashes dark heat, almost predatory. I blink and the heat is gone as though it were never there. Sam is reaching under the seat to get . . . a laptop? Oh, boy, there's definite HBP potential here, too. I need to be careful with this guy, or I'm going to be tying his blood pressure cuffs to my bed. Hmm. Kirby could help me with the equipment, if I want to try out a little light bondage, and . . .

"Jules?" Sam's looking at me quizzically, laptop screen lit up with a complicated-looking chart. The logo for Blake and Sons Construction flashes in the upper left corner.

I drag my thoughts away from silk blindfolds and chocolate-flavored body oil and look at him. "Are you Blake? Or Son?" Motel carpenter. Good one, Jules.

He laughs. "I'm one of the sons. My brother Sean is the other one, but he's actually a chef in San Francisco. Dad named the company when we were practically babies, and we never changed it."

"So, do you do set design full time, or house construction, or what?"

"We do building. Residential and commercial buildings. This is our first foray into set design, but I've been trying to break in for a while. Our company built Marshall's house, and he was happy enough with it that he gave me a chance." He's typing while we talk.

"Why set design? Isn't the building gig going well? The economy and all?"

"It's going fine. The movie/TV thing was strictly my idea. I've always loved movies, and I thought it would be fun and profitable to get the business involved. Dad thinks it's a little nuts, but he and I agree on most things, so we decided to go for it." He shifts a little in his seat, and his arm is pressed firmly against mine on the console. I briefly yearn for coach class, where there would be no console between his legs and mine. *Focus, Jules.*

The flight attendant stops again. She's not too happy to see me sitting next to Sam, judging by the expression cracking the layers of makeup on her face. She leans over to Sam. "Can I get you anything else?"

She's all but ignoring me, but too bad for her. "I'll have a Bloody Mary."

Sam whips his head around to look at me, a flash of something that looks like disappointment in his eyes. "I'll have a black coffee and some more water, please," he says quietly.

As the flight attendant moves on, Sam takes a deep breath and forces it out in a sigh. "Look, Jules, you can tell me that this is none of my business, but there are a lot of places that you can get help."

"Help for what?" This is it, I think. He's on to me. I don't know anything about TV production and it's obvious. He's recommending career counseling.

"Help with the drinking problem. If you're not into the AA philosophy, there are medically designed programs, and counseling, and . . ."

"*What? What drinking problem?*" I'm raising my voice. "What drinking problem?" I hiss. "I don't have a drinking problem. I got drunk one time, because I had a day from hell auditioning hundreds of little- and no-talent singers, my boss is a hypochondriac who thinks I'm Florence freakin' Nightingale, and the senior PC on the set is trying to poison me with bacteria-infested mayonnaise. I'm NOT an alcoholic."

Sam searches my face and can evidently tell the difference between denial and righteous indignation, because he appears embarrassed.

"God, I'm sorry, Jules. I'm doing it again. I see alcoholics everywhere, and I've got to stop it. Now *I'm* the one who's completely embarrassed. Please forgive me." He shakes his head and mutters, "Dad would kick my ass."

"Sam, it's no problem. I guess the evidence against me was pretty compelling this morning. But what's the deal?"

He looks at me, the sheepish smile fading from his face. "No big deal; my own demons to live with. Mom was a drunk. She was passed out on the couch every day when I came home from school. Finally, a couple of years ago, she ran her car off a bridge. She died, Jules. I guess I'm a little sensitive to seeing beautiful women drinking." He leans his head back and closes his eyes, but not before I see the anguish in them.

That clunking noise you heard was the padlock falling off of my emotions. My hands are shaking. I look at them and clasp them tightly between my knees. I'd already decided to try the relationship thing again—sometime, with somebody—but I wasn't bargaining for this. I haven't felt this lurch in my stomach since Mark. And look how *that* turned out. I'd be a lot safer having a fling with somebody who has no chance of engaging my emotions. Someone like . . . Roger. I glance at the seat in front of me, where I can see Roger's silky dark hair between the seat and the window. He's gorgeous, he'd definitely be hygienic, and I wouldn't have to worry about picking pieces of my heart up off the pavement for months when it was over. Roger is definitely a possibility.

"Jules? Are you OK? I'm sorry, I didn't mean to dump my neuroses on you. Shit. I *never* tell people that stuff. I don't know what's gotten into me. Let's forget it and start over, OK?"

That's it. Let's forget it. I smile and turn to look into the warmth of his eyes, knowing that I'm not going to forget anything. Tampa suddenly beckons like Xanadu. This is going to be an interesting few days.

Chapter Nine

Mark

OK, I guess I have to tell you the Mark story. Mark was—cue melodramatic clichés—the first man I ever really loved. Sure, I'd had flings and romances, and I'd even thought I'd been in love several times before. I mean, I was twenty-six years old and not exactly a virgin. Sexually or emotionally.

Then I met Mark and all the sappy, overused, trite love songs that have ever been sung *started making sense*. It was awful and wonderful all at the same time. We couldn't stand to be apart from each other for more than an hour. In fact, other than for five days during a medical conference Mark attended in Chicago, we never spent a single night apart, from the day we met until the day he dumped me only seventy-two hours before our wedding.

But I'm getting ahead of myself.

Mark was the complete opposite of me in all the ways we thought didn't matter. I was flighty and couldn't decide what I wanted to be when I grew up. He was in medical school, following the path carved by his father, his mother, his grandmother, his grandfather, his great-grandfather, and probably all the ancestral Stantons since the dawn of time. There was probably a Stanton in the operating room at creation. *We have to be careful about blood loss when God removes that rib from Adam. Prep Eve, stat.*

So Mark was going to be a doctor, and I was going to be a famous writer. (Or maybe an actress. Or a scientist.) His family loved me and I loved them, and my mom loved Mark, too. Dad was the only holdout from this interfamilial love fest. It was out of character for him, since he never says anything about my love life, but I remember he took me out for breakfast soon after Mark and I had joyously announced our engagement.

"Are you sure you know what you're doing?" he asked, over pancakes and country-fried potatoes. Our weekly Saturday morning breakfasts have been a tradition since I was about six months old. I didn't contribute much to the conversations back then, though.

"What do you mean, Dad? I thought you *liked* Mark." I poured extra butter pecan syrup on my pecan waffle. Redundancy is a good thing in breakfast food.

"I do like Mark, Jules. I'm not sure if I like him for you, though." He was staring at me pensively, as though wondering how far to go. "He's awfully, well, stodgy for someone so young, isn't he?"

"Stodgy? Dad, you've been reading too many of your own books. Mark's not stodgy, he's stable. He *is* in med school, after all. Would you want a scatter-brained doctor taking out your appendix?"

"No, of course not, Jules. But this is for the rest of your life. *The rest of your life.* Can you really live with this man for the next fifty or sixty years?"

Of course I was sure I could live with Mark for hundreds of years. He was my soul mate, after all. The yin to my yang. My heart's desire.

And I'd already picked out my wedding dress.

Later, when Dad told me during the week I was supposed to have been on my honeymoon that he and Mom were getting divorced, that breakfast conversation made more sense. But it was all moot, anyway. Because Mark had decided he wanted to be free to stick his yin in other women's yangs.

I still remember every word of *that* conversation. And the bastard didn't even have the decency to stand me up at the church, so I could be Bold, Undaunted Jules, bravely dancing at my husbandless reception until three A.M. and amazing everyone with my courage and loveliness. I even could have slept with an usher or two.

But no, he had to do his jilting in private. In our apartment. Where he was packing his suitcases when I came home from the library.

His seven suitcases.

"We're only going to Hawaii for ten days. I don't think you'll need seven suitcases," I said. I was laughing and tried to put my arms around him, but he did a weird two-step maneuver away from me.

"Jules, we have to talk." He was still fiddling with the pile of shirts on the bed, and hadn't even looked at me yet. I didn't have a clue. That's what amazed me the most, in the three or four hundred times I replayed the scene in my head.

We have to talk??? Could it have been any more clear? How could I not have guessed?

I remember bouncing onto the bed, throwing my arms over my head as if I were going to form a snow angel in the middle of his heaps of clothes. "OK, let's talk. Can you believe we're going to be married in," I looked at my watch, "in exactly seventy-two hours?"

It was three-eighteen in the afternoon on a Wednesday when my world shattered, in case you're interested.

"That's just it, Jules. We aren't." He sighed heavily and came to sit next to me on the bed. "We have to call off the wedding." He finally looked at me, and waves of sadness poured from him.

Naturally, I thought somebody had died. "My God, Mark, what is it? Is it your dad?" His dad had been through a couple of bypass operations in the past few years.

"No, Jules, no. Nothing's wrong. I mean, everything's wrong, but nobody's sick or anything. I can't go through with this. I don't want to get married, Jules. I can't marry you."

And then Time Stopped. I know why they call them clichés. It's because they're true now, and they've been true for thousands of years and millions of people. When the man you love crushes your heart under the soles of his Adidas running shoes, time actually does stop. With all due respect to Stephen Hawking, the laws of physics go straight to hell. It took three years for my hand to rise to my mouth, and another seventeen for me to run the few yards to the bathroom, where I threw up everything I'd eaten that week.

The rest of the story is pretty mundane. Mark had met another med student in Chicago, and he hooked up with her for the whole conference. They had an all-around great time, wining and dining and playing hide the stethoscope. When I asked him if he was in love with her, he laughed. No, he wasn't in love with her. He never planned to see her again. He just wasn't ready to give up all the women he could never sleep with again if we got married. So I wasn't even dumped for the Other Woman. I was dumped for all the nameless, faceless women he wanted to fuck in the future.

This didn't help with the humiliation, you understand.

But it took a long time to get to humiliation. First, I had to pass through the pain. Agony, really. Then Agony's friend Towering Rage showed up for a while. I had to work through quite a few of the gang: Despair, Hopelessness, Jealousy, and Revenge, before I ever got to Humiliation.

I was still in the Agony portion of our entertainment when my parents hit me with their divorce news. It wasn't how they'd planned it, of course. The breakup had been in the works for a while, but they hadn't wanted to shadow my joy and nuptial-planning excitement with their own sadness. Unfortunately, they'd already sold their house in Dublin, and Dad was moving to a new place in Upper Arlington, while Mom was going to be a Writer in Residence at Berkeley for a while. So it was kind of like, we're so sorry you're in pain; come get your stuff out of the house so the new owners can move in by Friday.

To be fair, it wasn't that abrupt, and they tried their best to lessen the blow. But after two weeks during which *both* of the Happily Ever Afters I'd cared about the most suddenly weren't, I locked my emotions up so far down in the wastelands of my heart I'd have needed a map to find them again.

Now here I am, five years later, sitting next to a man who has a built-in GPS unit. Am I really ready to be found?

Chapter Ten

The Under the Sea Theme Park

The plane must have crashed and I'm in Hell. There's no other way to explain it. I'm going to spend the rest of eternity in the Under the Sea amusement park, being tortured by singing auditions.

In ninety-five-degree weather. And humidity. It really is Hell.

I open another bottle of water (my sixth in two hours, but who's counting? At least they have Aquafina in Hell) and look around for Satan. All I see is Nellie, but after the way she shrieked at her staff this morning, she's a contender for the job. I've tried to talk to Nellie's assistant about standing up for herself over the past week, but the woman is literally afraid of her own shadow. I mean, her shadow must have beaten the crap out of her one day, and then hung out on the street corner smoking with all the other bully shadows.

Naturally, Nellie blames us for the heat. Because it's so *unusual* for it to be hot in Florida in August. Not that I'm catty, but I do get a teensy bit of amusement from what the humidity is doing to her hair. Especially now that we're being filmed constantly, and not only at preselected times.

Oh, didn't I mention the new development? Turns out U2's Bono called Roger's band Latent Earwax a "brilliant new development in the pantheon of music." Not that hanging around with all those world leaders talking about Third World debt forgiveness has made Bono a pompous egomaniac, or anything. He pretty much always was one.

But an *influential* pompous egomaniac. No sooner had *Entertainment Weekly* and *Rolling Stone* and probably all the London tabloids, who never let a little thing like consistency get in the way of their reporting, announced the news, than Latent Earwax was on its way. The band's album shot up the charts and suddenly all of its tour dates, which had been on the verge of being cancelled, are sold out. The bottom line of all this frenzy is that Roger is being hailed as the genius of new-talent spotting, and *POP STAR LIVE!* has raised advertising costs by about quadruple what they were going for before.

Now we've got a bit of a frenzy going on right here. There are actual journalists on site, reporting on the auditions, and we have our own film crew taping every minute, in case we need a shot for posterity of Q having his blond hair spiked by one of what he calls his "posse," or Nellie plumping up her nonexistent cleavage.

Break's over. Back to musical hell.

Flying Feathers

This contestant has got to be kidding. He burst through the curtain (we're using the ready-made stage that Under the Sea uses for its own Musical

Revue—don't ask; it involves dancers dressed up as bowling pins: Rock and Bowl) instead of walking out to the designated place on the stage as we've asked everyone to do. His outfit?—costume?—whatever he's wearing looks like Chippendale dancer crossed with Masai warrior. He has a loincloth on under a cloak made out of purple feathers. Plus, his body is painted with strange symbols that look oddly like the Powerpuff Girls.

Joe, Norman, and I are in total agreement for once. We're all staring at him with our eyes and mouths wide open. Roger, Nellie, and Q have identical expressions on their faces. (Now that we're in the public eye so much, the role of the production coordinators in prescreening has diminished; part of why Nellie was so hysterical is that *she* now has to listen to all of the singers. *All* of them.)

Then Loincloth Boy starts singing. And we thought it was bad *before*.

"In the jungle, the mighty jungle . . ."

"STOP!" bellows Roger. We've never heard Roger raise his voice before; all heads swivel in his direction. "I can't bloody STAND it. You are quite possibly the worst singer in the world. No, in the HISTORY of the world. What the BLOODY HELL do you think you're playing at? GET OFF THAT STAGE!"

He's kind of cute when he's angry.

Loincloth Boy froze at the first bellow and now looks like he can't believe what he's hearing. So he decides the way to ingratiate himself with the judges is to call them a bunch of assholes on national TV.

"You're a bunch of assholes! You don't know anything about music! You wouldn't know a good singer if he bit you in the ass!"

I don't understand why good singers would go around biting people in the ass, but people say strange things when they're under stress.

By now, our crack security duo of Sharp and Johnson is up on stage to escort Loincloth Boy off the stage. But LB doesn't want to be escorted. So he starts running around the stage in a wild circle, screaming abuse at the judges, especially Roger. Sharp and Johnson chase after him, yelling at him to stop.

It had to be cheap glue. That's all I can figure.

Cheap glue melts in the sunshine, as any self-respecting American kid who left her art project out in the yard for three hours after school knows.

It doesn't take three hours in the heat and humidity of Florida.

One minute LB is making a mad dash across the stage, howling his defiance, his purple-feathered cloak and loincloth flapping. The next minute, the feathers start flying off the cloak. But he's still running and howling. And Sharp and Johnson are still chasing after him, yelling for him to stop.

They're not exactly in good physical shape, our security team. So they're running and sweating and yelling and running and sweating and yelling.

And the feathers are flying: hot, goopy glue stuck to the ends.

You can guess the rest. Within another few minutes, Sharp and Johnson are covered in purple feathers that are sticking to their uniforms, hair, and skin. Q, Nellie, and Roger are gaping in disbelief. Norman and I are laughing so hard, I'm sure I'm going to pee down my leg any minute.

And Joe's even smiling a little.

Suddenly, the stage curtains part, and Sam appears right in front of the newly-plucked loincloth boy. Sam's arm shoots out and he grasps the boy's arm, yanking him to a stop. Sharp stops dead and leans forward at the waist, inhaling great sucking gasps of air. For a minute, we're all sure Johnson is going to run right into Sharp, starting a domino effect, but he manages to stop in time and drops to his knees right there on stage, coughing and hacking.

Those guys have got to get in better shape.

All of the boy's fight magically disappeared with his feathers; he slumps next to Sam, a picture of abject defeat.

The Under the Sea security guards show up (good timing, when everything is over) and announce that they'll escort him out of the park. They ask if we want to press charges, but nobody but Sharp does. We convince him that we need him to go shampoo the purple feathers out of his hair and come back to help us with the rest of auditions, instead.

As the boy is being marched through the huge crowd that gathered to watch the show, he turns and glares at us, hatred glittering in his eyes. "You haven't seen the last of me." (Teenagers can be so melodramatic.)

I turn around, still smiling and shaking my head, to a sight that crushes my amusement like a bug on a windshield. Nellie has all ninety-seven pounds of her insect-like body pressed up against Sam.

"Oh, Sam. That was so brave of you. You saved the day," she purrs.

I roll my eyes. This wasn't exactly ax murderers gone ballistic. It was one teenaged boy with unrealistic dreams of stardom, a big bag of feathers, and a defective glue stick.

Sam does appear to be enjoying the attention, though. I narrow my eyes and realize I'm feeling a lot less guilty about his shoes. Sam raises his head and catches me watching them. A slow, lazy smile spreads across his face, as though he can guess what I'm thinking. He peels Nellie's claws, er, fingers, off of his arm and murmurs something to her, as he starts walking.

Straight to me.

The man has a great walk, I'll give him that. No striding, swaggering, or swaying. Just a relaxed, self-confident walk that says "I want to have dinner with you."

Huh?

"Jules, I said I want to have dinner with you. Earth to Jules? Are you free tonight?" He's still smiling that dangerous smile.

"Um, yes, er, no, I mean, really?" Good, now he thinks I'm an airhead *and* inarticulate. "I mean, as long as we get done with auditions before midnight. We wasted an hour with our feathered friend. Thanks for stopping him before we all died of heatstroke, especially poor Sharp and Johnson." I grin and try hard not to look at his chest, which is sharply defined in his snug T-shirt. Doesn't the man own any baggy flannel, for God's sake?

He steps closer to me, so that I'm standing in the shade of his body. Oddly, my temperature shoots up. I tilt my head back to look into his eyes. I think the heat is affecting everyone, because his gaze is searing into mine.

"Don't you want to give me a hero's welcome? I did 'save the day,' after all," he murmurs, as he pushes a strand of my hair behind my ear with one fingertip.

"I'm sure Nellie will be glad to give you a hero's any-thing you want," I reply, somewhat snappishly. Did I mention the heat?

"I'm not interested in what *Nellie* has to offer, Jules." He steps back. "See you after auditions."

I'm not sure that dinner with Sam is a good idea, in

my newly emotional state, but it can be like a test. If I can have a fling with Sam without getting my feelings involved and being shattered when he leaves me, I can get through anything.

Love is so overrated, anyway.

Arson and Old Lace

Norman is my hero. He found a Starbucks and brought me two enormous iced coffees, so I think I may survive another morning of auditions. At least we're down to the finalists now. We finished all three hundred and eighteen auditions last night after midnight. I wasn't sure if I was relieved or disappointed that I had to take a raincheck on dinner with Sam. I collapsed in my Under the Sea Motel room bed for eight hours, then woke up disoriented, and screamed when the first thing I saw was the giant neon-blue octopus on the ceiling.

They go a little *overboard* with their Under the Sea theme here.

So now we're getting ready for the first of the twenty finalists, and her name is Shanicia. Well, her name is actually Alice B. Jones, according to her application, but a lot of the bees spend their time waiting in line coming up with stage names that they think will look good on the Billboard lists. She told us yesterday that she's a lead and solo singer for the First Baptist Church of St. Petersburg, and I can believe it. She has a voice that would make angels weep. It's so pure, and she has an amazing range.

(I've been working on my musical knowledge with some of the camera guys who are music junkies. Our entire camera crew consists of reformed garage band members. Anyway, I know all about range, pitch, and tone now.)

She sings the first lyrics of a pretty traditional rendition of "Amazing Grace." Then, when she has us lulled into complacency, she totally rocks out. OK, Norman said that first, but he's right. She throws her body, soul, and the full power of that incredible voice into a hot-tempo pulse pounder that probably knocks a few angels off of their harps.

I'm betting Shanicia is coming to Hollywood.

Sure enough, we work our way through the rest of the finalists and there are plenty of good singers that we picked yesterday, but nobody else with the kind of spark that shouts Star Quality. Until we get to number twenty.

Carlos Quintana walks up onstage in ordinary blue jeans and a simple long-sleeved white shirt. But there's nothing ordinary or simple about him, other than his clothes. I don't remember him as being particularly impressive yesterday, but he auditioned around nine-thirty last night. Carlos Santana would have bored me by then.

A good night's sleep must have done wonders for either his singing or my listening, because when he opens his mouth to sing, it's liquid heat. Nellie and Q, who've been bickering for the past ten minutes, both stop and look up at the stage in disbelief. Roger is smiling and drumming his fingers to the beat. It's—what else?—a Santana cover, but he makes it his own. His black eyes flash passion and power and pride as his body moves to the music.

The teenaged girls standing behind me are practically hyperventilating. Did I mention that he's gorgeous, too?

Carlos stops singing, and Roger stands up and slowly starts clapping. "Thank you, young man. You have single-handedly restored my faith in this competition. You are by far the best singer I have heard yet."

As much as he hates to agree with Roger (or Nellie) about anything, Q is nodding. "You brought it, man. You're in."

We only need two judges to agree, but Nellie so hates being superfluous. "I told them last night that you were the one," she says, eyeing Carlos like a sugar addict looks at a Krispy Kreme donut. "You're absolutely coming to Hollywood, José."

"It's Carlos," Norman whispers.

"Whatever."

The judges step up on the stage for the obligatory photo ops with the two winning finalists, and I slump back in my chair. I'm suddenly exhausted again, but it's nothing a cheeseburger, fries, and a huge Diet Coke can't fix. As I roll my head around on my neck to stretch my complaining neck muscles, I see something odd in my peripheral vision.

There's somebody on top of the stage roof. It's not a real roof, more like a wooden frame draped with loads of cheap, sparkly fabric. So it's even more alarming when I see the flames shoot up from in front of the crouched figure.

"Watch out!" I shout at the people on the stage, but they can't hear me, because of the explosion that blasts through the air. Suddenly, I can't hear anything as the force of the concussion slams into my eardrums.

I see the figures on the stage launch into the air, like some weird outtake from a Jackie Chan movie. Smoke billows up from beneath the splintered wood, and now I can't *see*, either.

I shoot to my feet, terror propelling me toward the stage. Sam is suddenly there, too, leaping up on the destroyed stage from the other side.

"Jules, stay back. We don't know if there's another

bomb," he shouts at me.

Another bomb? Did he say *bomb?* My steps falter for a moment, until I hear screaming. That high-pitched shriek has got to be Roger. I start running again.

The dust and smoke is clearing enough for me to see the results of the explosion, as I gingerly climb up on the wood. The boards in the middle of the floor have splintered and are sticking up at odd angles. Roger is lying sideways on the edge of the hole, his left leg wedged between two boards. Nellie is starting to pick herself up from where she has landed on top of Carlos. Shanicia/Alice is pulling herself up to stand nearby. They all look dazed, but unhurt.

Suddenly, I remember the figure on the roof. "Sam, there was somebody on the roof," I begin.

He whirls around. "I thought I told you to stay back," he says, his face furious. We hear a crackling sound from above. The lacy fabric roof is blazing, and part of it is coming down, headed straight for where Roger is trapped between the boards. Sam and I reach him at the same time and move as though we've choreographed every step and rehearsed for months.

Sam wrenches the board off of Roger's leg. I yank Roger away from the hole and out of the way of the flaming fabric. Sam dives underneath it and rolls as he hits the wood, then is immediately on his feet stamping the flames out with his boots.

By this time, security shows up with fire extinguishers and starts to put the fire out. We can hear the siren wail of approaching emergency vehicles. I help Roger to his feet, so we can move off what's left of the stage, after we determine that the worst of his injuries are scrapes and a really large chunk of wood stuck in his calf. It's not bleeding much and nothing appears to be broken, so of course he's sure he's dying. The emergency personnel show up on the run and take him off my hands, so I turn to see how everybody else is doing.

On the other side of the stage, Nellie is brushing the dust off of Carlos with a lot of unnecessary touching. At least both of them look fine. Shanicia is standing next to them. She has a scrape on her cheek, but appears otherwise unharmed.

I'm realizing I haven't seen Sam for a few minutes, when the shock sets in. I start shaking and feel icy cold, in spite of the oppressive heat of the day. Strong hands grasp my shoulders from behind and pull me against the warmth of a hard body. Sam.

"Don't you ever do that to me again," he grits out against my hair. He sounds angry, but his hands are gentle on my shoulders and he starts rubbing my arms from shoulder to elbow.

"You scared me to death, Jules. You could have been hurt."

Why would you care, I want to ask, but the warmth of his body is too soothing, and I don't have the energy to be confrontational right now. I sag back against him in relief.

"That's it. You're going back to your room to have a shower and rest." He pulls away from me as he speaks, and I feel an ache of loss. Then he turns me around.

"Do you need me to carry you?" He's peering intently into my eyes; I guess he noticed the shaking.

"What, like some helpless female?" I laugh. OK, it was wobbly, but it still qualifies as a laugh. "No, I'll walk. Just what I need, the crew thinking I'm sleeping with yet another member of the *PSL!* gang."

Sam looks at me sharply, questions in his eyes, but, mercifully, he doesn't ask them. He wraps his arm around my waist and we head for my room. The crowd magically opens up to give us space. The look on Sam's face is enough to discourage idle chitchat.

We reach the Octopus Suite in record time, and Sam pulls the key out of my shaking hand. He draws me into the cool dimness of my room, then closes the door and leans back on it, pulling me into his chest for a hug. I notice that he's trembling a little bit himself.

"How did you get to mean so much to me so quickly?" he mutters into my neck. My neck is really pleased to be singled out for the attention, I can't help but notice, but my knees are starting to buckle. I'm not what you'd call a swooner, but the heat, the smoke, and the shock of it all are getting to me.

OK, I've wanted to say something like this my whole almost-six-foot-tall life. Drum roll, please:

Then, Sam sweeps me off my feet.

He really does! He picks me up like I weigh nothing, and I've got a good fifty pounds on Nellie. I stare at him in disbelief as he carries me to the bathroom and sets me down gently by the door. "Do you need help with your shower, or will you be OK?"

I look at him, considering. Is this an elaborate ploy to get in my panties? Not that he'd need elaborate. Or even a ploy, at this point. But I only see concern in his eyes, no unbridled lust.

Not even *bridled* lust. Damn.

I shake my head. "Sam, thanks, but I'm fine. I think the heat got to me for a second. I'll, um, I'll see you later. Thanks for helping me get here."

He smiles grimly. "I'm not going anywhere until you're out of the shower and in bed. What if you get dizzy and fall down? I'll be right outside this door if you want me. . . ."

I nod and close the bathroom door behind me. The

first man who wants to get me naked and into bed in almost a year, and not a hint of passion from him. Nothing but sweet, kind, caring concern. I must be losing my touch.

The warm spray of the shower sluices the smoky smell and the wobbly feeling away. I wrap a towel around my hair, and pull on my favorite silk robe, a cornflower blue that exactly matches my eyes. I don't put my underwear back on, and I don't tie the robe all that tightly, either. Then I towel off my hair and shake it out around my shoulders.

I'll show *him* sweet and caring. HA. He's going to be begging by the time I'm done with him.

I open the door and step out into the room, almost running into Sam, who stands up as I open the door.

"Are you OK?" he asks.

"I'm fine, just a little wobbly. Thanks for staying." I shake my head, trying out Kirby's patented Hair Toss, and look up at him from beneath my lashes. *Hello.* It's working. Sam's jaw is clenched shut and his gaze is roaming over my silk robe and what it's barely covering. Did I mention it's really short?

"Let me get you settled for a nap, Jules, then I'll get out of your hair," he says, his voice husky.

OK, it's all or nothing time, folks. I draw a deep breath and step closer to him. "What if I want you *in* my hair, Sam?"

He inhales sharply, arms coming up around my waist. "Jules, you've been through a lot, and I don't think this is the time . . ."

"No, I haven't. I wasn't on the stage when it blew up. I'm fine. Except for the part where I want you to kiss me, and you're not doing anything about it." I trace the outline of his lips with my fingertip and he groans.

"I hope you don't regret this later. Because I have a

feeling I'm not going to let you get away from me after we're through," he murmurs against my forehead, then traces kisses down the side of my face and around to my lips.

"Less talking and more kissing, Blake," I reply. I'm suddenly sounding kind of husky myself, and feel a tiny twinge of fear. I was so sure I could be in control of this relationship and this man, but control is slipping away from me as quickly as my robe is slipping down my arms.

Then he's really kissing me, and I never knew lips could be so soft and so firm all at once. And the loneliness of the past year and the hunger of the moment combine to make me spontaneously combust. I rip at his clothes to get my hands under his shirt and feel his skin under my fingers, as he lifts me by the waist and moves me to the bed, all the while kissing and kissing.

After I stop to find the condoms Kirby always hopefully stashes in my flight bag, I pull back my head and look in his glorious brown eyes and start laughing and push him back on the bed and jump on top of him. He's laughing, too, and wrestles me over on my back and starts kissing me again, and suddenly we're not laughing anymore, because the heat and the flames between us make what happened back on the stage look like nothing.

I think, how could I have lived without *this* for a whole year, but I know I'm wrong, even as I think it, because I've never felt this kind of heat before. Then he's moving down my body, kissing and nibbling, and my breasts are begging for attention and he doesn't let them down. And he's moving farther down my body and pressing my thighs to the side and he's kissing me, and suddenly south of the border has come to be the center of the universe and his tongue sends me supernova.

As the shudders die down in my body and the planets start turning on their axes again, I almost believe that this man knows exactly who I am, yet he still wants me, so I'll never have to fake anything with him. The freedom in that thought pushes me back over the edge when he enters me, so I'm coming apart and coming apart underneath him and he's looking at me with surprise and joy and maybe even a little love in his eyes and then he's shuddering, too, and collapsing on top of me, and all I can think is,

Oh, this *is what I wanted all those years. What took you so long to find me?*

Chapter Eleven

Movie Options and the Midwest

Here I am, back in good old Columbus, Ohio, home to the Ohio State Buckeyes and not a whole lot else. I always feel lucky that I escaped, while simultaneously yearning to visit, so the old expression, "You can take the girl out of the Midwest, but you can't take her away from her mother's meat loaf" really rings true for me.

Auditions don't start until tomorrow, although I hear that the line of wanna-bees is already stretched all the way around the football stadium. The hype surrounding the show caused a huge jump in the number of people trying out. I hear the OSU football stadium can hold around ninety thousand people. Not that we're going to listen to more than one thousand, max, but the bees all bring friends, family, and anybody who can provide moral support. We had a fight with one girl who wanted to carry her Chihuahua onstage for luck.

So I have a relaxing day scheduled, for a change. I'm taking Nellie's assistant shopping at City Center Mall to buy her something—anything—that makes her look like she hasn't time-traveled from Puritan New England. Our goal: Get the brown and gray out! She's trying to grow a backbone, and I even heard her tell Nellie *No* about something. She cushioned it in huge, fluffy Martha Stewart-sized pillows of apology, but still, any No is a huge leap.

After shopping, I'm meeting Dad for lunch. He said he has some good news and some great news. His latest book probably hit the bestseller list in Liechtenstein or something. His books have been translated into every other language in the world. Although, who knows what they speak in Liechtenstein? [NOTE TO SELF: Learn more about geography.]

So I have about ten minutes. Maybe enough time to catch up on e-mail. I haven't been online in days and probably have a zillion messages to read.

I log on to my laptop and can't believe it's been so long. I pat the mouse in apology. Since the invention of e-mail and the Internet, my closest personal relationship has been with my Dell.

I'm not interested in Hot Russian Brides, having my breasts enlarged (half price!), or any of the pharmaceutical cornucopia of illegally-distributed sex enhancers, weight reducers, or mood lifters, so my inbox is quickly deleted down to three messages. Three messages in the last five days. I'm pathetic and need to remember to get a social life.

Kirby, Dad, and Jerry. I open them in order of projected length.

Dad: *meet me at Mandarin at 1:30; reservations for 2. See u then.* (Dad types his own books so doesn't like to waste energy or key strokes on e-mail.)

Jerry: *What's going on? How are you doing? Did you screw anything up? I saw a clip of the auditions in Tampa Bay on CNN. You didn't set that fire, did you? UPDATES,*

JULES, I WANT UPDATES.

Interesting how he *assumes* I had something to do with the fire. I mean, it's not like work-related catastrophes follow me wherever I go. Well, I mean, not always. I write him a quick note explaining the fire, and how the Tampa Bay police department caught Loincloth Boy, our scorned singer. Turns out he had enough bomb-making paraphernalia in his basement to blow up the whole theme park. The fire department determined that the bomb was very poorly constructed, though, which explained why we got so lucky with only superficial injuries.

Except for Roger, who's loving every minute of getting to hobble along on crutches, his calf swathed in bandages from knee to ankle. Turns out he had to have sixteen stitches when they removed that chunk of wood. He's in hypochondriac heaven—his injury is a medically-proven fact for a change.

I finish by telling Jerry that the job is going great, and I'm really enjoying it and realize, as I hit SEND, that I actually mean it for once. I can feel a stupid smile spreading over my face, as I open the e-mail from Kirby.

Kirby: *Where ARE you? Your cell phone has been turned off for days, and you're never online when I try to Instant Message you. Are you banging that British guy with the fungus? Gross, I can't even believe I asked that.*

Anyway, I have good news. I took the job at W&L and negotiated a $30,000 pay raise from what I made at the agency. Plus bonuses and stock options. We're having major champagne when you get back, my treat. I haven't asked my boss out to lunch yet, because he wore brown socks with a navy suit one day and fell about seventeen levels on my personal hotness scale. He's definitely up there on the HBP chart, though, and you know how I am, so there's still hope.

Write soon, you traveling slut. Kirbs
p.s. I heard from your dad that you'd be in Columbus for
a couple of days, so I sent you a present care of him from my
new company. Ask loverboy to help you play with your new
toys and, whatever you do, DON'T OPEN IT IN FRONT
OF YOUR DAD.

Oh, goody. I'm always afraid of Kirby's sample baskets. Half the time, I don't even recognize what the
heck the stuff is supposed to be. Plus, there was the
time Mom was over when I opened a box, and I had
to make up a story on the spot about how the 24-
karat-gold Ben Wa balls were a reproduction of an
ancient Chinese children's game. Then I had to keep
her from taking them home to show everybody at her
reading group party. Luckily, Dad's not the type to
open my mail.

There's a knock at the door, so I shut down my laptop. Time for a little *My Fair Lady* action at City
Center Mall.

"I'll have the sesame chicken," Dad says.

"You always have the sesame chicken, Dad. Be bold.
Live a little. Try something new," I say.

Dad tilts his head sideways and peers at me over the
top of his reading glasses. "Why do you care what I
eat for lunch, Jules? And Hunan beef with extra hot
sauce isn't exactly a new adventure in culinary experience for you, either." He's grinning as he hands his
menu to the waitress.

I draw circles in the ring of condensation my water
glass sweated on the table. "I'm only saying, having
new experiences is a good idea sometimes." I'm grinning, too. In fact, it's the same PermaGrin I've been
wearing since two nights ago, when Sam and I made
love for the first time.

And the second time. And the fourth time, but

who's counting? (Thank goodness for Kirby and the econo-sized travel condom pack.)

Dad breaks into my haze of sexual nostalgia by clearing his throat. "Jules, I have some great news."

"Let me guess, Dad. You signed a contract for *Professor Maxwell and the Hundred Harmonicas*?"

"No. Well, at least not yet. But I did sign a deal to have Professor Maxwell optioned for a movie!" His whole face lights up with childlike glee. "Jules, we get to go to Hollywood. I can take you shopping on Rodeo Drive."

"Dad, that's fantastic! Um, it's pronounced Ro-DAY-o, not like the thing with cowboys roping animals, but anyway, that's wonderful news. Tell me everything."

The waitress arrives with our potstickers (fried, of course) and egg rolls, so we pause briefly to smear hot mustard on everything. I got my taste buds from my dad's side of the family.

"Tell me, tell me," I say, mouth stuffed with egg roll.

"Well," he says, pouring us more green tea, "I don't really understand all of it. My agents—now I have two agents, my literary agent, of course, and a new Hollywood agent—are working out the details. I'm learning new terms like bumps, going-in vs. final approved budgets, set-up bonuses, novelization, sequels and remakes, floors and ceilings, major vs. mini-studio, separate card credit, and positive prints. It's a whole different universe from publishing."

"Someday you'll have to explain to me what all of that means. But how exciting! When do they start filming? Can I come watch? I am *so* totally coming to the premiere with you. I need a new dress. Wow! This is great news, Dad. I'm so happy for you."

He's smiling. "Slow down a minute, Jules. This is Hollywood. They talk big, and then things may or may not happen. I know writers who've had their books optioned for years, and still no movie. Right now, it means that I get a nice chunk of change for work I've already done, and get to see my name in *Variety*."

He pauses while steaming platters are placed in front of us, then starts unwrapping his chopsticks and flashes me an evil grin. "This will make your mom nuts, you know."

"Dad! She'll be happy for you. I mean, she'll rant about populist culture and the Hollywood-ization of society for a while, but she'll be happy for you. You know how she is."

We both know how she is. She keeps nagging me every other week to ask where the first three chapters of my literary novel are for her agent to review. I'm only on page six, unfortunately. But they're six damn good pages, if I do say so myself.

"The producer already has a couple of A-list actors interested in the lead. I always saw Sean Connery in the part, but he's too old these days. So I guess it'll be one of these young guys. I tried to get a veto over the casting, but no dice. As long as it's not that pretty boy Brad Pitt, or some idiot like Adam Sandler, I guess I'll be fine with it."

"We need somebody who's like a young Russell Crowe. He was so hot in *Gladiator*. He's old, now, too, but somebody like him," I say. I can see myself hanging out on the set, chatting with . . . Colin?

"Colin Farrell? Or maybe that totally hot guy who played Angelina Jolie's love interest in the Lara Croft movie. You know, the one she had to shoot in the end, because he wanted to sell Pandora's box?" Oh, yeah. I can *totally* see myself on Dad's movie set. Maybe Kirby could come, too.

I think of Kirby's effect on all men between the ages of nine and ninety. Maybe not. And, anyway, a visual of Sam keeps blocking Colin in my daydream. Hey, I adore Sam, but I can still look, can't I?

After a little chatting and a lot of eating, Dad pushes his empty plate to the side and rests his clasped hands on the table. Oh, oh. This is his let's-be-serious-now pose. What did I do this time? I remember Kirby's e-mail. Oh, God, did he open Kirby's present? I open my mouth to explain that it's all a practical joke from a distant acquaintance, when he says he's getting married.

What? My mouth snaps shut as I try to process this. From sesame chicken to movie options to Colin Farrell to getting married. Nope, doesn't compute.

"Huh?" I say. (Notice how articulate I am in stressful situations.)

"I'm getting married, Jules. She's a wonderful woman, and I've known her for almost two years and, well, I'm not getting any younger, as they say, ha ha. So we're getting married. I'd really like for you to be part of the wedding."

My fried rice swells up in my esophagus, choking me. This is my *father*. Fathers aren't supposed to get married before their daughters. Well, other than that first time, of course. And who's the bimbo? Probably some Anna Nicole wannabe.

(The rational part of my brain knows this isn't very flattering to Dad, but the rest of my brain tells Rational to shut the hell up.)

"Jules? Aren't you going to say you're happy for me? Or congratulations? There are certain traditional responses for situations like this, you know." Dad's smiling tentatively, but his eyes are concerned. "Jules?"

"Sorry, Dad, you caught me off guard. I didn't even know you were seeing anybody, after all. And I'm a little surprised you didn't tell me this news first. I mean, a wedding is higher up on the priority chain than a movie option." I'm stunned and trying to unclench my hands underneath the table. The childish part of my brain is screaming I Want My Mommy, and the rest of my brain is totally onboard with this idea.

"I know, but I wanted to get a chance to talk about lighter subjects before I told you. I wasn't sure how you'd take it. I know you had a tough time when your mom and I got divorced, especially right after that bastard Mark took off."

"Dad, of course I'm totally happy for you. When do I get to meet her? Have you told Mom yet?"

He leans back in his chair, relaxed now. Looking at him, I realize that his shoulders have been hunched up around his ears with tension the whole lunch. Why didn't I notice it before? Because I was too wrapped up in my hormone-induced haze. I'm a sex fiend and a terrible daughter.

"I was hoping you'd be happy for us. We'd like to take you out to dinner tomorrow night after auditions, if you're free."

"We're doing two days in Columbus, so I know we'll be finished at a reasonable hour. How about dinner at nine at The Refectory?" I name one of our favorite restaurants. "I'll meet you there. And is it OK if I bring somebody? I, um, I have someone for you to meet, too."

The smile on my face is a pretty big clue, even for somebody who doesn't write mysteries for a living.

"Jules, are you seeing somebody special?" Dad leans forward over the table to hold my hand.

"I think so. It's still way early, Dad, but he feels special. I haven't felt this way since Mark, and maybe not even then. I'd really like for you to meet him." Plus Sam can be moral support when I meet the girlfriend. Fiancée? Urk.

"I'm so glad for you, baby. Ever since Mark, you've been hibernating. Or at least your real feelings have. Your mother and I have felt so guilty that our divorce contributed to your fear of emotional involvement." My dad is the only father I know who will jump right in and talk about feelings, which is a good thing, since Mom sure never would. She pours all her feelings into her books.

"Dad, your divorce had nothing to do with it. All right, so I felt sorry for myself a little and sad for you two a lot, but you had to make the choice that was right for you. I just want you to be happy." I'm telling the truth about this, too.

News flash: The Earth seems to have quit revolving around me and my own despair, angst, and drama. Maybe I *am* growing up.

We stand up to go, and Dad hugs me right there in the middle of the restaurant. "I'm so glad you're here, baby. I can't wait till tomorrow. We'll make the reservations and I'll tell Amber you're looking forward to meeting her."

Amber? Her name is Amber? How old is this woman, twelve? I bite my tongue to keep from asking. Which hurts, by the way. [NOTE TO SELF: "Bite your tongue" is a figure of speech, stupid.]

My dad's getting married, and I'm seeing somebody I think I could have real feelings for. Maybe Happily Ever After isn't dead, after all.

I'm basking in the warm glow of contentment and Chinese food as we walk away from the restaurant, when Dad stops dead. "Oh, no." He looks like his sesame chicken backfired on him.

"Oh, no, what?"

"Jules, I forgot that I asked a friend to meet us for coffee after lunch. He, um, well, he . . ."

"HE? *HE?* Please tell me you didn't do this to me

again, Dad. Please tell me this isn't one of your lame attempts to set me up with the son of one of your buddies." I cross my arms over my chest and blast him with my meanest You Promised To Stop Doing This glare.

"Jules, he's, well, I . . . OK. I did. But I promise, I never will again. But you have to at least meet him. He's a really busy guy, and he took time out of his day to meet you, even though he has some important job in law or finance or something." Dad's eyes glaze over at any talk of left-brained careers.

"I don't care. I'm busy, too. I had a horrendous morning shopping with somebody who has to be arm-wrestled to the floor to buy clothes that actually fit her body, and tomorrow is going to last about fifty years. I want to go back to the hotel and take a nap." And find Sam to have a nap with me. We don't have to sleep, actually.

"Jules, you can't do this to me. I promised my friend that you'd meet her son. I talked up your TV career and, well, I can never show my face on the golf course again if you don't at least meet him."

"Oh, all right. I'll have coffee with him as long as you stay there, too. Twenty minutes, tops. And never again, Dad. Or I'll sic Kirby on you." Dad has been afraid of Kirby since the time we all had lunch, and she fired three people over her cell phone before dessert.

As we walk up to Java Master, I'm threatening Dad with various forms of hideous torture and death if he ever does this to me again, when I see Sam. I start waving like a fool, trying to get his attention across the lunchtime crowd, when I notice he's not paying any attention to his surroundings.

Because of who's right next to him.

He has his arm around the shoulders of one of the

most strikingly beautiful women I've ever seen. She's wearing a red suit that has to be silk, and she's tall, like me. Except she's not a bit like me. I glance at my denim skirt and tank top in despair, then look back at them. That suit fits her like it's tailored, which it has to be, because they don't exactly sell suits for the supermodel-thin body off the rack in Columbus, Ohio.

She laughs up at something Sam says, and I notice that her porcelain-perfect skin covers cheekbones Tyra Banks would envy. Of course, no ponytail for her, either. She has what Kirby and I sneeringly call the Career Woman Special; a chin-length bob that makes most women look like they have pumpkin-shaped heads. On *her*, it looks glamorous. Career Woman Barbie doesn't mind a bit being that close to Sam, either, if her body language is any clue.

I can't believe this is happening. That prick. It's only been a little more than forty-eight hours since we were doing the wild thing under the octopus, and he's already on a date with someone else? Of course, *we* never actually had a date. So he probably thinks I'm easy.

He probably thinks I pull the "fresh out of the shower, loosely-tied robe" routine on just anybody.

He probably thinks—who the hell cares what he probably thinks? I'll kill him.

"Jules? Jules? Here's Evan," Dad says, tugging on my arm. I'm still glaring at Sam, when he raises his head from Ms. Perfect Woman and happens to catch my eye. I can't believe this—he has the unmitigated gall to *smile* at me? Or is that a smirk?

I slowly and deliberately turn away and give blind date boy a big hug and a kiss on both cheeks. Take *that*, Sam. I'm over *you* already, too. "Hello, Ed."

"It's Evan."

"Whatever." I know I'm being rude, but I don't have one ounce of energy to carry on this conversation. Dad is gaping at me, but he's the one who got me into this mess with his stupid fix-up crap.

"I really have to go," I say. "I have a terrible headache and think I got a bad egg roll. I might vomit any minute. Maybe on your shoe, Edgar. I'm known for that, for shoe-puking. Famous in three states. You really don't want to take a chance. I'll, um, see you later, Dad. Bye, Edwin. Nice to meet you." I know I'm babbling, but I have to get out of there right away, before I do something even more embarrassing than shoe-puking. Like crying.

I turn to run away (in a calm, orderly fashion, of course, in case Sam and the slut are watching), when an ear-splitting shriek rips through the mall. We all whip around to see who's being disemboweled by chain saw, and I notice that Edmund is turning a hideous shade of green. Oh, great. Maybe he's a shoe-puker, too. We're the perfect couple.

"EVAN!! I see you, you two-timing prick!"

A very large woman carrying several shopping bags is bearing down on us, slicing a path through the shoppers. She's as round as she is tall, and I expect her to bounce when she screeches to a halt in front of us. She jabs Ed, sorry, *Evan*, in the chest with an amazingly long fingernail. Painted green. (The fingernail, not Evan, although the two shades of green are strikingly similar.)

"I told you if I caught you with another woman again, I would rip your balls off. Didn't I? *DIDN'T I??*"

With the pitch and range she can put into shrieking, I wonder if I should invite her to auditions tomorrow. At least she's not yelling at me.

"And YOU, you two-bit ho, what the hell do you

think you're doing with my fiancé?" she yells at me.

"Don't you dare speak to my daughter like that, you hussy. Evan's mom said he wasn't dating anyone, and we were having coffee." Dad is so sweet when he goes into protective mode. But, *hussy?*

"That evil woman don't want me having nothing to do with her son, because I'm only a lowly nail technician. And this hound sticks it in any bitch he can find. I don't know why I even want him, but I'm not letting anybody else have him." She advances on me, a towering rage of over-teased hair and quivering cheeks. "What do you have to say about that, ho?"

I back up a step, realizing that I'm perilously near the new City Center fountain and, if this were a B movie, one or more of us would end up in the fountain, soaking wet. Luckily, life is rarely like B movies.

"Well?" she repeats, menacingly stepping even closer. "What do you have to say, ho?"

I Have Had Enough. Prudence would say not to annoy a large woman brandishing shopping bags. But Prudence probably didn't see her potential boyfriend draped all over a supermodel-wannabe or get called a ho three times. Bite me, Pru.

I stand my ground, look her up and down, and say, "Your nails suck."

She gasps in disbelief, her eyes widening. Evan still hasn't said a word and is trying to sidle off, when she reaches out an arm that would make a truckdriver proud and grabs him. "Did you insult . . . *my nails?*"

"Yep. Your acrylic is cracking and *you give bad bevel.*" These are fighting words, and every woman in a fifty-foot radius knows it. "And you can keep your stupid boyfriend. I, at least, have enough self-esteem not to play around with a hound dog."

I walk away, dignity and pride intact.

I walk away, pride and self-esteem intact.

I walk away . . . oh, damn. Who am I kidding?

I turn to walk away and feel her claws digging into the back of my tank top and skirt, as she starts shrieking incoherently, and suddenly I'm flying through the air into the fountain. Head first.

You see, I forgot. My life is *always* like a B movie. Shit.

Luckily, I land on my hands and knees, so I don't have to add head injury to the day's tally. I come up, sputtering, and push my hair out of my face, to see her evil face leaning over the edge of the fountain.

"Don't you *never* insult my nails, bitch." She smiles and stomps off to the rock she lives under, dragging Evan behind her. I hope they never breed.

You know how people like to say "It can't get any worse than this" when life really, really sucks?

I know better.

Because as Dad helps me out of the fountain, sputtering apologies to me mixed with dire threats against Nail Bitch's person, Sam and Barbie show up.

Sam grabs my arm with one hand and raises my chin with the other. "Jules, are you all right? What happened? What did you do to that woman?"

"What did *I* do? Oh, let's see. I threw myself into the fountain fully dressed. That'll show her, won't it?" I yank my arm out of his grip and squelch off toward the exit. Sam catches up with me pretty fast.

"Jules, that's not what I meant. Are you OK? Did she hurt you? Did you hit your head? One minute we heard a weird screeching noise and the next you were in the fountain. Jules, STOP." He moves in front of me, to block my path.

I focus on the relevant part of what he said. "We? WE heard a weird screeching noise? Suddenly you're a WE? Did you tell the other half of WE that you were screwing me two nights ago? Or do you get sex from other people so she doesn't have to mess up her hair?" I can hear my voice getting shrill, but shrill is pretty mild, considering my day.

"Get the hell out of my way, Blake, before I hurt you." I shove past him and head for the door, barely hearing my dad telling Sam to stay away from my daughter, young man, over the cacophony of my own humiliation and despair. Happy endings, right. Glass slippers aren't good for anything but blisters, in my world.

Chapter Twelve

You've Got Voice Mail

I wake up in a fog, wondering where I am. Orange carpet, orange drapes, orange and purple bedspread. Got it. Another hotel. Yesterday's fiasco hits me in the face, and I cringe. I'm one of those women who never learns from her own mistakes. I'll be reduced to placing pathetic ads in Internet dating services when I'm fifty: *SWF, age 42* (everybody lies in those ads), *seeks SWM for long walks on the beach.*

Not that anybody walks on the beach in Seattle, but whatever.

I roll over and see the reason for at least part of the fog. The bottle of Ambien mocks me from the bedside table. Kirby made me bring them—*how will you sleep in cheap hotel rooms?*—and I took one yesterday afternoon, set my phone to Do Not Disturb, and crashed. Escaping through sleep is underrated; I've been out for about sixteen hours and never once felt like an ass in my dreams.

A sleeping pill hangover feels like the alcohol kind, I discover as I weave my way to the bathroom. I've always stayed away from drugs, so they have a big effect on me when I do take any. I have an addictive personality and was terrified of cocaine in college. The idea of something that would make me feel jazzed and energetic all the time, plus as a side benefit I'd get really thin, was too terrifyingly appealing. I knew if I ever tried it, I'd be just days away from selling my clothes on the street corner to buy more.

So I never did.

Kirbs has tried it all and has a low-level sleeping pill and happy-pill habit, I think. She has the energy of a crazed coke junkie naturally, so sometimes she needs help to come down, she says.

Speaking of coming down, I wonder how much coffee and Diet Coke I'll need to come back *up*. After my shower, I dig through my suitcase, trying to find something clean that says to Sam, *I was way out of your league, anyway, loser.*

I'm thinking the fuzzy pink sweater from J.C. Penney's isn't going to do it for me.

I pull out my basic black Donna Karan that I usually save for parties where the odds are so good I definitely have to shave my legs. And, in for a penny and all that, my Jimmy Choos with the stiletto heels that I "let" Dad buy me for my birthday.

OK, I tell him what I'm buying, and he sends me the money. It's a system that makes us both happy. Me, since I don't get any more repeats of the John Deere L100 Series Lawn and Garden Tractor (um, Dad, I live in an *apartment*), and Dad, because he really does have a ridiculous amount of money and doesn't know what to do with it. To my credit, I quit letting him give me cash or financial help of any kind when I turned thirty; a grown woman has got to have *some* standards.

Makeup. I need makeup. I grimly apply foundation, mascara, eye shadow, the works, trying to ignore the red message light on my phone that's madly blinking. If Barbie shows up at auditions today, there's no way I'm going to look underdressed next to her anorexic ass.

Not that I can look much worse than I did yesterday after my fountain adventure.

Pleased with my reflection—hey, the hair alone took thirty minutes of blow-drying and twenty dollars' worth of Kerastase, I deserve to be pleased—I sit down on the bed and pick up the phone.

You have eleven messages.

Eleven? I reach for the pad by the phone and make numbered notes.

"Jules, I don't know what you thought, but that was an old friend, well, an ex-girlfriend, but it was years and years ago, and she made partner in her law firm this month. She happened to be in Columbus for a trial . . . we were catching up on old times and celebrating her partnership. Call me when you get in."

1. Sam. Lying through teeth.

"Jules, it's Dad. Are you OK? I'm worried about you. Do you want to press charges against that obnoxious woman? I mean, really. Please let me know if we're still on for dinner tonight. And should I make reservations for three or four? I'm guessing that was your, um, friend that you were yelling at on the way out. Call me."

2. Dad. Call. THREE for dinner.

"Sam again. The front desk says you have your phone on Do Not Disturb. Jules, please call me. This is a stupid mis-understanding, and you're too smart to be mad at me over it. Plus, I'm worried about you. Are you bruised? Call me."

3. Sam. Passive aggressive. "You're too smart." HA! Only my heart bruised.

"Jules, it's Kirbs. Your dad called me. What the hell are you up to, crazy woman? Fires in Florida, fountains in Ohio, you're like a one-woman traveling disaster show. And who's the guy with the blonde you were screaming at? I'm worried about you. CALL ME, OR I'LL FLY OUT THERE AND BEAT YOU."

4. Kirby. Call her. Need sympathy.

"Jules, it's Joe. You failed to fill out your I-9 properly, so your next paycheck is going to be delayed until you see me and fill out a new one. In triplicate." (Cackling noise.)

5. Joe. Kill him. Joe = Wicked Witch of West from Oz in drag?

"Jules, it's Nellie. We've decided that you should be in charge of babysitting the contestants during filming in Hollywood, since you're so . . . maternal. And they really need someone older to look up to and keep them out of trouble, blah blah blah. So we need your cell phone number to give everyone. You'll be on call twenty-four/seven. Ta."

6. Nellie. Kill her, too. Murder spree. Babysitter for hormone-crazed teenagers with dreams of stardom Kill self next. Cell phone number.

"Jules, Sam again. I don't appreciate this. I'm worried about you. I thought the other night was special. I'm sorry if you didn't and can just convict me without a trial. Please call me."

7. Sam. Maybe telling truth?

"Jules, it's Roger. I, erm, I wondered if you'd be free for dinner tonight after auditions. I know you're from Columbus, and I thought perhaps you could show me some of the, erm, local sights. This is just a friendly dinner invitation between friends, in a friendly way, no sexual harassment of

any sort here, har har. Um, anyway, let me know during the day today or call my cell phone if you want to be private. I mean, private in a friends-only sort of way. Well, OK, I—"
BEEP.

  8. Roger. Dinner with Dad? Would serve Sam right. *Friendly.* Long winded.

"Jules, it's Kirby. Get your ass on the phone and call me RIGHT NOW. I'm not putting up with your melodrama."

  9. Kirby. Call now, before she flies out here.

"Jules, it's Dad. A package just arrived for you from Kirby, UPS. That girl scares me. I'll bring it to dinner. It's kind of bulky, so I'll just open the box this afternoon and bring along whatever's inside."

  10. Dad. OMIGOD, Don't let him open the package. *CALL IMMEDIATELY!!!*

"Sam again. I can't play these games, Jules. I was starting to really care about you, but I can't play games. Been there, done that, as they say. I'm sorry you won't listen to me. I won't bother you again."

  11. Sam. Giving up. No games. Telling truth? Trust????

As I hang up the phone, I look at the list. OK. I have to call Dad first and keep him from opening that package. Dad and I may have a great friendship and a parent-child relationship that was the envy of all my friends in school, but some things a woman just does *not* want her father knowing about her. Or even suspecting. Then Kirby, before she books a charter plane to get here.

Then I'll deal with the rest of it. It's only eight A.M.; I have an hour until I have to be at the stadium. I catch sight of myself in the mirror. Do I really want to wear stiletto heels at nine A.M.? Screw it. There is no wrong time to wear Jimmy Choo.

Dad's voice mail clicks on after the first ring. He must be writing. "Dad, DON'T open the package. It's some personal, um, feminine items from Kirby. You know, that-time-of-the-month stuff. Please don't open it, it would just embarrass us both. Bring the box for me, and you can just leave it in your car until after dinner. Thanks! Oh, and keep the reservations for four. See you tonight."

I know, you're thinking that's really lame, because why would Kirby mail me tampons from Seattle, when I can walk down the street to any drugstore? But Dad shuts his brain off at the slightest mention of female menstruation, like most men, so I'm safe.

Next.

"Kirby Green's office. May I help you?" Nice phone voice. Is that a hint of Australian accent? Why haven't I visited Australia? It's close to Seattle, kind of. I think. Really need to work on that geography thing.

"This is Jules Vernon. May I speak to Kirby?"

"Ms. Green is in a meeting, may I take a message?"

"Yes, tell her I'm fine, don't come to Columbus, and call me on my cell."

"Thank you. I'll be sure she gets the message."

We hang up, and I briefly consider going to work in the corporate world, so I could have a secretary. Wouldn't it be great to have someone screen your calls, take your messages, do your typing and get you coffee?

Although, I'd probably be so low-level, I wouldn't even get to have a secretary. I'd probably have to *be* the secretary. And not a talented, glamorous, executive assistant kind of secretary, but a temp who has to work for five people who never pronounce her name right and try to pinch her ass. Well, at least the guys.

OK, enough woe-is-me and other procrastinating. Should I call Sam or not? If not, is this really a conversation I want to have in person? I weigh the humiliation potential of my various options.

OK, I'm calling him. I do a little Lamaze breathing and dial the front desk. "Sam Blake's room, please."

"Mr. Blake has checked out."

"What? When?"

"Around an hour ago. May we be of any further assistance?"

"No, thanks."

Where can he be? We're not leaving Columbus until the day after tomorrow. Why would he have checked out? Is this about me? Is he so crazed with sadness he left? Did he give up on me because I didn't call back? Is he moving in with Barbie while we're here? Are they getting back together? Their kids will be gorgeous, the bastard. It didn't take him long. One evening of not being able to reach me, and he's having kids with that slut.

Does she even want kids? Won't that mess up her fast track at the law firm? Does he know this about her? I am anguished for Sam and the children he'll never have, before I remember that *he's* the one who left me for her in the first place. He deserves it.

What kind of father would he be? The first time his kid overslept, he'd want a new kid. He'd probably be sneaking out teaching the other kids in the neighborhood how to build birdhouses and ignoring his own kids. What a slimeball.

All righty, then. I've exceeded even my own quota for self-induced insanity for the day, so I arm myself with all three of the Diet Cokes from the minibar, and head for the door.

Chapter Thirteen

The Indiana Mob

As my personal escort (yes, we're a little less low-rent at *PSL!* since the buzz about Earwax and the media explosion over the bombing) strong-arms his way through the crowd lined up six deep in front of the stadium, I'm wondering, Where did all these people come from? I do a little calculating and figure there must be more than five thousand people in line for auditions.

This is going to call for a new strategy.

At the ten-yard line nearest the scoreboard, where the temporary stage is almost set up, I see that everybody else is already here, and the judges are fighting. A normal day, in other words.

I search for Sam without looking like I'm searching. He's standing by the stage, staring right at me, eyes narrowed. Barbie's nowhere in sight, either. Hmmm.

As I reach the judges' table, an important truth occurs to me. Maybe stilettos on a football field weren't the best idea.

Nellie is furious about something. Now there's a new development. Not.

"I am *not* listening to five thousand no-talent singers. I will get a migraine. I will absolutely lose my mind." She stamps her foot.

She stamps her foot? What are we, two-year-olds?

"As much as I hate doin' it, I have to agree with the old chick here. I ain't up for assault by tone-deaf wanna-bees, either. Let's make the PCs screen the first round, at least." Q isn't much for mornings, from the looks of the black circles under his eyes.

Nellie's not so irate she didn't catch the slur. "Don't. Call. Me. Old. Chick." She shouldn't grit her teeth like that. It's got to be bad for the cosmetic dentistry.

Roger breaks in. "Quit squabbling, children. We don't have to audition everyone who shows up. We can set limits. What do you think, Jules?"

I'm staring at Sam's back (OK, and his butt, too, which is truly a work of art), and I'm caught off guard.

"Well, limits. Yes, limits. Why don't we set a maximum of one thousand that come through the PCs, and one hundred that go to you, since you need lots of tape for the promo spots? Everything is more exciting when it's unavailable. Turning four thousand people away will create more buzz," I say.

We can whip through a singer a minute, generally, when the system runs smoothly. It doesn't take a whole minute to know that most of them aren't even close to what we're looking for, and then we have plenty of time for the truly talented (for finals) and the truly awful (for promos and teasers).

Q, Roger, and Nellie are all nodding. Norman is still zoning out, and I don't know where Joe is.

"Right, then. Brilliant as usual, Jules. One thousand it is. We'll do a little meeting and greeting for the B roll and then take a long lunch and come back around two for the first set of finalists. If you have any by then," Roger says.

I look for Bobby and Andy. Oh, that's Andy Sharp and Bobby Johnson, our security team. I've gotten to know them pretty well lately. Andy calls me Calamity Jules, for some reason. And he doesn't even know about the fountain incident.

There they are. "Andy, you look great! How's the Body for Life working out?" I gently nudged him on to a fitness program, after the wheezing and gasping stage chase in Tampa Bay.

"It's amazing, Jules. Look at this." He proudly pulls the waistband of his pants out and can get a finger in the gap easily. "I've lost almost ten pounds in a week on that low-carb thing. And I've been walking on the treadmill in the hotel gym, like you said. I miss bread and beer, though."

"There's new low-carb beer out, I heard," I say. "It may taste like crap, but it's worth a try. Great job, Andy!"

I turn to Bobby. "Got any new pictures for me?"

Bobby's son just turned a year old. He misses his wife and baby desperately, and is going home to Seattle for a visit as soon as we wrap in Columbus. Then the whole family is coming to Hollywood with him. We could have hired a local security team for Hollywood, but TV people are superstitious about everything. Marshall would never change anything that might "break his luck" when we're on a roll, and from the looks of that line outside, Bobby and Andy have job security for a while.

I ooh and aaah over the baby pictures for a while (why do babies all look the same? And when does the maternal thing kick in? Will I one day look at a baby picture and feel like renting out my uterus for nine and a half months to get one of these at the end? So far, no go.) and then tell the guys the new plan. They get the unenviable job of telling four thousand contestants to go home.

"Look, it's probably only about another thousand wanna-bees and their assorted friends and family," I say.

"That's reassuring, Jules. So somebody's boyfriend can punch me in the face when I say she can't audition. I feel much better," Bobby says glumly, putting his pictures back in his wallet and trudging off.

The Ohio State University assigned a team of perky students to help us, so I ask them to make up cards with the numbers one to one thousand and help distribute them to all auditioners until the cards run out. It goes pretty smoothly, all things considered, and we get down to the job of searching for the next Beyonce, Jay-Z, or Kelly Clarkson. (Not that we're allowed to even mention *American Idol*, since we're not, repeat not, a cheesy rip-off; but platinum on your first CD is not to be sneered at.)

The first hundred or so singers blur by in an unremitting drone of teeth-numbing boredom. Some of them might wind up singing on cruise ships one day, if they really practice hard. The rest are just mediocre. Nobody's even got the grace to be shockingly bad, to give us something to laugh at. The camera crew filmed a couple of shots of people tripping as they climbed onstage, but pratfalls can only take you so far.

After a short bathroom break and stretch, we motion the next contestant on stage. I see that Joe finally showed up, from wherever he was sacrificing cats or small children.

"Did you get my message, Jules?" he says.

"I got it. I mentioned it to my friend Jerry, the *lawyer* who runs the career placement service that sent me to you, and he said something about employee rights and lawsuits. I'll just forward Marshall his e-mail." I smile innocently.

Joe's pasty complexion turns even whiter. "No, no, that's OK. I'm sure it's a simple mistake. I'll talk to Marshall and get it all straightened out. There's no need for you to bother him about it."

It always surprises me that having a pet lawyer is more effective than having a pet pit bull. And the only shit you have to shovel is the verbal kind. Really, a good attorney is a woman's best friend.

Norman hisses at us to be quiet and tells the kid onstage to get started.

We're already tired and shuffle through papers to find number one-oh-nine's application form. Jack Arnold, from Indiana. The first notes of the Rolling Stones song zest through the air. Rolling Stones? Mick Jagger has *socks* older than this guy.

"Whoa. Not to sound like Q or anything, but this guy can bring it." We're all dancing in our seats, energized by the first serious talent to step foot in the stadium since Saturday's pre-season matchup between the Buckeyes and Cincinnati. (The senior quarterback has a passing game my mother rhapsodizes about.)

I feel a presence behind me. Sam? I whip around and look up. And up.

And up.

Talk about your offensive line. This guy could have been a linebacker. Heck, he could have been *all* the linebackers, twenty or so years ago when he would have been in college. The Incredible Bulk is peering over my shoulder at my notes.

"Excuse me?" I say, covering my notes with my hand. "Can I help you?" Which is polite-speak for get out of my face before I call security.

"I'm with Jack. He's the best, isn't he? He's a great singer. Don't you think he's a great singer?" Bulk is looming over me. I'm not sure if that's a menacing look or his normal expression. The guy has to be six and a half feet tall and four feet wide. He looks like his nose has been broken a dozen times and never fit back together right.

Norman turns around. "Dude, you're blocking the sun. And you're like, scary looking. Back off." Norman is nothing if not honest. It's like being around a small child. There's no filter between brain and mouth.

Bulk backs off a few steps, and we turn back to the stage to look at Jack. Joe is the first to speak, for a change. He usually waits for somebody else to speak up, so he has something to sink his weasel teeth into and make snide pronouncements.

"That was great. You didn't fill out your form completely, so if you'll step down here and do so, we'll pass you on to the finals." Joe's big on forms. He didn't bother to check with Norman or me about Jack, but I can't argue with his choice, so I stay quiet.

"Wise choice," says Bulk, who is right behind us again. "You'll want to make sure Jack goes to Hollywood."

Am I being threatened? What is this, some low-rent version of a Grisham novel? Maybe Denzel Washington will show up to save me. Or Tom Cruise, except he's kind of short.

Or Sam, the little voice in my head that has been making me keep an eye on Sam's whereabouts every second of the morning pipes up. (Why is it my conscience sounds like Jiminy Cricket? It's hard to take seriously a voice that sounds like it should be singing "When You Wish Upon A Star.")

Jack bounds off the stage and heads straight for Joe.

"Thank you, sir, you won't be sorry." Oh, Joe will love being called sir.

Jack bounces over to Norman and me. No lack of energy here. "Thank you so much for your time and dedication to this wonderful show. I hope I really can make my dreams come true on *POP STAR LIVE!*" Much eye contact and firm grip on the handshake. Corn-fed Indiana wholesome look.

This guy can work a room.

After we wave the next contestant onstage, I notice Jack and Bulk talking behind us. They're speaking in low tones, but with lots of gesturing. After a couple of minutes, Jack points to the EXIT sign, arm out-stretched and jaw thrust forward. The big guy looks sheepish and ambles off.

I can't help it; I'm curious. Plus, I'm the den moth-er now, right? So I get to know what's going on.

"What's going on?" I ask.

"What do you mean?" Jack asks, with a Who Me? Smile.

"The Incredible Bulk there. What's the deal? And come here, so I can give you my cell phone number. I'm the newly-elected den mother, not that there is anything resembling a democratic process at work here." I scratch my number on a scrap of paper and hold it out, closing my fingers when he tries to take it.

"Bulk?" I repeat.

He heaves a deep sigh. "Oh, OK. It's ridiculous and annoying, but Luigi is my bodyguard."

"Bodyguard?" *Luigi??* No way that guy was Italian.

"Yeah, my dad is the Bottled Water King of Indiana. We have all the vending machines and a lock on the corporate market. It's kind of cutthroat, and there have been threats. Long story short, these guys who work for Dad think they're Indianapolis's answer to the Mob. They've watched *The Sopranos* way too much, and it's warping their brains."

He laughs and shakes his head. "Luigi was Luke Abernathy until a couple of months ago. Now we have to call him Luigi. It's a joke. I promise, they won't be a problem. Please don't let this affect my chances."

I look at him, then at Norman, then back at Jack. This isn't really happening. We've gone from the Theme Park Terrorist to the Indiana Mafia. I look around wildly, suddenly sure that I'm on *Candid Camera* instead of *POP STAR LIVE!* Nope, no cameras except ours.

"Just keep Luigi out of my face, and we'll be fine," I sigh.

Maybe *I* need a Luigi. I fantasize for a minute about a Celebrity Death Match between Luigi and Nail Bitch, while some girl on stage shrieks out a hip-hop version of another Whitney Houston song from *The Bodyguard*. By four o'clock every afternoon, I'm ready to hurt Whitney and Kevin for ever making that movie.

We're breaking for lunch, even though we only found one finalist (Jack) and one really hideously bad singer (Carmen, whose costume as a transvestite Carmen Miranda impersonator had me cracking up until I read his/her application and saw that he/she really is a transvestite Carmen Miranda impersonator).

I mean, you don't want to laugh at somebody's livelihood.

Lunch, I find out, doesn't involve food today. Sure, there's food, the OSU alumni office has provided a catered spread. But not for me. I have a meeting with Marshall to discuss my new responsibilities.

Ever since the burning stage incident, and the

media hype that surrounded it (Mom left me a voice mail that said you could see the clip of me launching onstage to help Roger eighteen times a day on CNN), Marshall has been around a lot more. He's a pretty big name in TV, I've learned, but he had a couple of flops in a row and has gone three years since his last Emmy.

Remember *Lawyers with Stakes*? It was *Buffy* meets *Ally McBeal*, Norman told me. Right. I didn't remember it, either. It only lasted two weeks, before NBC yanked it with a mid-season replacement.

That's another thing about TV I've been trying to get used to: TV-speak. You can't say, This is a show about a man and a woman trying to find each other, in spite of the challenges life throws at them. No, it has to be something *meets* something else. So, *Gone with the Wind* meets *Shrek*. Or *Charlie's Angels* meets *Pirates of the Caribbean*. The secret code is that the stupider and more outrageous the comparison is, the more money the concept generates.

I learned last week that Marshall pitched *POP STAR LIVE!* to the network as *Survivor* meets *American Idol*. I'm living in terror of the day we ask the singers to eat bugs or build huts.

Only fifteen minutes late for our twelve-thirty meeting, Marshall rushes up and flops down in his chair. I know it's his chair, because his name is on it. Marshall has one assistant who has no apparent reason for existence except to carry Marshall's chair around for him. Marshall's butt is obviously too rarified for just any chair.

"Jules, I understand Nellie filled you in on the breadth and scope of your new responsibilities with the contestants?" He's out of breath. Being so important must be highly aerobic.

"No, actually, I just got a voice mail that said . . ."

"Good. Then we won't have to waste time. I've had cards printed up with your cell phone number, and they're being given to everyone on the cast and crew. Plus the finalists, of course. Now that the eye of the media is upon us," he paused, looking furtively around for any media eyes. "Now that the eye of the media is upon us, we have to be very careful of every move our finalists make. I don't want to find out that somebody is out doing body shots in a bar by seeing it on *The Today Show*." He leans forward to look me in the eye, with his I'm Being Serious expression.

"I'm being serious, Jules. The only body shots I want happening are the ones we choreograph and film. You have to watch these kids like a hawk. You'll be on call twenty-four/seven, of course. And I'll give you all my numbers, including my personal cell. Never, ever call me on my personal cell."

So why is he giving me the number? I nod, trying for an I'm Serious, Too, look, as the Assistant Chair Carrier hands me a business card with handwritten numbers on the back.

"Ask Joe, if you have any questions. He told me yesterday how responsible you are, and that you'd do a great job. You'll go far with a mentor like Joe. He's been around since I was a grip on *Days of Our Lives*." He leaps out of his chair, ready to rush off somewhere else, and looks down at me.

"Jules, don't screw this up."

I sit there with my mouth hanging open. I've noticed that my mouth hangs open more since I got this job than it ever has in my life. I'm usually much more easily pissed off than surprised. Joe said I'd do a great job? Joe, a mentor? I try to figure out his ulterior motive. This project must be going to suck, bigtime.

Net result of this meeting: I still know nothing

about my new responsibilities, but now everyone in any way connected to the show will be able to call me any time, day or night, to ask me about them.

There's no time for me to scrounge a sandwich from the buffet table, because Joe is calling for the next contestant. I haven't eaten since my lunch with Dad yesterday and may pass out from hunger.

I haven't called Jerry yet.

I haven't talked to Sam, who vanished around lunchtime after aiming a disgusted look at me.

I still have no clue what I'm supposed to be doing in my new babysitter job. It's only one o'clock, and I already feel like a total loser.

As I stand up to walk back to our judging table, I step forward but my shoes don't. As I trip over my own feet and fall face forward into the grass, I hear an ominous crack. The heel of one of my seven-hundred-dollar shoes, which sank into the turf while I was meeting with Marshall, just snapped off. I know it. I lie perfectly still on the ground with grass up my nose, wondering when my life became an *I Love Lucy* rerun.

Chapter Fourteen

Grass Stains and Bagels

Maybe if I just stay here, nobody will notice me. I turn my head to the side. This stadium grass is silky soft. Maybe it doesn't hurt that much to get tackled. Maybe . . .

"Jules?" Either I'm having a nightmare, or that's Sam's voice. I close my eyes and opt for nightmare.

"Jules, are you OK?" I feel hands under my arms, lifting me to my feet. Which are now bare, by the way. My Jimmy Choos are still stuck in the ground, laughing at me. I remember when I was a little girl, I thought if I closed my eyes, people couldn't see me. I lost at hide-and-seek for months.

I clench my eyes tighter. I'm a slow learner.

"Jules, you have grass in your hair. Please open your eyes," Sam says.

I open my eyes and look right into Sam's very amused brown ones. He's trying to look stern, but his lips are quivering. "Is this a daily occurrence with you? Fighting fires, swimming in fountains, taking headers into the dirt? I might have to rethink our relationship, if you're going to insist on being such a wild woman." He's brushing grass off my dress, which has a big green stain right across my left boob. Great.

Wait. Did he say our relationship?

"Did you say our relationship? Are we still going to have one?" I ask, my voice trembling just a teeny bit.

"Did you get my messages, Jules?" He doesn't look so amused now, but he's still holding on to my arms.

"I didn't get them until this morning. I went to sleep when I got back to the hotel and slept clear through the night. I wasn't avoiding you, honestly, Sam. We need to talk, and I called you, but they said you'd checked out of the hotel. Where did you go? Are you leaving?"

"Jules? Are you coming or not?" Joe yells from his seat at the table. I suddenly realize that everyone is staring at me. Joe, Norman, the contestant onstage, the entire crew, and pretty much everyone in the stadium has their eyes focused on me. My face turns about eight shades of red.

"Sam, we have to talk later. Will you be around? Can you have dinner with me and my dad tonight?" I whisper.

"I've got to go back to California and check on some jobs, Jules. I have a flight out at six. I'll call you tonight." He finally lets go of my arms, and wrenches what's left of my shoes out of the ground. "Here you go. You might try sneakers the next time you're in a football stadium."

I watch him walk off, then head over to Norman and Joe. As I sit down and try to clean smudges off my face, Joe passes a bulky, napkin-wrapped bundle and a semi-cold Diet Coke to me.

"I thought you might be hungry, since you missed lunch," he says, without looking at me. Wonder of wonders, it's two bagels. Maybe I need to rethink my opinion of Joe? I do have a tendency to categorize people pretty quickly.

Joe yells up at the girl onstage. "Now that Jules has deigned to grace us with her presence, go ahead."

Or maybe not.

Dinner with Daddy

Amber is not, as I'd feared, a teenager. She may even be older than me, though not by much. Dad's face is glowing with such happiness, I don't have the heart to give him a hard time about it. Who am I to decide what age range he should date in, anyway?

She's wearing a fedora that's so ugly, it has to be expensive, over the glossiest black hair I've ever seen. She has a bit of a Lucy Liu look.

When the coat-check girl tried to take the hat, I thought there would be a fistfight. We're now seated in the restaurant, and I wonder what the etiquette is for women wearing hats at the table.

I say, "Interesting hat."

"Oh, thank you. It's Prada, of course." She gestures down at her ripped-fabric plaid jacket and silky black pants. "I picked up the jacket at *Comme des Garçons* for a steal. And, of course, my sweet Tommy bought me the *Hermès* pants for the six-month anniversary of our first date." She giggles.

My sweet Tommy? Six-month anniversary of our first date? I may be sick.

"Oh, and Jules, I adore your pants. Whose are they?"

Even I know she doesn't mean who owns them, but which designer. "The Gap. Pre-season sale last year. Nineteen ninety-nine."

Dad breaks into this scintillating conversation about articles of clothing. "Amber lives in New York, of course. She's an executive assistant in my literary agency, and she's a fine judge of talent. In fact, you might think of sending her the first chapters of your spy girl novel."

I have about twelve pages of the spy girl novel finished. What can I say? I try to be all things to all parents. I think of Dad's hard-charging literary agent, and wonder what she thinks of her staff screwing the clients. OK, let's *so* not go there. I order another drink.

I look around the restaurant while Dad and Amber chatter, enjoying the elegance, the candlelight, the murmur of conversation, and the muted clinking of silverware and glasses. This was always my favorite restaurant, and Dad and I celebrated each of his new book deals here. Mark and I used to come here, too, which ruined it for me for a while, but the bad memories faded and the good ones surfaced again, enticed by the gloss of excellent service and the palate-teasing pleasure of exquisite French food.

I'm a little annoyed that Amber is here, encroaching on my special place with Dad. But I'm not a ten-year-old railing against an evil stepmother, so I decide to make an effort to get to know her.

"So, Amber, will you be able to work with the agency long-distance when you and Dad get married?" I smile and try to look interested.

"Long-distance? Work? Oh, you silly girl," she trills. I've never met anybody who trills before. It's as irritating as you might imagine.

"I'd never move away from New York, of course. I mean, it *is* the center of the universe. Although I'll be quitting my job to serve as a full-time muse to my darling Tommy." She puts her hand on Dad's and gazes at him adoringly. From the looks of the boulder on her ring finger, I'm guessing the Muse has already helped darling Tommy find a way to spend some of his money.

Stop, Jules. *Give her a chance before you judge her.* *Remember Joe and the bagels.*

I take a deep breath and smile again. "Are you moving to New York, Dad? I thought you hated big cities."

He opens his mouth to answer, but the arrival of the French country terrine, shrimp tian, and smoked salmon and poached salmon rillette interrupts whatever he was going to say. Dad and I are big on appetizers.

(Amber looked at us in horror when we ordered, of course. "You're not really going to eat all that, are you? Think of the cholesterol. Why Jules, I'd be big as a house if I ate like that," she said, brushing nonexistent crumbs from her size two pants.)

The hors d'oeuvres served and more wine poured, the waiter disappears quietly, and Dad begins again. "I know, I used to hate big cities, but it never hurts to try new things. We're looking at apartments in a nice little neighborhood, but they seem to be pretty costly."

"It's Central Park West, darling boy. You get what you pay for, you know. It's not like living out here in the wilderness." Amber shudders at our frontier existence in Columbus. She was probably surprised to find out we had electricity. No covered wagons, either. My determination to like this woman is fading fast, so I stick a forkful of salmon in my mouth to keep from being rude.

"Tell us all about your new job, Jules." Even in his besotted state, Dad's picking up on my attitude and wants to change the subject.

"It's weird, Dad, but I love it. Half the time I have no idea what I'm doing, and the rest of the time I feel like I'm the only one on the crew solving any of the problems. It's fast-paced, and it's crazy, and everyone involved with television in any way is completely insane, but I really love it. I think once we get to Hollywood, I'm going to have a blast." As I say it, I discover that I mean it. This isn't one of the rote pep talks I give Dad or myself at the beginning of a new job. I'm not trying to convince anybody it's true.

It really is true.

Dad seems unconvinced. "Well, um, that's great, Jules. But, well, you said that about media escorting, too. I just hope this is the right track for you. I know you're not crazy about writing, no matter how much your mother and I try to foist it on you, and I've been hoping you'll find something that makes you as happy as writing makes me."

The mention of Mom makes Amber nervous. "Oh, isn't it just so exciting to watch children find their own way?" she says.

"Oh, do you have children, Amber?" I tilt my head.

"Er, no, of course not. All that noise and mess. I mean, euwww." She's giggling again. I've never known a grown woman who giggles, at least not before she's twice the legal limit for blood alcohol.

"It's just that I can understand what your father is saying, Jules. And when I'm part of the family, I hope you always feel like you can turn to me for advice."

God help me, my life has become a fairy tale. Enter wicked stepmother. My evil mind whispers, "Does this mean Sam is Prince Charming?" Shut up, I tell it.

Somehow I manage to make it through a dinner that lasts for seven years, but I draw the line at dessert. I'm pretty full from the filet mignon, anyway. I might be hungry later, though, so I take a lovely chocolate mousse and a slice of pecan-encrusted caramel cheesecake to go.

Amber is staring at me in dismay, horrified eyes going back and forth from me to my carryout bag. As Dad confers with the server, she leans across the table and whispers, "You know, Jules, there are programs I could help you find. If you're not into O.A., there are private clinics and individualized plans . . ." Her voice trails off, and she leans back in her chair, the picture of a concerned soon-to-be-stepmother.

O.A.? What—oh, please tell me this is a joke. She's talking about Overeaters Anonymous. I've been referred to two different twelve-step programs in the space of two weeks.

"Really?" I whisper back. "Where do you go for your anorexia treatment?"

Unbelievably, she ducks her head and looks pleased. "Oh, Jules, I'm not anorexic. How nice of you to say, though."

I'm not kidding. This beautiful, allegedly intelligent career woman is so twisted, she considers a life-threatening disease to be a good thing. Wow. The fashion industry has so many reasons to be proud.

We say our good-byes outside, so Dad can transfer Kirby's box, which is, miraculously, unopened. My cab is waiting, in spite of Dad's urgings that they drop me at the hotel. I've just had all the Amber I can take for one night. Plus, I can check my cell messages in the cab without being rude. Sam may have called by now, or Kirby. And maybe I have a message or two about my new den mother gig.

As the cab pulls out of the parking lot, I call in to my voice-mail, nose over the top of the dessert bag, inhaling deeply. Maybe I have just a teensy bit of room left for a bite or two.

"You have forty-seven new messages."

I'm going to *kill* Joe.

Chapter Fifteen

Access Is Money

I'm limping and shell-shocked by the time I get to the hotel. I must have sprained my ankle earlier with the graceful faceplant trick, and the swelling is showing up now. Lovely.

As I hobble my way into the lobby, awkwardly balancing Kirby's box and my desserts, I have a brief fantasy that I hear Sam calling my name.

"Jules, over here," says imaginary Sam.

"Jules, stop." He sounds annoyed.

People aren't annoyed with me in my fantasies, so I stop and look. Sure enough, it's the real Sam crossing the lobby to me.

"Are you OK? Why are you limping? Is it from your fall earlier?" He's taking the box and bag out of my hands, as I stare at him in disbelief. He's supposed to be in California.

"Sam, why aren't you in California? And do you realize that most of our conversations consist of you asking me if I'm OK? You need to get better pick-up lines." I smile in what I hope is a flirtatious manner, but probably comes across as an I'm-in-pain-and-need-to-get-off-my-ankle manner, considering what happens next.

Sam waves a bellhop over and thrusts the packages at him. "Follow us, please," he says, as he picks me up.

(He picked me up again. I could get used to this.)

"Let's get you to your room and put some ice on that ankle. Do you feel like it may be broken? Should we take you to the ER? Where's your room?" His face is even more beautiful up close. He has the most amazingly long and thick eyelashes. How unfair is that? Oh, room number.

"I'm in one-ten. Right down the hall to the left. I don't think it's broken; maybe sprained a little."

Sam walks down the hall, carrying me like I weigh nothing. I'm rethinking my overall contempt for the Prince Charming concept by the time we get to my door. He sets me down gently with one arm still around my waist, supporting most of my weight, opens the door, and then swings me back up and carries me across to the bed.

As Sam retrieves my packages and tips the bellman, I study him closely, wondering why he's here. Our relationship so far, other than one night of really great sex, hasn't been all that auspicious. I doubt he'd cancel plans for me. Maybe he missed his flight.

"Did you miss your flight?"

"No, I canceled it and rescheduled for tomorrow morning. I wanted to talk to you in person before I left. I'm even more glad that I did, now." He flashes his trademark dangerous smile and grabs the ice bucket. "I'm going to go get you some ice for that ankle. Don't move while I'm gone."

As he walks out the door, I lean back against the pillows with a goofy grin spreading across my face. I could definitely get used to this. I'm imagining a world where Sam brings me breakfast in bed and, generally pampers me all day tomorrow when my cell phone rings.

My whole body jerks, and I can feel my left eye start twitching. I listened to every one of those forty-seven voice-mail messages in the cab and, if this is going to be my life for the next twelve weeks, I may have to quit now. Six from Marshall, all marked "URGENT," reminding me to do parts of my job I've been doing just fine without reminding since I started.

I sigh and answer the phone.

"Jules, it's Marshall. Where the hell have you been? Never, ever turn your cell phone off from now until the end of the season. Do you understand?"

"Yes, Marshall, it's just that . . ."

"I don't care. Access is money. Don't be unreachable again. And if you have a crisis, you have all my numbers and my personal cell, right?" He doesn't wait for an answer this time. "Never, ever call me on my personal cell."

Click.

I close my phone, wondering what that was all about. Does he just need to know I'm available at all times to be contented deep in his Machiavellian soul? Am I going to be chief flunky for the rest of the show? Media escorting is starting to look better and better. Even Chef Francesca wouldn't be that bad, if we just confiscated her sauté pan . . .

The rest of the forty-seven phone messages were equally fun. Three from Kirby, asking me where the hell I am, and why I bother to have a cell phone if I keep it turned off all the time.

One from Norman, asking if I want to go out for beers with him and Nellie's assistant tonight. That's interesting. She's never gone out for drinks with us before. If clothes make the man, then what do shimmery form-fitting dresses do for the mouse-woman? Go, Norman.

The rest of the phone messages were from the finalists. All thirty-six of them. (Messages, not finalists, thank God.)

"What should I bring to L.A., Jules?"

"Will we have makeovers, Jules?"

"Will somebody pick my songs, Jules?"

"Did you make flight arrangements for me, Jules?"

"Jules—Jules—Jules—Jules."

One thing is clear: I need an assistant. I'll talk to Marshall about it Monday. And I'll call everyone back tomorrow. Working on the weekend is bad enough, but I'm not working on Saturday night.

And especially not this Saturday night, I think, as the door opens and Sam walks in with the ice. I turn my cell phone off, mentally sticking my tongue out at Marshall.

The whole growing-up thing is a process, remember.

A Carpenter and Chocolate Mousse

Sam wraps ice in a plastic bag and a towel and gently tucks it around my ankle. "It doesn't look that swollen, Jules. I'll bet you'll be fine in the morning." He's tracing circles around my knee, and I feel the heat starting, in spite of the ice on my leg.

"It's not all that bad now," I admit. "I'm glad you're here, though. It might get, um, worse in the night, and I'd need somebody to help me." I'm looking down at my lap when I say this. All it takes is five minutes around this man, and I become Wanton Woman. Why didn't I just say, *Stay here and DO me, big guy?*

I groan, and Sam instantly looks concerned. "Is it hurting worse? Maybe we should get you to the doctor, Jules."

"Sam, I was groaning because I'm always making a fool out of myself around you. Why would you possibly be interested in me? I jump to conclusions. I'm a klutz who attracts disasters. I'm like the character in the cartoons who has the little rain cloud following her around all the time. Why me?" I laugh a little, but it's painful to put my thoughts into words like this. Especially when it's all so true.

Sam is smiling again. *Oh, my.*

"Life around you is never dull, that's for sure. But you left out a few adjectives: interesting, funny, sexy, passionate, beautiful. Even with grass in your hair or water dripping off your head. Those are enough reasons for me to want to get to know you better."

He stands up to move around to the other side of the bed. "Now, move over, klutzy, and we'll watch *Saturday Night Live* together and share the desserts I'm betting you've got in this bag."

OK, *SNL* mostly sucks these days, except for Tina Fey and sometimes Jimmy Fallon, but who cares. I've got Sam and chocolate mousse. All is right with my world.

I jolt awake, wondering where I am and why it's so warm. Then I see that I'm curled up against Sam's chest, his arm around me, with the muted TV flashing the closing credits of *SNL*.

"So you're awake, sleepyhead? Have a nice nap?" Sam reaches up with his other hand to stroke my hair away from my forehead.

"I guess I dozed off. I remember part of Kate Hudson giving the welcome, and that was it for me. I must have been more tired than I thought." I snuggle closer.

"Thanks for staying to take care of me, Sam. You're

really a nice guy, aren't you?" I start drawing aimlessly on his chest with the tips of my fingers, stroking from his collarbone to the top of his blue jeans.

"Just a really, really nice guy," I murmur.

"Maybe you should stop doing that, if you want me to stay nice," he says, his voice low and husky.

"I'm sorry, is that bothering you? What if I do this instead?" I say, and walk my exploring fingers down past his belt to the muscular legs tempting me. I trace ever-expanding circles on the tops of his thighs, noticing that his breathing is speeding up.

"Jules," he groans, trapping my hand under his. "You're tired, and your ankle hurts. Now may not be the right time for this. And we need to talk about yesterday and clear up that misunderstanding."

Oooh. Absolutely not. "We do not need to talk about Barbie, er, yesterday. You told me what you were doing. I have old friends who are men, too. Even old boyfriends who are still friends," I announce airily. Not really, but I had a crush on a boy in second grade, and he fixes my dad's plumbing these days, so I see him once in a while and that kind of counts, right?

"And my ankle is fine, see?" I wiggle it around, and it doesn't hurt a bit. Either the ice helped, or lust is a great anesthetic.

I turn his head to face me. "I'm fine," I say, as I gently bite his lip.

"You're fine. And we're here." I lick his earlobe, enjoying the shudder that rips through him.

"Did you have other plans for the evening?" I bat my eyelashes in a ridiculously exaggerated way that makes him laugh.

"No plans," he says as he leans into my kiss. "No plans at all."

Our last time was all about fire and flames and frenzy. This is a gentler passion. I lean back as Sam unbuttons my shirt slowly, kissing the skin revealed by each button, as he works his way down my chest and belly. He pushes the fabric aside and just gazes at me for a moment in what looks like awe.

"You're so beautiful, Jules."

"So are you," I whisper, glad I wore my pink lace bra. (My panties even match, by some miracle.)

My fingers are trembling as I grasp the bottom of his shirt and pull to lift it over his head. He helps me and suddenly the shirt is gone, and I'm inches away from his glorious chest. I give in to an urge I've had for days and lick his nipple. I can feel his body clench, and he moans. My clever hand reaches for the part of his jeans that just got a whole lot fuller, and I cup him and squeeze gently.

"Jules, I want to go slowly with you this time. I want to cherish you like you deserve. You're not helping me with the *go slow* part of the plan," he says, eyes closed and head flung back.

I smile to myself, smug in my newfound power.

"You're right," I say, pulling away from him a little.

"What? Right? Right about what?" He opens his eyes and looks dazed.

"You're right about going slow. Besides, I'd really like my dessert," I say innocently.

"I'd like to *be* your dessert," he says, his eyes darkening, his swift grin somehow amused and predatory at the same time.

"That sounds lovely, but I was really talking about my chocolate mousse," I tease, pointing to the bag.

"Your, um, right. Mousse," he says, taking a deep breath and sitting up. "It's probably melted by now, Jules. I should have put it in the mini-fridge for you."

"Oh, melted is fine for what I have in mind, Sam," I say, trying on a predatory grin of my own.

He blinks, then throws his head back and laughs. "Never, ever dull, Jules. I was so right about that."

The power balance has shifted, I think as I watch Sam draw chocolate designs on my naked body and then tenderly, thoroughly clean them off with his tongue and lips. He still has his jeans on, which is so unfair.

"That is so unfair," I complain. "You still have your jeans on."

He smiles at me lazily, eyes sparkling. "I don't want to distract you with my Greek-god-like body."

I laugh. With most guys, they wouldn't *say* something like that because they actually believe it. With Sam, you can tell he's poking fun at himself, which is adorable. But, still.

"Take them off, Blake. Now."

He looks at me, the amusement in his eyes darkening into pure heat. "We need to be careful of your ankle, but I'm going to have you. Right now, Jules."

Suddenly he's off the bed and shoving his jeans down his legs and swinging me back up into the air. I put my arms around his neck and turn toward his body, rubbing my breasts against the silky hair on his chest, shivering from the exquisite friction, the explosions and electricity shimmering on a direct circuit from my breasts to the big C. The skin on my entire body pebbles in chills and flushes with heat, my thermostat gone haywire, as he turns and leans forward to take my lips in a kiss that has little gentle about it.

Then I'm seated on the edge of the dresser and wrapping my legs around him, pulling him forward, pulling his heat into my own, frantically digging my nails into his back. He resists me, leaning down to draw one nipple into his mouth, sucking so hard I feel like I'm going to fly off the dresser and into space. I cry out and clutch his shoulders, thrusting my pelvis forward helplessly while he turns to my other breast and gives it the same attention, but this time biting until the wanting spikes to the edge of pain and it mixes with the pleasure and I'm begging him, Please, please, please.

And he stands up and lifts me with those strong, wonderful hands and thrusts into me, looking into my eyes the whole time. His expression is somber and yet happy, too, and he says, "You're mine, Jules," so quietly I almost don't hear him.

I gasp and feel myself tighten around him, and he's just the right size to fill me up, fill my body, fill my neediness and my neuroses, and fill the place in my heart that's been empty for so long. And I can't wait for him because I'm flying and yet tethered to the gravity of his thrusts, and the explosions keep coming and coming, and then he's exploding, too, and holding me so tightly I feel him under my skin and I'm under his and it's so right and so good and finally, finally, I think. Finally, I'm home.

After what seems like hours, Sam lifts his head off my shoulder and draws a deep, shuddering breath. "Are you OK?"

We both start laughing.

"I'm so beyond OK, it's almost obscene to admit it," I whisper. "But I'm going to collapse any minute, so we'd better get back to the bed."

He smiles ruefully and says, "My knees are a little weak, so maybe I'll just help you hop over there this time. I hate to ruin my He-Man reputation, but I think dropping you on the floor would be even worse."

I whimper a little when he pulls out of me, feeling a loss, the tiny death the French call it; the loss of intimacy and connection. But he must understand, because he traps my face between his hands and gives me a kiss that reaches clear down to my soul, to the dark places labeled Jilted and Failure and Impostor, and his kiss shines a gentle rosy glow in the shadowy spaces. It's not a floodlight or even sunshine, yet—I know that's up to me—but a small flashlight beam of hope for what comes next, and maybe even the end of hiding from my emotions and myself.

As I curl up around him on the bed, I remember that tomorrow is Sunday and, for the first time in several years, I may not need the full two hours for my stress break. I reach out to turn the lamp off, and my gaze falls on my cell phone, crouched in menacing glee on the table.

Well, maybe an hour and a half.

Chapter Sixteen

Sundays Are Looking Up ...

Sam has to leave at the repulsive hour of seven A.M. to catch his flight, but he'd set the alarm on his watch for six. He says that breakfast isn't really a priority and pulls me into his arms. In the dim light of the dawn glimmering through the curtains, we rediscover the slow and gentle rhythm we'd lost in our haste last night, and it's heart-achingly lovely to be held and loved and cherished.

Then he has to leave, and I roll over and go back to sleep. On his pillow, with the scent of him surrounding me.

I wake up at nine and shower and get dressed, girding myself for the Battle of the Phone Calls. First, I spend a hedonistic ten minutes deciding on the most extravagant and expensive breakfast on the room service menu, because Mr. Never, Ever Call My Personal Cell owes me. As I list my lengthy order, I smile at the expression that would be on Amber's face if she could hear me ask for this decadence of cholesterol and calories.

I stretch my pleasantly sore muscles. My ankle feels pretty good, but I have some aches in places I didn't even remember having muscles. This isn't necessarily a bad thing.

It's Sunday, but I can't work myself up into a pre-stress anxiety attack. Usually I spend the morning thinking about the many reasons why I need to freak out at the appointed time, but today I'm thinking I might just take a nap from one till three instead. As Dad said, we have to try new things. Maybe the new Jules can give up Sunday Stress-Outs. I hang up the hotel phone and pick up my cell.

This will be the test.

Chapter Seventeen

... Or Not

After such a great start, my morning crashed downhill like a runaway train. It's almost three o'clock now, and my tray of cold breakfast is sitting, untouched, on the edge of bed where I put it four and a half hours ago. I started returning phone calls, and it was literally one crisis after another. I listened to whining, worrying, and barking.

And that was all from Marshall.

The rest of the eighty-three, yes, that's right, *eighty-three* phone calls I've placed and received today were brain-suckingly awful. Mostly the contestants, wanting more details about their trips to L.A., or what's going to happen there, or how the shows will be formatted, or any of a million other details about which I have no idea and about which, right now, I couldn't care less. Not to mention that the future of our country is in big trouble if these contestants represent tomorrow's leaders.

Here's a sample conversation with, oh, let's call her Diva A:

Jules: Hello?

DA: Thank GOD you finally got back to me. I've been losing it, just totally losing it. OMIGOD, you don't understand the panic.

Jules: What's wrong? Just calm down, we can fix it. Are you all right? Is anybody hurt? Are you in jail?

DA: No, I'm not all right. How could I be all right? My friends told me that everybody in L.A. wears designer clothes. I don't have any designer clothes. All I have is a Gucci knockoff skirt I bought from a guy in Times Square last fall. This is a CANTAS-TROPHE, Jules.

Jules: A *what*? Do you mean catastrophe?

DA: Whatever. The one that means serious bad shit.

I had variations on that exact same conversation eight times this morning. I guess it's sexist, but I didn't expect to have to deal with this from the guys, too. HA. I think they're even worse. Eighty-three phone calls. I vow never to answer a telephone again.

Oh, shit. It's ringing.

I look at my cell phone, which I now hate with the richly layered passion I formerly reserved for poisonous snakes and polyester, and contemplate throwing it out the window for the sheer joy of watching it shatter on the pavement.

Sadly, my room is on the first floor.

I answer the damn phone. "What? And this had better involve blood gushing out of your eyeballs, or hang up now and call me tomorrow," I hiss, in full Cross Me and Die mode.

"Jules? Jules, is that you? It's Marshall. What's wrong with your eyeballs? Look, I'm in Vegas for the weekend, hanging out with—*no, I said Hit Me, you idiot, I'm not going to stand firm on twelve*—hanging out with some friends and—*Dammit! Can't I ever catch a break at this game? Busted.* Anyway, Jules, Ellen says we need gift baskets. So get 'em. OK? You've got all my numbers, even my personal cell. Never . . ."

"STOP," I shout.

". . . ever, er, what? Why are you shouting?"

"Ellen who? Gift baskets for whom? What are you *talking* about?"

"Ellen DeGeneres, who else? She did the Emmys and some standup; has a TV show; maybe you've heard of her? World's most famous lesbian?"

Condescension is more than I can take right now. "I KNOW who Ellen DeGeneres is, Marshall. Now explain about the gift baskets."

"You know, the gift baskets full of comped goodies all the Emmy presenters pull just for showing up. The ones last year were worth about ten K. They create huge buzz, and we can auction one on eBay or something. Anyway, I'm in an important meeting, and I don't have time for this."

I got your important meeting right here, I think, channeling Chris Rock.

"Marshall, I know you're busy. I'm trying to get the most information I can, in order to do a great job for you and remove stress from your life. God knows, I wouldn't want you to have stress in your life." I'm shouting again by the time I finish the sentence and, even with the image of a pink slip flashing in front of my eyes, I can't force myself to care.

"Get 'em. Better yet, let Roger, Nellie, and Q get their publicists off their fat asses and work it. But get 'em. I want gift baskets for every show. Got it? Call me if you need me, but never, ever . . ."

"STOP!! Why did you *give* me your personal cell phone number, if I'm never, ever supposed to call it? Why is it so important? Is it a hot line to the Pope? Do you think His Holiness might suddenly feel the need to GIVE YOU INSIGHTS ON YOUR STUPID REALITY TV SHOW??"

I feel a lot better for getting that out, even though he hung up midway through "stop." Even a lowly Production Coordinator has to stand up for herself some times.

I can't bear to relive the agony, so I will just relay some of the highlights of today's exciting and important telephone conversations:

With Kayley: "I don't think you should bring your mink or your fox, Kayley. Enough people oppose the wearing of dead animals that it might cost you in the ratings."

With Kirby: "No, we didn't try out the Amazing Anal Plug and Electric Clitoral Stimulator. Don't you think that's a bit much for a second date? And, let me just say, EUWWWWW."

With Jack: "I don't care if he's harmless. If that nutjob leaves one more message on my voice mail about somebody sleeping with the fishies—and who writes his dialogue, for God's sake; the freaking fishies?—you're off the show. He's *your* bodyguard, fix it."

With Derek: "No, you cannot give my cell phone number to the three different girls you're simultaneously dating, so I can tell them they can't come to L.A. to be in the audience. Figure out your own love life, Derek. No, I'm not single. Don't try your cons with me, babe. I am the Queen of Con Artists. Bow to the master."

With Shanicia: "I don't know what to tell you about camels and needles, Shanicia. It's Sunday, go talk to your pastor. Yes, if you win, you can donate any profits to your church. I don't know, do I look like a tax accountant?"

And so on, and so on, and so on.

I have to escape. I don't care about access being money. Marshall can put it on my tab or deduct it from my paycheck, which has become laughingly inadequate over the course of the past forty-eight hours. I grab my room key and head out for a walk.

The demon cell phone stays behind.

Concussion, Redux

I walk past the elevator in the lobby and run into Roger, who's stepping out. I mean, I literally run into him. I crack him in the nose with my bowed head.

"Can't you watch where you're . . . Jules! Where are you going?" He's clutching his nose, which makes it hard to hold his crutches. One starts to slide to the floor. I retrieve the errant crutch, and we move away from the elevator door.

"Roger, I'm so sorry. I'm in a foul mood, and I wasn't paying attention at all. It's all my fault. Let me check to make sure it's not bleeding." I gently remove his hand to examine his nose. It looks a little red, but no blood.

"No nosebleed. Just put a little ice on it, Roger. Again, I'm sorry." Not sorry enough to help him get ice, though. I've had enough of anybody connected to *POP STAR LIVE!* for one day.

"If you call room service, I'm sure they'll send up an ice pack. I'm sorry, but I really have to get out of here, Roger." I'm close to hyperventilating. The hotel has become a trap; the walls are shrinking to pull me closer and closer to the switchboard, where I'll be forced to talk on the phone until the world ends.

Not that I'm prone to exaggeration.

"Jules, for once I'm not worried about myself," Roger says. He chuckles sheepishly. "I know I'm a bit, erm, fragile at times. But you're white as a sheet, and I'm worried about you."

"Fra-JEEEL-ay," I mutter. "Must be Italian."

"What?"

"Nothing, never mind." Maybe they don't watch *A Christmas Story* in England. I'm losing it here.

He peers at me, searching my eyes for something.

"Pupil dilation," he says.

"What?"

"I think you have a spot of pupil dilation. Perhaps you struck your forehead against my nose a bit hard. You may have a concussion, Jules. Why don't we pop over to the café for tea?"

I grit my teeth and try not to rip his appendix out through his throat. "I don't have a concussion, Roger. I don't want tea. I hate tea. The only dilation you see in my pupils is that of a woman who has been forced to sit on the phone for five straight hours talking to crazy people. If I don't get out of here right now, I'm going to lose my mind. Now, either get out of my way or come with me, but I'm going out that door right now."

Roger looks startled to see me turn into the Shrieking Shrew of Death right before his eyes but, to his credit, doesn't run away screaming. "Right, then. I'll just stroll along with you for a bit."

He lifts both crutches and walks over to the front desk, limp barely noticeable in spite of the massive bandage still covering his calf.

"If you'll just send these to my room, please. Roger Scowl. Thanks." He turns back to me.

"Are you coming or not, Jules?"

I shake my head, but follow him out the door to the humid furnace that is Columbus in the summer.

Once we're outside, I don't want to go anywhere in the heat, but would feel too stupid after my outburst to turn tail and go back in. Not to mention that I have to get out of the range of that phone.

Plus, I'm starving.

"Roger, how do you feel about good old American barbecue?"

"I don't think I've ever tried it, but if you promise me ale, I'm your man." He smiles and raises his hand for a cab.

"Take us to Damon's, fast," I tell the driver. "It's a rib emergency."

I relax back against the plastic-covered seat and, for the first time since Sam left this morning, my shoulders unhunch from around my ears. (It's a family trait. We're the Quasimodos of stress. Except for Mom; she bites her nails.)

I smile at Roger. "Thanks. And sorry for biting your head off. And for the head-butt thing. This has been one of the worst Sundays ever and, for me, that says a lot."

"I think I'll wait till you've had a beer or three to follow up on that intriguing line of thought," he says, and, perhaps sensing that I need it, turns to look out the window in silence the rest of the way to the restaurant.

Artery Clogging and a New Friend

Damon's is filled with the Sunday sports crowd, but they're mostly in the bar. The restaurant is nearly empty at four o'clock. We order platters of ribs, fries, and sides of artery cloggers, with a pitcher of beer.

Roger holds his glass up. "To you, Jules. I don't know how you manage to stay so sane in the midst of chaos, but here's to Jules and sanity."

I touch my glass to his and smile ruefully. "I'm not sure how sane I am right now, Roger, but that's sweet of you to say. I returned eighty-three phone calls today. That's more phone calls than I usually make in a week. Two or three weeks, even." I take a long swallow of Killian's.

"And these people are nuts. I mean, what is Marshall's deal? Is he like a Quentin Tarantino wanna-be? What the heck is up with this 'Never, ever call me on my personal cell' crap?"

Roger starts laughing. "Oh, the personal cell. That's a bit of a quirk. His most recent ex-wife, his fourth or fifth, I think, called him on that cell to say she was leaving him for somebody in development at HBO. So now he's superstitious and doesn't want to talk about the show on that phone, in case the bad luck rubs off."

I stare at Roger in disbelief. "Why the hell doesn't he get a new cell phone? Is everyone in TV insane? I mean, not you, of course."

"Yes, we're all a little nuts, and thanks, but I know I'm as weird as the rest of them. I'm always sure I'm dying, Nellie is obsessed with her youth in a land that worships it, and I'm not really sure about Q. I've heard some rumors but, well, I don't really care to spread unverified gossip." He pours us both more beer, draining the pitcher.

"In any event, we're all nuts, and now you're in the thick of it. Although you're quite refreshingly sane. And thank you, by the way, for your heroic actions in Florida. I might have been badly burned, had that blazing fabric landed on me while I was unable to pull free of the stage. You and Blake were fantastic."

I smile again. Roger's much nicer up close and personal.

Our dinners arrive, and we spend a happy half-hour

gorging ourselves on vastly unhealthy food and chatting about anything and everything that has nothing to do with the show. Another pitcher of beer manages to disappear, too. Finally, I push my plate aside and sigh.

"I can't eat another bite. Not even dessert." The thought of dessert reminds me of what Sam and I did with that chocolate mousse last night, and I can feel my face heating up.

"Jules, you were right. This is fantastic. I'll have to eat barbecue more often. Are you feeling well? Your face is turning an alarming shade of red." He peers at me.

"I'm fine, it's just a little warm in here. Especially after all that food. Should we go?" I reach for the check.

"No, let me pay. The judges have expense accounts. You should make Marshall give you one, too, now that you've taken on additional duties." He slides his credit card into the bill folder and holds it out to the passing server.

"I get all I want from room service as part of my luxurious perks. I think it's part of Marshall's evil plot to keep me chained to my room and working. I'm surprised he hasn't looked into having that damn cell phone surgically implanted in my head," I mutter.

"Speaking of cell phones," Roger says, and opens his. "That cab driver gave me his number, so let's get him back here, shall we?" He makes the call, while I excuse myself to go to the bathroom and check my teeth for hunks of dead cow. (This is never a good look.)

On the drive back to the hotel, I'm relaxed (read: tipsy) enough to ask Roger about something he said at Damon's. "Roger, if you know you're a, um, well, a teensy bit overly concerned with your health, why can't you just let it go? Chill out a little?"

I turn to face him in the cab. "I mean, if you— BRAAAAAAAP."

We look at each other, stupefied.

I just belched on my boss.

The cab driver says, "Good one, girlie. We'll make a Buckeye out of you, yet."

Roger and I burst out laughing. "N-n-n-not bad manners, just good beer, my dad always says," I manage to gasp out, then collapse into another wave of laughter.

"I heard even the royal family enjoys a good belch now and then, Jules," Roger chokes out.

"I think you're both nuts," the driver says cheerfully. Roger and I stop in mid-laugh, look at each other, and collapse again. I haven't laughed this hard in a long time.

We're still laughing, as we climb out of the cab in front of the hotel. Roger gives the driver a twenty-dollar tip. "I never can figure out the exchange rate. I either just insulted the poor man or made him quite happy."

"Quite happy, I'm thinking. Although he deserves it for putting up with us." I wipe tears from my eyes and take deep breaths, trying to calm down.

"Thank you so much for coming with me. I needed a break so badly, and I thought I wanted to be alone, but this was much better. Even the thought of the four hundred phone messages that are probably waiting for me by now can't get me down." We walk inside and I stop by the elevator and hold out my hand to shake his.

Roger takes my hand in his and pulls me closer, leans down and presses a brief, but firm, kiss on my lips. "No, thank *you*, Jules. I'm so glad we were able to spend a little time together. I truly look forward to seeing more of you in L.A."

The elevator door opens, and he steps in, leaving me still standing there, speechless. I turn to walk down the hall to my room and see Nellie next to the soda machine, smiling at me malevolently. I force myself to walk calmly past her on the way to my room. "Hello, Nellie."

"Well, well, well. Looks like we found the crew slut for this show. Sam hasn't even been out of your bed for one whole day yet, has he? I'm sure he'll be very interested in hearing about this."

"Nellie, I don't appreciate your tone or your comments. Nothing happened between Roger and me, and Sam is my business, not yours." I keep walking, shaken by her nastiness. How did she know about Sam and me?

"Sam may be your business now, but I'm betting not for long." She flips her hair and struts off, content in spreading havoc and malcontent in her wake.

Bitch.

I realize I'm digging my nails into my palms and force myself to unclench my hands. She's simply trying to stir up some drama, so she can enjoy the fallout. I'm not going to let what she said get to me.

Not much.

Chapter Eighteen

Mom

I manage to make it through the night with only twelve new phone calls. (Sam wasn't one of them; he must have gotten in to L.A. late.) I probably scared the contestants enough that they won't be calling me on Sundays from now on. Marshall calls again, of course, and I'm even nice to him. He is the executive producer, after all, and, as much as I complain about it, I do want to keep this job. It's a short call, anyway.

"Jules, get BenQ Camera Pocket digital cameras for the baskets. They were in the 2003 MTV Movie Awards Baskets. Probably a new version by now. Find out. *I said STOLI on the rocks, what is this rotgut?* Jules, *People* magazine will be by for your interview tomorrow. Don't screw it up."

Click.

I hesitate for a long, long time with my finger poised over my phone to dial Marshall's personal cell and find out what he's talking about. *People?* Interview me? I finally snap my phone closed, undialed.

He must mean interview the contestants, and I'm

supposed to coordinate it. I can see how he'd get confused, in the middle of his vodka and blackjack, er, I mean, important meeting.

Mom calls next. She's on her way back to Columbus from her latest round of speaking engagements, but she won't get here until after I'm gone. We chitchat a while about nothing important. I'm squirming, wondering if she knows about Dad. She finally brings it up herself.

"So, did your father tell you about his midlife crisis?"

"Um, I, what do you mean?"

"The walking issue of *Vogue* magazine that he's going to marry." She laughs. "Poor Tom. Why couldn't he just buy a red convertible, like all the other fifty-five-year-old guys? I think this one may stick, Jules."

She doesn't sound angry or bitter, I'm pleased to hear.

"I don't know, Mom. I met her last night and, well, she's not exactly a deep thinker, is she?" We both laugh, and I immediately feel disloyal to Dad. "I mean, she was nice. And, um, certainly well-dressed. She seems to be nuts about Dad, too."

"I hope so, Jules. I really do. I've been hoping since we divorced that your dad would find the great passion that we didn't have for the last half dozen or so years of our marriage. He needs that; needs to be the center of someone's universe and have a person he can spoil and pet and pamper." She sighed.

"I wasn't that person for a long time, but he had you. I envied your relationship with Tom for the longest time, you know. You talked about your feelings and boys and school with him, but you and I could never talk about anything but books or philosophy."

"Mom, that's not true. We talked about stuff. We talked about, um, well, we talked about . . ." I trail off, realizing that she's right.

"Mom, I'm sorry. I never knew you felt that way. But you weren't interested. I'd try to talk to you, but you'd glaze out. And if you did focus in on me, I could tell you were zooming in on a vignette for your next piece for *Story* or your next book."

I laugh a little. "Underneath the literary microscope is a tough place for a teenager to live. Especially with her own mother."

"Oh, Jules. I've wanted to have this conversation with you for so long, but not on the phone. I'm sorry it took your dad's getting remarried to force us into it. I'm so sorry for not being there for you. I was always far too selfish to have children. I wanted to be able to stay up until four A.M. working out a plot, or hang out in the coffee shop with my friends all day. But your dad wanted a baby so badly, and so I gave him you. It was kind of a trade, almost. Here's a baby, so you won't cling to me so much."

She pauses, and I feel a little sick. Who wants to be told that her actual existence was nothing more than a deal: *I'll loan you my uterus for nine months, if you leave me alone for the next eighteen years.*

"Why didn't you just buy him a dog?" I ask bitterly.

"Oh, no, Jules. Oh, honey. Once you were born, I looked in your eyes and was lost. You were so tiny and perfect. And you were mine. I made you; you came from my body. You looked at me with all the mystery and wisdom of the ages in your solemn little eyes. And I loved you, instantly and completely. And I always have."

We're both crying now. I'm not sure I want to have this conversation on the phone, either.

"I love you, Jules. But loving you didn't magically

make me understand how to be a mother, or deal with a child. So I let Tom become the primary parent by default, and I guess I've been trying to play catch-up ever since."

"Oh, Mom, you don't have to play catch-up. I love you, too, and we can talk about all the feelings and girly stuff you want." I'm laughing and crying at the same time, and it sounds like Mom is, too.

"OK, then. Enough of this emotional catharsis nonsense. What are we going to wear, Jules?"

"Wear to what? Oh, the movie premiere? You heard about Dad's movie deal, right?" I'm wiping my eyes, and wedge the phone between my ear and shoulder to blow my nose. I'm pretty much done with this emotional roller coaster, thank you.

"Ah, yes, cultural imperialism at its best. We can sweep the world with dubbed versions of Professor Maxwell's Hollywood-ized adventures. I can't wait," she says drily. "I'll buy the popcorn."

I start laughing. "Do they even have popcorn at premieres? Wouldn't the ordinary people be in danger from all those size-zero actresses attacking them for their butter?"

"I can't really see Amber with a big old tub of movie popcorn, either."

"Mom! No jokes about Amber. We're both going to try to be nice to her, OK?"

"Well, actually, Jules, that's what I was talking about. What are we wearing to the wedding?"

This is a surprise. She's going to the wedding? But, on second thought, I can't imagine anything of any importance happening in Dad's life without Mom there. They've been best friends since they were twenty-one years old. The divorce didn't change that.

"I don't know, Mom. What do you think?"

"Who knows? I'm thinking traditional mourning

black might be too obvious, even for Amber, so we'll figure it out once they nail down the date. I don't think she's too happy about me coming, but too bad."

"Have you met her?"

"Only once, for a quick lunch. I think she ate two leaves of lettuce, no dressing. Your dad and I were talking about your trust fund, and she met us after. I'm not sure how she's going to feel when she finds out that his money is tied up." She sighs again. "I just hope your father is happy. He deserves it. And maybe Amber will be it for him. Maybe she's a *Do-me-right-here-on-the-desk-Tom* kind of woman."

"Mother! Stop right now. Don't ever, ever say something like that to me again, or I'll have to gouge out my eardrums. This is my father we're talking about. I mean, euuwwwww."

She howls with laughter. "Did you think we turn fifty and die, Jules? I can't wait until you meet Fernando. I met him in Venice, and we've been hooked up ever since. He's a delightful traveling companion, if a little . . . tiring." She snickers.

"That's it, Mom. I swear I'll hang up." *Fernando?* Sounds like a gigolo. And did my Mother just say *hooked up?*

I repeat, euuwwwww.

"Jules, I'm so glad we talked. I love you, baby. I've got to go; we've got opera tickets. Take care of yourself and call me from L.A. And don't think you got out of telling me about Gorgeous Man. Tom told me all about the hunk who pulled you out of the fountain. If I'd been there, I'd have decked the bitch for you, by the way. Love you, bye."

"Bye, Mom. Love you, too."

Divorced parents really shouldn't talk to each other so much. I'm happy, though. That's more of a personal conversation than I've had with my mother since I was twelve and started my period, and she had to figure out whether virgins could wear tampons or not. (They can. Kirby told me how.)

Chapter Nineteen

He-Man and Fendi Shades

Saturday feels like four years ago, instead of the day before yesterday, but here we are again at the OSU stadium, with another line stretching for what looks like a mile. We quickly run though our one-to-one-thousand drill with the numbered cards, and get started on auditions. I don't see any of the judges here this early (it's eight), but Norman and Joe and I are ready to go.

We're even in good moods. Because today we pick the very last finalist and never, ever have to hold auditions again. I might live through this after all.

Norman lines up his lucky action figures on the edge of the table. I know them all now. He has Darth, Luke, Hans, and Leia, of course, but also He-Man, Skeletor, Aragorn, Legolas, and Gimli. Frodo stays in Norman's pocket. I'm vaguely worried that I recognize and remember all these characters, and what that might say about me, but Norman brought me a grandé latte, so I don't care.

"Hey, those are the new Fendi One shades that dude's wearing." Norman points to the contestant climbing onstage. "Those are hot."

I look at the sunglasses, at the action figures on the table, and then back at Norman. I was surfing the 'net last night for gift basket ideas, and Norman's comment triggers a tiny light bulb in the as-yet uncaffeinated dimness of my brain. "Norman, we need to talk about gift baskets at lunch. Don't go anywhere."

He looks at me, puzzled, but says, "Whatever, dude."

Joe leans over from Norman's left and glares at both of us. "Are you ready, children? Can we get this over with now, please?" The tuft of gray hair standing up on the back of his head is quivering in indignation.

"Sure, Joe. And, hey, thanks for recommending me to Marshall for the contestant supervisor role. It's an important job, and I'll do my best to make you proud," I reply, doing my best Sweetness and Innocence impression.

He narrows his eyes in suspicion, searching my face for some hint of the misery he must have known he'd be causing. I smile happily. I won't give him the satisfaction.

I smile at the leather-clad contestant on stage, who must be sweltering in that outfit. It's got to be ninety degrees out here already. "Please begin."

Die with dignity, I always say. OK, I actually never said that before. But I can start now.

We make it to lunchtime without finding a single talented singer. My cell phone didn't ring once, either. I wonder where Sam is, and why he's not calling. Nellie and Roger showed up to shoot some B roll, but nothing exciting. Nothing that will boost our ratings and make us network darlings. I don't know where Q is. Norman and I wander over to the buffet of cold cuts and cheeses and fill our plates. I take two of my drug of choice, Diet Coke, out of the barrel of ice, and we head back to our table to eat.

"OK, Jules, what's up?" Norman says around a mouthful of roasted turkey sub.

"What do you know about gift baskets? Specifically, the kind of gift baskets that companies fall all over themselves to donate stuff to; the kind of baskets that all the presenters at awards shows get." My fingers and toes are all figuratively crossed.

"They're awesome, dude. I hear the presenters needed a forklift to get the Oscar baskets into their cars last year. The MTV Movie Awards basket had a Mattel Castle Grayskull and He-Man action figure in them. Totally intense. They weren't the originals, of course. Just reproductions. I have an original He-Man, mint in its original box from the early 1980s, that I got for two bucks at a garage sale. Can you believe that people don't know the value of what's in their own garages? Once, I . . ."

"Norman. Stop talking now," I break in before lunchtime is over, and I'm no closer to my goal.

"What? Oh, OK. What about baskets?"

"Marshall wants them. We need to arrange them. I want *you* to be in charge. You're a gadget hound, you certainly know about the trends and what would be hot and what would be lame to put in them. I'm going to make Nellie, Roger, and Q direct their publicists to go out and get the stuff donated, but you get to decide what kinds of goodies we should be aiming for. Sound good?"

"I'll be like Santa, dude. Score!" Norman is definitely onboard with the idea. I lean back and finish off my first Diet Coke. Multitasking and now delegating. I could get into this management thing.

* * *

Granny Hawkins and Sweet Mary Ann

Lunch runs late, after all, because we've got some kind of loud racket up in the bleachers, and it looks like our security team is involved. I'm thinking we have contestants trying to sneak in, or spies from rival TV shows, and run over to investigate.

I can hear the yelling from twenty yards away. (I know because I'm on the twenty-yard line.)

"You cheated! I don't care if you are somebody's grandmother. You cheated, and we can prove it. There's no way you turned up with all four aces twice in seven games, you, you . . . card shark!" Andy sounds pretty ticked off.

Four people stand up as I reach the bleachers. Sharp and Johnson. One of our camera guys. And a tiny woman who must be a thousand years old. I've never seen so many wrinkles in my life. She looks just like the baked apple doll my dad bought me when we drove up to Amish country for dinner one October.

Baked apple Granny is waving a fistful of cash. "I won this fair and square, sonny. Don't you try to cheat me, just because you're a sore loser and the fates were smiling on me. Would you take the Social Security check right out from under a poor old woman?"

She climbs down from the bleachers toward me. "Young lady, you're my witness. These boys lost to me in a fair game, and now they're trying to weasel out of it. You better help me, 'cause I'm afraid they might try to strip-search me for these cards they think I'm hiding."

All three of the guys instantly turn green at the thought of doing a cavity search on Granny.

"Oh, no, not again. You PROMISED, Grandma," wails a voice speeding toward us. I turn to see who it is, just as Granny mutters to herself and starts stuffing five-dollar bills in the pocket of her dress.

I may be wrong, but it sounded like Granny said "Oh, shit."

The whirling dervish grinds to a halt in front of me. "I'm so sorry, I'm so sorry; she promised. I just left her alone for a second; I was nervous, and I had to use the little girls' room, but I'm so sorry. I'll make her give the money back." The girl is tiny, no more than five-foot-two with her two-inch heels, and she's wearing a contestant number pinned to her sleeve. Granny belongs to contestant seven hundred seventy-seven, a tiny girl with freckles and—get this—braids in her red-brown hair. Raggedy Ann come to life in a blue-flowered dress.

Interesting contestant number.

Seven-seven-seven turns to Granny and holds out her hand. "I want the money, Granny. Now."

She's actually called Granny. This is getting better and better.

Granny pouts. "I won it fair and square this time, Mary Ann. These boys just can't take being beat by an old woman."

The 'boys" and I are looking from Mary Ann to Granny and back like we're watching a tennis match. Mary Ann narrows her eyes and turns to Sharp. "Did she run the Four Aces on you?"

His eyebrows shoot up. "She did. That old bat, I mean, sorry, miss, your grandmother had four aces in two different hands."

Mary Ann quirks an eyebrow at him. "And you fell for it not once, but twice, and kept playing with her?" She crosses her arms over her chest and starts tapping her foot. "Grown men like you?"

Sharp and Johnson look sheepish, and the camera guy slinks off toward the set. Granny smiles, puffing up her chest like a tiny, wrinkled sparrow.

"You tell 'em, Mary Ann. Why, I . . ."

"Stop. Right. There. You give them back their money right now. This audition is about me, and you promised not to cheat anybody connected with the show out of their money. Running the Four Aces trick not once, but twice? You ought to be ashamed." Mary Ann scowls fiercely at her granny, who wilts under her granddaughter's stare and starts digging in her pockets.

"Oh, all right. I was just having a little fun with the boys." She shoves a wad of cash at Sharp and Johnson. It looks a little smaller than what she'd put in her pockets earlier but, hey, I figure she's entitled to a percentage.

I judge it's a good time to break up the party.

"OK, you two make sure you divide that up three ways," I say, pointing in the direction of the camera crew.

"You, seven-seven-seven, you're up now. Let's go."

"Oh, no, we're only in the six hundreds. I'm not up for a while yet."

"Listen, Mary Ann, I'm not letting Poker Alice here wreak havoc on our crew any more than she already has. You're up now, I said. Let's go."

Mary Ann grabs her errant grandmother's wrist in a firm grip and follows me back across the field. "Yes, ma'am," she says politely.

Ma'am? I can't be more than twelve years older than this girl, but suddenly I'm a *ma'am?* Now it's my turn to mutter "Oh, shit."

Granny grins at me. "I heard that."

Mary Ann sings with all the wholesome purity of farmland America wrapped up in the notes of her song. She's too tiny to make the sound that comes out of her throat. It's physically impossible, and yet there it is. She's singing "God Bless America" and, for once, I don't check the sky for frogs.

When she finishes, I feel wetness on my cheeks. Norman and I look at each other in awe. Joe beats us to it, though.

"Young lady, you're going to Hollywood." He looks a little misty himself. We don't have to wait for the judges to know that she's going to be a finalist. Little Mary Ann may actually win this whole thing.

Watch out, Los Angeles. *POP STAR LIVE!* is coming to town.

Chapter Twenty

People *Magazine and Other Annoyances*

We're on our way out of the stadium to go back to the hotel, when Marshall finally breezes in, trailed by a mousy guy in jeans and a T-shirt. (The judges showed up long enough to agree about Mary Ann, then left for the airport.) I didn't get a chance to talk to Roger before he left, but he kept aiming his killer smile in my direction. Even Norman finally caught on and asked me about it. I pretended I didn't know what he was talking about.

"I'm here; the day can start." Marshall's suddenly big on dramatic entrances. The closer we get to Hollywood, the more dramatic he gets.

"We're done, boss," Joe says. "We picked a real winner for you."

"Oh, well. OK, then." Marshall is visibly deflated, but recovers quickly. "Everybody, meet Irving Rosenberg from *People* magazine. He's here to interview everybody about the show, and might follow us around for a few weeks. Let's be nice to him and persuade him to stay. Jules, you're up."

The reporter rolls his eyes at Marshall's pep talk.

I'm betting with the kind of celebrities he interviews on a daily basis, Marshall's Not All That.

"Oh, and plans have changed. We're all flying to L.A. now. Our plane leaves in less than two hours, so we'll go straight to the airport from here. Questions?" He's walking toward the exit as he talks.

"Marshall, wait. I'm not even packed. I have to go back to the hotel first," I yell at his back.

"No worries, J-Vo, I told the hotel to have their people pack you guys up. Your suitcases will meet us at the airport."

I stop dead in disbelief, causing Rosenberg to run into my back. This is *so* not happening. It's just wrong on so many levels.

First, I don't want strangers touching my underwear. Second, *J-Vo?* He must be kidding.

Third, wait, I know there's a third, but what . . .

"Ms. Vernon, Irving Rosenberg;" reporter guy says, holding out his hand. "I'm sorry I ran into you, but you need to put on your brake lights, ha ha. Marshall said we could talk in the limo and get started on your interview."

My interview? No, no, no.

"Please call me Jules," I say automatically. "I think you misunderstood, Mr. Rosenberg; I'm not a contestant. I'm just one of the production coordinators on the show. I'm supposed to coordinate your interviews with the finalists."

"Call me Irving. No, you're not. We're not interested in the finalists. There are over one hundred reality shows on TV right now. Do you know how many contestants that makes? We don't write squat about any of them until Nielsen blesses you with the ratings or you get the buzz." He's almost running to keep up with me, but I don't slow down.

"Ms., ah, Jules, Marshall offered us an unprecedented look behind the scenes to report on the show behind the show. We get total access to everything that goes on, an inside look at how a reality TV show is built, from the ground up. And you're the face."

"I'm the what?" I stop and turn to look at him. He's panting a little and sucks in a huge breath before he responds. Must not clock too much cardio time at *People*'s corporate gym.

"You're the Face," he says. I catch the capital F this time.

"I'm the Face of what?" I ask slowly. I add Marshall to my rapidly increasing list of People to Be Slowly Tortured to Death.

"You're the Face Behind Reality TV," he says, grinning. "I get twenty-four/seven access to you from now until the first winner of *POP STAR LIVE!* is revealed ten weeks from now. And I have to say, I'm glad you're not a dog. I mean, usually the production coordinators look like that old guy there or weigh three hundred pounds."

I lean close to him, and he smiles even wider in anticipation. "This is not happening. No way, no how. I will cut my head off with a rusty pair of nail scissors before I let you invade my privacy like that."

I stride off, leaving him standing there with his mouth hanging open.

The Face Behind Reality TV Turns Red

So, of course, now I'm on my way to the airport in the limo with Irving, giving him an interview, and figuring out how the Total Access is going to work. I've vetoed most of his ideas, already:

I can be your roommate! NO.

You can be my roommate! NO.

We can get a suite and be roommates with my photographer,

too. NO.

I'm thinking Irving doesn't get laid much. Pathetically eager doesn't come close to describing him. I wonder what Sam will think of this. Not that I really give much of a shit, considering Mr. Have Your Fun and Fly Across the Country Without Calling still hasn't. Called me, that is.

What is that third reason? If I could just think . . .

My cell phone rings. "Excuse me, Irving, this is more of my Total Access lifestyle in action."

"Hello?"

"Jules, we're going to have to get you clothes. What is that shit you're wearing? We need hot. Set something up with Nellie as soon as we get to L.A. You can have five, no, ten grand, max. That's gotta last for the first five weeks of the show, so don't blow it all in one place. And never, ever, call me on my personal cell."

Click.

Ten thousand dollars for five weeks' worth of wardrobe? Is Marshall nuts? That's more than my last car cost.

Luckily, we're pulling up at the airport as I close my phone, so I don't have to talk to Irving anymore for a while.

"Jules, we can check in and get seats together."

Terrific.

I wonder how to go about retrieving my luggage. We walk inside, and I look around for Joe and Norman, who took a separate limo.

"Jules, isn't that your name?" Irving is tugging on my arm. He reminds me of a Chihuahua: little and bouncy. I expect him to say something about Taco Bell any minute.

"What?"

"Your name? I think they're paging you."

"JULES VERNON. JULES VERNON. REPORT TO THE TSA STATION IN FRONT OF THE DELTA COUNTER IMMEDIATELY. JULES VERNON, REPORT TO THE TRANSPORTATION SECURITY ADMINISTRATION STATION IN FRONT OF THE DELTA COUNTER IMMEDIATELY."

Suddenly I remember what number three is.

Oh. My. God.

It's that damn box.

You know that expression, "she saw her life pass before her eyes"? It doesn't only apply to near-death experiences. I can see the headlines now:

POP STAR LIVE! PRODUCTION COORDINATOR TRIES TO SMUGGLE DANGEROUS PHALLIC OBJECTS ON AIRCRAFT.

Film at freaking eleven.

I literally can't move. Irving is looking at me like I'm a little slow. "Jules? We have to go see what's up. They probably found those rusty nail scissors you were talking about earlier." He grins and starts pulling me toward the Delta counter.

Dear Lord, if ever You wanted to send a lightning bolt to strike me dead for all the blasphemy, now would be a good time. Please. Pretty please.

I let myself be dragged along the concourse, nearly immobilized with horror. But, OK, how bad can it be? Maybe it *is* just something like the nail scissors, right? Or, if not, whatever Kirby sent isn't likely to be a threat to public safety, right? And I can check that bag. Or maybe they're just calling me to claim my luggage.

That's it. That's got to be it. I heave out a huge breath, relieved. I don't know why I always get so worked up about things.

We approach the TSA station, which has a huge

crowd around it, and go to the end of the line. There's uproarious laughter blasting from the front of the line, and I start to feel a little sick. The page begins again.

"JULES VERNON, REPORT TO . . ."

"She's Jules Vernon," Irving pipes up helpfully, and drags me to the front of the line. "Jules is right here."

Remind me to add him to the Death List. His name can go right after Kirby's.

The line parts like the Red Sea and right in front of me is the TSA screening table. My opened duffle bag is on one side and the opened cardboard box is on the other. In between, what looks like the entire stock of your average neighborhood sex shop is lined up. (If you live in that kind of neighborhood.)

An enormous woman in a TSA uniform is fondling a gigantic latex penis. "I gotta get me one of these! Damn, but I ain't never seen the guy who could bring it home like this baby will!"

The crowd roars with laughter. I feel like I'm going to faint.

A sweet-faced, elderly man who reminds me of my late grandfather looks at me. "Are you Jules Vernon?"

"Yes," I whisper.

He looks at me in disgust. "Are these your, your . . . items?"

"Yes," I admit, looking at my shoes. "But they were a gag gift from a friend. I hadn't even opened the box, as you saw. I didn't know what was in there, I swear. Let's just . . ."

The TSA woman breaks in, playing to the crowd. "Well, honey, I guess we know whether you're traveling for business or pleasure."

What witty repartee. Party Woman's a comedian. She should keep her day job.

Oh, shit. What is the reporter thinking? I turn to him, afraid to look at his face. "Irving, I can explain. I . . ."

"Jules, no need to explain to me. The idea of Total Access is sounding better and better." His smile is so huge I'm surprised his face doesn't crack. Irving thinks he's getting twenty-four/seven access to a nymphomaniac.

"Miss, if you don't mind. We need to examine your, ah, possessions." Grandpa is still looking at me like I'm an escaped child molester. The crowd seems to be growing by the second.

He points to the first item on the left, and nods to another guard with a clipboard, who takes notes. "What exactly is this?"

I sigh in defeat. May as well get it over with.

"That's the Alexander the Great."

"The what?"

"The Alexander the Great. The conquering hero of dildoes. Available in three different appealing flesh tones; it vibrates for maximum pleasure."

Did I mention that Kirby and I got really drunk one night and wrote the catalog and website copy for several of W&L's new products?

The Grandpa guy is in total shock. Party Woman is saying, "Oh, yeah," and Irving is panting.

"What about this?"

"The Easter Egg. Provides both clitoral and nipple stimulation in one pink-glitter package."

It occurs to me that I probably don't have to recite the sales copy, but I'm hearing my voice from somewhere far, far away.

"And this?"

"That must be the Amazing Anal Plug and Electric Clitoral Stimulator. Use your imagination."

Irving is taking notes now. And is that, oh, no. My

life is over. There's Marshall, Joe, Norman, and the entire camera crew, wondering what the hell is going on.

"Finally, this last item?" Party Woman is eyeing it covetously. I should give her Kirby's card.

"That's the Super-Sized Rabbit, made popular on *Sex and the City*. Can we please just throw it all away and be done with this, now?"

"Oh, we don't have to throw it out. We just needed to know what it was, to be sure you weren't smuggling any illegal items or explosive devices." Clipboard Man aims an evil smile at me.

"You're free to go."

"Thank God." I'm going to throw up. I'm going to throw up and then quit my job. I can never show my face around these people again.

"*After* you turn it all on, so we know it really is what you say it is."

My head snaps up in disbelief. The expressions will haunt me for the rest of my life. Party Woman's avid anticipation. Norman's consternation. Grandpa Guy's disgust. Irving's lust-induced hyperventilation. And all this on an empty stomach.

That's it. I'm done. For the first time in my entire life, I wonder if I can pass out.

In a zillion years, I could never have predicted what happens next.

Joe saves me.

I'm rooted to the floor in abject dread, when I hear his familiar, pissed-off grumble.

"Get out of my way. Move, you morons."

He fights his way through the leering crowd to stand beside me and glares at the TSA agents.

"What the hell do you think you're doing? Harassing an innocent passenger in front of all these people?"

Party Woman, twirling the dildo, says, "I wouldn't exactly call her *innocent*."

Joe wheels to scowl at her ferociously, and she takes a step back. Joe in full fury is quite a sight.

"You know damn good and well that this woman is no terrorist, and these are not dangerous objects. You're just having a little fun at her expense. Don't you have a private room that you could have used for this inspection?" He turns to glare at Grandpa Guy.

"You ought to be ashamed of yourself, letting this happen."

The old guy looks a little sheepish and clears his throat. I want to hug Joe. I don't know why he's standing up for me, but I'm pitifully grateful.

"I intend to file a formal complaint and see that Ms. Vernon does, too, if you don't put her possessions back in her bag and clear her to go to her flight immediately. I know TSA is under federal mandate to reduce ranks. How happy do you think your boss would be to have a concrete reason to take three people off the payroll?"

I bask in the glow of having Joe's devious mind working for me instead of against me for a change. The TSA people are stuffing everything in my duffle hastily. A much-subdued Clipboard Man tells me I'm free to go, and they're sorry for any inconvenience, just doing their job, blah blah blah.

Joe grabs my arm and pulls me through the crowd. When Irving tries to follow, Joe turns and snarls, "Back off for a minute, pal, or you'll be getting Total Access to *me* for the next few months."

We push past our crew and keep going. Joe pulls me all the way down the concourse and around a corner, then stops.

"Are you all right?" he asks gruffly.

I burst into tears. The humiliations and stress of the

past couple of weeks have finally caught up with me. Joe looks painfully uncomfortable, but he awkwardly pats my shoulder.

"Now just calm down, Jules. It's not that big of a tragedy. You'll get razzed for a few days, and then the crew will find something else to talk about. Now, now. Calm down, girl."

I try to pull myself together with a few deep breaths. I wipe my face and blow my nose, then look at Joe.

"Why?"

He doesn't pretend not to know what I'm talking about.

"Because they were being bullies, and I hate bullies. Plus, you don't deserve it. My daughter is about your age, and I can't imagine what I'd do if they were harassing her. Not that she'd ever have stuff like that," he adds hastily.

"It's not my stuff! It was all a gag gift from a friend, Joe. I hadn't even opened the box. And, anyway, I thought you hated me," I wail. So much for the eye makeup.

"No, I never hated you, Jules. I just get sick of the age discrimination in this business. I've been doing this job for thirty years. Hell, Marshall the diva and I go way back. But he makes me babysit his kid brother and hires you off the street—with no experience— to do the same job I'm doing. It's always the same thing; they want the young, pretty face." He stops, snorting with disgust.

"How would that make *you* feel?"

"That sucks. I would be furious. No wonder you hate me." I blow my nose again.

"I said I don't hate you, Jules. Hell, you're the first of the pretty faces I've come close to liking. You're not afraid to admit you don't know what you're doing and ask for help. You don't act superior. You're not always cutting out of work for auditions. Hell, you even pretended that you were happy about the contestant watchdog job, just to spite me. You've got balls, Jules." He grins.

"Sorry about that, by the way. But somebody who won't chain those kids to the wall has got to do it, so that leaves me out, and Norman would be out partying with them."

I smile at him. "It's OK. They're going to buy me lots of expensive clothes and shoes for doing it, so it's not a total loss." We both laugh.

"All right. We have to get out of here, or we're going to miss our flight. Don't go getting all girly on me now, Jules. Nothing has changed."

I smile at his rapidly-retreating back. *Everything* has changed. OK, I'd better get moving or I'll miss my flight. My vibrators and I are on our way to L.A.

Chapter Twenty-one

Shopping with Spider Woman

Downtown Hollywood is a lot dingier than I expected, but we're staying in the "dormitories"—a mansion in Hollywood Hills. Although maybe this isn't an actual mansion by Hollywood standards. Marshall snorted at me when I said as much, as if to say, What, this old thing?

Compared to my one-bedroom in Seattle, it's the lap of luxury. A wraparound pool circles the entire front of the house. Four bedrooms and eight baths (I don't understand the math, but there you have it. I guess, with five female divas-in-training sharing the same house, eight bathrooms is a good thing.)

But I don't have time to explore much, because we got in late last night. So after five hours of sleep, I have to be semi-coherent and at Marshall's offices. KAT network is a relative newcomer, trying to follow the path of Lifetime, TBS, TLC, and, of course, the miracle success story FOX, and break into the big time. If we're lucky, we may become KAT's anchor show, like *Trading Spaces* is for TLC, or that *other* reality singing show is for FOX.

I can't relax and enjoy the scenery, even though my driver (yes, I have my own car and driver; how cool is that?) is a cheerful guy who points out the sights and celebrity homes on the way. We pass Nicolas Cage's house and the little shack where Tori Spelling and her dad hang out. Practically a double-wide, really.

Now that I want it to ring, my cell phone has been ominously quiet. The rational part of my brain says I should call Sam and see what's going on; I have his cell phone number. The high-school girl in me says he's probably in the hot tub with some starlet laughing at me and my provincial chocolate mousse ideas.

I'm a little anxious about my meeting with Nellie, too. Shopping with her is not going to be a girls' bonding experience. Nellie's not what you'd call warm and fuzzy.

Not to mention that I'm not all that excited about going shopping with someone who weighs twelve pounds.

We pull into the parking lot, after passing through a security gate where a guard practically wants a blood sample and retina scan to let us through. That's Ashton Kutcher walking down the sidewalk with some old guy in a suit. And . . . YES! There's our potential host walking up to them. He's the hottest host MTV has ever had, and I hear rumors that he's being wined and dined to try to get him to host *POP STAR LIVE!*

OK, I can suffer through fittings of designer clothes for MTV Guy. And *Sam?* says the little voice in my head.

"If I keep hearing voices in my head, I'm going to have to go on Prozac," I mutter.

"Miss? Ms. Vernon?" The driver is holding my door open and looking at me like I'm a total wack-job. Wonder how long he's been standing there while

I played Drool over the Celebrities? Although, who cares at this point? I've been painfully humiliated in better places than this.

Nellie's dressed all in black today, which is a bad idea for her; it makes her look like a spider. She's dressed to kill (probably me), too. I don't know enough about designers to tell you much about the silk blouse unbuttoned nearly to her waist (thank God for double-stick tape but, even so, I'm a little nauseated looking at all that exposed skeleton), or her suede micro-mini, but she sure didn't get that outfit at Target. The stiletto boots, either.

"So, I have to take you shopping," she says, walking around me slowly, as if she's examining a particularly nasty flea infestation in the carpet.

"It wasn't my idea. Marshall wanted . . ."

"It's *my* job to know what Marshall wants, Jules." She sneers, waving her left hand in my face. Maybe she's showing me the enormous yellow diamond ring? This is new. Oh, please tell me she and Marshall didn't get engaged.

"Marshall and I are engaged to be married. So I'll thank you not to *translate* him for me." She's still circling me like she's trying to decide where to spray the Raid first.

OK, that's about enough. Kirby is a master at the "study them like they're an inch tall" game, so Spider Woman doesn't intimidate me.

Much.

"Look, Nellie, I'm not looking forward to this any more than you are. So either cut the crap and let's get going, or just give me the damn money and I'll buy my own clothes."

She is speechless for a brief and glorious moment and then narrows her eyes.

"So, the country mouse has teeth, does she? Well, Jules, Marshall asked me to waste a perfectly good day and ten thousand dollars trying to make you presentable. So let's get to it. I'm sure we can find *someplace* that caters to the, shall we say, plus-sized woman?" She grabs what even I recognize as a Louis Vuitton bag (the LVs all over it are my first clue), and slithers toward the door.

"Let's just get it over with. I always like to do the most painfully depressing tasks on my schedule first, leaving me to recuperate in the afternoon." She sighs in abject despair.

Oh, yeah. This shopping trip should be fun.

"Oh, goody, is it just us girls?" I say brightly, grinning like a crazed lunatic.

Nellie flinches and heads for the door. I honestly have no idea how she can walk in those boots.

First, we go to Rodeo Drive and the very exclusive boutiques. In spite of myself, I feel a thrill of anticipation and mention it to Nellie.

"This will be fun; doing a makeover with so much money will be like *Pretty Woman*."

Nellie looks at me, lip curling. "What, you're a whore, too?"

Chant. Breathe.

I am the Zen-like Production Coordinator.

Breathe. Chant.

I will NOT kill my boss. I will NOT kill my boss.

[NOTE TO SELF: I have way too many bosses on this stupid show.]

The boutiques each have one-word names and no more than ten items on display in the whole shop. There are always two or three clerks (Fashion Stylists, I'm told, excuse *me*) to handle the arduous task of ignoring any potential customers who enter the shop with the hope of perhaps trying on or—gasp—even buying one of the ten items. There's also usually a security guard who looks like he could double as an exotic dancer.

I remember that this is L.A. They probably *are* exotic dancers.

We spend three quality hours searching through *Risqué, Scandal, Blanc, Nirvana, Suede, Teardrop, L'Affaire,* and *Onyx,* only to emerge victorious with one shirt. One shirt. For three hours of enduring Nellie. She earned her place on my death list about five minutes into the first store, and she's rising up with a bullet, as they say in the music biz.

"Jules, I don't mean this in a bad way, but how do you fit in airplane seats with such a wide ass?"

"Jules, gravity really isn't your friend. Now that you're in your forties, you need a support bra."

Forties? I clench my hands together, to keep from snapping her twiglike neck like a, well, like a twig.

"Jules, have you thought of a girdle? They come in pretty colors these days."

"Jules, as a friend, if you do two hundred ab crunches a day like I do, you can get rid of that unsightly belly bulge."

She's a dead woman.

Finally, after an entire morning of abject humiliation as Fashion Stylist after Fashion Stylist commiserates with Nellie about the hopelessness of ever trying to get something to fit my "obese" five foot eleven inch, size-ten body, my cell rings. It's Marshall.

"Marshall, your fiancée is driving me insane. I am not fat just because I don't fit into something designed by the team of Anorexics R Us and Liposuction, Inc. I'm going to wear my own clothes. You can keep your money." Nellie is imperiously holding her hand out for the phone. Screw her. She can get her own phone. I turn my back on her.

"Bananas?" Wherever he is, there's a lot of static.

"What, Marshall? What about bananas?"

"Why don't you just go to Banana Republic? They're a big sponsor of the show, and we're supposed to wear their stuff as much as possible. You have to set up the shopping spree for the contestants, anyway, so you could kill two birds and all that. And hurry up! I know when you girls get together you like to giggle and have fun, but we have a show to run here. The finalists are flying in this evening. Bye."

Click.

Giggling? With Spider Woman? Not likely.

I grit my teeth and turn to Nellie. "Did you know all this time that we're supposed to be shopping at Banana Republic, instead of buying this hideous, overpriced designer crap?"

She rolls her eyes. "It's so plebeian, Jules. I thought you'd want at least a few signature pieces first. I should have known better. Let's go. Perhaps we can stop at Payless Shoes on the way and find you some Birkenstocks."

That's it. That is *so* it. I saunter over to the wall and pick up the most exquisite and ridiculously impractical pair of shoes on the display. Lipstick Red, of course. Brushed velvet pumps with a strappy slingback and four-inch heels. Hermès, I'm pleased to note.

"I'll take these. In a size nine."

The Stylist reaches for them reverently, as though I were handing her the Holy Grail of footwear.

"I'll wrap them up for you right away, Miss."

Nellie looks shocked. "Those are four-thousand dollar shoes. You're going to wear four-thousand dollar shoes with Banana Republic?"

I smile sweetly. "You did say I need a signature

piece. I'll take that Dolce & Gabbana bag, too. Oops, silly me. Guess I'll only have two grand for the rest of my wardrobe. Whatever will I do?"

"You can't . . . you can't . . ." Nellie is sputtering now.

"Oh, yes, I can. Marshall gave me the money to spend as a reward for my new responsibilities. *People* already has the first article at the printer. Do you really want to make me so unhappy I have to quit?"

I pull out my trump card. "Should I call Marshall *on his personal cell* and ask him about it?"

Nellie pales. She's not what you'd call gracious in defeat. "Don't mess with me, Jules. I've worked with him for five years, and I share his bed. You'll always lose."

The visual of Nellie and Marshall doing the nasty is more than I can take. "Nellie, I just defended my dildoes to the Transportation Security Administration. You got nothin' that scares me."

We wait in a painfully tense silence, while my packages are wrapped with the care befitting the crown jewels, and then take the car to Banana Republic.

I've never been so happy to walk into a store in my life.

Chapter Twenty-two
The Finalists

$\mathscr{I}$'m back at the mansion with a whole twenty minutes to myself before the first wave of finalists arrives. I check my cell phone messages, and there's one from Kirby. She sounds buzzed.

"I threw Daniel out again, Jules. Going to try to meet somebody higher up on the BP scale this time. Bye."

I still haven't heard from Sam. So much for Prince Charming. Kirby's been right all these years. There's no such thing as happy endings.

After hanging the clothes in my closet (I have a private room; the finalists are going to be sharing rooms with bunk beds), I try on my new shoes. I'm practicing walking across the floor without overbalancing and breaking my neck, when my cell phone rings.

I lean carefully down from my new altitude and grab the phone. It's Sam. Speak of the devil.

"Hello."

"Hi, beautiful. What are you up to?"

"About six feet, three inches, in these shoes."

"What?"

"Never mind. Where are you? I thought you'd call."

"I know, sorry about that. We had an accident on a job site and one of my foremen got hurt. I spent the evening at the hospital with his wife, waiting while he got his leg operated on. It was fractured in three places."

"Sam, I'm so sorry. Is he OK?"

"Well, he's going to be, after some long and painful therapy, from what they tell me. They've got three kids, and I needed to reassure his wife that the company will keep him on full pay and benefits while he's out, and that we'll hold his job for him. He's been with us for eighteen years." He sighed.

OK, maybe not the devil. This guy sounds pretty angelic, actually.

"It was a stupid accident caused by a subcontractor we won't use again. So now I need a new foreman for this job. I've been interviewing our guys who are ready for a bump up, and I think I found somebody. Anyway, enough about my stuff. What have you been doing all day? Caused any landslides, earthquakes, or other natural disasters?"

"Very funny. I almost caused an *un*natural disaster when I was forced to strangle Nellie with her own scarf. Probably Hermès, knowing her," I mutter.

Sam's voice sounds concerned. "Jules, you should be nice to Nellie. What she says carries a lot of pull with Marshall, and she wouldn't lose any sleep over costing you your job."

Suddenly, I'm not in the mood for job advice. "I don't know why you're suddenly so worried about me, Sam, when you haven't bothered to call me for so long."

"Jules, I explained about the accident. I didn't realize I had to check in with you." He sounds frustrated. Too bad.

"No, you certainly don't have to *check in*. But, since I know you have a cell phone, a five-second call to let me know what was going on would have been nice." But he never bothered, did he? Why am I so easy to walk away from?

"You're right. But I haven't had anybody close to me in a long time, and I'm just out of the habit. I should have called. I will next time. Are you OK?"

"Yes, I'm OK. I just know from painful past experience what happens when men go out of town and don't call. So all my fears and anxieties creep up to choke me from behind. I don't know what else to say." I can feel the tears coming and fight desperately to keep them at bay.

"I'm not *him*, Jules. It's not fair to judge me by what he did to you. And we have to talk more about this bastard at some point, by the way." His voice is gentle, and that very gentleness releases my tears.

"I know, Sam. And I'm sorry, too. But I'm not sure I'm ready to serve my heart up on a sacrificial platter right now. I have to go. I can't talk now."

"Jules—"

"I can't, Sam. I just can't."

It's oddly satisfying to be the one doing the hanging up for a change. So why can't I stop crying?

They're Heeeere

A wave of noise and excited laughter rolls upstairs, and I go down to greet the finalists. As I walk down the stairs (in my old shoes), I see that Marshall and his assistants are here, too. Looks like Carlos, Amanda, Lucas, Shanicia, and Lisette are in the first wave.

"Jules, we need to talk. Over here. Where is my

chair?"

Marshall is gesturing for one of his lackeys to put his chair down in the foyer. I stop on the bottom step, and wave a hand for quiet.

"Hello, and welcome to L.A. and *POP STAR LIVE!* We're so delighted you're here. One of Marshall's assistants will show you to your rooms. Please unpack and get to know each other a little bit. We'll be going out to dinner around eight, when the rest of the finalists arrive. You all know me, but in case you've forgotten, I'm Jules Vernon. And I don't want to hear anything about Eighty Days," I quip, but I'm looking at blank expressions on four out of five faces. Don't they teach kids the classics these days?

As they file past me, Carlos, the only one of the finalists who smiled at my attempt at a joke, murmurs in my ear, "I preferred your *20,000 Leagues Under the Sea*, personally."

I grin at him. Oh, my. He is a luscious guy. And smart, too. And if Sam and I are calling it quits . . . I feel an unexpected pang at the thought, but ignore it and watch Carlos walk up the stairs. He has a delicious butt, purely objectively speaking. And I'm really good at running away from my emotions. Why stop now?

We must not sleep with the finalists, we must not sleep with the finalists, we must not sleep with the finalists, we must not . . .

"JULES! If you're done playing Vanna White, I need to talk to you right now." Marshall is not a patient man.

I hurry over to him. "Yes, Marshall, what's up? We're working on the gift baskets, and . . ."

"I don't care about the gift baskets right now. Listen, Nellie told me about today. She was really upset; said you were rude to her."

"But that's not true. I . . ."

"I don't want to hear it. I don't care. Look, you're a strong person, but Nellie is really fragile. You need to handle her with care. Got it?" He stands up and Assistant Chair Boy rushes to retrieve Marshall's throne, er, director's chair.

"Fragile?" I'd like to handle her. I'd like to handle my fist in her face.

It dimly registers in my brain that I'm having a lot of free-floating hostility issues these days, but I'm not the kind of woman to let a few unresolved murder wishes get the better of her.

"Yeah, so just be extra nice to her for a while and this will blow over. OK, gotta go. Irving's meeting you and the finalists at dinner to start the Total Access program. You've got reservations at the Hard Rock Café. Call me if you need me, but never, ever . . . well. You know." Waving back at me over his shoulder, he's gone.

That's it? He didn't say anything to the finalists, so he came all the way out here to chastise me for being mean to Nellie? Of all the unfair, unbelievable, unfair, monstrous things to happen, Marshall's mad at me for being unpleasant to *her?* Did I mention *unfair?* And now I have to be extra nice to her?

I taste something vaguely metallic in the back of my throat, and I know I'm about to cry. The one thing I've never been able to take is criticism, and to get it from my boss, when it's so undeserved, is sending me over the edge. I run for the bathroom, before I lose it and one of the finalists sees me.

The door is barely shut behind me when the tears start. At least I didn't cry in front of Marshall, like I did with Joe. I think of the scene in the airport, and the phone call with Sam, and I cry even harder, muffling my face in a towel.

That's it. I'm done. I can't take this. Even Jerry won't expect me to work with these people. He can send somebody else. I don't care. I'm out of here. I can't face working with Marshall every day, watching Nellie smirk, or dealing with reporters in my face. It's way above and beyond the call of duty, and I'm finished.

I splash water on my face, and trudge back upstairs to call Jerry. This must be some kind of record. My big debut in Hollywood lasted one whole day.

Chapter Twenty-three
Second Chances

Excited and high-pitched chatter floats down the hall from the girls' room as I reach my bedroom and, for a moment, I'm tempted to join them. They're having so much fun, and this whole experience is going to be amazing for them. Then I remember my conversation with Marshall and firmly close the door behind me. I'm reaching for my phone when it rings. Caller ID displays Kirby's cell phone number, for the first time since I left voice mail messages on all three of her phones, yelling at her about the gift box and how much trouble it caused for me.

Knowing Kirby, she'll expect me to have forgiven her by now. HA! Not likely.

"Hello?" My voice is suitably frosty.

"Jules? Are you OK? God, girlfriend, I'm so worried about you." Kirby sounds near tears. I didn't mean to make her feel that badly about it. She had good intentions, after all.

"Kirbs? What's wrong? Don't worry about those screaming messages I left you; I just had to get it out of my system. Trust me, I've survived worse. This very week, even." Kirby never cries. Never. I'm not sure I can handle it if she starts now.

"Jules, I know how sensitive you are to public humiliation. My God. If I'd had any idea that so many people would see you with that stuff, I would never have sent it. Please believe me. I'm so sorry. I, I, oh, Jules. Can you ever forgive me?" She *is* crying. Oh, no.

"Kirbs, calm down, calm down. It's OK; I overreacted. Not all that many people saw it and hardly anybody I know. It's not like it's public knowledge that I was trying to get dildoes on an airplane, after all," I laugh. Now that I'm trying to cheer Kirby up, I can see the humor in the whole thing. Sort of.

"Not public . . . Oh, shit. Jules, you don't know, do you?"

"Know what? What are you talking about?" Somebody's banging on my door.

"Hold on a second, Kirby." I open the door to find the rest of the finalists grouped outside of my door with their suitcases, looking excited and young and scared to death. They all start talking at once.

"Where . . ."

". . . here . . ."

"Dinner . . ."

"Rooms . . ."

"When . . ."

"OK, OK, one at a time!" I smile and hold up a hand for quiet. "Kirbs, I've got to go. I've got a hallway full of finalists to get situated and take to dinner. I'll call you tonight."

"But, Jules, we really need to talk . . . ."

"It's OK, Kirby. I forgive you. Don't worry about it another minute. I'll call you tonight. Gotta go!" I snap my phone shut and herd Wave Two of the finalists to their rooms. It occurs to me that Kirby's remorse and the enthusiasm of the contestants have given me an attitude adjustment. Maybe I'll just hold off on that call to Jerry. What can a few more days hurt?

Just When You Thought It Was Safe . . .

All eleven of us are squeezed in around two tables at the Hard Rock Café on Universal Studios Boulevard. Most of the kids have been to Hard Rock Cafés before (they're everywhere these days), but this is *the* Hard Rock Café. I don't know why I keep calling them kids; they're not much more than ten years younger than me. But they act like kids. All wide eyes and open mouths. They're so excited when they see any celebrities, even the minor ones, like the group of castaways from the latest *Survivor* show eating a disgusting amount of food two tables away. Although I guess if I'd lived on nothing but rice for that long, I'd be shoveling down the cheese fries, too.

All except Carlos and Kayley. Carlos has an air of stillness around him and watches the room from eyes that are too hard and cold to belong on a twenty-two-year old face. He made a point to take the chair in the corner, too, so he can scan the room ceaselessly. Not in a Spot the Celebrity way, like the others, but wary and watchful, like he's looking for trouble. Or maybe I'm finally turning into a fiction writer, like Dad, and imagining things.

Kayley, on the other hand, is as transparent as the glass heels of her Prada pumps. (No, I didn't recognize them as Prada; she told us. Repeatedly.) She's making a point to show that she's above the celebrity-watching and fun.

She's also a catty little bitch. She managed to hurt Lisette's feelings in the first five minutes we were here

("Do you really want to order that fried food? You know the camera adds ten pounds and you certainly can't afford them").

Then she moved on to Shanicia ("Oh, you sing in church? How provincial . . .") and Mary Ann ("Is that a homemade dress? Even our maid can afford to buy clothes. Don't worry, I'm sure I have some old things I can loan you for the show").

At the same time Kayley is stabbing knife-edged comments in her fellow female contestants, she's weighing the men, trying to decide which to go after. I've known women like Kayley before. Who hasn't? So I know she's not after these guys for sex, although sex will probably happen.

No, Kayley's looking for weaknesses she can use. She catches me watching her.

"Jules, you're so lucky to be on the crew of the show. I mean, we're so glad you'll be part of our support staff." She smiles oh-so-innocently, putting the servant in her place. I think I'll just nip this in the bud right now.

"Kayley, for as long as you're a part of this show, you'll be *my* support staff. You will each do exactly what I tell you to do, every single day, all day long. We're going to have rehearsals, clothes fittings, rehearsals, public relations opportunities, makeup and hair sessions, and more rehearsals. You'll all be working harder than you've ever worked in your lives, and a lot of it will be on film." I look at each one of them in turn, impressing on them how serious I am. They all look suitably awed, except Carlos, again, who has a smile playing at the corners of his lips, and Kayley, who looks miffed to be out of the center of attention.

"You will never, ever leave the house without my permission, or on your own without the group. If the show does as well as we hope in the ratings, we're going to have a lot of press trying to get you alone for photo ops and interviews. Don't give them any chances. If you give unsupervised interviews, you're out. If you leave the house without permission, you're out. If you do anything you're not supposed to do, or *don't* do anything you *should* be doing, you're out."

Kayley sneers at me. "Look, I know you're trying to 'scare us straight,' or whatever. But we all know that the network is not going to drop us early and take a chance on not having enough finalists to carry the full nine weeks and support the ads they've sold."

I knew she'd be trouble.

"You're absolutely right, Kayley. And that's why I have a list of ten alternates we selected during auditions, each of whom would probably cut off his or her right arm to have the chance to take your spot. So if you're planning to break my rules, tell me now so I can call the first name on the list." I stare into her eyes, unblinking, and she's the first to drop her gaze.

Jules: One, Kayley: Zero. I hope I can stay on the positive side of this game for the next nine weeks.

After that, we relax, talk, and generally get to know each other. Kayley pouts for a while, then joins in the conversation. Turns out Anton, our young Barry White, has never been away from home before. He smiles a little sheepishly and raises his hand.

"Anton, you don't have to raise your hand, man. This isn't school." Derek rolls his eyes.

The hand goes down. "It's just, um, are we allowed to call home? I promised my mama I'd call her every night."

Everybody laughs and, amid some good-natured ribbing about mama's boys, I tell them we're giving them personal cell phones as part of their perks.

They'll have to star in a Nokia commercial for the privilege, but we can talk about that later.

My phone rings. I fish it out of my purse, saying, "And speaking of cell phones . . ."

They laugh, and I answer.

"Hello?"

"Jules, it's Irving."

"Irving, where are you? Marshall said you'd join us for dinner."

"And, ah, you were fine with that?"

"Sure, why not? I know I didn't like the idea at first, but Marshall promised you total access for your articles, and I agreed."

"Jules, you didn't see the magazine today, did you?"

"What? No, I've been swamped. How did the first article turn out? Did you get us good coverage, or are we a tiny blurb in the back?"

"Oh, God. Jules, you're the, you're, ah, you're actually the cover story," he mumbles.

"What? That's fantastic! We should get a huge spike in the ratings for our first live show. Thanks so much!"

He groans. "Jules, don't thank me, I can't take it. Listen, it wasn't my fault. The pictures were on a roll of film I left on my desk, and my department secretary had them developed. I guess the managing editor rewrote my copy entirely after he saw the photos and, ah, I just want you to know I had nothing to do with it. I'm so sorry."

I can feel my chicken fingers and fried cheese sticks congealing into a cold, greasy ball in the pit of my stomach.

"Irving? What are you talking about?"

"The pictures, Jules. The airport. The TSA screening. It's you on the cover. The headline reads, '*POP STAR LIVE!* Producer Creates A New Kind of Buzz.'

Jules, I'm so sorry. Jules? Jules?"

But I've dropped the phone. I look up, and I can literally feel all the blood draining out of my face and pooling somewhere around my ankles. I stare wildly around the restaurant, panicked. Has anyone seen it? Does anyone recognize me?

"Check! Check! NOW!" I yell for our server, and then look at everyone at the table.

"Come on, guys, we're out of here. Early day tomorrow. We, I, let's just go. Now." I throw my new corporate Amex card at the server and tell her to hurry up, frantically looking around for telltale signs that the other patrons read *People* today and are laughing at me. Nobody seems to be paying any attention to me except for Carlos. He tilts his head and raises one eyebrow.

The server is back. She's smirking. Oh, no. Oh, please God, no.

"So, I see from your card that you work for *POP STAR LIVE!* We've all been watching the audition teasers and the promos and can't wait for the first show."

Derek breaks in. "So do you want my autograph now, to avoid the crowds later?"

The server laughs, but she's still looking at me. "No, I'd rather have Julie's autograph. Maybe on my magazine?"

She smirks again. "I'm so impressed with how you, what did they say? Oh, how you're 'starting the show off with a *bang*.'"

This is not happening. I freeze in my chair, speechless. I can't take public humiliation again. And how many people read that stupid magazine? Thousands? Hundreds of thousands? Millions?

The finalists don't know what she's talking about, but everyone's starting to notice the expression on my face. Somehow, I answer her through numb lips.

"Yes, well, anything for a PR stunt, right? Is that my check?" Like she's getting a tip.

"Yes, you'll notice a tip is already included, since you're a party of more than ten." She smirks at me again and walks off.

I take the receipt and my card and stand up. I can't look anyone in the eye. I stumble as I walk woodenly toward the door and our waiting cars. Carlos is at my side, suddenly, and catches me before I run into the dessert cart.

"Is it bad?" he murmurs, voice pitched low so nobody can hear him.

I don't have the strength to pretend. "It's worse than bad. It's a disaster."

For the entire ride back to the house, I stare fixedly out the window and say nothing. At one point, I flinch, as it hits me that this is what Kirby was trying to tell me. And I was *nice* to her.

An eternity later, we arrive back at the house. I tell everyone good night and set the security alarms, still as if sleepwalking, and then somehow make it up the stairs to my room. Once there, I lock my door, turn my phone off, curl up on the bed in a fetal position, and lie there, awake and unseeing, until morning.

Chapter Twenty-four

What Doesn't Kill Us Makes Us Stronger.

*I*t's eight A.M. and I haven't slept. I haven't moved. For the first time since college, I didn't take off my makeup or brush my teeth last night. I seem to be trapped in a fugue state; immobilized by the depth of my own haplessness.

I've spent the past eight hours examining my life and what brought me to the point of being on the cover of *People* magazine, undoubtedly fondling a phallic object. I'm thirty-two years old, and I haven't accomplished anything. There's no place to hide from the truth. Let's just count it down, shall we?

First, I have no job, again. Well, technically I still have a job, but that's only because I haven't turned my phone back on to get Marshall's screaming messages firing me.

Second, I have no relationship. The first man I was attracted to in more than a year abandons me at the drop of a hardhat.

Third, I claim I want to be a writer, but I can't get beyond chapter one in any of the books I start. (I have thirty-nine first chapters in the trunk underneath my bed, if you must know.)

I'm merely the ghostwriter of my own life. And the worst part is, I don't know how to fix it.

There's a knock on the door. Aargh. I can't talk to anyone. Maybe not ever. Maybe I'll move to the mountains of Montana or Missouri or one of those M states and buy sheep. I could be a shepherd. I wonder where they buy those long poles with the hook they carry around?

Another knock. Louder.

I close my eyes, willing the intruder to go away.

"Go away."

"Jules, I need to talk to you. It's important." It's Mary Ann.

"Go away."

"Jules, let me in, or I'll pick the lock. Granny taught me how, years ago."

Oh, shut up.

"Go away; I'm sick."

I hear a clicking sound, and the doorknob twists clockwise and then back again. About three seconds later, Mary Ann is walking into my room. She closes the door behind her and re-locks it, snorting dismissively.

"A baby could pick that lock. Pikers." She turns to me.

"Jules, you look terrible."

"Gee, thanks, Mary Ann. You're so charming. But I warn you, sucking up to me won't help you win the show."

I pull the pillow over my head. Maybe she'll go away if I stop talking to her.

"You need to snap out of this. So what? So what if you were in a stupid magazine, and so what if Letterman made fun of you?"

I move the pillow and wail. "Letterman made fun of

me?"

"And the *Today* show. And Leno. But who cares? Here's the thing, Jules. This is L.A., for Pete's sake. You think anybody cares what's in your luggage? Do you have any idea what kind of twisted nonsense goes on here? It makes your, ah, episode look like nothing."

She sits on the edge of my bed and reaches for my hand.

"What doesn't kill us makes us stronger. Trust me, I know. My folks died when I was six, so I had to go live with Granny. She's a dear, but she's always gambling away the grocery money and whatnot. My college fund is long gone."

She draws a deep breath. "You think I *like* dressing in *Little House on the Prairie* chic?"

"Anyway, Jules, here's the deal. How people react to this—and to you—is up to you. If you act like it's getting to you, they'll blow it up into a huge, ugly deal. If you laugh it off, it's going to blow over. You have two choices in life. You can let other people's opinions of you dictate your reality, or you can create your own perception and screw 'em if they can't take a joke." Her eyes shine with defiance, and I have the feeling we aren't just talking about me anymore.

I sit up in the bed. "You know, that's pretty wise coming from a kid like you," I say, trying to smile. It makes my face hurt.

"Yes, I know. But you can get past this. I know you can. And we need you right now."

She stands up to go, leaving me staring at her, feeling about three inches high for the way I labeled her Raggedy Ann at auditions.

"Mary Ann?"

"Yeah?"

"Tell everybody to hurry up with breakfast, and I'll

meet you in thirty minutes to leave for rehearsals.
And, Mary Ann?"

"What?"

"Thanks."

We smile at each other, two women with very different lives, yet in complete empathy for one brief
moment.

The moment over, Mary Ann moves to the door.
"I'm going to win this competition, you know," she
says, with quiet determination.

"Mary Ann, I wouldn't be a bit surprised."

After the world's quickest shower, I check voice mail.

"You have thirty-seven new messages."

Oh, goody.

But the new Jules-channeling-Mary Ann me takes a
deep breath, sits down with my notepad, and listens
to them all.

*"Jules, it's Dad. What is this magazine photo about?
Honey, you don't have to do those publicity stunts; put your
foot down. They wanted me to go work on an archaeology
dig site for my fifth Professor Maxwell. Just say no. Amber
sends her love. Call me."*

"Jules, Sam. Call me. Please."

*"Jules, it's your mother. What the heck is going on? Are you
OK? Did you wash your hands after you touched that . . .
stuff? (whispering noises) What? OK, um, Jules?
Fernando wants to know where you buy stuff like this. Call
me."*

This must be the all-time zenith of mother-daughter
relationships: My mom just asked me where to buy a
dildo. That is wrong on so many levels.

"Jules, Sam. Call me. Now. Please."

"Jules, it's Kirbs. I tried to tell you, but you cut me off and

then had your phone turned off later. Are you OK? Do you
want me to fly down there and get you?"

"*Jules, Jerry. I'll start looking for somebody to replace you*
right away. I'm sorry I ever got you into this mess. I should
have known you were too nice to get mixed up with TV peo-
ple."

"*Jules, Sam. Call me. Now. Or I'll come over there.*"

"*You are a GENIUS!! Why didn't I think of that?*
Although, being executive producer, they would have caught
on to me, but YOU have that sweet, innocent face. Jules,
you get a RAISE!! TODAY!! Somebody write that down—
Jules gets a raise today. I don't know where a pen is, you
moron, that's your job. *Jules, call me right away!!*"

Marshall thinks I'm a genius? I get a raise? What? I
listen in a daze to the remaining twenty-seven messages, all from various reporters, including six from a
very apologetic Irving Rosenberg.

Sam sounded pretty upset, too. I'd better call him.
I start to dial his number, when I hear loud yelling
from downstairs. OK, time to put my personal crisis
on hold and pop into the phone booth for my switch
to Super Jules, Finalist Babysitter Extraordinaire.

I run down the stairs toward the front door. Our
security guards are yelling at somebody who's speaking in low tones. "No, we said you can't come in.
Orders from Marshall. Nobody in or out until we
drive the bees, er, finalists to rehearsals. Sorry, Sam,
but that includes you."

So Sam made good on his threat to show up, I muse
as I slow down. Wonder what this is about?

Now I can make out Sam's words. That dulcet voice
is sharp-edged with menace. "Bobby, Andy, you're
great guys. But I'm going in to see Jules right now.
If you want to stop me, you're going to have to shoot
me."

OK, that's about enough with the alpha male non-sense. I reach the doorway and stare at the three of them bristling on the porch.

"Let's tone down the testosterone, shall we, boys? Andy, Bobby, please let Sam in. I'd like to talk to him."

Andy looks at me, concerned. "Sure, Jules, but we wanted to make sure you didn't have to talk to any-body until you were ready."

"Right. Nobody," Bobby adds, glaring at Sam.

"Thanks, guys. I really do appreciate it. But I'll be fine. And I do want to talk to Sam. Thank you so much, though. You guys are the best." I want to hug them for being so protective but, considering the way Sam is looking at me, maybe not.

I turn to go inside and walk right into Lisette. All ten of my gang of finalists (flock of finalists? phalanx of finalists? concert of contestants?) are grouped in the doorway, watching avidly.

"Show's over, kids. Line up for the limos. It's rehearsal time. We'll be having lunch catered in at one at the studio, and we're going shopping for your outfits for the first show this afternoon. Have a great morning. I'll see you after lunch." I move aside hur-riedly, before I get crushed in the mad stampede for the cars.

Carlos is last, and he stops, then deliberately posi-tions himself in front of me. He's talking to me, but looking at Sam.

"Is there any problem, Jules? Want me to stick around while this bozo is here?" His gaze flicks con-temptuously up and down Sam, sizing him up and finding him wanting.

Sam, I can tell, has reached the limit of his patience.

"This *bozo* will be glad to put you in the car person-ally, if you need help, Junior," he grits out.

If any more testosterone gets released into the atmosphere this morning, I'm going to grow hair on my ass. I rest my hands on Carlos's shoulders lightly. "It's OK, Carlos. This is Sam Blake, our set designer. Go to rehearsals, please. Thanks for your concern."

Carlos saunters past Sam, turning his head to spit on the ground as he passes. I sigh. This is going to be a long, long nine weeks.

"Come in, Sam, before you do something we'll all regret. Plus, you've got fifteen years on Carlos. He might hurt you." I can't resist the dig, after the Nellie news.

Sam looks up at me, eyes narrowing. "Yeah, let's go inside, Jules. We have some things to talk about."

I watch Andy and Bobby herd the chattering contestants into the limos and drive off, before I close the door and turn to Sam. "Coffee?"

"Sure."

We start toward the kitchen, and I'm hoping I can find the coffeemaker, and wondering if we even have coffee, when Sam puts his hands on my shoulders and pulls me to a stop.

"Jules," he groans. "Please turn around."

I think about it for about half a second before I do. Well, he *did* say please.

"What?" I try for truculent, but come off as slightly whiny. Damn.

"Jules, how do you do it?" He's smiling, although somewhat reluctantly, I think.

"Do what?"

"Awaken the protective instincts in every man within a five-mile radius. First the security guards, then that gangbanger. And how did *he* get on the show, anyway?"

"What gangbanger? Carlos? He's not in a gang. We don't take anybody with a criminal record, and we

had them all checked out this week. Other than
Kayley having a few speeding tickets, and Lucas getting a little rowdy at a Faith Hill concert, they're all
clean. Why do you think he's in a gang?"

"Come on, Jules. Dad built our company from the
ground up. We lived in some pretty rough neighborhoods when I was a kid. I can recognize the type."

"The type? Sam, you don't seem to be *the type* to discriminate against Latinos."

Sam laughs in disbelief. "Discriminate? Because
he's Latino? I don't care if he's green and from Mars,
Jules. The look in his eyes, the way he dropped into
a defensive stance in front of you, and the long-
sleeved shirts? Don't tell me you didn't notice? And
the gangs I grew up around were *white*, for your information."

"I, er, what about his shirt?"

"A long-sleeved shirt in this heat? Have you seen
him in a T-shirt?"

"No, but that's just his style thing. Like Amanda
and her crop tops; All Navel All the Time."

"Amanda doesn't have gang tats on her abs, like
Carlos does on his arms. Probably back and chest,
too."

"Tats? Tattoos? How do you know?"

"Jules, you'd better ask him about it. Better yet, I'll
ask him about it. I want you to stay as far away from
him as possible."

I've been pretty calm all morning, considering people across the country think I'm a perverted nympho.
But now I'm getting seriously pissed off.

"Excuse me? You want me to stay away from him?
You want? Since when did what you want factor into
my life? You picked the wrong woman, if you're looking for a doormat." I storm down the hallway into
the kitchen. I need caffeine to deal with this.

"No, I don't want a doormat. I appear to want a damn walking tornado. Everybody and everything around you gets swept up in your wake. Especially me." He puts his hands on top of mine on the coffeepot, holding them still.

"And I haven't felt the way I did when I made love to you for a very long time. Maybe never. I want to feel that way again, Jules."

I stare at his hands covering mine, feeling the heat of his body behind me. The reasons I was angry at him seem distant somehow.

Sam slowly turns me to face him, gazing down into my eyes. "I'm sorry, Jules. Let's try again."

How can I refuse? I've always been a sucker for puppy-dog eyes. I close my eyes and tilt my face up for his kiss, then he whispers in my ear.

"Now, about those dildoes . . ."

Talk about ruining a mood. I chase him all the way out of the house, snapping a wet dish towel at his gorgeous behind. I'm not sure who's laughing harder.

Chapter Twenty-five
Dive-bombing Birds and New Drapes

Three times the number of people I've ever seen in a staff meeting are crowded around the conference table. I'm the last one to arrive, of course. Nothing like making a dramatic entrance when you're trying for incognito. Everybody stares at me, and then the snickers and smirking start.

In any normal work environment, they'd say things about you behind your back. But this is Hollywood. It's all right there in your face.

"Hard time getting out of bed this morning, Jules?"

"Too busy creating all that *buzz* to get to work on time?"

"If you need a real man, baby, come sit on my lap. I've got your Alexander the Great right here."

For a moment, I freeze with my hand on the doorknob, like a deer caught in the headlights of Arnold Schwarzenegger's SUV. Then I remember Mary Ann, and I start laughing.

"Listen boys, if you're the best this town has got, I'll stick with my pal Latex. Thanks for offering, though." I force myself to smile nonchalantly and saunter through the room, taking a seat near Marshall. Nellie never condescends to join us at staff meetings, fortunately.

"Shut up, you mouthy assholes! If one of you'd had the brains to get your plastic dick on the cover of a national magazine, you'd be half as talented as Jules is twice over."

Marshall does have a way with words. I try to decipher what that sentence meant; I think it was good for me, and bad for the sycophant guys.

"Enough already with the shit. We've got buzz now. Sorry, Jules, but you know what I mean, and this first show on Wednesday has got to kick major ass. What've we got?"

One of the clones speaks up. There are maybe half a dozen of them, reminding me of that guy in *The Matrix* who kept replicating himself. They're wearing identical all-black outfits and pasty-white complexions. I can't keep them straight, but only three of them talk, while the others frantically take notes. I notice Norman is nowhere to be seen, and Joe is seated away from the table, back against the wall, with his arms folded over his chest and a look of disgust on his face.

Clone One: "We pitched this as *American*, um, ah, as a singing show meets *Survivor*. Let's make them eat disgusting stuff like native Californian bugs."

(We're not allowed to say *American Idol*; Marshall says it's bad juju.)

Clone Two: "What native Californian bugs? What have we got here, cockroaches? That's old news. Everybody makes 'em eat cockroaches. *Survivor, Fear Factor*, even that new dating show weeds out the potential girlfriends with the cockroach gig. We need New. We need Hot. We need Different."

Clone Three: "What about birds?"

One: "They can't eat birds; we'd get crap from the environmentalists."

Three: "No, not eat the birds, you idiot. Make 'em sing with predatory birds dive-bombing their heads."

Marshall: "Can we do that? What about the nutjobs from the Sierra Club or ASPCA or some such crap?"

Two: "What predatory birds? Like vultures? Bats? Wouldn't that be gross? What about birdshit and stuff? Costume and makeup would have a coronary."

I can't believe this conversation. My head is whipping back and forth like an André Agassi groupie at Wimbledon. Are they insane?

Clone One: "It's gonna take some time to set up the bird thing. We'll have to get clearance from some damn agency or something. Somebody call the zoo."

Three: "I know! The theme of the week can be bird songs!"

Marshall: "What? They have to warble and shit?"

Three: "No. They have to sing songs from bands with the names of birds in them. Like Counting Crows, The Eagles, The Byrds, Sheryl Crow."

Marshall: "I like it. Make it happen for Week Two. I love Sheryl Crow. She's hot. Not that Nellie's not hotter," he says hastily, looking around as if Nellie might suddenly appear to castrate him.

One: "But what about this week? We need high concept. We need hot, hip, and happening. We need to steal from the best reality shows out there. What have you got, people?"

I can't keep my mouth shut any longer. Plus, I'm getting a crick in my neck.

"Um, shouldn't we try to be original, fresh, and different, instead of derivative of other shows?"

Everybody looks at me in total disbelief and dismay.

"What the fuck are you talking about, original? This is TV, Jules. Three hundred different cable channels playing the exact same show at any given time. We hate original. We despise fresh. *We LOATHE different."* Marshall spits out, looking at me as if I were something nasty he had to scrape off his shoe.

How fast you go from hero to zero in this town.

The clones are at it again.

One: "What about *Fear Factor*? We can hang them upside down and make them sing while we bungee them."

Two: "Yeah, 'cause that's going to make for such great singing. Idiot."

I break in again. (One, I never learn and, two, I hate long meetings. Plus, my humiliation threshold keeps climbing exponentially. Imagine that.)

"What about *Trading Spaces*? Everybody loves that show, and the host, Paige Davis, is a wholesome, America's sweetheart kind of woman. The show would be a perfect match with our contestants; sweet young people redo each other's rooms in the contestant house. We could get media coverage and *People* can write something positive for a change. We can even contact home improvement stores for ad dollars, and they might not usually buy time on a reality singing show." I lean back in my chair, smiling.

All the clones start talking at once, telling me what a stupid idea it is, when Marshall interrupts.

"I love it. You're a genius, Jules, you really are. I love that show. That Vern dude rocks. Anal little guy, but his rooms are the best. Make it happen. Get them for this week's show. And, hey! No Doug. Guy's a freak." He stands up, which is apparently the cue for the meeting to end.

"Jules, how's the babysitting going? Don't tell me; I don't care. Are those the new clothes? You still look like a refugee from grad school. Trendy it up."

He turns and points at Joe. "You. Show Jules

around the set and tell her what's what. I don't want her to embarrass us with *People*. Anything I need to know?"

Joe shakes his head. "Nope. Got it covered. Meeting with Blake later. Final details for the set. Let you know."

Joe makes laconic seem loquacious.

"So, um, Sam's going to be here?" I try for casual, but Joe's not buying it.

"You and Blake, huh? Didn't see that one coming. Good guy. Don't screw it up." He strolls toward the door, leaving me staring after him.

I swear to God, if one more person tells me not to screw something up, I'm going to scream. Or say some very, very, very bad words. Which reminds me of Kirby. I need to call her and Jerry and tell them I'm staying with the show.

As I walk out of the room, contemplating all the hundreds of details I'm mandated to "not screw up," I pass Marshall whispering urgently on his cell phone. Wow. *Wonder who's important enough to call Marshall on his personal cell?* I grin and start to pass by, when Marshall clutches my arm in a grip that will probably leave fingerprints.

"Hold on." He mumbles something else into the phone that I can't quite catch, then flips it shut and looks at me. He's still got my arm in a vise grip, and all color has deserted his face like advertising sponsors from a show tanking in the Nielsens.

(Oooh! My first TV-speak analogy. I'm *so* in with the in-crowd.)

Marshall finally pries his fingers off my arm.

"Jules, you're fired."

OMIGOD!!

I fall back against the wall and stare at him; my mouth is opening and closing, but not making any sounds.

"But, but . . . what do you mean, I'm fired? We just walked out of a meeting where I was the best thing to ever happen to this show. Remember *talented?* Remember *if you had half the brains Jules has?* What happened to that? Why are you firing me?"

I can feel the tears forming just behind my eyelids and in my throat. This is what I get for caring about something. A job, a man, whatever. If I care about something, I always screw it up.

Marshall won't quite meet my gaze.

"It's not me, Jules. It's the head of KCM Records. They're pretty conservative in Texas, and he had a cow about the *People* cover. I've been ordered to fire you, or else he's going to pull KCM out of the show."

Oh, *fine.* Marshall isn't exactly Mr. Loyalty, anyway, and if it comes to a choice between me and a million bucks, guess who's packing her suitcase? The tears burn down my face, and I don't even care.

"Marshall, give me another chance. That wasn't my fault. I explained the situation—the gag gift—what happened. Let me personally apologize to KCM and see if that helps." I can't believe I'm pleading to keep a job. When did I cross the border from Nonchalant into Determined?

Marshall's shaking his head *No*, though. "No way, Jules. That man is more stubborn than a New York agent. You can't talk to him. I'm sorry, but you've got to go."

Then he walks away, leaving me standing there in shock, *You're fired* ringing over and over again in my brain.

About ten feet down the hall, Marshall stops and turns back toward me.

"Jules, there might be a way. I really like you and want you on the show. Plus, who else is stupid enough to take on the babysitting job?"

I start to answer, but he stops me with an upheld hand. "Hah, that last bit was just a retortical question. Look, if you can *promise* me you'll stay out of trouble, I think I can convince KC to leave you alone. After all, he *did* sign a contract. I may not have much, but I do have ballbuster lawyers." He grins and rubs his hands together.

"I'll just tell him that we promised *People* that they'd get access to you for the entire show. We'd be in breach if we backed out now." Marshall pats me on the shoulder a couple of times and then turns to go, apparently not noticing that I can't choke out a single word.

"I still think it was fucking brilliant, Jules. *New Kind of Buzz*. Ha! Brilliant.

As he strides off down the hall, I sink to the floor. I *love* that man, even if he can't say *rhetorical*. I still have my job.

Barely.

Impostor Unmasked

I walk into the studio where we'll be broadcasting live for the next nine Wednesday nights. Except it's more a giant auditorium than a studio. The place is huge.

"There must be seating for a couple thousand people in here."

"Three thousand, four hundred, to be exact," says Sam, walking up behind me. I can't help the chill that races through me at the sound of his voice. My heart does a funny little lurch, too. Unless that's indigestion from my healthy breakfast of two Diet Cokes and a Snickers bar.

"Hey, Joe, Jules. How was the command performance?" He grins at us. I get the feeling he knows

Marshall pretty well.

"Same shit, different day," Joe grumbles. "Now they want to have dive-bombing birds attacking the contestants. Don't be surprised if you get a demand to build an aviary for next week, Sam."

Sam laughs. "This stuff always blows over, Joe. I can handle Marshall," he says, shaking his head. "Birds. What will they come up with next?"

"Well, blame your girlfriend there for what they came up with next. She had some damn fool idea about those kids painting each other's bedrooms or changing the drapes or some such nonsense, and we're going with it." Joe stomps off in disgust.

Sam smiles at me, his entire face lit up with delight. "My girlfriend? Are you my girlfriend?"

"I think it's way early for the 'G' word, Sam." I'm smiling, too, though.

"I like the 'G' word. I like all sorts of 'G' words." He steps closer.

"Like glowing." He traces my cheek with one finger.

"And glistening." He continues on down to my neck with that evil finger.

"Groaning," he whispers against my ear. "Growling. Giving. Gasping."

"And even G-spot." He finishes, biting my earlobe.

"How about Get back?" I ask, pushing him away, and pretending lightning didn't just sizzle straight from my earlobe to the 'G' word in question.

"Or Grow up? Or Get to work?"

"You're no fun at all," he says, grinning at me and shoving his hands in the pockets of his jeans, which I can't help but notice seem a tad more snug than they did a minute ago. Not that I'm standing around staring at his crotch, but it's hard to miss.

Sam's not a bit embarrassed about it, either. He starts whistling and walks back toward the stage. "See you tonight around nine, Jules. Wear heels."

What? I can't, he, I, ohhhh. *Men.*

I deliberately ignore him and go in search of Joe. He's in the production control area, which looks like the deck of the Starship Enterprise, only more complicated.

"Hey, Joe. What's up?"

"I thought I'd give you a tour, rookie. Done live TV before?"

"No, never. I'd appreciate anything you can tell me."

He gestures at a wall of what look like TV monitors.

"This is your bank of preview picture monitors. Through these images, the director will continuously monitor pictures from each video source. The production switcher/vision mixer lets him cut, fade, or mix between picture sources by sending the selected channel to line, to be recorded, or to be transmitted. Since we're live, it's pretty intense. Like one person playing chess against five opponents at the same time."

He walks across to some kind of control board.

"This is the sound desk, critical for a show like ours, where the quality of the singing will influence America's vote. And of course, lighting controls here, where production lighting is switched and relative intensities balanced. Got your character and graphic generator, in case we want to superimpose names or images on the screen, while people get to know the contestants' names, and a special effects generator, but we won't use that much on this show."

My head is spinning. I'm sure it takes four years of college to understand all this equipment. I start to ask a question, and a tiny woman dressed in a tangerine tube top and lime-green satin parachute pants runs in. My pupils contract against all that brightness, as she scans the room frantically. She spots me and rushes over.

"Are you the AD? Where have you been? We need to talk about opening shots. Do you want ECUs, knees, or what? How are we placing the pedestals? Slung mike, PZM, or baton for the host's short monologues? Well? Speak up, woman. We need answers now."

I have no answers. In fact, I have no clue what the heck she just said to me. I'm standing there gaping, trying to frame the right answer, when I don't even understand the question. Joe rescues me again.

"No, she's not the Assistant Director. She's a PC, and she's in charge of herding the contestants. This is Jules Vernon."

She rolls her eyes. "Great. I just wasted three-point-five minutes of my life on a glorified babysitter."

She turns to go.

"No, she's not a babysitter. She's a team-builder. So lighten up. All that nastiness will stunt your growth." Joe smiles down at the top of her head.

She flashes an affectionate grin at Joe.

"You old goat, how'd you land this gig?"

"I pulled strings to be near you, sweetie."

She grins again and runs back out of the room, presumably in search of the real AD.

"So what the heck was she talking about?" I ask Joe.

"OK, let's see. Opening shots are pretty much what they sound like—what the TV audience will see when we start the show. ECUs are extreme close-ups, to capture the emotion on the singers' faces during the songs. Knees are knee or three-quarter-length shots; cuts the body just below the knees in the frame. Still gets some emotion, but more of the body language, too. The pedestals look kind of like robots with wheels; they move around with cameras on them."

He pauses to draw a breath.

"OK, I've seen pedestals when I was a media escort to morning news shows, then."

"Right. Same thing. The slung mike is a hanging microphone suspended over the action. It will come in handy when we have a group of the finalists singing together. PZM is a personal zone mike; we can attach it to a table or chair or even the wall where the host is chatting with the singers. Finally, a baton is what it sounds like. Just a simple hand mike. The problem with those is that they're controlled by the person holding them. If they don't have experience with mikes, they're likely to forget about it and hold it at waist level or something and screw up the sound. Got it?"

I grin. "Not really. But, luckily for viewing America, I'm just a glorified babysitter and don't have to worry about the PZM or the ECU or the ABC or whatever."

Joe doesn't grin back. "You know, Jules," he says slowly, not quite meeting my eyes, "you do that a lot, and I don't get it."

"I do what?"

"You put yourself down. You're always taking a poke or jab at yourself, and they all add up to the same thing: I'm not really smart enough/good enough/talented enough to do this job, so don't hold me accountable if I screw it up."

The indigestion roars back up my esophagus with a vengeance.

"I—"

"No, let me finish. You're talented and you're smart, but a lot of people miss it at first because of the way you treat yourself. You're one of the best team-builders I've ever seen. Hell, you have Sharp and Johnson eating out of your hand, and they almost came to blows with our previous PC. You can even calm Roger down, and you understand Norman."

He shuffles his feet and clears his throat.

"I like you, too, but don't tell anybody, because I'll deny it. Got a reputation to maintain. Quit selling yourself short. Now go take those kids shopping."

He walks out of the control room, leaving me standing there, stunned, in his wake. Those were the most sentences I've ever heard Joe string together at one time. Somehow, what he said carries more weight because of it. That's the first time anybody's ever called me on my Impostor Syndrome. Maybe I'm finally ready to be caught?

Chapter Twenty-six
Week One: And Then There Were Nine

The days until Wednesday whisk by in a frenzy of clothes fittings, promo and commercial filming, and rehearsal after rehearsal. Sam and I even have a chance to go on an actual date. (He talked Joe into being den mother for the night; Norman's been in Florida at a *Star Wars* convention all week.) We have dinner and walk for hours, talking about everything and nothing. After a few minutes—OK, a lot of minutes—of steamy kissing in his car, I'm back at the house to sleep, alone. I'm determined to take it slow with him this time, because I've got a tiny flame of hope that maybe there's really something here.

Through some miracle of scheduling, luck, and Marshall's sheer persistence, we arrange for the *Trading Spaces* show to fly to Hollywood and redecorate the contestants' dorm-style rooms for the show.

It's hilarious, and we have a great time. The guys' room is now a replica of the Hollywood Walk of Fame, and the girls have the inside of Mae West's dressing room. Paige Davis and I walk around all day saying, "You know how to whistle, don't you? Just pucker your lips like this," and collapsing in laughter, but nobody gets it. Not old movie buffs, I guess.

As we watch the *Trading Spaces* van drive off, our high spirits drain out the soles of our shoes. (Jimmy Choo, Prada, Nine West, Adidas, and Nike.) There's nothing else to distract us now from the specter of our live show tomorrow night, and tension drapes the finalists like a shroud. A few of them head for the games room to try to Game Boy or eight ball in the corner pocket the stress away. Several others wander off to various corners of the house, where I can hear them rehearsing yet again. I wonder if anybody will still have a voice by tomorrow.

I mentally shake off my sudden despondency and realize Carlos followed me into the kitchen.

"Hey, Carlos. What's up? Want to have a snack with me?" I'm searching the fridge for Diet Coke, but all I find is mineral water. Health food freaks must stock this thing.

"No, what I need is a beer. Are you all right, Jules? Who was that guy?"

"What guy?" Ah HA. There's one shiny silver and red can wedged in the back corner. Score. "Sorry, no beer."

"That set designer guy. Was he bothering you?"

Oh. This is the first time we've talked about the scene outside the house between him and Sam. Sam's admonition about gangs strikes a warning note in my mind. I know he's wrong, but we may as well get it out on the table. I look at Carlos in his long-sleeved shirt.

"No, Sam wasn't bothering me. In fact, we're kind of seeing each other. He said something about you, though, that I was hoping you could clear up. He thinks, I mean, it's crazy, but Sam thinks . . ."

"He thinks I'm a banger," Carlos said flatly.

"I, er, yes. I told him it was ridiculous, but he grew up in bad neighborhoods and has this stupid idea, I mean . . . Oh, damn. I shouldn't have even brought it up. I'm sorry, Carlos."

"He's right."

"I . . . what?"

"He's right. I was in a gang. The Dragon's Tears, based out of Miami. I was eight when I started. In my neighborhood, you got protection from a gang, or you died. So pardon me if I scoff at your boyfriend's 'bad neighborhoods.'" His eyes are as dead as his tone.

I don't want to continue this conversation. I wish I'd never started it. But I need to know the truth.

"What about now? You said you *were* in a gang. Not any more?"

"Not anymore. I've got an eight-year-old sister. Just the age I was when I joined up. She was making noises about joining. It's never gonna happen. The only way I could stop it was to get out myself and get her and my mama the hell out of that neighborhood. No way my baby sister's gonna get gut-shot in a drive-by." From the bleakness in his voice, I know that his knowledge of gutshot children is very real.

He aims a measured look in my direction. "Don't mess this up for me, Jules. This is my chance to make enough money to get out for good. I plan to win."

"Carlos, you know enough about what I've been through lately to realize one thing: Second Chance is my middle name. Good luck."

He grins and, for the first time since I've known him, he looks like the boy he still is.

"Oh, and Carlos?"

He freezes, wary again.

"Some day when this is all over, I want to see your tattoos. I always thought a little dragon tattoo on my belly would be cute."

He roars with laughter. "Mine are anything but cute, babe, but I'll show you my tats anytime. After all, you're pretty hot for an old chick."

"Hey!" But I'm yelling at empty air. He can move fast, the brat. I decide to haul my old chick bones up to bed, to get some sleep for tomorrow. It's going to be a long day.

Jedi Knights and Bubonic Plague

It's six hours until show time, and the studio is Chaos Central. From the way the crew members are running around like maniacs, it's hard to believe we'll pull off a live show tonight, but Joe reassured me that it's always like this. Something about TV people feeling more indispensable if they're frenetically freaked out of their minds on air date. OK, whatever works, I guess.

I don't have time to worry about it, though, because I'm trying to keep the contestants from losing what's left of their overstressed minds. And voices.

We had to show up early for sound checks and lighting checks and all the checks I thought they finished in rehearsal last night, but evidently which could have changed dramatically in the eighteen hours since then. Joe is double- and triple-checking costumes, props, and even sequencing. I've been looking for Norman since we arrived, but he's nowhere in sight. If he dropped the ball on the gift baskets because of his *Star Wars* convention, I'm going to beat him over the head with his own light saber. Speaking of light sabers, is that . . . ?

Oh. Good. Grief.

Either Norman is here, or a Jedi Knight in full regalia beamed down from the mother ship. (Or maybe that's *Star Trek*; I can't really keep them straight.) He's heading straight for me. I wonder briefly if I should try to defend myself.

"Jules, long time no see, dude. What's up? I had the most awesome week. I got a photo taken with me and *Anthony Daniels*."

He says this with the same awestruck tone a child would use to say *Santa Claus*. I hate to burst his bubble.

"That's great, Norman. Who's Anthony Daniels?"

Bafflement and disappointment mix in his expression. "Who's Anthony Daniels? *Who's* Anthony Daniels? Jules, Anthony Daniels is just THE voice of C3PO in both the original *Star Wars* series *and* the new episodes. *Just* one of the greatest voice-over talents of all time. *Just* the man who brought humanity to the greatest robot in the history of film. I mean, you've got your R2D2 afficionados, but how can they even compare a bunch of mechanized beeping and burping to the emotion—"

"Norman. Norman!"

He comes back from wherever the Force took him and looks at me dazedly. "Yeah?"

"Norman, that's fantastic, and I can't wait to see it, but it's less than six hours till the show, and I haven't seen the gift baskets. You did remember the gift baskets, didn't you?"

Norman's huge smile relieves me immensely. "Sure I did. I wouldn't let you down, Jules. No way! I did five baskets, like we discussed. One for each judge, one for a randomly selected member of our studio audience, and one for caller number one million who votes for tonight's winner."

"That's great, Norman." It is great.

"I never had any doubts." I had huge doubts.

"Where are they?" The acid test.

"Where? Oh, right. Um, I think I left them in my car." He scratches his head. "No, that can't be right, because I lost my license after that thing with the Vespa. I must have left them in the cab."

"The cab? The *cab?*" I'm running for the door. "Norman, are you saying the cab driver just drove off with our gift baskets filled with thousands of dollars' worth of merchandise?"

"Calm down, dude. It's my buddy—he drives a cab part-time, in between auditions. I'll call him on my cell."

My steps and my heart rate slow down simultaneously. Yet another Lamaze breathing moment.

"Call him right now, please, Norman. I want to see those gift baskets before show time."

Are we having fun yet?

"Jules. Jules!!" It's Marshall, and he sounds panicked. What now?

"Jules, get down here right now!"

I run in the general direction of his voice, yelling as I run. "Where are you, Marshall?"

"I'm at the door to the men's room, where else would I be?"

Of course, right. Where else?

I slow to a stop in front of him. He is, in fact, standing in the door of the men's room, with the door wide open, in spite of the wall of urinals facing the doorway and the two men who, by the sounds of it, are not quite done doing what men usually do at urinals. Not that I've ever seen them before. Doing it at urinals, that is. Oh, God.

"Marshall, what is it? And don't you think you should close the door and give those poor men some privacy?" The men are frantically nodding their agreement.

"Fuck privacy! We've got a crisis in here and you'd

better fix it. Now!" He reaches out as if to grab me, and I back up a step, wondering if he's washed his hands yet. I mean, euuwww.

"What crisis? In there? Why would you need me for a crisis in the men's room?" There's no way I'm going in there. They don't pay me nearly enough for this.

"Jules, listen. Just listen!" He flings the door open even wider, if possible, and points down the bathroom toward some stalls. I listen, and the distinct and entirely disgusting sound of retching is coming from the first stall. Did I mention, euuwww?

"OK, one of my contestants is getting rid of a few butterflies. It's not a crisis; it's just stage fright. Serenity now, Marshall. Serenity now."

"Don't serenity now, me, Jules, or I'll fire your ass. Your *contestant* with butterflies is actually my *judge* who thinks he has bubonic fucking plague, and says he's not going to do the show. Fix it. NOW." Marshall grabs my arm and drags me into the bathroom.

In all the times I envisioned the day of our first show, hanging out in the men's room while a hypochondriac judge puked his guts out was never in the picture. But, OK, I am an Important Production Coordinator.

I am in Show Biz.

I have a Can-Do attitude.

I'm going to puke. Don't they ever clean in here? This is nasty.

We reach the stall, and Marshall hammers on the door.

"Roger, open that door, or I'll break it down, you malingering slime ball. If you screw up my first show, I'll chew your guts up and feed them to the horses for glue." Marshall's not especially picky about keeping his old sayings straight.

"Go away. I told you I'm dying. I want Jules. I want Jules. I want JUUUUUUULLLLLES. . ."

The ululating moan is a nice touch, I think, as I breathe through my mouth. Marshall jabs me in the side.

"Ouch! I mean, Roger, I'm here. It's me, Jules. What's going on, sweetie? Talk to me." I'm using my cousin's talk-to-her-toddler voice, for some reason.

"Jules, thank God. You have to get me to hospital right away. Call the CDC. Get me quarantined. I have bubonic plague. It's hideously contagious."

It briefly occurs to me that he's not worried about *me* getting infected.

"Roger, you don't have bubonic plague. There's no such thing as bubonic plague anymore. It's been eradicated since the Dark Ages or something, hasn't it?"

"That just shows what you know. From 1967-1993, an annual average of 1666 cases of the Plague have been reported by the World Health Organization. The number of actual cases is probably much higher, given the failure of many countries to diagnose and report the plague. More than fifty percent of cases occur in males, Jules." He pauses, and we hear more retching noises.

Marshall throws his hands up in disgust. "*You* deal with this. But I don't care if he has the bubonic plague, scarlet death, or chicken fucking pox, you get him on that show tonight," he hisses at me, and then stalks off toward the bathroom door.

Leaving me alone in the men's room with a guy carrying the first-ever reported case of the black plague in Hollywood.

I sigh and lean against the wall.

"What are your symptoms, Roger?"

"Fever, chills, myalgia, sore throat, headache, weakness,

malaise . . ."

"Myalgia? What the heck is myalgia?"

"Pain in one or more muscles. All of my muscles hurt, Jules."

Especially the one between your ears, I think, and then an unpleasant suspicion pops into my mind.

"What did you say about the World Health Organization, Roger?"

"I'm not done listing symptoms, Jules. I have rose-colored purpuric lesions. . . ."

"STOP! I Do Not Want To Hear About Your Lesions. *What did you say about the W.H.O.?*"

"I, erm, well, I said that from 1967-1993, an annual average of 1666 cases of the plague have been reported by the World Health Organization. The number of actual cases is probably much higher . . ."

"Ah HA! You've been surfing MEDLINE again, haven't you? I cancelled your Internet account, after you thought you had scurvy in Tampa Bay. How did you get back on?" I'm standing outside a stall in the men's room, mere hours before show time. I can't stand it.

"Jules, I don't know what you're talking about. I simply happen to be the victim of a dreadful disease, and we're wasting the few precious remaining moments of my life discussing the Internet. I really thought you'd care a bit more about my fate." Roger combines Haughty Aristocrat with Injured Sufferer really well.

"Roger, of course I care about you. Come out and we'll take you to the doctor. You'll miss the show, though, and all of your fans will be so disappointed. Plus, you'll be letting the contestants down, and they've worked so hard for this night. But it can't be helped, since you'll be in quarantine and all. Come on, we'll get you to the hospital quick, so I can find another judge. Better get an American this time, so we can have somebody with a little more of the-show-must-go-on spirit, if you know what I mean. No offense, of course." I grin and start counting. Three, two, one . . .

The door bangs open. Roger, who does look a little pale, I must admit, shoots a wounded look at me.

"You're awfully eager to get rid of me, Jules. I must say, I expected more of you. May have to rethink my job offer, after all. And, of course, it was the Brits who invented the saying The Show Must Go On, not you upstarts over here. No offense to Americans, you understand."

I swallow my grin, which is trying hard to resurface, and walk toward the door.

"Please wash up, Roger, and then I'll take you to the hospital."

"Well, not so fast. It's possible I was overreacting. Come to think of it, there's only one lesion, on my arm, and it may be a mosquito bite. And my muscles may be sore from the Swedish massage I got from that sadistic masseuse last night. In fact, I feel better now." He marches over to the sink, the fate of the British Empire firmly astride his thrown-back shoulders.

"Actually, I'm sure I can do the show tonight. Can't let my fans and the finalists down, as you say. Quite right. I'll just wash up and see you in a while, Jules. I'll have a bit of a rest in my dressing room before the show."

"That sounds like a great idea, Roger. I'll check on you in a little while. I'm so glad you're feeling better."

I escape out the door and run right into Norman. He, Joe, and about ten of the crew members are lined up outside the bathroom. Either they all need to pee, or they're worrying about Roger.

All but Norman and Joe shove past me into the bathroom. All righty, then. I guess we answered that question.

Joe cocks his head. "He OK?"

"He will be. I pulled out the 'we'll replace you with an American' threat, and he snapped right out of it." I shake my head and start walking off toward the contestants' dressing rooms.

"What was it this time?" Norman calls after me.

"Bubonic plague. Don't ask. Just don't ask."

As I walk down the hall, I make a fatal mistake.

I wonder what else could possibly go wrong.

Irving and the photography crew from *People* are back, I see, as I reach the girls' dressing room. They're lugging camera equipment toward the door. To be precise, the all-male photographers and reporter are starting to push open the door to the all-female dressing room.

"Freeze!" I yell, as I run the last few feet to meet them.

"Just what do you think you're doing?"

Irving knows he's still in the doghouse with me over the cover story, and now he's not getting out any time soon. Not to mention my future pink slip is on the line here if KCM Records sees pictures of my contestants in their Victorica's Secrets. No way am I losing this job.

"Well, Total Access and all that. We were just going in to get some intro shots. You know, Preparation for the Big Night, and all."

"Total Access does not include shots of our female contestants in their underwear, you pervert. I'll let you know when we're ready for you. And what's wrong with you, anyway? You're *People*, not *Playboy*."

Irving at least has the decency to look sheepish.

"It's about ratings in our business, too, Jules. For us, it's ad sales, subscriptions, and in-store sell-through. Sorry, though. I'll come back when you say you're ready."

One of the photographers, who doesn't look all that happy with the new turn of events, speaks up. "And speaking of *Playboy*, we saw a photographer with *Playboy* handing out business cards to your contestants earlier. The chicks, at least. Probably not that fat one, though."

Nice. A guy who hasn't washed his hair in at least three days is judging my contestants on their looks. I stifle the urge to point this out, and zero in on the other part of what he said.

"How do you know he was from *Playboy*?"

"He was a she. And I know her from around. We have a guild, you know." He aims one last disgusted look at me before trudging off after Irving toward the guys' dressing room. I'm not worried about defending *their* privacy. Carlos can take care of them just fine, I'm thinking.

It looks like an unreported tropical storm struck the dressing room in my absence. There are clothes and shoes everywhere. Mary Ann is arguing with the makeup artist. (We have three people on the makeup team and they each have a specific place in the hierarchy. The makeup designer *designs* the makeup for the entire production. This is Very Important and asking him to touch up someone's powder, as I did last night during dress rehearsal, is a serious faux pas. The makeup artist does the actual makeup, and the makeup assistant does, well, assisting, I guess.)

"I don't want to look like a clown. I like the natural look, not that tarted-up loose woman look." She has her arms firmly crossed over her chest, and a mutinous expression on her face.

Loose woman? Does anybody even say that anymore?

The makeup artist looks disgusted and throws his brush down on the table.

"The natural look is fine, as long as we use makeup to effect the look. Those lights will wash you out so badly, you'll look like you've been in your grave for a week without it. Trust me, Mary Ann. I know what I'm doing. You met my wife; does she look like a . . ." He laughs. "A 'tarted-up loose woman'?"

Mary Ann shakes her head slowly. "No, she's lovely. I'm sorry; this has been too much, and I get overwhelmed. So much going on all at the same time. I'm a long way from Ohio, you know."

I'm still stuck a few lines back. His wife?

"Your wife?"

He glares at me. "Yeah, my wife. Hey, I only act a little gay at work because nobody believes straight guys can do makeup. Trust me, you grow up with six sisters, you know makeup." He shudders in exaggerated horror.

"They were putting dresses and lipstick on me from the time I was a toddler. It's a wonder I'm not Norman Bates, the sequel."

OK, maybe the horror's not all that exaggerated. In any event, Mary Ann has calmed down and is letting him do her makeup. I see she still hasn't changed out of her cotton plaid dress, but decide to wait until makeup is done to talk to her about costume.

I walk over to where two of our hair stylists are working on Shanicia's hair extensions. Her eyes are closed and she's mumbling to herself. As I get closer, I realize she's praying. I hesitate, not wanting to interrupt, when she stops and her eyes fly open.

"Jules? Is it close? Are they almost done? I'm not

even dressed yet. I'm scared to death."

I look at the stylists to answer the easiest question first.

"About ten more minutes," one of them answers my unspoken question. "It's going great, and she has lovely hair."

"Yes, what a beautiful girl. You'll do just fine, sweetie." The other chimes in with a sing-song cadence I recognize vaguely. Ah, the talk-to-toddler voice. These people are very familiar with pre-show jitters, obviously.

"You're going to be great, Shanicia. You're all going to be great. You've worked so hard and, in a way, you've been rehearsing for this night your whole lives. You're going to be magnificent."

They all look at me solemnly. My pep talk hasn't made anybody forget that one of the ten will be going home this week. And each of them knows it could be her.

Except maybe Kayley. She's stretched out on another chair, getting manicured and pedicured at the same time. She lifts one of the cucumber slices off an eye and peers at me.

"Yeah, yeah, we get it. We're all magnificent, blah, blah, blah. Don't you have something better to do than bother us with your bullshit? Daddy wants to talk to you before the show, by the way."

I take a deep breath. Patience is a virtue, right?

"Kayley, if it's about the tickets again, I'm not selling him extra front-row seats. Each contestant has an allotted number of friend and family seats in the first two rows. If they want to work something out with your dad, that's fine. But tell him to quit leaving me cell phone messages about it."

She snorts in my general direction and replaces the cucumber slice. I shake my head and evaluate the rest of my finalists.

Amanda is behind the screen, getting dressed, and I see Lisette waiting calmly on the couch, doing what looks like breathing exercises. Things are basically under control here; I'd better check on the guys. And, no, the thought of catching Carlos stripped down to his underwear has nothing to do with it.

Although, let's face it. My new let's-take-it-slow strategy with Sam drives me into All Horny All the Time mode.

Speaking of Sam, as I step out of the dressing room and close the door firmly behind me, I see him leaning against the wall a few feet down the hall.

"Hey, beautiful. How are you doing?" He unfolds his yummy body and smiles at me.

Taking it slow isn't always the best idea, I think.

"I'm good. Good to see you. Are you? Good, I mean." How many times can I say good in the same sentence? Aargh. Why do I always get flustered around him?

"Yes, you are. Good. And here we are back at 'G' words." He's aiming that lethal smile at me again. The one that can melt panties at fifty paces.

"Let's get together after the show tonight, Jules. I'm tired of taking it slow. Or maybe I'll just take *you*. Slowly. Would that be all right?" He brushes my hair away from my face.

"I, um, that would be, well, slowly is good, actually. But what about my contestants?"

"*Your* contestants? You really have taken this job on, haven't you? Your contestants will be fine. Joe's going to babysit. I'd better go check on the set. Wait for me after the show, and we'll take my car and go get some dinner. And see what kind of *slow* we can get ourselves into." He bends down and presses a brief, hard kiss against my mouth, and is gone before

I can mention that he was awfully sure of me.

On second thought, why quibble? Slow sounds like exactly what I need. Especially after today.

Break a Leg

"I'm going to break your freakin' leg, you pompous windbag!"

Somehow, that doesn't sound like traditional show business well-wishing. I round the corner, to see Kayley's dad squaring off against Jack's bodyguard. Kayley's dad must be the pompous windbag, because he's answering back.

"Not a chance, you hairy ape. And if you lay a hand on me, I'll have your ass thrown in jail so fast your Neanderthal head will spin."

This is my penance for wondering what else could go wrong.

"Break it up, you two. What's going on?"

"He said I couldn't . . ."

"The hired help isn't going to . . ."

"Whoa! One at a time. You first." I point to Luigi/Luke, the bodyguard.

"This rich prick said I have to give him my seat for one of his buddies, because I'm just the hired help and I don't get to sit in the first row. I practically raised Jack and I'm not gonna miss his big show biz moment." He's actually growling. I've positioned myself between a four-hundred pound growling man and his adversary, which forcibly reminds me that I'm braver than I am smart.

"Luke, you are *not* going to miss his big show-business moment. Jack had the same number of tickets for the first and second rows as each of the other contestants. If he gave you one of them, he must think very highly of you. You do not have to give your ticket up *to* anybody, or *for* anybody. Please go wait out in the seating area."

"And you," I begin, whipping around to face Mr. Got Rocks. "I'm a little sick of your attitude. Just because you have money to burn does not give Kayley a better or worse chance than any other contestant. It does not give you a right to more or fewer seats in the audience than those of any other contestant. And, finally, it does *not* give you the right to leave annoying messages on my cell phone voice mail all day long. Now, stop it!"

He's breathing hard through his mouth, with his head down and his fists clenched. Maybe I was afraid of the wrong guy. He takes a step toward me, and I involuntarily step back. When I see the evil glee spread over his face, I get seriously pissed off.

"OK, that's it. Back off now. If you take one more step toward me, I am going to get Kayley kicked out of this competition. You know I can do it. We have alternates standing by their phones who don't have parents who are total assholes. I don't want to hurt Kayley, but I've had enough of you. Just give me an excuse, just one. Please."

He takes half a step forward and then pauses. I can see rage battle hesitation on his face. Finally, he steps back.

"Fine. I'll back off. But you don't want to mess with me, Jules. I've destroyed entire companies. It's not a threat; it's just a fact."

"You know what? I've had way too much melodrama lately to give a damn about your hot air. So stay out of my way, and we'll be fine. Now please go out to the seating area with the rest of the families and friends."

I turn to walk off, clenching my jaw against the urge to sneak a look back at him. I can feel the flames from the look he's aiming after me searing holes in my back, but I don't hear footsteps, so my shoulders relax infinitesimally.

Of course you won't hear footsteps if he has a gun, my mind says.

You shut up, too, I tell my mind, aware that I'm developing a raging case of schizophrenia to go with my new ulcer. I can get a T-shirt made: *I went to Hollywood, and all I got was this lousy mental condition*.

Show Time

The hours until show time race by as I check hair, makeup, outfits, and attitudes. The mental states of the guys vary as widely as those of their sister contestants. Carlos is relaxed and watchful. Jack cracks jokes that arc an edge of cruelty against their attempt at humor.

What's the difference between a diva and a five-dollar whore?

About a thousand bucks.

He notes my raised eyebrow but ignores me. Lucas and Anton are quiet, but Derek is white-faced under his makeup. I steer him off into a corner.

"How're you holding up?" I ask quietly, trying not to draw any attention to him.

"I'm fine. No problem. Just like the senior class play, right? Times about five freakin' million, right?" He's sweating.

"It's OK, Derek. When you're out there, just talk to the host like you're chatting with a friend, and sing directly to Nellie. She thinks you're great, and you'll do fine." I pat his arm.

"OK, guys. Time to head for the green room. You're going to be great. Break a leg out there and all that show biz stuff." I'm smiling. Sam was right.

They are *my* contestants. I already know that I'm going to cry with whoever gets voted off this week.

From that moment, the frenzied rush begins. I supervise the contestants in the green room in between the times they're on air. A preternatural calm settles over me, as I help them work through their nerves and jitters. I'm the oasis of sanity in the middle of chaos.

This is an unfamiliar role for me, but I like it.

Even Norman and the gift baskets can't throw me off, I hope, as I see him walk into the green room with the first basket, trailed by a couple of the stage hands with the other four.

"What the hell is that?" I hiss. So much for calm.

"Isn't it great? I got everything I needed for the baskets at the *Star Wars* convention. Jules, there's a light saber, action figures, official Storm Trooper masks, CDs of the soundtracks from all the movies . . ."

"You got *STAR WARS gift baskets*? Are you nuts? Marshall is going to have a cow."

"Nah, he's used to it. And Mom says he has to quit being mean to me, or he doesn't get to come to Sunday dinner anymore." He smiles angelically.

I am momentarily bemused by the thought of Marshall and Norman at a Sunday dinner presided over by someone who can out-Marshall Marshall.

"Oh, Norman. It was my responsibility. He won't fire you, but your mom's protection doesn't cover me. Well, it's been nice knowing you."

"Trust me, it's going to be fine."

And, somehow, it is. Our host announces the gift baskets as an exciting, exclusive homage to classic film and, in a unanimous gesture of benevolence, all three judges donate their baskets to be auctioned off on eBay for charity. (Benevolence = they don't like

Star Wars, either.)

Nellie attacks Marshall on a commercial break. "I wanted my Louis Vuitton Cell Phone Case and Nokia 9990 Wireless Phone Limited Platinum Edition. Marshall, you'd better go get me one. Now."

Unfortunately, because of my supervising slash babysitting slash calm-everybody-the-heck-down duties, I don't get to see much of the actual show. I can hear the singing, though it's muffled, and see a few moments of the show on the monitor in the green room.

Carlos sings with even more power than he fired at us during auditions and whips the audience into a frenzy of clapping and hip-twisting.

Derek hits a few flat notes and walks offstage, bewildered at how he might have failed at something.

Shanicia blasts a gospel remix through the rafters that has even Q saying *Amen* at the end.

Roger slams Amanda. "Poor song choice, terrible outfit, and, actually, the worst singing I've heard from anyone in this competition. You'd better improve, or you're going to be out."

(I spend a good ten minutes calming a hysterically weeping Amanda after that delightful incident.)

Mary Lou, still in her plaid cotton dress, but with makeup on, I note, sings with such power and purity the entire audience is silent for several seconds after she finishes, then they go wild in the first standing ovation of the evening.

From what I manage to see of the other contestants, they're all good, but nobody stands out from the pack. Not that I have the time or inclination to make that decision.

Finally, it's over. All ten of them are on stage singing the final notes of—what else?—"Hooray for Hollywood" as the closing credits roll. We made it through our first show. Only eight weeks more of this. The thought collapses me into a chair, feeling weak, headachy, and the onset of what must be myalgia.

Maybe I have bubonic plague, too.

Chapter Twenty-seven
Aftermath

Sam and I go out for dinner after the show, which is code for Sam and I pick up take-out Chinese and have each other for dinner after the show.

We spend hours exploring each other and thinking up new 'G'-words.

Like Glorious.

And Great and Grand and Glad.

He tries Groovy, but I laugh him out of bed. Then I come up with Gnarly, and he tickles me viciously for it. I get away with Gaga, when I tell him that it means "marked by wild enthusiasm." (We played a lot of Scrabble at my house.)

Sam almost makes me cry with Galatea-like tears, but we have a fierce debate over whether Aphrodite or Artemis brought her statue to life for lovelorn Pygmalion. I make him look it up and don't even rub it in when I'm proven right. Of course it was the Goddess of Love. I mean, duh. OK, I don't rub it in *much.*

I redeem myself with Gallant and Gentle, which he is, oh, so much. And Giving and Generous and

Good.

Then he tells me he thinks he's falling in love with me.

And all I can say is, "Gamble. Going. Gone." But I'm thinking Ghastly, Gruesome, and Grisly. Ghoulish, even. Because the last man to tell me he loved me is off sticking his Gimlet in other women's Girdles.

Enough with the damn 'G' words, already.

"Gamble, Jules? Going, Gone?" Sam is smiling, but he looks sad.

"I'm sorry, but you caught me off guard with that. I mean, I thought we were having a great time, I mean, a good time, er, AARGH. I can't get these stupid 'G' words out of my mind. Fun. I thought we were having fun. I didn't know we were getting our emotions involved." I'm frantically scooting back up the bed toward the headboard, covering myself with the sheet. The emotional police sound a blaring retreat. WARNING. WARNING. STEP AWAY FROM THE FEELINGS.

"I told you about Mark, and why I'm not sure I'm ready for emotional entanglement again. I thought you understood. I, you, wow. I'm not ready for this, Sam. It's too soon."

He throws off the sheet and springs up to pace the room. He's all lean, lithe muscle prowling like a caged panther. Oops, need to focus. Where were we?

"It's been six years, Jules. Six years since that moronic asshole dumped you. How long are you going to hide from your own feelings? When will you be ready? Ten years? Fifteen? Twenty?" He sweeps his hair back from his forehead with an impatient hand and then whips around to face me.

"It's hard for me, too, Jules. I've been let down a lot. Women who want the Blake and Sons money but aren't too picky about little things like love or loyalty. But I feel something special with you that makes me want to take a chance again. Don't you feel it? Or am I just something to amuse you during the show?"

I have to make him understand; to break through the bitterness in his voice. But I suddenly don't understand myself. What am I so afraid of? Is avoiding the lowest of the lows worth hiding from all the amazing highs?

I look at him, trying to formulate an answer that will make sense. Suddenly it's clear. "Sam, I want to try. I want to try, with you. Please help me not to be afraid."

Suddenly I'm crying and he's right there holding me and his eyes are so warm and his arms are so strong and safe. And, as I fall asleep, still wrapped in his arms, I realize I may have found my way to Grace.

The Day After

We got the ratings! The critics blasted us, but in a good way. For example:

A total rip-off of American Idol, *right down to the cheesy British-accented judge, but with a twist. Upbeat imagery of the contestants* Trading Spaces, *in a unique crossover with another network, beats the schmaltzy sentimentality of video postcards from home any day. Sadly for this reviewer, no video of the pleasing (or should we say self-pleasing?) production coordinator caught on the cover of a certain national magazine . . .*

OK, maybe not *great* reviews, but Marshall is ecstatic. Our first show hit big, and the ad dollars are pouring into the network. Tonight is our first results show, where we tell America the results of the voting—live. Marshall's still tinkering with the format and trying to bribe the network for more airtime, but, as it looks now, after this first week we'll be giving the results live each week during the show. We're holding an emergency staff meeting tomorrow morning to see how we can pump up the excitement for next week. We need to top the *Trading Spaces* concept. My head is ballooning from the praise the clones are heaping on me about that, by the way.

"Knew it was a great idea, Jules."

"Way to go, Jules. I always knew you were on to something."

People in Hollywood lap up the smell of success the way Seattle-ites lap up lattes. When you're on top, everybody's your buddy. Not so much different from other places, after all.

My cell phone is ringing madly, too. Mom, Dad, Kirby, and even Amber call to congratulate me on the wonderful show, as though I were solely responsible for the entire production. I don't actually correct them, but I don't take the credit for it all, either. Not technically.

But it's a weird place to be emotionally, celebrating the show's success, when one of my contestants has the ax hanging over his or her head. It makes me feel Marie Antoinette-ish, so I veto the idea of ordering a celebratory cake.

Tonight's results show hovers ominously over our heads. The contestants are jazzed up on nerves and caffeine, and I'm right there with them. We're all speculating—some openly, most in whispers—on who will be voted off. I'm pretty sure that either Amanda or Derek is in trouble, from what I saw when Sam and I watched a tape of the show late last night. Or maybe early this morning.

Hey, what can I say? We took it slow. Real slow. The man turned Slow into an art form.

And the Loser Is . . .

Thank goodness the results show only lasts thirty minutes, because this is torture. First, we make them all sing two songs together. Then we play footage of each of the contestants during the past week and at auditions, with a lot of attention on Carlos, Kayley, Derek, and Amanda, I notice.

Finally, the moment I dread arrives. The host announces the bottom two: "Derek and Amanda."

We cut to commercial. Derek looks dazed, and Amanda starts crying in earnest. I rush out to offer tissues and comfort, knowing it's not enough. The director waves me offstage.

From behind the curtain, I hear the words.

"I'm sorry, Amanda. You will not be America's new *POP STAR LIVE!*"

Mercifully, we roll tape of Amanda singing from last night with the closing credits, instead of asking her to sing to America after the ax fell. I run out onstage to offer my support, but her family is there before me, and they elbow me out of the way, glaring.

I'm part of *POP STAR LIVE!*, which makes me as much the enemy now as I was "part of the family; come visit anytime" just hours ago. Understanding that this is all part of the show, the game, and the drama of live television doesn't make me less sad for Amanda. Who are we to raise the hopes of these dreamers and then crush them? The thrill of the ratings wears off fast.

I gather my greatly subdued flock to return to the house. Tomorrow we'll order cake and start a new round of clothes fittings, rehearsals, and promo filmings. But just for tonight, we'll all be a little solemn, thinking of Amanda. And, for the nine of them at least, wondering if they'll be next.

The Reality portion of Reality TV has arrived.

Chapter Twenty-eight
I'm Up; I'm Down

Thursday: An actual round of applause greets me when I walk into the staff meeting, late again. (There was a long line at CoffeeWood.)

"Good job on the *Trading Spaces* deal, Jules. The public eats that happy shit up. Way to go with Roger, too. And keeping everything smooth backstage. You're doing a great job for somebody who's only been in TV a few weeks." Marshall loves me, but I'm immune to his praise. I've seen him transform into Evil Dictator too many times.

Nellie would *hate* it, though. I smile hugely.

"Thanks, but Joe deserves most of the credit. He's been teaching me the ropes, and he supervised everything that happened last night. Plus, Norman's brilliant twist on the gift baskets brought us a lot of attention with the press; even CNN picked up on the eBay auction plan."

I look around for my colleagues. Joe is ducking his head, but I can see the corners of his grin, and Norman is sprawled back in his chair, clutching a Diet Coke, eyes half closed. Norman's not a morning person, either. He smiles at me.

"Jules, I totally told you the gift baskets would rock. You gotta trust me, babe. The Force is with us."

Marshall rolls his eyes. "Don't start that Force crap, Norman. I promised Mom, but no more dressing up like a Wookie or whatever the hell you were supposed to be yesterday."

Norman snaps to attention. "A Wookie? Man, you are so lame. That was a genuine replica of the original Jedi . . ."

I'm frantically shaking my head No and holding a finger to my lips, when Norman finally sees me and subsides back into his chair, grimly muttering. "Fine, whatever. Move on, dude."

"OK, so where are we with the predatory birds? We had the warm and fuzzies last week; this week we dive-bomb the shit out of them and make America wet their pants." Marshall spears one of the clones with his stare.

"You. Progress report. Now."

The clones all have gray linen pants and white shirts on today. I can't figure out how they do it, unless they really do call each other the night before:

"Gray pants, white shirt, pass it on. "

"Got it."

Missed some of that. What? No birds.

". . . no chance of permissions. Endangered species, endangering wildlife for commercial gain, yada yada."

Marshall's glaring again.

"Now what do we do? The contestants are already practicing their bird songs. I even asked Sheryl Crow to be a guest judge." He smiles beatifically for a second, and then his mouth falls open.

"Make sure she's not sitting next to Nellie." He shudders.

To be honest, a shudder goes around the whole table. It's collective horror in action.

Joe speaks up from his place against the wall. He's in his usual uniform, jeans and an old cotton shirt. Very un-clonelike.

"Keep the bird songs. Forget Sheryl Crow. Your life and impending marriage would be in danger. Stick a few tame parrots near the singers. Lay in some footage about endangered rainforest species or something. The tree-huggers will eat it up." Joe being Joe, that's all he has to say.

The rest of us spend the next forty-five minutes translating Joe into TV production and, by the end of the meeting, we've hammered out a plan. My part is trivial enough; I have to help my nine kids find jewelry or clothes with birds on them. I wonder briefly about Carlos's tattoos. Nah, maybe not.

As we're leaving, Marshall makes another announcement. "To shake things up, this week we're going to have the contestants vote each other off. Go do it."

I stop dead on my way out the door. What? I intercept Marshall on his way to chew the wings off butterflies, or whatever he does during the day.

"What? Marshall, we can't do that to these kids. They're becoming friends."

"Friends. Yeah, right. Jules, we have a million-dollar contract up for grabs at the end of this thing. You're a naive fool if you think there's a single one of those kids who wouldn't sell his own mother down the river to get it." He laughs at me, and then he's gone.

I think of Carlos, and the mother and sister he's trying to save. Marshall is wrong. But the Executive Producer is never wrong, so we're doing it his way. Those poor kids. I trudge down the hall, feeling like predatory birds are dive-bombing *me*.

Botox and Blowjobs

Monday: After a fairly calm weekend, I wake up to a cell phone call from Nellie that is the equivalent of a royal command to see her today. I consider dawdling or, even more fun, blowing her off completely, but think I've used up my quota of free passes where my job is concerned. I pass various crew members in the hall and ask if anybody's seen her. Somebody eventually mutters something about her dressing room, so I head that way. I don't know why she'd be in her dressing room this morning but, as she'd be the first to point out, it's not my job to question her actions.

I knock on the door and hear her gentle bellow.

"What?"

"It's Jules. You wanted me?"

"Come in, already."

I walk in the door and see a bizarre sight. A man in a suit is leaning over Nellie, sticking a needle in her forehead. A big needle. Oh, gross. Nellie's assistant hovers in the background, still wearing gray, I see, but at least with a pink scarf on today. Maybe there's hope for that girl, yet.

"Nellie? Are you all right?"

"Of course I'm all right, you idiot. Why wouldn't I be all right?"

"Um, I just wondered. . . . What are you *doing?*" The well-dressed man keeps stabbing that needle in her face, between her eyes.

"My doctor is giving me my Botox injections. What the hell does it look like?"

It looks like torture in the Spanish Inquisition, but I figure she doesn't want to hear this.

"You know," she says, looking at me consideringly. "You could use some Botox yourself. His services are written into my contract; go ahead and hop up here."

Her forehead looks like a swarm of tiny, angry bees have attacked her. Nellie and her doctor are both looking at me.

"Uh, no, but thanks. The idea of injecting poison into my head isn't up there on my list of fun things to do. But thanks for the offer."

She shakes her head in disgust. "Whatever. You can't expect to get far if you don't try to improve yourself, Jules. Now what do you want?"

"Nellie, you left a message for me. I thought *you* wanted something."

"Oh, right. Marshall wants me to arrange makeovers for all the contestants. I'm far too busy this week. You handle it. Make sure to get it on tape; hair color, makeup, the works. And be sure to get some damn clothes for our little country mouse. Mary Jean, Mary Ann, whatever her name is. She looked ridiculous the other night. Completely embarrassing." She's sneering at the thought.

"Not that having you do a makeover for somebody else isn't the blind leading the blind. But I've written down the names of my stylist team, and the hair and makeup people for the show are going to help. We're going to use clips in the promos and during the show, so don't screw it up."

I'm clenching my hands into fists again. I'm going to have permanent indentations on my palms from my fingernails, if I don't get away from her soon.

"Fine, Nellie. I'll do my best not to screw it up." I snatch the sheet of paper out of her hand and turn to go.

The doctor, silent up until then, speaks up as I reach for the doorknob.

"You know, at your age, you really should start thinking of having some work done. I'll leave my card with Nellie. I could give you the bulk rate discount."

I'm so proud of myself for not slamming her dressing room door. Out in the hall, I pull in a deep breath of relief. One close encounter of the unpleasant kind done for the day. The actual makeover thing should be fun. I glance at my list. I have to see Roger next. He left me a rambling message about friendliness and how the weather in London isn't nearly as bad as I might expect. I hope he doesn't think he has another disease; I haven't figured out where the closest emergency room is yet.

I find him in the break room, sneering at the tea bags. "Hey, Roger."

"Hello, Jules. You people and your pitiful excuse for tea. No wonder you can't play rugby." He casts the tea bag down in disdain and grabs a bottle of water from the bin on the table.

"I don't actually get the connection between tea and rugby, but whatever. Rugby shirts are cute. I used to date a guy in college who . . ."

"Erm, Jules, as fascinating as that may be, perhaps we could get to the point."

"Fine, Roger. Why should I get to ramble just because everybody else around here does?" I'm muttering like a petulant child, albeit a child who evidently needs bulk cosmetic surgery and Botox.

"Right," Roger says, looking confused. "Well, then. Here's my proposition."

"Oh, *no*. I mean, Roger, I'm very flattered, but I've been seeing Sam and, well, we didn't say we were exclusive and maybe he's not, but he'd better be after that whole Barbie thing, but I can't. I mean, you're totally gorgeous and adorable and nice, but it's just that I'm kind of not available right now."

Now he looks *extremely* confused. Then he starts grinning. "Oh, Jules. You thought I—that I was—no, it's not that kind of proposition. Although I, in turn, am very flattered that you think I'm gorgeous and, what was it? Adorable and nice? But I was merely going to ask you to consider taking a position with me, when the show is on hiatus, as my executive assistant."

His executive assistant? The proposition wasn't . . . Oh, no. Not again.

I bury my head in my arms on the table and groan. It may be muffled, but it's loud.

Roger starts laughing. "Please don't be embarrassed. I think it's quite charming. And perhaps I've led you to believe that I'm attracted to you. The truth is, maybe I am a little attracted to you. But I've seen you and Blake together, and I don't like starting on an uneven playing field. On the professional side, however, it's a different matter."

He sits down next to me, and strokes my head. "Look at me, Jules."

"No," I say into my arms. I bring a whole new meaning to the term Blithering Idiot. See what budding self-esteem can do for a woman?

"Jules, look at me. Now." He's using his stern voice now.

I look up at him through my hair. "I'm such an idiot, Roger. I can't believe I thought, well, you know what I thought. And you were trying to offer me a job. That's probably off, now isn't it?"

He smiles. "You're not an idiot. I did kiss you in Ohio, remember? If I thought I had a ghost of a chance, I may have offered a proposition of a more personal nature. But let's move on. I think we work well together, and you're even understanding of my, shall we say, eccentricities."

He offers me a bottle of water, which I accept, pushing the hair out of my mouth. (At least I didn't start crying again. I hate mascara running down my face when somebody's offering me a job.)

"I'd like for you to come work for me. My assistant at my record label quit to go off and have a baby with her new rock star husband and doesn't plan to come back. You're such a quick study, you'd learn all about the record industry in no time. It's as exciting as TV, but with a whole different cast of oddball characters. You'd love it, and you'd be fantastic at it. And, if they pick up the show for next season, we can both come back to L.A. then."

"Back to L.A.? Oh, is that what you meant about London on your message? You want me to move to London and work for you? But wouldn't I need a work visa or something?"

I tend to focus on trivial details when I'm overwhelmed.

Roger laughs. "We can work all that out, Jules. But do you think you'd like the job? I can't promise never to come down with any more medieval diseases, but I'll do my best."

I don't know what to say. From a career in TV to a job for a major record label in London just like that? I've always wanted to travel. Kirby would adore it; she'd spend all her vacation time with me, shopping and exploring.

A voice I hadn't heard before among the teeming cast of characters in my head (yes, my Thorazine is on order) spoke up: Do you really want to run again? Or drift, or wander aimlessly, or whatever euphemism you care to use for the fact that you're thirty-two years old and can't decide what you want to be when you grow up? I thought you liked this gig. I thought TV was finally it for us. I mean, you. I mean, me. Whatever, you get my meaning.

Schizophrenia issues aside, the voice made a lot of sense.

Plus, what about Sam? I can't imagine a construction company owner would find much chance to travel to England. It's not exactly a quick plane trip from California.

You're not planning your life around somebody you just met, no matter how much he makes your toes tingle, my feminist side says grimly.

Toe tingling is really important in life, the rest of me says.

Roger is watching me, head tilted to the side. I'm having a split-personality moment right there in front of my potential future boss. Great.

"Roger, I don't know what to say. Or even what to think. I need a little time to think about it. I'm very honored that you're asking, in spite of the way one crisis after another seems to follow me around. But uprooting and going to England is a big deal, and I need some time to think it over. I think I might have finally found my own reality here—in Hollywood of all places—so I'm not sure that this is the time to plunge into something new like the record business, either. I'm so very flattered that you'd ask, though."

"Take your time, Jules. We have a little more than seven weeks left of the show. But do think about it, and try to let me know in a month or so, so I can start making the arrangements. We'll get you a flat, of course. Unless you want to room with me?" He grins slyly, brushing a lock of hair out of his eyes. He really is adorable. I can't help it; I have to hug him.

I throw my arms around him. "Roger, you're wonderful. Thank you so much for the offer and the opportunity. I'll let you know as soon as I can."

He's startled, but hugs me back. "You're very welcome. I really think we'd be great together."

I start to pull back just as the door opens, and Sam walks in. His friendly expression and demeanor change in a split second. Suddenly a very large and very dangerous-looking set designer is standing in the doorway.

"Get away from her, Roger." This isn't a Sam I've seen before. He's making me mad at the same time a tiny, completely and utterly un-politically correct part of me is thrilled at his possessiveness. (A *very* tiny part of me.)

"Sam, back off. I was just thanking Roger for his kind job offer, not that it's any of your business. I'd really appreciate you limiting the displays of unrestrained testosterone in the future." I shove my chair back from the table and face him.

"You," I poke him in the chest, "don't own me."

I turn back to Roger. "Thanks again. I'll let you know."

Roger tosses me a jaunty salute and quirks a smile at me. "Later, Jules."

I push past Sam and storm out into the hall.

"What the hell was that all about? Do you know that guy has a reputation as one of the worst playboys on two continents? Was he working on your sympathy for one of his many imaginary illnesses?" Sam's voice is grim, and he's matching my stride down the corridor.

"Look, Sam, the 'Me Tarzan; stay away from my woman' days are long gone. We're in the sensitive-man era now, thank you."

Sam grasps my arm and pulls me to a stop, looking down into my face.

"Hell, I know that. I'm usually as sensitive as the next guy." He blows out a frustrated breath and clenches his eyes shut for a moment.

"I don't even know where that came from. I've never been a jealous man in my life. But somehow, when I saw you with your arms around that British windbag, I went nuts. I literally wanted to smash him." He steps away from me.

"You're turning me into a crazy man, Jules. I'm not sure I'm up for this tornado crashing through my emotions. Maybe you're right about taking it slow. Although the only *slow* I want with you is to slowly drive you wild with passion. Right now, for example, I want to drive myself so far inside of you that you can never get me out." He stops, breathing harshly.

I am frozen in shock. I put my hands on his arms and can feel him trembling.

"Sam, I . . ." Footsteps approaching the corner next to us jolt us both back to the moment. I step away from him, trembling a little myself now.

"Yeah, I know. I'm sorry. I need to think about this, Jules. I'll call you later."

Then he's gone, leaving me wondering what the heck just happened. I slide down the wall to sit on the floor, wondering how I manage to ruin—on such a grand scale—anything I care about.

Or anyone.

I'm at a total impasse. Terrified to care too much and terrified not to.

Tuesday: It's show minus one day, and the makeover teams arrive at the house early today. All nine of the remaining contestants will be transformed through the science of makeup and hair wizardry. Plus a little arm-twisting in the case of Mary Ann, who is determined not to ruin her "luck" by wearing clothes that her granny didn't sew for her.

"I know they're not beautiful or trendy, but I'm superstitious, Jules. I made it this far wearing them, and I want to wear them all the way through to the end."

We're in the kitchen, scrounging for something to eat that doesn't look like seaweed. What is it with Californians and this crap they eat?

"I understand all about superstition. But you were ranked pretty low in the voting last week. If you don't dazzle them with a hotter look this week, you could be going home sooner than you think. Can't we compromise?"

She's considering what I said, I can tell.

"What kind of compromise?"

"What if we reworked one piece from your wardrobe each week and paired it with a new, trendier piece?" I have my fingers crossed behind my back.

"Well, I suppose that might work. As long as I have something that Granny made for me. It's kind of like the something borrowed, something blue thing at a wedding. Or how baseball players will wear the same socks every game when they're on a streak. I don't want to break my luck."

"That's great, Mary Ann. I'm sure our costume people can figure something out." I'm so relieved, I reach out and hug her.

"They don't change their socks? Really? That's disgusting."

We walk down the hall, discussing the finer points of baseball. I try not to have favorites, but I really like this girl.

The stylists have transformed the games room into Makeover Central. Irving and the crew from *People* are everywhere at once, filming and interviewing. Marshall will be thrilled. I wander among the laughing, chattering contestants, noticing that a few are missing. Carlos, which doesn't surprise me. But Jack and Kayley aren't here, either, and that does. Jack never misses an opportunity to work an angle, and Kayley would at least want to be around to belittle everyone else. I decide to go searching for them.

Nobody's in the living room, and the pool's empty.

I head up the stairs to the bedrooms, feeling a dull worry start to puddle in my gut. I reach the guys' room and knock on the door. "Anybody home?"

"Come in." I recognize Carlos's voice and push the door open. He's finishing buttoning up another of his long-sleeved shirts, this one black silk. He flashes a smile at me.

"Just getting dressed, Jules. Wanna help?"

The man radiates heat. I'm betting there are a lot of heartbroken girls back in Florida.

"Be careful, or I'll take you up on it. Then where would you be, stuck with a naked old chick?" I grin, but his smile fades and he's across the room and standing in front of me in two strides.

"Any time, babe. Any time." He reaches out and twirls a strand of my hair in his fingers.

I feel like a goldfish surrounded by sharks lately. Sharks of the male kind. I force a laugh.

"OK, Junior, you can quit bluffing. You're safe with me. Have you seen Jack or Kayley?"

Carlos raises an eyebrow at my backpedaling, but doesn't move to stop me from stepping away from him. He finishes his buttoning, then looks at me, serious again.

"No, not lately. I'd watch out for them, Jules. They're trouble, like the person who pretends to be your friend at night, and then you find his knife in your back in the morning. I've seen them plotting together a few times. I don't know what they're up to, but it can't be good."

I don't want to gossip about any of my contestants, but I tend to agree with him.

"Thanks, Carlos. I'll watch my back. I need to find them, so I'm going to keep looking. Why don't you go downstairs and get in on the makeover bandwagon?"

He opens the door for me. "Jules, you wound me. You think I need making over, *querida*?"

I tilt my head and slowly give him the once-over, from head to toe. "Maybe only your ego. It could use a little shrinking."

He laughs and puts a friendly arm around my shoulder. "You're probably right. The funny thing is that it's been so long since anyone but my mama would dare to tell me something like that. I kind of like hearing it."

"Gee, thanks. First I'm an old chick, and now I remind you of your mother. I'll just hobble my ancient thirty-two-year-old bones off to look for Jack and Kayley now."

Carlos starts down the stairs. "Good luck. And remember what I said about those two."

I watch him descend the stairs, smiling in spite of myself. If I were only twenty-two, or twenty-five, or even . . .

I shake it off. Having fantastic sex with Sam must be rattling all these hormones loose and melting my brain.

It's only ten feet down the hall to the girls' room (past mine; the threat of me hearing is supposed to deter midnight coed visiting) and I'm still smiling to myself about Carlos, which explains why I don't bother to knock before I push the door open.

I really, really regret not knocking.

Jack is sitting on the bed nearest the door with Kayley. And I do mean *with* Kayley. They're both naked, and she's kneeling in front of him and pumping her head up and down with wild enthusiasm. I'm frozen at the sight, my mouth dropping open in horror. No, no, no, no, no. I don't want to see this. I don't want to deal with this.

I start to stumble backward, pulling the door shut,

when Jack opens his eyes and sees me. He yells, and Kayley . . . ah . . . stops what she's doing. She whips her head around to look. Our gazes lock, and she deliberately smiles at me, turns back around and dives in on him again.

He says, "Kayley," in a strangled gasp, but I don't wait around to hear any more. Or, God forbid, see any more. I yank the door shut and back away. Oh, crap. What do I do now? There's nothing in the Production Coordinator handbook about dealing with intra-contestant blow jobs.

There's not even a PC handbook, actually.

Shit. This hideous vision may be burned into my eyelids, like a porn movie gone bad. I can't stand it. I *so* did not want to see that. Now what do I do? Is this a matter for Marshall's personal cell?

I cringe at the thought. I can just imagine Marshall's sensitive response. *So they're fucking. Kids fuck, who cares? I thought I told you never, ever . . .*

As usual, when life hands me lemons, I call the Queen of Bitter. "Kirby, my contestants are screwing each other, what the hell do I do?"

She's not in, but her voice mail assures me she'll get back to me as soon as possible. *Damn.*

There's a knock on my door. I'm not ready to deal with this. It's not my job to keep oversexed, hormone-crazed adults in line. (Hey, after eighteen, they're adults.) OK, actually it is my job to do just that, but it sucks and I don't want to do it anymore. I'm way too young to be the prom chaperone.

There's another knock. "Jules, I know you're in there. Can I talk to you?" It's Jack.

"Sure, come in, Jack." Waiting is going to make it worse; we may as well have the talk now. I wish I knew what I was going to say.

"Jules, I'm sorry you saw that." He looks contrite

and very solemn. You never know with Jack if it's sincere or an act, though. I'm guessing this is an act. How sorry can he be, considering the way Kayley was using him as her own personal lollipop?

"Jack, you're not half as sorry as I am," I say, wearily. "I don't even know what to say to you. Just, use a condom if you, um, you know. And be careful. And, oh, hell. I'm not really the chaperone type. Just try not to have sex in public places anymore."

"It wasn't a public place, Jules," he points out, in a reasonable tone.

I have no patience for reasonable right now.

"It's a public place when any of four roommates of the naked girl on your lap could have walked in at any moment to retrieve a hair brush or lipstick. Just stop it! Can't you control your hormones for seven more weeks?"

He nods, still the picture of remorse. "I'm sorry, Jules. It won't happen again."

"Fine. Where's Kayley?"

"She, ah, she went downstairs. She didn't want to, ah, discuss this right now. She's a little embarrassed."

I narrow my eyes. We both know she's not a bit embarrassed; she just doesn't give a shit what I think, and she's flaunting it in my face. Trouble is, I can't figure a way to get rid of her without having it blow up in my face and hurt the show with bad publicity, so I have to put up with her.

My no-favorites policy is wavering. I hope Kayley gets voted out soon.

"Fine, Jack. Just go downstairs and get made over. You might want to take a shower first." I bury my head in my hands and don't watch him leave. Why, again, did I agree to this?

* * *

Show Time

How does Wednesday get here so fast? It's thirty minutes until show time, and I've herded my contestants into the green room for the final checks. Joe is discussing the new procedures with them and reassuring Lisette that the parrots won't get anywhere near her. Norman is onstage, doing a final prop check.

I feel like Benedict Arnold. Marshall wouldn't let us tell the finalists that they'll be voting each other off this week. He wanted to capture "real emotion" for the cameras. I'm worried about how they're going to take it, and I don't like lying to these people I've grown close to over the past weeks. I glance at Kayley and Jack, heads together in one corner. Well, close to most of them.

I mentioned the incident to Marshall earlier today, but he responded pretty much as I'd expected.

"Jules, you need to get out more. Maybe I'll have a talk with Blake, if you're really that naive." He laughed uproariously and ended the conversation.

I hadn't realized my relationship with Sam was common knowledge, but not much is private or personal among the cast and crew of a TV show. It's not that I'm trying to keep secrets or anything. I just don't like living in a fishbowl.

"Jules?" Mary Ann's timid voice interrupts my self-pity session.

"Yes? Wow, you look fantastic!" I start clapping. She does look fantastic. The stylists took one of the red-and-white-checked dresses from her closet and ruthlessly shredded it into a tiny, low-slung miniskirt. She's wearing a close-fitting white cropped T and a pair of Celine stiletto boots.

"Jules!" The agony in her expression clues me in that she's not as enamored of the outfit as I am.

"I can't wear this on TV. I look like a . . . a hooker!"

I can't help it; I laugh. "No, you look like a pop star. Remember? The name of the show? And you're perfectly decent. No cleavage, no butt cheeks. Just a little of your incredibly flat belly. Must be nice, by the way."

I could look like that, if I'd give up dessert. No way it's worth the trouble.

"Juuuules." She's not convinced. But it's too late. We're live.

Bird Poop and Other Shitty Things

The show progresses like last week; I'm too busy to catch much of it. I hear laughter from the audience at a spot where there shouldn't be laughter, and peer at a monitor to see that several of the parrots have escaped and are winging their way over the audience, pooping freely, as birds will do.

The bird-themed songs play well to the crowd, though. Carlos sings a spicy version of the Eagles' "Desperado" that makes all the women in the audience gasp and shriek. Mary Ann does a fun Sheryl Crow, with "Soak up the Sun," but she's wobbly on her boots and nervous about the clothes, so it's not her best effort. Roger proclaims that she'll probably be out after tonight's performance, and my heart sinks. He was right last week, and I hope his pronouncement doesn't carry too much weight with the contestants.

The tense moment comes after the singing, when the host announces that the finalists will vote each other off tonight. Their faces are a mix of shock, horror, thoughtfulness, and, in the case of Jack and Kayley, glee. Those two almost look as if they knew it was coming. I wonder.

On a commercial break, I catch the brunt of the unhappiness.

"Jules, did you know about this?"

"How can they—"

" . . . can't expect us to—"

"Why didn't you—"

"It's not fair—"

Joe cuts them off. "Thirty seconds."

"Look, I'm so sorry about this," I say. "Marshall just came up with the idea a few days ago, and he wouldn't let us tell you. Just do your best and vote your conscience. You're all stars."

Then it's a two-second dissolve to the open, and the cameras are hot, filming contestant reaction in the green room. As they trudge back onstage for the vote, I feel a heaviness in my heart.

Please let it not be Mary Ann. Not yet.

And, somehow, it isn't. The votes are counted onstage and, though Mary Ann is in the bottom two with Lucas, he's the one ultimately voted off. His country style has already captured Nashville's attention, but it doesn't play well on *POP STAR LIVE!* I wish him the best as he walks backstage, surrounded by his family, and feel guilty at how relieved I am.

But it's Wednesday night, and we've lived through Week Two. At this rate, I'll have the gray hair to go with my "old chick" label by Week Nine.

Chapter Twenty-nine

Death Threats and Kidnapped Cats

Thursday: Our staff meeting is subdued. The ratings sank from the first week's high; the birds format didn't win any new viewers and may have lost us a few. The critics poked at us for stealing the voting scheme from *Survivor*.

Of course, everything else on TV is so fresh and original. Not that I'm bitter.

We're tossing around ideas for perking up our third show, when I notice a glaring difference in one of the clones. They're all still dressed the same, down to their Casio sports watches. Except for Clone Two. He's wearing a very bright and shiny Rolex that he alternates between trying to hide under his sleeve and peering at with a goofy smile on his face. My basic suspicious nature kicks in, as I remember something I thought about last night during the show.

"So," I interrupt Clone One mumbling something about *The Bachelor* and point to Two's watch. "Nice watch. Is it new?"

Two covers his watch with his other hand and looks at me, stricken. "No, no. This old thing? Not new.

Just don't usually wear it."

This is fishy. He's not meeting my eyes. Two better never play poker with Granny Hawkins.

"That's interesting, because I've never seen you wear it before, and it's such a nice, shiny watch. Looks new."

Marshall cuts in. "Can we cut the accessory appreciation minute, Jules? We've got a show to plan, in case you forgot. Sheesh. Women."

I turn to Marshall. "Yes. A show to plan. Just like last week's planning meeting, where you specifically told us not to let the contestants know about the voting scheme. And yet two of them knew all about it. In advance of the show. What do you think about that?" I'm still talking to Marshall, but I turn and trap Two with my gaze again.

Now he's sweating.

"I, well, um, really? Which contestants knew?" His gaze is darting wildly around the table, trying to figure out who knows what, I bet.

"Kayley and Jack. And she ratted out her snitch. She said she's not going down for it alone." (Yes, I'll admit to being a closet *CSI* fan. I'm going to say *perp* any minute.)

"It wasn't my fault," Two wails. He wasn't all that tough to crack.

"Her dad made me. Have you talked to that guy? He's scary. He said he had pictures of me with Fluffy, and he'd ruin me." He sniffles and waves his Rolex-clad wrist around.

"The watch was on my car seat after the show last night. I can't even prove that it's from him. I, well, it's probably from him." His shoulders slump as he mumbles his confession.

I want to circle back to the really important part of this conversation.

"Who's Fluffy, and what were you doing with or to him or her that makes these pictures worth blackmail?" I figure, after the dildo incident, I have a right to know about my stone-throwing colleague's perversions.

"She was my neighbor's cat, but he was mean to her and he kicked her, so I stole her. Well, rescued her, really. She's very high-strung and delicate and only likes Fancy Feast and he made her eat that dry kibble," he says in utter horror.

Damn. No closet bestiality going on here to top my vibrators-at-the-airport story. Back to the point, I guess.

"So, Marshall. We have a traitor, for whatever well-intentioned cat-rescuing reason. The important part of this story is that we need to keep an eye on Kayley's dad. He came pretty close to threatening me in the hall the other day." I remember the look in his eyes. It wasn't entirely sane.

Joe stands up abruptly. "I think I'll have me a little chat with Daddy. He's banned from the show from now on. Any more shit from him, and I suggest we kick Kayley off the show."

Marshall is shaking his head even before Joe finishes his sentence. "No way. It's not her fault Daddy is a wackjob. And the TV cameras love her. That fishnet body stocking was damn near transparent. We're getting a lot of buzz in the women's magazines and on *Entertainment Tonight* about Kayley. She stays. Fix it with Daddy, but she stays."

He stands up, signaling the end of the meeting. "We're going with the *Bachelor* thing. Whoever gets the most studio audience votes this week goes on a date next week. Figure it out and report back. I want those audience vote machine thingys installed ASAP. Do it."

Then he points at our feline-favoring traitor. "You! You're on lunch duty the rest of the month. I want Italian next. Don't ever, ever let me down again or you'll never work in this town again."

As Marshall stomps his way out of the room, I hear his growly chuckle floating back over his shoulder. "I always wanted to say that thing about never working in this town again."

Q's Coming Out?

Saturday: I haven't seen much of Irving or *People* magazine lately; he and his photographers are spending more time with the contestants than with me, thank goodness. We hit high enough in the ratings to make the singers interesting on an individual basis. I'm not especially worried when he calls me on a weekend; probably wants some more background on Kayley. Much to my dismay, she's becoming a media darling.

"Hey, Irving. How's it going?"

"Jules, I wanted to give you a heads-up about the new issue." The squirrelly tone is back in his voice. My stomach plummets, as I frantically search my mind for something embarrassing I've done lately. Nobody knows about mistaking Roger's job offer for a lewd proposition, and he wouldn't have told a reporter about it, anyway.

I haven't seen or talked to Sam since the incident in the hallway, I realize in surprise. I'd usually be obsessing about not hearing from a guy. For the first time in my life, my work has a more central place in my life than my insecurities.

"Jules. Jules? Are you there?"

"Sorry. Just trying to figure out why you sound like that. What is it, and why do I have the feeling I'm going to hate it?"

He laughs. "It's not about you this time, Jules. It's about Q. He told us he's planning to 'come out' live on the show. A rap star who's famous for songs filled with gay-bashing says he's going to 'come out' live on TV? You know that's cover story material. Hey, this will be good for you! The ratings will shoot up." He sounds cheerful about the whole thing, the rat.

That's it, then. A gay judge coming out live on the show equals the end of KCM Records. I don't have to worry about being fired. The whole show will be over.

Wait. I know for a fact that two of KCM Records' hottest acts are openly gay. Guess old KC doesn't mind gay, he's just anti-vibrator-in-the-airport. I blow out a sigh of relief.

Irving's right, too. The ratings will probably soar. I'm just concerned about the portion of our studio audience, usually a good third, who are Q fans, and how they're going to take the news. I hope we don't have rioting in the aisles. I make a mental note to get Andy and Bobby more help with security.

"OK, thanks for the heads-up. Anything else?"

"Yeah, how about a date with Kayley?" He's almost panting.

"Irving, that girl is way out of your league. And trust me, you're better off." I hang up the phone, thinking about Sam. He said he needed time to think. Well, he's had about enough time. I dial Joe for a little Saturday night babysitting relief.

Monday: My date with Sam never happened. Turns out he had to go to San Francisco to meet with a crew on one of his job sites for the weekend. But I made Joe hang out with us Saturday night anyway. Watching him beat the guys at pool and then grouch and snort his way through the chick flick video the girls were watching was a great stress reliever. It's hard to remember that only a few short weeks ago, I thought he was trying to poison me with bad mayonnaise.

This morning, the fallout from the Q cover story has started already. We have to drive through two groups of antigay protesters to force our way into the studio parking lot. The first group carries signs misquoting Bible verses and wears suits and dresses. The second group carries signs spewing obscenities and wears grunge. It doesn't matter how you dress up hatred and intolerance; it all looks the same to me.

I'm a little surprised that Q is gay, for no other reason than the sparks he seems to touch off in Nellie, but I'm the first to admit that I don't exactly walk around playing Spot the Sexual Orientation.

When we enter the studio, the first thing I hear is loud shouting coming from the conference room. I can't handle strife this early in the morning, before I've had caffeine, so I try to sneak past the open doorway. No such luck.

"Jules! Get in here. What the hell is your buddy Irving up to now?" Marshall is frothing at the mouth.

"*My* buddy? Since when did splashing a humiliating photo of me across the country count as friendship?" I'm not taking the heat for this one. I see that Roger and Nellie are in the room, too. Roger's slouched in a chair at the end of the conference table, nursing a cup of coffee, and Nellie is right up in Q's face; her body language is shouting vile and vicious things at him, if I'm any judge.

I sidle over to the coffeepot. Empty. Damn. Roger hands his cup to me without looking up. It tastes like crap, but it's caffeine. I drain the mug.

"And what the hell did you think you were doing,

making an announcement like that anyway?" Nellie shakes her finger right in Q's face. He looks amused, I notice. None of this is bothering him.

"Listen, sweetcheeks, I make the announcements I want to make. You're off the market, right?" he says, capturing her left hand and shoving her ring toward her face. "So why are you so upset? Marshall not keeping you satisfied?" A grin slowly spreads over his face.

"You can come over any night and try to help me change teams if you want, baby."

I love that Q has the amazing ability to render Nellie speechless. It's a priceless talent.

She slaps him so hard a crack rings out, and we all flinch. The red imprint of her hand is clearly visible on Q's face. He stands very still for a moment, eyes narrowing. Then he grabs her hand and pulls her even closer.

"That was it, peaches. One free shot. And that's only because of Maui. If you ever hit me again, I'll turn you over my knee and spank your delightful little ass. We both know you like it." He releases her hand and steps away from Nellie and turns to the rest of us.

"This isn't really any of your business. We don't need a meeting. We don't need a discussion. I'll make whatever announcement I want to, *whenever* I want to, and you'll get over it. If that's not acceptable, tell me now, and I'll leave the show today." He scans our faces.

Marshall starts blustering. "Now, nobody said anything about anybody leaving the show. We're just trying to deal with the fallout from some of our sponsors at having a gay judge. We'll handle it. You're not going anywhere."

Q heads for the door. "Fine, then. And you might

wanna remember one thing. I never used the word gay in that interview. The reporter came to his own conclusions. We're free to print a denial, if you want. I don't care what you do." And then he walks out, leaving us all looking at each other in silence.

Well, not for long. Nellie starts shrieking.

I've never heard a shriek like this one. It ranges from a hideously cacophonous wailing sound, to a list of all the foul names she can come up with on short notice, to suggestions as to the animals of which Q's mother may have had intimate knowledge. It's actually quite creative. I'm guessing the spanking suggestion didn't go over so well. And *Maui?* This chick gets around.

Roger stands up, grabs my hand, and drags me out of the room, shutting the door behind us. "Let's just leave the lovebirds to deal with this, shall we? I don't quite grasp the implications of Q's sexual orientation on the future of the show. However, you seem to have quite an antigay movement in the parking lot, judging by the eggs and tomatoes currently residing on the hood of my car."

The filter between my brain and my mouth must have melted, considering what I hear myself saying next.

"So, Roger, have you slept with Nellie, too?"

He looks at me, startled, then laughs. "God, no. She reminds me of one of those black widow spiders who mate, then kill. She's doing quite a job at castrating our producer, isn't she?" He shudders.

"Nellie and I. How hideous, Jules. Now you've ruined my appetite completely, and I had a lovely eggs Benedict in mind for brunch." He starts to walk off, then turns back.

"Flattering that you'd be interested, though." He winks at me and is gone.

Show Time

The finalists rehearsed like crazy this week. The possibility of being voted off has supplanted the excitement and newness of the TV experience for most of them, and they buckled down to work. The faces I see in the green room are all determined to prove they've got pop star potential onstage tonight.

They're ranged around the room in their usual positions. Kayley and Jack huddle together in a corner; she shoots dirty looks at me periodically. Lisette and Anton focus on breathing exercises on the couch. Mary Ann practices walking in her kitten-heeled Miu Miu pumps.

Derek and Carlos talk quietly with Shanicia over by the stage entrance. Only eight left; seven after tonight. I watch them and wonder which one won't be here next week.

Joe calls time, and the host segues smoothly into his opening sequence. (He's smooth, all right. Marshall actually focus-grouped his face.) Everyone jerks as though an invisible current were switched on that runs from their bodies to the televisions across America. Which, in a way, it does.

"Jules," somebody hisses.

"What's up, Norman?"

"We've got a problem, dude. Maybe two problems. First, I heard that some of Q's fans are staging a riot after the first commercial break. Second, Kayley's dad tried to bribe the company that set up the audience voting machines, and the guy from the company says he thinks they might be rigged. The guy who was in charge of installing the machines never showed up for work today. Third—"

"You said *two* problems."

"So don't kill the messenger. Third, don't you think Carlos and Mary Ann are going to freak out at this *Bachelor* thing if either of them are the ones?"

"What Bachelor thing?"

Norman looks at me in disgust. "Jules, you really need to stay awake in staff meetings. Since we're doing an audience vote tonight—you know, vote for your favorite—to determine the bottom two and the loser, we're taking the person with the most votes and making them go on a date with a random member of the studio audience."

He smiles bashfully. "Well, not all that random. I get to pick. Marshall said you can help, if you want."

This is what I get for solving the Mystery of the Traitorous Clone at the staff meeting, instead of paying attention. Norman's right. Carlos and Mary Ann will have fits if they have to do this stupid date thing. I close my eyes. This is still part of the penance for that "what else could go wrong" question, isn't it?

I hear a loud groan from the audience and rush to the monitor. Mary Ann fell out of her shoes and is sitting awkwardly on the stage, tangled up in the microphone cord. She waves everyone off who rushes to help her, and rises to stand by herself, now barefoot. In a gesture of rare self-possession, she dazzles a smile at the audience and the camera and tosses first one, then the other offending shoe into the crowd.

"I hope you have better luck with them than I did!" she calls to the girls who catch them. The crowd roars with delight and approval. In one of those stranger-than-fiction coincidences, she launches into her planned song for the week, something about "Whose Bed Have Your Boots Been Under," and the crowd goes wild, clapping and cheering. Mary Ann is redeemed from last week in a big way.

I hover by the monitor for the rest of the show, but

there are no big surprises. The planned riot turns out to be a few grumblings and some heckling from the balcony, but our security team quashes it quickly.

In the singing, Carlos is as consistently wonderful as usual; the others all do fine. If I had to pick who the audience will vote out, though, I'd go with Derek or Jack this week. They're both off tonight. Just a little, but enough to make a difference with such stiff competition.

My super psychic powers must be on the fritz. Our host announces the bottom two with much fanfare, and it's Derek and Kayley (which is pretty good confirmation that her daddy's planned vote rigging didn't work). She looks as incredulous as I feel. Our crowd tonight is mostly female, though, and women are in no way Kayley's target demographic.

The final tally reveals Derek as tonight's loser, so Kayley is safe. The expression on her face bodes ill for somebody, though. She's as crazy as her father, and I wouldn't want to meet either of them in a dark alley tonight.

The funniest part of the show, though, is the expressions on Carlos's and Mary Ann's faces when the judges reveal the new Win a Date with a Contestant component of the show. In a true best case/worst case scenario, they received the highest number of votes from the audience. Good news: They're both likely to go the distance on the show. Bad news: They have to go on a date with somebody Norman picks.

I rush to help Norman find suitable dates, and we come up with a fun-loving coed type for Carlos and a shy boy with braces for Mary Ann, so as not to scare her too much. In the chivalrous high point of the evening, Carlos slings an arm around Mary Ann's shoulders and announces that they'll double date. I have the feeling he's treating her like another baby sister. For all his surface scariness, Carlos is a sweet man. Not that he'd ever admit it.

I give everybody time to commiserate with Derek and exchange addresses and phone numbers they'll never use, and then I round them up to head for the house. The limos seem really empty with only four of us per car. It's a quiet ride back after a few good-natured jokes about the upcoming dates. Even Kayley is lost in thought. I notice she pushes Jack out of her way when we reach the house. Trouble in Conspiracy Central? Could be another interesting week.

Checking my voice mail, I see there are still no messages from Sam. He'd better have a good explanation. As I turn out the light, I realize I'm afraid I already know what it is. Then I notice an envelope behind the lamp with *Jewels* written on it. Either somebody doesn't know how to spell my name, or my free diamonds are finally here.

I grin at my own lame attempt at wit and open the envelope. A single sheet of paper flutters out, and I unfold it to read the single line printed there:

BACK OFF OR DIE.

Chapter Thirty

Week Four

Thursday: The staff meeting is upbeat this week. We're back up in the ratings and everybody loved letting the studio audience vote. The critics bashed us, as usual, calling us a "hodgepodge of mismatched concepts stolen from other shows." (Well, duh. We have more interesting judges, though.) We decide to run clips from the big double date and also of the other four contestants roller skating, so they all get equal air time.

I looked around at everyone carefully, trying to decide if any of them wrote the death threat. The Clones don't like me much, but don't seem prone to violence. I'd given the note to Bobby and Andy to check out, but asked them to keep it quiet. I'm pretty sure it's just a bad practical joke.

At least, I hope so.

When the meeting breaks up, Marshall's secretary stops by to hand me a note that I'm needed on the set. I wander off in that direction after chatting with Norman and Joe for a few minutes.

As I walk onstage, I hear a familiar voice calling out

directions. I stop to watch Sam overseeing his crew renovating the set for this week's show. We've decided to jazz it up, of course. Now it's supposed to scream Broadway musical, I think. As Sam steadies a ladder and hands tools up to one of his men, I enjoy the way he fills out his shirt. This is new for me; the mere sight of somebody's back never turned me on before.

Then I remember I haven't heard from him in a week and a half.

"Did somebody out here leave a message for me?" The ice in my voice could sink the Titanic all over again.

Sam swings around, then calls to someone else to take his place. As he walks toward me, I'm struck by how quickly I've memorized the planes and angles of his face.

He's smiling, but there's a shadow of something dark in his eyes. "Hi, Jules. How are you?"

"Fine, thanks. I received a message that someone needed me?" My tone is cool; he needn't think he can just pop in and out of my life whenever he feels like it.

"It was from me. *I* need you. I spent a week trying to deny it, and another few days trying to come to terms with it. I need you, Jules. It's too soon, and it's too sudden, but there it is."

His honesty and need blast through my ice and defenses. I'm trapped in the furnace of his emotions, and he's right. It's too soon. I panic.

"Sam, you can't just—you can't take off for a week and a half with no word and then come back and hit me with a statement like that. In a public place, no less. I'm sure you feel like you've worked things through, but back here in the real world, all I've worked through is that you feel free to abandon me with no word and disappear on a whim." I'm backing toward the stage entrance and finally turn and bolt. But he's right behind me.

"What will it be next time? You won't like the way I'm talking to Norman? I had popcorn and watched a movie with Joe Saturday; how many days' free pass does *that* give you to take off?" I whirl around.

"You said no games, Sam, but you seem to be a master player. I told you how I feel about being abandoned, but it's 'now you see him, now you don't.' Well, here's a clue. I don't like games, either."

His hands fasten on to my shoulders. "Jules, you're right. My only excuse is that I've been hurt in the past, too. The woman I thought I loved dumped me in a heartbeat, when she had the chance at a guy with more money and more power. The money and power were all she ever wanted. When I saw you hugging Roger, it brought all that back to me." His hands are stroking my arms now.

"I'm sorry, Jules. I worked my way through it, and I'm back. Please give me a chance to explain. Please give me a chance to be with you."

My shoulders slump under his hands, and I laugh a little.

"We're quite a pair, aren't we, Blake? Both afraid of our emotions. Both running away at the first sign of entanglement. Did it occur to you that two broken people don't make a good match?"

He wraps his arm around my waist and looks into my eyes. "Yes, to be honest. It did occur to me. I also realized that there must be something pretty strong between us to make us both run so hard and so fast away from each other. Don't we deserve a chance to discover what it is?"

He leans down and presses a gentle kiss on my lips. "Give us another chance, Jules. I won't screw it up this time."

I burst into laughter, a real laugh this time. For once, somebody isn't telling *me* not to screw something up. For that alone, he deserves a second chance.

"OK, Blake. But you'd better not." I kiss him back, winding my arms around his neck, and we put about ten days' worth of loneliness into that kiss. The floor has started to blister from the heat, when I hear a not-so-discreet throat-clearing.

"Uhhhm-hmmmmm. All right, that's enough. This is a place of business, you two. Get a damn room." It's Joe, of course. And he's not moving.

Reluctantly, I try to pull back from Sam, but he's not having it. He keeps an arm draped over my shoulders when I turn to Joe.

"Is there something we can help you with, Joe?" I'm smiling and gritting my teeth at the same time. It feels fairly unpleasant.

"Blake, thought you ought to know that Kayley's dad, the rich nutjob, threatened your girlfriend there. I've been checking him out and he's a scary guy. We need to talk about it. Nobody else around here is taking it seriously. Glad you're back. See me in an hour or so." He heads for the door.

Oh, sure. *Now* he's in a hurry.

Sam, whose arm tightened around me back at the word *threat*, turns me back to face him. "What the hell is that about?" The scary look is back on his face. I sigh. We were doing so well.

For almost ten seconds, I consider telling him about the note.

Nope.

"Sam, it was nothing. Just a stage parent going a little nuts. Don't worry about it, and please don't go all alpha male on me and beat him up or something.

You know he's the kind who would put you in jail *and* sue your company. It's so totally not worth it. Besides, if you're in jail, how can I do this?" I rise on my tiptoes and stick the tip of my tongue in his ear.

Sam makes kind of a growling sound, then starts laughing.

"OK, consider me distracted. But this conversation is not over. Not by a long shot. I've got a lot to do, and I know you do, too, but I'll pick you up for dinner tonight around seven. Bring an overnight bag. Please."

I watch him walk away, thinking that his final *please* tempered the smugness of what came before it. He's an interesting mix of contradictions, my Sam Blake.

My Sam Blake? I roll it around in my mind. Maybe. Just maybe.

Show Time

How is it Wednesday again? The week flew by. Sam was true to his word, and we spent a lot of time getting to know each other better. I asked him to attend every event we scheduled for the contestants all week long with me, and he agreed without a murmur of protest. About halfway through the Michael Jackson song playing in the roller rink where Sam skated in a conga line with Anton, Lisette, and Shanicia, I realized I may be falling in love with him. I wonder how many of life's most important discoveries are accompanied by "Thriller"?

We also had a wild attack of the "we've just met and I'm crazy about you, so I'm going to tear your clothes off at any opportunity" kind of sex. Not that I'm proud of it, but I have rug burn on my elbows. Too much information, I know, but it was that kind of week.

Now I'm floating in a pheromone-induced haze, which is much better than drugs, as I've informed Kirby. But the tension in the green room slices through my contentment. Not even the humor in the video clips of Carlos and Mary Ann's double date can ease the white knuckles of the seven singers.

But it *was* a funny date. In the video clips we're watching, Carlos takes on the role of overprotective big brother and manages to insert himself in between Mary Ann and her date anytime the poor boy looks like he might actually touch her. By the third time her date tries to hold her hand, everybody in the studio audience chants "Carlos, Carlos" and, right on schedule, Carlos steps between them. His poor date is starstruck enough to go along with whatever happens, and she smiles vacuously at him in all of the clips. The final shot is of Carlos kissing his date lightly on the cheek and escorting her back into the limo, while conveniently walking between Mary Ann and her date. The poor boy almost kissed Carlos.

Now *that* would have been funny.

The singing begins. We're doing alphabetical order tonight, so Anton is up first. The tension hits him hard, and his voice wavers some on the ballad he performs. In an unusual move for her, Nellie is the toughest on him.

"You know, Antonio, if you can't keep up with the amateurs in this competition, you're never going to make it in the bigs. We have to be ready to perform anytime, under any conditions."

Roger and Q look at her in surprise. The most she's had to contribute so far has been the occasional critique of a performer's outfit.

"I'd have to agree," says Roger.

"It's *Anton*," says Q.

"Whatever," says Nellie.

Carlos and Jack are both electric gold, and the crowd blesses each with standing ovations.

Kayley is next. She's determined to recover from last week's moment in the bottom two, and she's changed her look. More Britney Spears, less Christina Aguilera, to try to pull the female vote back her way. Plus, she sings a spicy version of a Beyoncé tune I recognize (but can't remember the title of) and has the crowd eating out of her beautifully manicured hands.

Lisette seems a little off to me, too. Kayley's campaign to belittle her about her weight has been working, in spite of my efforts. Lisette started a no-carbs diet, and has lost some weight, but she'll never achieve a size zero during the course of the show. She has a false start and falters her way through a song that should be perfect for her.

Mary Ann is radiant and belts out an old Faith Hill standby, "Breathe," like they wrote it just for her. I can see Granny in the front row, and the pride in her face beams out across the stage and rivals the lights for incandescence.

Finally, Shanicia wraps things up with one of her favorite Whitney Houston ballads, but can't quite bring it off tonight. The tension is getting to all of them.

Roger stands up. "It's clear the pressure is ratcheted up, and most of you have quite an awful case of nerves. Try to work it out before next week, so America doesn't die of boredom."

We're at our last commercial break of the evening, which means studio audience voting time (a very unwieldy process involving weird kiosks that look like ATMs). I'm sick to my stomach again; I'm not sure how much more of this voting I can take, and I'm not even one of the contestants. I can't imagine how hard it must be for them.

We all strain to hear the words. "In our bottom two tonight: Anton and Lisette."

Grief and shock on those two faces; sadness and relief combine on the faces of the others.

And, finally: "I'm sorry, Anton, but you will not be America's next *POP STAR LIVE!*"

And then there were six. This is the worst part of my whole week.

Chapter Thirty-one

Week Five: Halfway Through

Thursday: This is not a good day. In fact, today sucks. I have grinding, crushing, miserable PMS. Not just the cramps. Not just the headache. Oh, no. The full-on, step-away-from-the-chocolate-and-nobody-gets-hurt PMS. I call Kirby for sympathy.

"What?" Oh, oh. She sounds like she's chewing nails. Or a new hole in somebody on her staff's ass.

"Kirbs, it's Jules."

"Oh, fine. Hang on. *Do we really need to pay for four freaking drafts of this copy? It's not literature, it's an ad for body oils. Can't anybody at that damn agency get anything right since I left? Call over there and tell them I'm not paying this bill.* Jules, you still there?"

"Troubles in paradise?" I curl up on my pillows and resolve not to leave my room until tomorrow. The finalists are at rehearsals already, thank goodness.

"The agency hired some moron to replace me when I came here, and I'm getting ridiculously padded bills. I'm not paying it. Screw it. But how the heck are you? And thanks ever so much for these damn cramps." She sounds as bad as I feel.

"Hey. You can't blame me for your cramps." I turn the heating pad up a notch and settle it more snugly across my abdomen.

"Wanna bet? You switched me around to your schedule when we had that vacation in Mexico last year. I'm never, ever rooming with you again."

It's a medically proven fact that when two or more women live together, their bodies will coordinate menstrual cycles. Creepy, but true. Our dorm at UW was pure hell one week a month.

"Well, then, you can imagine how good I feel. Shanicia cried all night because Anton was her best friend on the show. Jack and Kayley are up to something; I know it, but I can't figure out what. I called in sick to the staff meeting, which means they'll probably decide to do something thrilling for this week's show, like throw the contestants out of an airplane just for fun. You know, whoever splatters the least gets to go on to next week."

"Wow. And I thought *I* was a bitch today. *Hey, can I get some coffee in here some time this century?* Stupid cow of an assistant thinks she's too good to bring coffee to a woman boss."

I start laughing. "I called you to cheer *me* up. This is not working out how I'd planned."

"Hey, you want cheerful, watch the fucking morning news shows. I saw *POP STAR* last night, by the way. I gotta tell you, that Roger is gorgeous. And what's up with the rap star going gay? I thought there was something going on between him and Nellie."

I sigh. "Who knows? Yes, Roger is gorgeous. And he's offered me a job in London. I don't know what to tell him, and he's going to want an answer soon."

"A job in London? That's fantastic, Jules! I'd visit a lot. Maybe I'll move over there, too, and we can show all those British men what they're missing." She whistles.

"Unless producer boy really just wants to get you alone to play hide-the-tea-bag?"

"I doubt offering me a job in one of the most populated cities in England is about getting me alone, Kirby. And, no, I already made the mistake of thinking he was trying to get me into bed. Of course, being the sophisticated, high-class kind of girl I am, I turned down his nonexistent advance very sweetly."

"Oh, God. You're turning into a walking comedy channel, Jules. Your life is like *Candid Camera*. How are you holding up? How's Sam?"

"Sam. That's the problem. I think this thing between us could be huge, but we're both scared. I can't seem to get past Mark. Before you say anything, it's not that I'm not over him—I am. It's that every time the slightest thing goes wrong, my mind says, *See, it's just like Mark.* And I can't blame Sam for what Mark did."

"At least you realize it. I think that's the first step to getting past it. But you said 'we.' 'We're both scared.' What's his deal?"

"He had a bad relationship, too. She just wanted him for his money, so she dumped him for somebody with more of it."

"Ouch. That's hard on a guy's ego. At least he knows you can't possibly be after him for his money, considering who your dad is."

"That's just it. I haven't told him yet. I'm not ready to bring all my baggage into this yet."

Kirby laughs. "I'm sure your dad would adore being called baggage. By the way, I e-mailed him and told him if he'd wanted to date a younger woman, he should have called me."

"Kirby, you did not. You leave my poor dad alone! He's already terrified of you." I shake my head.

Kirby will never change, thank God.

"I think you should—*what now? Oh, OK*—Jules, I've gotta go. We're in talks to open a chain of upscale retail stores; very classy, pleasure for your marriage sort of thing. I've got to take this call. Call me tonight, OK? And remember: PMS Hell, Medicate Well. Love ya. Bye."

"Bye Kirbs. Good luck."

As I hang up my cell, it rings again. It's Norman. I made him cover for me at the staff meeting and then meet the kids at rehearsals to take them for new clothes. I couldn't deal with any of it today.

"Hey, Norman. What's up?"

"Jules, are you still sick? Dude, you gotta get better soon and get me out of this." He sounds panicked.

"What's going on, Norman? I'm sure you can handle it." Where are the drugs? I need something with an A. Advil, Aleve, even aspirin would do in a pinch.

"Shanicia has gone Sybil on me. She got a call from somebody at her church and burst into tears. She's been crying about Anton all day. And then she screamed at Kayley and called her an evil bitch. Not that I don't agree."

"Shanicia?" The B word is getting a lot of use today, but I can't believe Shanicia said it. She's never said an unkind word to anybody. She's more likely to pray for us than yell at us.

"Kayley made some crack about Lisette being fat, and Shanicia just let Kayley have it. Now Lisette's crying. Shanicia's crying. Kayley stormed off, and I don't know where she is. Of course, Irving got it all on film. We're gonna look like a bunch of freaks in *People* this week. Jules, you gotta help me. I'm desperate." His voice is literally shaking. Even men who are more firmly grounded in reality than Norman have a hard time handling women's tears. He must be losing it.

"All right, Norman. I'm on my way. Give me forty-five minutes. And send someone to find Kayley, before she gets into trouble."

"Sure, OK. Thanks, Jules. You're the best."

Yeah, yeah. I'm the best. I drag my crampy, crabby body into the shower, wondering, Best at what?

Saturday: We spent most of the rest of the week figuring out how we're going to solve crimes on the show. Marshall watched an episode of one of the *CSI* spinoffs last week, so now he wants us to solve crimes. I'm back at my room after a late dinner (and even later dancing) with the contestants and our ever-present and ever-increasing media entourage, when Sam calls.

"Hey, beautiful. I'm sorry I missed dinner and dancing with the kiddies tonight, but I needed to spend some time with Dad. He can't wait to meet you, by the way."

"I'd love to meet him, too. Can we do it when the show is over, though? I'm not going to be very good company during the next few weeks." I sigh and stretch out on the bed in an old Stanford T-shirt of Sam's, with a blue Bioré mask slathered on my face, and wet toenails glistening. There's something to be said for nights without a man around.

"You're always good company, but that's fine. I miss you." His voice has that husky note that makes me crazy.

"I miss you, too. Let's get Joe to babysit—oh, damn. Tomorrow night's not good. Actually, the whole week isn't good."

"You know, Jules, you can still spend time with me when it's that time of the month." He chuckles.

"How did you—? I mean, I know."

"It wasn't that difficult. You almost bit my arm off when I tried to steal a bite of your chocolate cake at lunch the other day."

"Hey, stay away from my triple-fudge layer cake, and nobody gets hurt; that's my motto."

"I'd better let you get some sleep. But first, tell me what you're wearing and torture me a little."

I look down at myself. Hmmm. I drop my voice down to a whisper.

"I'm just back from dancing, and I've gotten as far as taking my dress off. Then the phone rang, so I'm wearing my strapless black lace bra, matching thong panties, and dangling drop earrings. Perfect hair. Perfect makeup. Nothing else. Now don't you really wish you were here?" I try for a sultry laugh, and it must work, because his voice sounds a little ragged.

"God, Jules, I expected you to say an old T-shirt and jogging shorts or something. You're killing me here. I'm going to hold that visual until I see you again. Get some sleep. Bye."

I grin as I hang up the phone, looking at the hem of my old blue jogging shorts peeking out from under Sam's shirt. OK, so the guy knows me pretty well. Nothing says I can't throw in a few surprises, right?

My face cracking (or at least the face mask), I head to the bathroom to wash the goo off, thinking of Sam. Maybe I'll try that cold-shower trick, too.

I walk out of the bathroom humming and drying my hair, then swing it up out of my face and look right into the eyes of a grinning Carlos.

"Nice body for an old chick, Jules."

Oh, shit. I'm wet and naked, and there's a contestant in my room. I run back in the bathroom, covering myself with the towel from my hair. My thoughts are careening around in my head like pinballs.

I'm going to get fired, I'm going to get fired, is followed closely by, *What the hell is he doing in my room at two in the morning?*

I throw my damp clothes back on and storm out into my room.

"What the hell are you doing in my room at two in the morning? Don't I deserve a little privacy? Did anybody see you?"

He holds up his hands in surrender. "Hey, I'm sorry. You deserve privacy. But I knocked, and you didn't answer. I didn't want to lurk around in the hall and take a chance somebody would see me. I didn't know you'd be doing a personal strip show for me."

OK, so that's what a wolfish grin looks like.

"It's called taking a shower, you jerk. Which most people do without clothes on, for your information. What do you want, and why does it have to be in the dead of night?" I stalk past him, grab my comb, and point it at him before I drop into a chair and start detangling my hair.

"Make it quick."

"Jules, I don't like this *CSI* crap. I don't want to do it."

"Carlos, it's just going to be some hokey version of the game Clue come to life. It doesn't have anything to do with a real crime. Why does it bother you, anyway?"

He's pacing the floor, looking more wolflike every second. (In purely objective terms, there's something to be said for the sheer potency of these alpha males. Not that I am into that or anything.)

He stops in front of me and pulls me to my feet. "Listen. I didn't exactly hang out with people who watched a lot of TV back home. They were too busy drinking, doing drugs, and committing real crimes to sit at home on weeknights. But I just have a sick feeling in my gut about this. You put the words Crime and Carlos up on the same screen, and somebody is going to connect me to the Dragon's Tears. And then some way, somehow, the shit's going to hit the fan."

His hands are still circling my wrists, and he's staring into my eyes intently.

"Jules, I think I can win this. I have a real chance to win Mom and my sister a new life. I can't let it get screwed up now."

I let out the breath I didn't know I'd been holding.

"Carlos, I'll do what I can. I don't have much power over this kind of thing. Maybe we can figure out a way that you're left out of it, since you had to do that stupid double date."

I gently pull my arms out of his grasp and step back. "I'll do what I can," I repeat. "Please go get some sleep now, before somebody wakes up and finds you missing. And try not to worry."

He smiles and steps closer, and suddenly his hand is on the back of my neck, and he's pulled me into a kiss. It's a quick kiss and there's no tongue, so I don't have to slap his face, but I glower at him all the same.

"I'm off limits, Carlos. I'm involved with Sam, and you're a contestant, and I'm old enough to be your . . . older sister, and, for about a thousand other reasons, don't ever do that again."

He steps away from me and grins, then raises his eyebrows and looks right at my nipples, which are standing at attention beneath my shirt, the traitors. "Whatever you say, Jules. But don't tell me you're not curious."

I fold my arms over my breasts and shake my head. "Only about your tattoos, Carlos. Only about your tattoos. Now get out! I'll do what I can, you brat."

He stops at the door, all humor gone from his expression. "Thanks, Jules. For everything. You ever need anything, you call me. Anytime, anywhere."

Then he slips out the door, leaving me shaken and wide awake. In spite of his over-the-top antics, I care about what happens to Carlos and his family. I set my alarm to get up early and track down Marshall, then lie awake in the darkness for a long time.

Show Time

Wednesday: At the last possible minute tonight, I learn that my pleas and attempts at logic worked on Marshall.

"Marshall, we don't want the show associated with anything negative, like crime. Why don't we call it a treasure hunt or a mystery and give the contestants clues to figure out?"

At the time, he'd barked at me and hung up. Which I guess translates into, *Sure, Jules, what a good idea.* Who knew?

So we give each of my six remaining finalists a clue, and they have to put their heads together to puzzle out that the celebrity host is Sheryl Crow. The challenge of it has the added benefit of smoothing nervous edges; when they sing, they're incredible.

After the halfway-point commercial break, Q decides to play with us a little. He takes an unscripted walk over to the host and asks for the microphone. As he walks to the center of the stage, leaving our host gaping and Marshall jumping up and down backstage, he slows his pace until he's barely moving. Then, with much drama, he looks at his shoes, takes a huge breath and says, "I have a serious announcement to make."

Our studio audience gasps in unison; everyone has seen the press over his coming-out rumor. Roger looks amused; Nellie is clenching the edge of the table, white-knuckled and white-faced.

Q slowly, slowly raises his head, sweeps his gaze over the audience and the judges, and smiles. "It's been coming for a long, long time. I'm . . . I'm . . . I'm going to go back on tour when the show is over. The Q Live World Tour will kick off in early October right here in L.A. and I expect to see you all there!"

He punches his fist in the air, and the crowd roars with approval. Nellie and Roger look at each other in disbelief, and Marshall starts choking.

I pat his back.

"Are you OK?"

"Swallowed. Gum. Bastard."

I keep patting and make soothing noises, but a smile is quirking the corners of my lips. *Way to go, Q.*

Before we know it, it's That Time again. The contestants solve the lame puzzle and cheer for Sheryl Crow. Then the host, whom I've grown to despise, through no fault of his own, announces the results of the studio audience vote.

Lisette and Shanicia are in the bottom two, and they both break into hysterical tears. Mary Ann is crying, too. Joe won't let me go onstage to comfort them, so I start crying. Why couldn't it be Jack or Kayley? Why do the good guys always have to finish last?

I stand in the green room, sobbing in Joe's arms, as Lisette becomes the fifth contestant to get voted off the show. Our singer who was Destroy-the-Death-Star good met her own destruction on live TV. I wonder again how I'm going to make it through the next four weeks.

Chapter Thirty-two

Week Six

Thursday: Will somebody take Marshall's damn TV away from him? He was up half the night watching reruns of *24*, and now he says we're doing next week's show in the same format. I can literally feel myself aging a year each week during the staff meeting.

"What do you mean, like *24*, exactly, Marshall?" I ask wearily. Joe snorts from his corner by the door. Joe communicates more and more nonverbally in staff meetings as the weeks go by, I've noticed.

"We'll start filming everything the finalists do Tuesday night at eight, and round the clock until the show. Then we'll run clips of the highlights." He's delighted with himself; you can tell from the thrown-back shoulders and wide grin.

My shoulders are almost parallel with the table, on the other hand. Not so delighted on this side of the room.

"Marshall, since a good eight hours of that time will be sleeping, then there will be bathroom time and eating, instead of battling international terrorists like Kiefer Sutherland does, don't you think America will be a little bored with it?" I try for my reasonable tone, instead of my will-you-pull-your-head-out-of-your-butt tone.

Norman lifts his head off the table, where I swear he was snoring just seconds ago. "Bro, be reasonable. Instead of the twenty-four-hour thing, why don't we just shoot tape of them getting ready and doing the clothes thing and rehearsing and stuff, then have your production dudes use a little CG magic to make it look like it's continuous?"

The CG team always likes to demonstrate that they're underutilized by creating elaborate computer-generated effects that they show off to us on commercial breaks. They'd be thrilled to have something to do.

"All right, you bunch of babies. I don't know why I let you shoot down my ideas, but let's do it your way. We're done. Jules, I need to talk to you."

Everybody else escapes the room, like rats deserting a sinking production coordinator.

"What's up, Marshall?"

"Jules, Nellie says Shanicia is freaking out. Crying all the time and screaming at people and shit. Fix it."

"Well, she's upset about Anton and Lisette, and—"

"I don't care. I don't want to know. Just fix it. Can't have some psycho on the show. Fix it and report back. And never, ever call me on my personal cell."

He slams the door behind him, leaving me wondering for about the ten thousandth time why he doesn't just pitch that damn cell phone into the ocean.

Friday: I try to have a long talk with Shanicia. She cries.

And cries.

And cries.

In fact, I spend most of Friday handing Shanicia tissues.

* * *

Saturday: We're going to a movie premiere. I have no idea what movie, because I've been too busy comforting Shanicia and refereeing fights between Jack and Kayley all day. Oh, and let's not forget the exciting conversation with Mary Ann.

She finds me in my room, preparing for the premiere. At least she has the courtesy to knock.

"Come in." I'm dressed, too. What a nice change from Carlos's visit.

"Jules, I can't go to the premiere. In fact, I have to leave the show."

"What? You can't leave the show. You have a great chance of winning, Mary Ann. What's going on? Sit down and talk to me."

Her eyes are red from crying. Oh, God. Not her, too.

"Granny's in jail, Jules. She tried to pull the Four Aces on a trucker she'd conned before, and he's accusing her of stealing. She was drinking at the Squat and Bobble, or she wouldn't have been so stupid. I have to go home and bail her out."

"Wait. Let's think about this. You can—the Squat and Bobble? Where are you from? Some kind of stereotype of rural Appalachia?"

"That's not funny, Jules. Cutter's Crossing is an up-and-coming urban community just outside of Forestville." She lifts her chin and glares at me.

"I won't have you making fun of my hometown."

"I'm not making fun of anything, Mary Ann. I'm just trying to figure out how we can help your grandmother, and the whole Squat and Bobble thing threw me. Has she been in jail before?"

"Why do you ask? What kind of people do you think we are?" Her glare is furious now, but I'm not the one in jail.

"I think Granny, at least, is the kind of person who cheats at cards. And the kind of person who's cheated at cards in the past. So it was an honest question. Get that board out of your butt and let me help you."

She visibly deflates. "Yes," she mumbles.

"What?"

"Yes, she's been in jail before." She won't look me in the eye.

"Right. What did you do then?" I'm reaching for my phone. This may actually be something I need to call Marshall on his personal cell about. It definitely qualifies as horrible news, especially if the press gets wind of it.

"Nothing. The sheriff's wife has been Granny's best friend since they were in diapers. She took care of Granny for me."

"Great. Let's call the sheriff and see what we can come up with. And, for God's sake, don't tell anybody else about this." I flip my phone open.

"What's their phone number?"

She gives me the number and then clears her throat. "I told Carlos. I just, well, I somehow knew that he'd understand. I'd never say anything in front of Kayley or Jack, and Shanicia is a wild card these days. Being from the country doesn't mean I'm stupid, Jules."

She's right, but I don't have time to feel guilty about it. I have to get Granny out of jail before the premiere. Plus, I need to return Dad's calls. I sigh and start dialing. *Tomorrow, Dad. I promise.*

Armani and Wet Spots

It's my first time on a red carpet, and I admit to a teensy thrill. Not that anybody's paying attention to me. Mary Ann was right, of course. A few sex toys isn't nearly scandalous enough to capture the attention of this town for long.   As we approach the entrance and say hello to Jackie Chan and Owen Wilson (this must be *Shanghai Knights, the Eighth* or something), I catch a glimpse of the most gorgeous man I've ever seen, standing just past the actors and photographers.

Sam is eye candy in jeans and a T-shirt. In a black suit and white silk shirt, he's so hot I want him to do me right here on the red carpet. I can feel the heat coiling between my legs. Oh, man, I have to sit in this theater for two hours. Please, please, no damp spot on the back of the Armani.

From the look in his eyes, he wants to drop me to the floor, too. I walk up to him and strike a mock fashion-model pose.   "Do you like the Armani, dahling?"

His gaze rakes down over my body and back up, and he leans toward me to murmur in my ear. "I love you in that dress so much, I can't wait to get you out of it. My place, later. You'll be the one writhing, hot and wet, on the carpet while I lick you all over."

He puts an arm around my waist and steers me down the aisle toward our seats. This is helpful, since I'm having trouble walking after swallowing my tongue.

Sunday: The movie was frothy and fun, and the sex was wall-banging and knee-weakening, and that's all I'm going to say. Sam brought me breakfast in bed and taught me a whole new way to think about maple syrup, before I had to go back to the house and resume babysitting duty. When he's not making me want him so much I ache, he makes me laugh or makes me breakfast.

I could get used to this.

* * *

Show Time

Wednesday: Shanicia broke a shoe, so I have the great luck to catch Kayley and Jack going at it in the costume closet about twenty minutes before air time. I'm torn between surprise that Kayley would risk mussing her hair and nausea at the sight of Jack's naked butt pounding away. Luckily for me, I don't get a full frontal of anyone, or I might have to gouge my eyes out.

I back out, close the door, and call for Joe. Hey, he's the senior PC; he can deal with some of this crap.

As I walk back to the green room, I can hear him yelling something about turning the hose on them, like dogs in heat. I'm smiling by the time I hand Shanicia her shoe.

The CG-enhanced clips of the contestants rehearsing, buying new outfits, and being made over delight the audience and have the added benefit of filling up the empty space in the show left by the five finalists who are gone. I have more time to watch the monitor tonight, and love the way Mary Ann transforms in front of a microphone. It's like watching a plain dove transform into a nightingale, pouring her life and light and soul into the music. Her relief at hearing that the sheriff dropped all charges against Granny, and that he and his wife are keeping her in "protective custody" in their home for the next month, probably has something to do with the glow on her face, too. Standing ovation.

Carlos owns the stage. He's the personification of bottled sex, and even the guys in the audience love him, because they're all imagining they're him. Second standing O.

Jack's up next. I put my prejudices aside to listen to

him, and he's a fantastic singer, as much as I hate to admit it. He's even more "on" than usual tonight. Guess wild closet sex does it for him. Euwww.

Kayley and Shanicia sing well, but both are a little flat. Roger goes into mad-dog mode. (He's already an Englishman.)

"We're too far into this competition for you two to sound this terrible. Didn't you rehearse at all this week? You'd better pick it up, or you'll be out."

Q says, "Easy, man. Kayley, try more vocals, less pelvis thrust. Shanicia, quit crying. This isn't about the sympathy vote."

Nellie says, "Can we just get this over with, already?" Rumor has it that she's still pissed about the Sheryl Crow appearance.

But the studio audience is fickle. They love Kayley, in spite of an off night. Jack and Shanicia are in the bottom two, and it's a really close vote. I cross my fingers, knowing that the right vote means I never have to see any naked part of Jack again.

"I'm sorry, Shanicia. You will not be America's next *POP STAR LIVE!*"

I'm crying again, but a tiny part of me is relieved that there will be no more crying jags to deal with this week. I start to pick up the scattered clothes in the green room, when I hear a shriek from the stage. I run to the monitor.

Shanicia is standing mid-stage with the microphone, screaming and pointing at Kayley. "You losers! How could you vote me out over that bleached blond bitch? Well, I'm not done. You watch! I'll be huge! I'M GOING TO POSE FOR *PLAYBOY*!!"

Q stands up and starts clapping wildly. He's a big fan of dramatic gestures. The director is waving wildly for the cameramen to cut, "CUT NOW DAMMIT," and the cast, crew, and studio audience are all screaming simultaneously. Irving has a huge smile on his face—boy, are *his* ratings going way up.

I stare at the monitor. *Only three more weeks. Only three more weeks. Only three more weeks.*

I sigh and trudge on stage to collect my final four for the ride back to the house. To hell with A words. I'm up to V now. I want Valium, Vicodin, or vodka. Where's Kirby when I need her?

Chapter Thirty-three

Week Seven

Thursday: Our ratings skyrocketed last night. The clones keep singing some weird song they made up about money.

Money, money. We have it. You want it. Money, money. That's pretty much it. There are no other lyrics. Come to think of it, it sums up Hollywood's one-note raison d'être fairly well.

Marshall finally cuts off the singing and general sucking-up marathon.

"OK, OK, settle down. I was watching TV last night—"

We all groan.

"Shut up. Remember who signs your paychecks. I saw this great show at three in the morning. *Queer Eye for the Straight Guy.* So we're going to get those guys to redo Jack and Carlos and get a bunch of lesbos to make over Kayley and Mary Ann."

Norman and I look at each other over our tall double-shot caramel lattes (no whip). He rolls his eyes.

"Uh, bro. The whole *Queer Eye* thing is an inside joke about how the stereotypical gay guy is a much better dresser and has a better fashion sense than your average straight guy. There's not the same perception thing going on with lesbos, er, I mean, gay women."

Marshall looks stymied for a moment, then beams. "We can get Kayley and Mary Ann to make over the lesbos!"

I contemplate banging my head on the table. I decide to speak up instead.

"Marshall, while I think it's a great idea, I wonder about how our sponsors will react. I think the gay angle may be outside of what mainstream America is going to want to see in connection with our kid-next-door image. Did you—" I can't believe I'm even asking this "Did you see anything else on TV that you liked?"

He tilts his head and closes his eyes. "Nah. Nellie spent most of the night spending my money on the home shopping channels. Who the hell ever heard of *citrine?*"

"That's a great idea, Marshall. You're a genius!"

He looks at me, perplexed. "I am?"

"Yes! Americans are the world's greatest consumers. Let's give a breakdown of where they can buy the looks that our finalists are wearing and how much the pieces cost." This will be great.

Except Joe, Norman, Marshall, and the clones are all looking at me in disgust.

"That's such a chick thing. No way, dude." Even Norman is against me.

"We'd lose the entire male demographic, Jules. Are you nuts?" Marshall of the "lesbo makeover" fame speaks.

"I got an idea," says Joe.

We all whip around to look at him in amazement. He's never volunteered a show idea in all the time we've been doing this. This should be interesting.

"I've been watching that *Antiques Roadshow*. What if we let some of the studio audience bring their old junk in and have some appraisers and stuff? Plus, we could get our finalists to all autograph something, have the appraisers give it a value, and then auction it off for charity on eBay." He looks down at his shoes, exhausted from the effort of stringing so many full sentences together.

"That's actually a great idea," I say.

"Classier than the lesbos," Marshall says.

"That rocks, dude. And I can bring in some of my vintage *Star Wars* stuff, just to see what it's worth," Norman says.

"Make it happen. Report in. We're done." Marshall is halfway down the hall before I manage to stand up. Thinking up these high-concept shows keeps a man busy, I imagine.

After the meeting, I wander over to the coffee room to find some more caffeine to jump-start my brain for the day. I'm halfway in the room before I notice Nellie lurking by the artificial sweeteners.

It's too late to escape. For some reason, the theme music from *Jaws* starts playing in my head.

She pounces. "Hello, Jules. Marshall told me all about firing you. Aren't you just the lucky one that he needed to keep you around to do the babysitting? It's not like you do anything else worthwhile around here."

I channel peace and gentleness. *Think of flowers. Think of the ocean. Think not of dropping coffeepot on her smug little toes.*

Didn't work.

"Nellie, don't you have enough to do without torturing the staff? Namely, me? I'd think you'd be way too far above me to take the slightest notice." I clench my hands together and feel my fingernails dig into my palms.

Nellie studies her nails. "Normally you'd be right, Jules. But I feel I have to watch-guard the integrity of this show."

The smile on her face is truly hideous. (Think of the Grinch stuffing Cindy Lou Who's tree up the chimney. Yep, that's it.)

"What integrity? It was just a practical joke and a few pictures. Everything blows over. The story will be somebody else in a day or two." I try to believe it, even as I say it.

"Perhaps that might be true, if your very own mother weren't some freak who writes books about . . . about . . . female parts!" She almost screams the latter part of her sentence. People in the hall stop to see what the fuss is about.

"Nothing to see here, boys. Jules and I are having a friendly chat. Just girl to girl."

As the crowd disperses, I'm torn between the desire to defend my mother and the need to protect what remains of my dignity. Not to mention my job.

"Look, Nellie, I . . ."

"Just forget it, Jules. I ordered a copy of *Conquerors and*—um, er, you know, the other word. Who knew that Sylvia DuPree would be our little Jules's mom? As soon as I read it, I'll know whether to report to Marshall that you should be out." She crushes her paper cup and tosses it on the floor, then stomps on it. Crushed, tossed, and stomped, like my hopes for a career in TV.

(OK, that *was* a little melodramatic, but there's no way Nellie will comprehend what reviewers called "the intrinsic genius and brilliance" of that particular book. Especially the part about the clitorectomies. I'm *doomed*.)

I bang my head against the wall a few times. It doesn't help with my dilemma, but it is oddly satisfying. I decide to pull a Scarlett O'Hara and worry about it tomorrow.

I've had enough for one day.

Friday: I decide to go to rehearsals with my finalists this morning. I haven't been in a while, and maybe I can help lighten up some of the tension that is choking all of us. We're wandering around this huge house, listening to the echoes of the six who are gone, and wondering who will be next. Kayley keeps cracking remarks about how she'll be so glad to have the room to herself next week, but even her viciousness is blunted by stress. Mary Ann ignores her, I'm glad to see.

The Jack and Kayley sex fest is over, it looks like. They were arguing a lot last week, and now they ignore each other pointedly. My relief at not having to wonder when or where I'll trip over them going at it like rabbits trumps the added tension in the air.

We arrive at the rehearsal studio in our limo (we only need one now) and see the welcome wagon on the front steps. If you want to call Jack's bodyguard and Kayley's dad in a fistfight welcoming. We all jump out of the car and run over.

Kayley's shrieking, "Don't you hurt my dad, you big ape!"

Jack's yelling, "Stop it, Luke. One more assault charge, and you're going away!"

Mary Ann's moaning, "Oh, no, oh, no, oh, no."

Carlos stands silently, body slightly crouched on alert.

I stop right next to them and yell as loudly as I can. "Stop it RIGHT NOW!"

They ignore me completely. Kayley's dad lands a

punch on Luke/Luigi's jaw that rocks his head to the side. He's got a great right hook for a rich guy.

But how stupid do you have to be to get in a fight with the Incredible Bulk? Luke/Luigi almost gently taps his massive fist against Dad's jaw, and we all watch Dad's eyes roll up in head before he staggers backwards. I think he's down for the count, but he fools me.

"You troglodyte! I ever catch you fucking with my plans again, I'll kill you," he gasps at Luke and Jack.

And Jack?

"What's a troglodyte?" Bodyguard is fisting his hamlike hands again.

"It means handsome Italian man," I say quickly. "Now would somebody like to tell me what the heck is going on?"

"None of your business, you interfering bitch. I've warned you before. You keep him away from me and his bastard buddy away from my daughter." Dad is leaning heavily on Kayley now.

Carlos is suddenly standing in front of me. "I suggest you apologize to Ms. Vernon," he says silkily.

Kayley's dad spits on the ground. "Get away from me, you greasy Spic. Kayley told me you were fucking the bitch. Guess she was right."

My mouth drops open. Kayley sneers in my direction.

"Yeah, that's right. Miss Holier-than-thou was lecturing us about a little innocent kissing, and she was spreading her legs for a guy fifteen years younger than she is."

A little kissing? Forget that, FIFTEEN YEARS younger?

"I certainly am not having any kind of relationship with any finalist on this show, which includes Carlos, who is *ten* years younger than I am, actually. Not that it's any of your business. And you might want to tell

Daddy that your idea of innocent kissing involves being naked with Jack's . . . parts . . . in your mouth, before he winds up in jail defending your nonexistent honor." I can't believe I just said that, but I haven't been this furious in a long, long time.

I wheel around to Jack and his pet goon.

"What the hell is *your* problem?"

Luigi/Luke points at Kayley's dad. "We just found out that this rich prick tried to fix the voting machines. The Union guys told me about it. They made sure it never happened. Us Union guys stick together. But who knows what he's up to now? If he tries once, he'll try again."

"You got no proof, other than the word of some slimeball buddy of yours," says Kayley's dad.

"Look." I'm trying for the voice of reason. "We checked out the allegations of voting machine rigging, but, except for that one worker, nobody else on the machine crew knew anything about it. Plus, Kayley was in the bottom two that week, so that's pretty clear evidence that it wasn't fixed on her behalf. If you have proof, let us know. Until then, check the attitude.

Bodyguard growls, and I've had enough.

"ENOUGH! I have had enough. I'm throwing both of you out of the studio audience for this trick. I'm going to make sure security doesn't let you in, so don't even try. The next negative word I hear about either one of you—even a single breath—your finalist is OUT. You know I can do it, and I don't make empty threats. Are you leaving, or should Jack and Kayley pack their suitcases now?"

Kayley stamps her foot.

"Daddy, if you cost me this competition, I'll never forgive you." She storms inside without looking back, and her very wilted father starts to leave.

"I mean it. No more. There will be no more chances," I call after him, then turn to Jack.

"I am *so* not kidding, Jack. Keep him in line, or you're out."

I grab Mary Ann's hand and drag her along beside me. I notice that Carlos falls behind to follow us, eyes never leaving Jack and his bloody-nosed bodyguard.

Once we're in the building, I sag against the wall.

"I don't know how much more of this drama I can take. Carlos, I'm very sorry you had to listen to those evil accusations."

He laughs. "Hey, it's kind of an honor that they think you'd sleep with me, J. Made my whole day," he teases.

I look up at him and am forced to smile. Mary Ann calms down a little, too. Some woman is going to be very lucky in the future when this man finally falls in love.

"Well, rehearsals should be interesting. Never a dull moment on *POP STAR LIVE!*"

Monday: Kirby calls at six A.M. and wakes me up. She's whispering.

"Daniel's back."

"What? Who? Kirbs, it's six in the morning. Are you nuts? You know I hate mornings." I blearily reach for the light switch.

"Jules, Daniel's back and I don't want him in my house." She sounds frantic.

"OK, calm down, Kirby. Why is he back? I thought you got rid of him for good this time. What's going on? Slow down and start at the beginning."

"I was lonely, that's all. All my friends are married or in serious relationships, even you now, and I just got lonely. I saw him out at the Waterfront Saturday night, and I was drinking and, well, it's Monday morning and he's still here. What am I going to do?"

Daniel can be frightening when he's thwarted, and all he wants is Kirby. Her body, her undivided attention, and her money. The last time she threw him out, I came over for moral support, and the menace in his eyes scared me. He's one of those guys who thinks domination and obsessive jealousy are proof of love.

"Kirby, get out and go to work. Call him from the office and ask him to leave. Tell him your brothers are coming over for dinner. Then, for God's sake, get your locks changed and don't ever invite him back. He scares me, and I don't know what the hell a smart woman like you ever saw in him."

But I'm lying. I know exactly what she saw in him. She saw the first man in her life she hadn't been able to steamroll over. It took a while for her to figure out the difference between self-assurance and a psychotic need for control.

"OK, OK, you're right. He knows I never, ever skip work, so he won't be suspicious. I'd better get going. Hey, Jules, I miss you. Come home soon. Please?"

"As soon as the show is over, I promise. Now get out of there and call me later. I'm going to be worrying all day, so don't forget."

I roll over and stare at the ceiling. We're smart women. How do we always get so screwed up when it comes to our love lives? I pull the pillow over my head and drift back into an uneasy sleep.

Show Time

Wednesday: Forty minutes until air, and I'm doing my usual frantic hamster-on-a-wheel routine, when Sam walks into the green room, looking like hell.

"Hey, Sam. Was the job in San Diego rough? You

look terrible?"

He grabs my arm and keeps walking.

"Oh, OK. *'Hi, Jules, nice to see you, too. How have you been? I've missed you these past few days.'* These one-sided conversations are so fun, Sam." I'm not in the mood to be dragged, especially after Kirby's drama with Daniel earlier in the week.

He swings me around so my back is to the green room wall and kisses me so thoroughly I forget what I was thinking. When he finally pulls back, my eyes are huge.

"What was that all about? And you're lucky there's nobody in here, or I'd punch you."

He takes a deep breath. "I've just been chatting with Joe. Forget to mention anything to me about the brawl in front of the studio the other day? Threats against you? Any of that ring a bell?"

"Hey, you were busy and had a lot on your mind. I wasn't going to bother you with trivial stuff over the phone. I handled it." I push against his chest, which is about as unyielding as a rock wall.

"I can live without the cave-man routine, you know. I'm a grown woman, perfectly capable of handling myself."

"The hell you are." His jaw is clenched so tightly, a muscle in his cheek is jerking.

"It's always you taking care of yourself, isn't it, Jules? Ever since what that bastard did to you before your wedding, you're all about taking care of yourself and not letting anybody else in. Not letting anybody else help. Well, you'd better get used to help, Hurricane Jules, because I'm not going anywhere."

How does somebody make a warning sound like a beautiful promise? Or is it the other way around?

"Sam, I'm glad you want to be here for me, but I'm telling you I handled it. It was no big deal."

"Let me tell you about 'no big deal,' Jules. I had my people run a check on Jack's family and Kayley's dad. First, Jack wasn't kidding about the Indiana mafia. It sounds like a joke, but his competitors have a nasty habit of running into accidents. One business owner who didn't want to play ball watched his wife and daughter get run off the road in their minivan. Luckily, nobody was killed, but not for lack of trying, from what I can tell." He slams a fist against the wall.

"Second, Kayley's dad is nuts. Not just the ordinary, garden-variety Hollywood kind of nuts. Completely fucking insane. He divorced Kayley's mom when Kayley was only a little girl, and destroyed his ex in the custody fight. Hired people to make her look like a total whore and druggie to the court. She killed herself soon after losing the custody battle. Since then, he devotes all of his time to two things: success as a corporate raider and giving Kayley everything she wants. Everything. The mother of a girl who beat Kayley out for a spot on the junior varsity cheer-leading team ended up in the hospital with a broken arm and a few busted ribs from a 'random mugging.'"

Sam stops suddenly and crushes me into a fierce hug. "Just how do you think I feel about finding all this out when the woman I love is being targeted by this mob of ruthless bastards? Jesus, Jules. If any-thing were to happen to you . . . And then I find out that something already has, and you didn't even let me know."

He lifts my chin, and I can feel his hand trembling. "It's over, Jules. You're never alone again, for the duration of the show. This stupid TV show is not worth you getting hurt. In fact, I'd tell you to quit right now, if I thought you'd listen."

I take my own deep breath and move away a little. "I . . . you're right. I'm not quitting. But I'm glad you're going to be with me. I'm glad you're worried about me. And, I—"

I fall silent and look at him in bewilderment.

"Did you, ah, did you just say you love me?"

"Yes, dammit, I love you. In spite of my determination to have a quiet and peaceful life, Hurricane Jules swept her tornado-style life through mine, and I was a goner."

I laugh weakly. "Hey, pick your tropical storm metaphor and stick with it. You only get one."

He pushes a hand through his hair and barks out a laugh. "Hell, Jules, you're a meteorological nightmare. You're a monsoon and typhoon and all the other –oons, as you would say, rolled up into one. Chaos follows you wherever you go, and I guess I'll just have to get used to it, because I'm sticking. I love you, so deal with it."

"That's just the kind of hearts-and-flowers declaration a girl dreams of, Blake. And don't think you get points for saying it first, because I knew I loved you first, clear back at the roller rink." I shove him out of the way and start to storm off, but he grabs my arm.

"Say it again," he demands.

"That's just . . ."

"No, the other part. Say it again." The heat in his gaze is searing into me.

"I love you, Blake. And I'm sticking, too. So you *can* just deal with *that*."

And the kiss that follows is pretty fantastic for two people who can't say *I love you* without turning it into a competition.

"Can't you two just get a damn room?" It's Joe again. His timing sucks. Of course, we *are* in a public place. To hell with that. I kiss Sam again, briefly this time, but with the promise of much more to come in my eyes.

"What?" I still sound a little surly.

"It's twenty minutes till show time, and your finalists are going to be coming in soon. You might want to get back to work, you slackers." But he's grinning in a very smug way.

"Knew you two were right for each other. You'll have cute kids." He whistles tunelessly and heads for the door.

Sam and I look at each other and burst into laughter. "We should have just listened to him from the beginning," he says.

Kayley "accidentally" poured coffee all over Mary Ann's dress, so I spend most of the show dealing with a costume emergency. From what I overhear, the *Antiques Roadshow* theme plays well, and there are a couple of real finds in the audience. Norman's *Star Wars* collection turns out to be valued at more than one hundred thousand dollars, shocking everyone, especially Norman, who has to be helped to a chair.

And, of course, in between all the silliness and hype, there is singing. The singing that brought us here in the first place, the singing that will make one of four dreams come true.

Mary Ann's a touch quavery in the beginning, shaken by the costume crisis and Kayley's cattiness. But she recovers quickly and brings home one of my personal favorites, "Come Away with Me." It's the same song so many bad singers butchered in auditions, but with Mary Ann's soulful touch, I feel goose bumps break out on my arms. The judges give her a standing ovation; one of the few they've awarded so far.

Carlos, for the first time in the competitions, delivers a performance that is merely good. Q, Nellie, and Roger are all speechless. Q finally says, "Whoa, man, are you actually human?"

Jack blisters out a rock medley that has the audience up dancing in the aisles. Stress and strife, like sex in closets, must be a catalyst for him.

Nellie practically leaps out of her seat to heap praise on him; she's one step away from fawning. I wonder what Marshall the enormous-yellow-diamond-giver thinks about this.

Kayley is in rare form tonight, dancing wildly in her best Britney Spears imitation, but she's flat on the song and the judges crucify her about it.

"You're not going to be able to dazzle the people who buy your record with your dancing," says Roger.

"Still with the pelvis, Kayley. Work on the vocals, babe. Vocals," says Q, shaking his head.

"That was awful, Kayley. I mean, I hate to be unkind, but that was the absolute zenith of awfulness. You're just not going to be able to count on being cute when you have no singing talent," says Nellie, completely unaware of the irony of those words coming out of her one-hit-wonder mouth.

Maybe all that Botox affected her memory.

But the audience agrees. Kayley and Carlos are in the bottom two, and Kayley is the seventh contestant voted off *POP STAR LIVE!* As she storms past me in the green room, she hisses a warning.

"You just wait, Jules. All of you. We're going to get even."

She scoops up three pairs of Manolos that don't belong to her and slams her way out into the hall. I feel a chill on my spine that has nothing to do with the air conditioning. Maybe I will mention this latest threat to Sam.

After all, he's in love with me. Tropical storms and all.

Chapter Thirty-four
The Most Original??

Thursday: I convey Kayley's threats and the background on her dad to everyone at the staff meeting. Sam's right; there's no reason to take this all on myself. Let Marshall deal with it. That's why they pay him the big bucks, right?

"He's a windbag. Lot of 'em around. Don't worry about it, Jules. Have the security guys stick close to you the next few weeks. What's next?" He looks expectantly at one of the clones.

Two, I think. The man has been squirming around like he needs to be excused to go to the bathroom. Mom used to call it the Potty Dance. Isn't it weird, the stuff you remember from when you were three?

Two pops up out of his chair. "I have an announcement to make."

So make it already.

He clears his throat dramatically and pauses to grip the edge of the table.

"*TV Guide* will be presenting Marshall and *POP STAR LIVE!* with an award Saturday night for Most Original New Programming in a Reality Series!!

We're a hit!!"

All the clones get up and start dancing around, while Joe, Norman, and I watch them in stupefaction. I can't stand it. I know it's stupid, but I can't contain myself.

"Original programming? Marshall, I'm happy for you, but *we stole every single idea on this show from somebody else!*"

"Of course we did, Jules. But we stole it in the most original way!" He roars with laughter.

"You still don't get it, Jules. There are no new ideas. Boy meets girl. Hell, boy meets boy, even. Man fights nature. Man fights himself. We've only got three concepts to work with, and they were already old by the time the Bible premiered. Adam and Eve, the plagues, Job, all that shit. Anything we could put on TV was an overworked cliché before TV was even invented. Hell, before electricity was even discovered."

"Or fiber optic cable," pipes in Clone One.

"Shut up, you moron. My point is that there are only new ways to present old stuff, and sometimes you play around enough and you hit gold!" He grins at me.

"You'll be fine in ten or twelve years, when that naiveté wears off, kid. But in the meantime, the network is renewing us for a second season! Champagne for everybody!"

The cheering and hugs start; everybody on the crew is suddenly in the room. The good news has spread as fast and mysteriously as light travels through those fiber optic cables that One mentioned. I sit in my chair, wondering why I'm not happier.

It *is* good news. Isn't it?

Roger and Nellie enter the room, jolting me out of my musings. Nellie makes a beeline for Marshall and the champagne, smirking at me.

Great. I wonder if she's read Mom's book.

I shake my head, determined to enjoy the moment and hold off any thoughts of my impending doom.

Roger walks over to me.

"So," he says, dropping into the chair next to me. "What do you think? Are you signing on with this madhouse for next year? And what about my offer for the off season? It still stands, you know."

I look at him and smile, but it's a sad smile. Somehow, over the course of the past few months, I've come to care about him. Even like him a lot. If it weren't for Sam, I'd be tempted. London would be a blast.

Roger looks into my eyes, and he sees everything that I'm thinking. Guess I'd better not play any poker with Granny Hawkins, either.

He sketches a rueful salute at me and smiles. "That's what I thought. But it was worth a chance. You and Blake, hmm?"

"Yep, me and Blake. I think it might be something great, Roger. Be happy for me."

"I am, Jules. And he'd better be good to you, or he'll answer to me. I was a champion boxer at Eton, you know." He grins that wonderful, insouciant Roger grin. Maybe Kirby . . .

Oh, no. Now I'm thinking like a married fixer-upper. Aargh. But maybe . . .

Roger takes two glasses of champagne from Norman and holds one out to me. "Shall we?"

I smile. "We shall." I stand up and propose a toast. "To Marshall and *POP STAR LIVE!* May our total lack of originality continue to be the most original around!"

Echoes of "To Marshall" and "To *POP STAR LIVE!*" echo around me as I take a sip, and then Roger leans over and kisses my forehead. "I'll miss you, you know."

"I'll miss you too, Roger."

"Just don't miss her too much," says a familiar voice, as hands lightly grasp my shoulders.

"Well, the best man didn't win, so I won't say any of that drivel, but you'd better take care of her, Blake. Or else." Roger's smile almost reaches his eyes.

Oh, no. We're not going to start the pissing contest again, are we? But Sam surprises me. He reaches around me to hold out his hand.

"No worries, Roger. I plan to take very good care of her for the rest of her life."

As they shake hands, the implication of that "rest of her life" thing hits me, and I fall back into my chair. Looking up at Sam, I drain the rest of my champagne and hold up my glass.

"Next!"

Everybody in the room starts laughing at my unwitting imitation of Marshall on a roll. Even Marshall. I look around at my team—this team I helped build and make strong, and hope that the Impostor is gone forever. I have a job—no, a career—that I love. This is definitely a champagne moment. For the first time in many, many years, I'm perfectly happy.

In spite of the death threats. Well, I wouldn't want life to get *too* boring, right?

Sam has a meeting with subcontractors he has to leave for, and I have to meet my three remaining finalists for lunch and another round of shopping. I'm heading for the door, rummaging in my purse to make sure I have my company credit card, when one of the grips yells down the hall at me that I have a phone call. I think it's odd, since everybody calls me on my cell, but stop in the sound room to find a land line.

"Hello?"

"Jules Vernon?"

"Yes, may I help you?"

"This is Riverside Memorial Hospital in Columbus, Ohio. Your father has been in a very bad automobile accident. You'd better fly back here right away. We're not sure he'll make it through the night."

The phone falls out of my hand and slams against the table. The sound guys look at me in surprise and then jump up to grab me as I start to fall. I can hear their voices from far away, as though I am plunging deep in a well and all sound and light are spiraling away from me.

I shake my head, hard. I don't have time to faint.

"My dad's been in a bad accident. I have to get to the accident. He's not . . . he might not . . . it's bad. Tell Marshall, tell everybody for me. Sam. Tell Sam." I'm running for the door. Have to get a cab.

I fly out of the studio and, miraculously, there's an empty cab waiting at the curb. I run to the door and yank it open.

"Airport. Get me to the airport. Now. Emergency." Now the tears are starting, and I can hardly force the words out through lungs burning in despair.

Phone. I need to call people. God, does Mom know? What about Amber? I have to call Kirby. She'll come. And Sam. Have to reach Sam. *Why didn't I return Dad's calls this week? I was too busy, and now I may have lost him forever.*

I scrub the tears off my face and dig in my bag for my cell phone. As I pull it out, I hear a voice I'd hoped never to hear again.

"Just give me the phone, Jules. Now."

It's Kayley's dad, and he's pointing a gun at my face. I can't make sense of this. Why is Kayley's dad in my cab?

"You don't understand. My dad has been in a terrible accident. I have to get to the airport. What are you doing? Why do you have a gun? I didn't have anything to do with your daughter getting voted off the show; that was the studio audience. And WHAT IS YOUR DAMN NAME? I'm sick of thinking of you as 'Kayley's dad.'"

If any of that made any sense to him, I'd be surprised. I'm not sure I understood it myself.

He smiles at me, and I see an empty nothingness in his eyes that terrifies me more than any of his previous blustering ever did.

"My name is Martin. But you can call me Marty, seeing as how we're going to be so close." Without moving the gun, he looks at the driver.

"Take us to the beach house."

"Look, Mr., ah, Marty. You don't understand. I don't care what you do to me. Well, actually, I do care. I don't want to die. But I have to get to the airport and get to my dad. My dad. You should understand that. If you were in the hospital, wouldn't you want Kayley to be with you?"

He smiles, but there is no humor in it. It's an evil smile, leached of hope and life.

"You stupid idiot. Your dad isn't in the hospital. We made that call to get you running out here to the cab. You're too stupid to figure that out? And Kayley," he snorts with disgust.

"Kayley wouldn't give me a glass of water if I were dying of thirst. She told me we were through if she didn't win this competition. Kayley would have won if you hadn't turned on her. I've given her everything to make her famous. To make her a star. But now it's over and she's gone, and you have to die."

I stare at him in fear and repulsion. What is he talking

about? What did he do to his daughter that turned her into such a conniving, manipulative person? I hope I'll live to find out. My terror is mixed with the huge relief that Dad's OK.

I offer up a little prayer of thanks. *I promise to call him all the time, God. I'll even be nice to Amber.*

Martin glances out the window. We're on Venice Boulevard. The crowds of people surrounding us are slowing the car's progress and making him nervous about holding a gun to my head in plain view. He snarls at me.

"Make even one move, and you're dead right here. I have nothing to lose."

But he turns halfway back into his seat, keeping his gaze on me, and lowers the gun.

It's now or never. Please don't let it be locked.

I launch myself at the door, wrenching the handle. It opens, and I fall out the door onto the road, hitting my shoulder hard and rolling. Somebody screams. Oh, that was me. My arm may be broken. Oh, man, that hurts.

Suddenly I'm surrounded by people.

"Don't move her."

"Give her some air."

" . . . bleeding?"

"Call 911."

" . . . head injury?"

I try to get up but gentle hands press me back down. I stare wildly around for Martin, but all I see is the back of the cab, driving off. I hope he's too afraid of all the people to shoot me in the middle of the street. Sirens are screaming nearer and nearer, and I manage to hold on until they lift me on to the gurney and somebody bumps my arm. Then it all goes black.

* * *

Safe

I wake up in the hospital with Sam slumped next to me in a chair, holding my hand. Lines I haven't seen before etch his face.

"Hi," I whisper. "Can I have some water?"

I see that my arm is bandaged, but no cast.

"It wasn't broken?"

He's holding a cup of water to my lips.

"What, sweetheart? Oh, your arm. No, it's not broken. Just banged up pretty badly. Jules, you could have been killed." His hand is shaking, and he puts the cup down and leans in to touch my face with his hands.

"Thank God you're all right."

"I *did*. I even promised to be nice to Amber." I laugh shakily.

"What?"

"Nothing. It was Kayley's dad, Sam. Martin. We have to call the police." I try to sit up in the bed, agitated.

Sam props the pillows around me.

"Shhhh, Jules. We know. Just stay calm. You've been through a lot. Martin's driver turned him in. Just drove up to the police station, turned Martin's own gun on him, and forced him out of the car. The guy's telling a lot of tales about what they did to you and a lot of other stuff that bastard's been up to. I guess he'd told the driver they were just going to scare you, and when Martin threatened to kill you, the guy wanted no part of it. He claims he was going to help you."

"Sure, that's what he says now. All I know is that I was headed to a deserted beach house with a lunatic and his gun. And Martin said some scary stuff about Kayley, too. It made me feel almost sorry for her,

Sam. She was just the conduit for his warped ambitions."

"Maybe so, but it seems to me that she's not trying too hard to get out from under evil Daddy's influence. She's, what? Twenty years old? She can choose a different life. Anyway, I never want to talk about them again. How are you feeling?"

I take inventory out loud.

"My arm—OUCH—my arm hurts like hell. I have a killer headache, and my ribs hurt. All in all, I feel terrific."

I beam my brightest smile at him.

"I love you, Sam Blake. Amazing what a near-death experience can do to a fear of commitment. You can commit to me any time."

He laughs. "I'd like to *have* you committed sometimes, Jules. I blame myself for leaving you alone for a single minute. But you promised me you'd keep Sharp and Johnson with you whenever I couldn't be. What happened?"

I look at him, somberly. "Martin had somebody call me and tell me my father was in the hospital, dying. I ran for a cab to the airport, and he was hiding in the front seat of the cab that was so conveniently waiting on the curb just outside the studio. I told the guys in the sound room to tell you, and I was trying to call you from the cab when Martin pulled that gun."

"Oh, Jules, sweetheart. I'm so sorry. So sorry. I'll never leave you alone for a minute until that psycho is locked away for good." He moves to sit on the edge of my bed.

"I really need to just hold you, Jules. I won't touch any place that hurts, but I need to hold you and know that you're safe."

"Sam, I can't think of anything I'd like better."

And we're still sitting just like that twenty minutes

later, with me leaning against his chest, my bad arm propped up, when Joe and Norman bang the door open and come running into the room.

Our Heroine Returns

Monday: I bully Sam into taking me back to work, after he spent the entire weekend spoiling and pampering me (which was just fine with me). I confess to maybe laying it on a teensy bit thick with the *Oh, my poor arm hurts*, but how often does a girl get the chance to be the center of the universe?

When we arrive at the conference room for our staff meeting, the crew spontaneously bursts into applause and gives me my own personal standing ovation, and I almost cry. Even Joe hugs me, then pretends my hairspray made him sneeze when he gets a little misty-eyed. (I don't mention that I'm not wearing hairspray; gotta protect his crusty old guy image.)

Marshall waves everybody back into their seats.

"I just want to say good job, Jules. You're practically dead with a hole between your eyes Friday, then back at work Monday. A lot of people could take a lesson from a work ethic like that."

Everybody claps while I wince at the visual of the hole between my eyes.

"Thanks, Marshall, but I was—"

"I'm not done yet, Jules."

"Sorry."

"As I was saying, in honor of Jules's adventure and that prick Martin going to jail, I think we should do the show in a Court TV theme this week."

My headache is suddenly back. Carlos will have a fit. Wait, I can use my invalid status one more time.

"Marshall, if I could just offer a suggestion?" I try to make my voice sound weak and quavery. Sam looks at me suspiciously, since I don't sound anything like the woman who was yelling at him this morning to take me to work or I'd call a damn cab. (Sam has appointed himself my bodyguard for the rest of the show, since I refused to quit.)

"In honor of the emergency medical personnel who helped me, and the police who put Martin behind bars, what if we twist your idea a little and do a Hometown Heroes show? We could honor the local EMTs, police, and firefighters. Maybe even get a bunch of them to sing a song with our contestants." I give my best poor, orphaned waif impression. Can I make my lip quiver?

Marshall is nodding. "I LOVE it! What a great idea! New York isn't the only city in the country with great police and firefighters. Let's freakin' do it! Make it happen, boys. And, Blake, watch out for our Jules. She's a big part of this show, and we need her back for next season."

Sam flashes a wry grin. "I'm trying, Marshall. She's taking years off my life, but I'm trying."

Show Time

So now it's show time, and I haven't done much to contribute to the show all week. Mary Ann and Carlos spent a lot of time watching over me, while trying to pretend that they weren't, and Jack even brought me some flowers he'd picked.

We lined up a huge contingent of local firefighters, EMTs, and police officers to recognize as Hometown Heroes, and I'll even have my fifteen seconds of fame when I go onstage, just before a commercial break, to help present a plaque to the representatives of each. Then they're all going to sing the national anthem with our three remaining contestants. I'm probably going to cry. I always cry at the national anthem and tonight is more personal than most; I was a bullet away from never hearing the Star Spangled Banner again.

Jack seems nervous tonight. He and Kayley split up before last week's vote, so it's not like he misses her. I wonder what's up. Then we're live, and Jack's up, then Mary Ann, so there's no time to do anything but watch and cheer and enjoy the show.

On a commercial break, Carlos sits next to me on the couch.

"Jules, I hate to bother you with this, but you might need to know." He has the dead look in his eyes that I hate so much.

"What's wrong, Carlos? Is it your mom? Your sister?" I reach for his hand.

"No, shhh, nothing like that. It's just that, you know how I was kind of jumpy last week?"

I do remember that his singing was off, for the first time since the show started.

"Yes, what's wrong? Just spit it out, you're making me crazy here," I hiss.

He looks around to see who's watching and pulls his hand out of my grasp.

"It's just that some friends from home said some of the old gang were poking around, asking a lot of questions, flashing cash around to get answers. Might be just big talk; might be about whose *cojones* are bigger. Or it might be that the media has caught on to me and is paying for information. I just wanted you to know."

"Oh, no, Carlos. Not now. You don't need this now." I'm suddenly a mother wolf (OK, a big sister wolf)—feral and determined to protect her cub.

"Let me talk to Sam and Marshall, and we'll figure out what we can do."

"No. I don't want to cause an uproar if it's nothing. Even if it is something, maybe it'll blow over for a week. That's all I need, is one freaking week. Damn."

"FIFTEEN SECONDS." Joe bellows out the time cue.

"Look, Carlos, let's talk after the show. Sam is really levelheaded and won't say anything if you don't want him to, but three heads are better than one."

He smiles down at me as he stands up and ruffles my hair. "Especially if one of them's yours, J."

Carlos doesn't let the tension, or his nerves, or anything else affect him this week. He's singing last, and Mary Ann and Jack were fantastic, so he knows the heat is on. He pauses to dedicate the song.

"This is for the EMT personnel who rescued our very own Jules from danger last week. The media attention about this incident focused on the deranged man behind it. We at *PSL!* want to focus on the heroes who saved the day."

Then, after a soulful pause that leaves us all expecting a haunting ballad, he fires out a version of "Living La Vida Loca" that knocks the collective socks off the studio audience. People in the balcony are dancing on their seats. The power and excitement of his performance blast a hole in the stress and tension and drama of the week to let the clean, cool air through. I'm singing along on the couch, and I notice that even Joe is snapping his fingers.

Good for you, Carlos. Good for you.

It's a tight vote, and Marshall and Joe oversee a systems analysis of the voting machines, but the results check out.

Mary Ann and Jack are in the bottom two. I hear a roar of pain and denial from the balcony, and see that Luigi/Luke managed to get past security.

But he's too late. The studio audience voted Jack off. Mary Ann and Carlos are going to the final round.

The three of us, plus Sam, are headed out the door to the car, when Norman runs down the hall. "Jules, Carlos, you'd better get in here and see this. Now!"

We dash back inside to see what could possibly be going wrong this time. The entire crew is huddled in front of the TV monitors in the production room, tuned to the local ABC news affiliate.

Kayley and Jack are giving a press conference about a block from here on the sidewalk in front of the Hilton. Oh, shit.

" . . . and deliberate pressure exerted by the judges to influence the audience to vote a certain way, since one of the production staff was having sexual relations with one of the contestants, Carlos Quintana," Kayley says.

That hateful bitch. I hope her dad's legal fees eat all of her inheritance, so she has to shoe shop at K-Mart.

"Not to mention the threats made against my friends and family," adds Jack.

Prick.

"But, worst of all," Jack continues dramatically, before Kayley pushes in front of him and cuts him off.

"Worst of all," she continues, "is the deliberate deception being perpetrated against America by this show that claims to be all about *family values*."

Jack shoves his way back in front of the microphones and cameras. These two deserve each other.

"This 'family value' show manipulated the show results, and now a *known gang member* is in the final two. The same person who sneaks in and out of a production coordinator's bedroom in the middle of the night, Carlos Quintana, is a known principal of the dreaded gang known as the Dragon's Tears, in Miami, Florida."

On the screen, flashbulbs and questions pop wildly. In our production room, everyone is staring at me and Carlos. Sam's standing behind me, and his fingers tighten on my shoulders.

"It's not like that," Carlos says. "The gang stuff, yeah, I'll own up to that. But I've never committed any crime, and I got out of the gang. I just wanted to build a new and better life for myself, and you never would have taken me if you'd known."

He shakes his head in disgust. "That shit about 'innocent until proven guilty' works better if you're rich and white. But, anyway, there was never anything between Jules and me. I did go to her room late one night to talk to her. I was worried about my mom and baby sister, living in the projects. Jules talked to me for a few minutes, and then she packed me off to my own bed. That's it. End of story."

He's speaking to the whole room, but staring right at Sam. I turn to look at Sam and see him nod slightly to Carlos; seeming to signal both his acceptance of the truth of Carlos's statement and his respect for a man whose chivalry and honor match his own. They both want to protect me.

Well, fuck that.

"That's very noble, Carlos. But I don't need for you to stand up for me. I can speak for myself. No, I wasn't sleeping with Carlos, or with *any* of the contestants under my supervision. I wasn't sleeping with Mary Ann either." I jerk my head in her direction, and she gasps.

"But, regardless of who I was or was not sleeping with, the real point here is damage control. We have to get our spin on this out there tonight or we'll lose ratings, viewers, and sponsors. Let's meet right now and map out our battle plan."

I start walking toward the conference room, when I realize I don't hear any footsteps. I turn around.

"What are you waiting for?"

"You just don't get it, do you, Pollyanna? We're fucked. We are *so* fucked. We are so *royally* fucked." Marshall's shouting echoes off the walls of the narrow corridor.

"There is no battle plan or strategy that will fix this. We can't have a gang member in the final two. We're going to proclaim Mary Ann winner by default next week. But first we apologize to America and tell them we didn't know anything about this loser and his gang shit."

Mary Ann looks horrified and puts a fist in her mouth, tears pouring down her face. I *know* Mary Ann. This isn't how she wanted to win.

Carlos clenches his fists. "I am not a loser," he says in a dangerous voice.

"I am somebody trying to make a better life for myself and my family. Isn't that what America's all about? Isn't that what the American dream is supposed to be about? So you're as fake as your bullshit *reality* show. Just glitter and flash with nothing underneath."

Marshall's face is beet red. "You're out! You ruined me! You ruined my show! Get out before I have security throw you out, you lying little weasel!"

I step between Carlos and Marshall. "He's not a liar. You take that back right now. He has more integrity than almost anyone I know."

I raise my chin and repeat it. "He's *not* a liar. We asked if they were convicted of a crime. He never was. No lies. Got it?"

Marshall looks like he wants to take a swing at me.

"It's a damn lie, Jules. You think he didn't know we'd want to know about a little detail like a gang history? On a family show? Give me a fucking break. If he wasn't a liar, he would have told somebody."

I take a deep breath. I have to do it. There's no other way.

"He did. He told me. I knew about his gang history."

Marshall's mouth drops open, and he stands there gaping like a fish.

"You . . . you're telling me you *knew* this? And you didn't tell me? Earlier, when we could have kicked him out without ruining the show? You *knew??*"

"Yes, I knew. I also knew, and still know, that he deserves a second chance. Please let him have that second chance, Marshall. Please."

Marshall looks at me, sheer loathing all over his face.

"You're fired. Get out of my sight."

Jules Stands Up

So now I'm dragging Mary Ann, Carlos, and Sam down the street to the Hilton. They want a press conference? They're going to get one.

As we run up to the front sidewalk outside the hotel, the press are just starting to pack away their equipment. I dash out in front of them.

"Stop! You want the truth about this little fiction those two sore losers cooked up? Well, I'm Jules Vernon, the object of the attack, and I've got Carlos Quintana with me. Do you want to hear our side of the story, or do you just want to air unsubstantiated slander?"

I've got their attention now. The reporters are racing to unpack and set up microphones and cameras.

"What are you talking about?"

"Carlos, what is your statement?"

"Are you two sleeping together?"

"What—"

"How—"

I hold up my hands for silence.

"OK, OK. We'll answer all of your questions. But first I have a statement to make."

I wait until they're all ready, cameras jostling for position, mikes in my face, pens poised over notepads; then I take a deep breath.

"I'm the Production Coordinator on *POP STAR LIVE!* about whom you've already seen and heard too much. But I'm here to tell you the truth about the horrible allegations you aired earlier. They're all wrong."

I look around, trying to make eye contact with each reporter, with every blinking camera lens.

"Carlos is an incredible singer and an amazing man. He has too much integrity to become personally involved with one of the staff. And I would never do anything to hurt—or help—the chances of *any* of the contestants on this show. It's my job to take care of them, to keep them focused on realizing their dreams. And, let me tell you, it's a job I've tried really, really hard not to screw up."

I find Sam in the crowd and meet his gaze for strength.

"Because here's a little secret about me. I've always been a screwup. At jobs, at relationships, you name it. I always quit, because I never found anything worth fighting for. I just found the most wonderful man in the world, and I tried to run away from him. Well, you probably don't want to hear about me and Sam." Sam is smiling at me with all the warmth of his love in his eyes.

"But I've also found a job worth fighting for. I just got fired from the show because of these terrible allegations. Our boss thinks we can't recover from them. But let me tell you this: I don't agree. And I'm going to fight for our show. Because somehow, sometime, this show became about more than TV. *POP STAR LIVE!* is about making dreams come true. And if I can't fight for that, then I deserve to be fired."

I pull Mary Ann and Carlos in front of the cameras with me.

"This young man used to be in a gang; it's true. But he told me about it; he didn't hide it. He never committed a crime, and he got out. He wants to make a better life for himself and his mom and baby sister. Isn't that what this country is all about? Second chances? Bettering ourselves in spite of any obstacle life throws our way?"

I can see some of the reporters nodding; I'm reaching them.

"There are a lot of people who don't believe that. Who think our show is over, because America won't forgive Carlos for his childhood, for choices he was forced into. But I know that's wrong. I know this country is all about hope and hard work and striving to improve ourselves. So I'm asking you, America, to call your local TV station. Call your local radio station. Heck, call our show directly! Let us know that you agree."

I push Carlos in front of the mikes and nod to him.

"I'm Carlos Quintana. Yes, I was forced into a gang when I was a child, and the streets were too dangerous without protection. But singing for you is my chance to make a real life for myself and my family. Thank you for giving me that chance."

He ducks his head and backs away. The reporters call out questions, but I hold up a hand again.

"First, I'd like you to hear from Mary Ann Hawkins. She is, as of a few minutes ago, the official winner of *POP STAR LIVE!* per decree from our executive producer, who cut Carlos from the show. I haven't discussed this with Mary Ann yet, but I know her as a woman of integrity, too, and I'm betting this isn't how she wanted to win. Mary Ann?"

I gently pull her in front of the microphones, and she stands there, tears running down her face, and squares her shoulders.

"I will not win the competition this way. Carlos is an honorable man. So I'm begging you, America. Give Carlos a second chance to help his family make a better life for themselves. Give us a second chance to show you what quality television is all about. Do it for me, for Carlos, and for the American dreams we all share. Thank you."

Then we're all laughing and crying and hugging each other, and the reporters are shouting questions at us. Sam walks up behind me and hugs me and then shakes Carlos's hand and hugs Mary Ann.

As we answer questions in the glare of the camera lights, I feel peace and contentment wash over me. I did my best. I made a stand. No matter what happens after tonight, today is the day I finally grew up.

Chapter Thirty-five
Week Nine

$\mathcal{S}$am takes us all back to his hotel with him. I'm not usually a fan of the dramatic gesture, but I loved how he shoved Marshall away from me at the studio and told him to go do something anatomically impossible to himself. (Not how he actually said it, but I'm trying to cut back on the F word.)

Now Mary Ann is checked into the room next door for the long bubble bath and sleep she wanted, and the rest of us are all stretched out in chairs on the balcony of Sam's hotel room. We're drinking large quantities of anything we can find in the mini-bar and staring off into space.

Carlos keeps trying to apologize.

"Jules, I—"

"Shut up, Carlos. Don't you dare apologize to me. You're one of the best people I've ever known, and I won't have you belittle yourself to me. Shut up before I punch you."

"She means it, kid," Sam advises.

Carlos shakes his head and looks from me to Sam and back again. "What have you got that I don't, amigo?"

Sam smiles, showing a lot of teeth, and throws his arm around my shoulders. "Her."

"Shut up, both of you. I'm sick of this pee-in-the-snow crap. Carlos's life is probably ruined, and you're acting like teenagers with your first hard-ons. Who knows if our little press conference did any good." I open another mini-bottle of wine. Zinfandel this time.

I hate zinfandel.

Sam smiles at Carlos. "You a teenager when you got your first one?"

"Nope."

"Me, neither."

"Guess she's gonna be in for a surprise when she changes your son's diapers, man."

They both laugh, and I want to crack their heads together. We need to figure out—*son? Diapers?* I am *so* not ready for that.

Back to the subject at hand.

"We have to figure out a way to get Carlos back on the show. Appeal to Marshall's conscience. Something."

"He doesn't have a conscience, *querida*. But thanks for trying."

Sam lifts an eyebrow. "You might want to watch those terms of endearment around me, kid. She may not speak Spanish, but I do."

"You quit calling me kid, Methuselah, and it's a deal." Carlos grins a challenge.

Here we go again.

"I'm calling room service. I want a big, no, two big bottles of something that resembles real wine, instead of this fake Kool-Aid-flavored crap. Anybody want food?" I stand up and head for the phone.

No takers on the food. I order some anyway, just to spite Marshall, since it's our last night on his dime.

I think back to a very different experience with room service.

"You know, way back when Roger wanted to show me his testicle fungus, I should have gotten out of this show."

Two voices yell at me in unison. *"What?"*

"Oh, never mind. Long story, kind of like the bubonic plague thing." I plop back down in the chair. The room is swaying gently.

"It pisses me off. I finally find something I like, something I'm great at, and it's ruined by those two social outcasts. Bad press clings to you like tar in this town; nobody else in TV will hire me after this. I may as well buy Chef Francesca a new sauté pan and go for it."

Carlos looks at Sam. "Do you have any idea what the hell she's talking about?"

Sam stretches his legs out and slouches even further down in his chair. "Yep. Don't ask. Long story about a concussion and an Italian woman who's really from New Jersey. Please. Don't ask."

I look at him with one eye. I don't know why, but the room stops spinning so much with only one eye open. He gets points for listening and remembering that story. He's really kinda cute, in a blurry way. Oh, I almost forgot.

"Sam, I have to take your blood pressure, so I can tell Kirby the perfect HBP/LBP ratio. Hey! I haven't had to use my Sunday Stress Solution since we started having sex, either!"

Suddenly a horrible cacophony blasts through the room. My cell phone rings in my purse. Sam's cell phone rings from his belt; Carlos's cell does the same. The hotel room phone rings, and there's a knock on the door.

We stare at each other in stupefaction, not moving

to answer any of them, when a new noise chimes in.

Bzzzzz, bzzzzzz, bzzzzzz.

It's Sam's pager. We all crack up, right there in the middle of all those ringing phones and what must be the SWAT team banging on the door, from the sound of it.

Sam looks at his pager.

"It's Marshall."

I look at my cell caller ID.

"Mine, too."

"Mine's Joe," says Carlos.

"Let me in, RIGHT NOW," shouts Norman from the other side of the door.

I run to the door, ignoring the phones for a while longer.

"Norman, I always loved you like a brother. You're the Luke to my Princess Leia; you know, not the early part, but the part with the little fuzzy teddy bears, where she says she's his sister." I throw my arms around his neck and burst into tears.

"You mean the Ewoks? Jules, are you OK?" He's patting my back.

"Yeeeesssss. You're my little bittle Ewok, Normie," I wail.

"OK, that's enough, Princess Leia." Sam is unpeeling my arms from around Norman's neck.

"'Normie' is going to tell us why he's here, and you're going to drink some coffee." He snatches my almost-empty wineglass out of my grasp, leaving me staring at my empty hand in surprise.

Guess that zinfandel packs a punch, too.

"The heck with that. I want more WINE. Where is that room service guy? Hey, Normie, remember when you stopped by my room in Reno, and Roger was there and I was holding my panties? That room service guy was late, too." I smile goofily.

The phones are still blaring, but now I notice that everybody is staring at me.

"Your panties, Jules?" Sam says, rather grimly for somebody with four eyes and two noses. Oh, no, I guess that's me.

"Oh, another long story. Fungus. Nasty. Just chafing, really. But then we had to rhyme British penises with Kirby. And humongous. Which, coincidentally, does. Rhyme, I mean," I conclude triumphantly, and then trip over my own feet and land on the bed, face-down.

What the hell. While I'm down here, I think I'll take a little nap.

"Oh, no, you don't, Sleeping Beauty." Sam is rolling me over. Am I really sure I love this guy? He's awfully bossy.

"Will somebody answer the phone?" he barks. Norman rushes for the hotel phone, and Carlos opens his. Mine, mercifully, stops ringing.

Then it starts again. I look at it. Marshall again.

"OK, Mr. Never, Ever Call Me on My Personal Cell. Here's what I think of you." I stand up and very carefully make my way to the bathroom and close the door.

Sam is at the door really, really fast. "Jules, are you sick? Do you need help?"

"Nope and nope. And don't worry about your shoes, this time." I flush the toilet once, then again, then turn the door knob and walk out.

"Um, Jules, don't you need to wash your hands, dude?" Norman looks embarrassed.

"What? Oh. No, I didn't pee, Normie. I flushed the six-hundred-dollar cell phone the show gave me down the toilet. Twice." I collapse on the bed in giggles, and Norman rushes to the bathroom.

Hey, I'm giggling. I might have something in common with Amber after all.

"Oh, dude. I think the phone busted something." Norman sounds freaked out.

We all look at the door to the bathroom, where a rapidly advancing wave of water is pouring out onto the carpet.

"Oops," I say, grinning at Sam. I know this should be embarrassing but, really, how embarrassed can I be over a broken toilet, considering the past few months?

Sam looks at me, then at the water, then back at me. Then he throws himself on the bed next to me and howls with laughter.

"Hurricane Jules strikes again! Now we have, we have f-f-flooding!" He's laughing so hard, he's gasping for air, his cell unnoticed on the floor where he dropped it.

Carlos cracks up. He's bent over at the waist and clutching his stomach, he's laughing so hard.

Norman looks at the three of us and starts laughing, too.

I lean over and pick up Sam's phone.

"Hello? Nuthouse Central, may we help you?"

"Jules? Is that you? Where the fuck have you been? Is Carlos with you? Turn on the TV right now!"

I look at the phone, considering flushing it, too. The water flooding out of the bathroom has slowed down, but I don't really feel like wading through it.

I hand the phone to Sam and reach for the TV remote.

"Hey, look what's on Pay Per View. Where the hell is our food and wine? We can watch a movie and have a party."

Sam gently takes the remote out of my fingers. He's on the phone. Wonder who called?

"What channel, Marshall?"

Oh, right. Butthead Boy.

And there it is. Carlos is on CNN.

"Hey, that's me!" I'm on CNN, too. It's a clip of some of the finalists and me walking into Banana Republic. I miss shopping.

Wonder if I'll get to keep my new clothes? Nobody else would fit them, and . . .

"Jules! Listen!" Carlos is waving at the screen wildly.

". . . *POP STAR LIVE!* finalist Mary Ann Hawkins, in a follow-up press conference to tonight's shocker from two former contestants on the show . . ."

Mary Ann is onscreen, live.

". . . help his family make a better life for themselves. Give us a second chance to show you what quality television is all about. Do it for me, for Carlos, and for the American dreams we all share. Thank you."

"In other news, the trial of suspected NFL . . ."

Click.

We all stare at each other. I'm suddenly a little more sober. There's a knock on the door.

Norman lets the room service guy in, even though the guy's a little squirrelly about the water. I mean, it *did* stop flooding.

I sit up straighter. "Take the wine back. We'll pay for it, but get it out of here. Bring a pot of coffee. No, two pots of coffee. Lots of cream and sugar. Lots. None of this two packets per cup crap. There's fifty bucks in it for you if you have it back here in ten minutes. Leave the food."

Sam jumps up and gives him a twenty and signs the receipt. I point to Norman.

"You. Call the front desk and get somebody to fix the toilet."

I turn to Carlos. "You. You may be back, baby." I

shriek and jump in his arms to hug him fiercely.

Carlos returns my embrace, then holds me out at arm's length. He looks at Sam over my shoulder.

"I don't envy you this one, Blake. You're going to need a lot of patience. And never, ever let her drink."

Sam laughs. "Who needs a sunny day when you can have Hurricane Jules?"

Squawking noises are still coming from Sam's cell, abandoned on the bed. I pick it up.

"Hello? Oh, hi, Marshall. Can we help you with something?"

"It's Marshall," I tell everyone.

"Jules, Jules, do NOT put the phone back down. I want you all back in here. We need to plan a strategy meeting right now. The networks are all over this; CNN, the papers, too. *USA Today* just called. *A Boy from the projects trying to improve his life: the American dream come true.* It's fucking brilliant, Jules. You're a genius. We're going to blast so far up in the ratings, they'll need a telescope to find us." He makes a weird sound that's a cross between a victory yell and some kind of Marine hoo-yah thing.

"What are you waiting for, Jules? Get off the damn phone and get down here. We have to plan! We have to strategize! And prioritize! Well? Jules? Jules??"

I smile and think about it for a few seconds. It would be so wonderfully satisfying to tell him to take his job and shove it.

For about two minutes.

Then I'd spend the rest of my life regretting not being part of the big finish. Not being there for two people I'd come to love: Carlos, whose first instinct, in spite of seeing his hopes crash down on his head, was to protect me; and Mary Ann, the country girl with the courage and integrity to face down Marshall and half the reporters in the city.

"Marshall wants me back. He wants us all back," I announce to everyone.

"Dude, that's what I've been trying to tell you since I got here," Norman says in exasperation.

Sam looks at me intently. "What are you going to do, sweetheart?"

I lean forward and kiss him on the mouth, hard. "Sam Blake, I love you. I love you for *asking* me what I'm going to do, and not trying to *tell* me. I love you for putting up with the chaos and disasters that follow us around. And I really, really love you for that thing with the maple syrup."

Sam clears his throat, but he's grinning like a loon. "Um, Jules, perhaps we could talk about maple syrup when the room isn't so crowded and your—boss?—isn't on the phone.

"Right. Good idea. Where is that coffee?"

The cell phone starts squawking again.

"Oh, yeah. Marshall."

I put the phone to my ear.

"Marshall. Marshall, shut up and listen. Yes, we're coming back. But you're giving me a raise. And Norman gets a raise, too. And Joe gets a raise *and* a promotion. He's been putting up with your rookie hires for long enough. What? No, we're not negotiating. Put up or shut up."

I stick my tongue out at the phone. Still a teensy part of that growing-up process going on, I guess.

I listen again. "Yeah? OK, it's a deal. We'll see you tomorrow for that meeting. No way. We need food and coffee right now." I take the remote back from Sam, who's been tossing it from hand to hand.

"And we need to watch *The Lord of the Rings*. I'm in the mood for a good swordfight or thirty. Good night, Marshall. Oh, and Marshall?" I start laughing.

"Never, ever call me on my personal cell. I just flushed it. Bye."

When the room service guy gets back with our coffee, on the run to beat my deadline and earn fifty bucks, he stops dead in the doorway and stares. All four of us are draped over various pieces of furniture, laughing so hard I'm expecting somebody to pee him or herself any minute.

The room service guy gingerly picks his way through the flooded room, as the engineering staff from the hotel shows up behind him. He carefully arranges the coffee tray on the table, as I try to grab my purse. Sam hands him a fifty, and he takes it and pauses.

"I gotta get some of whatever you guys are on."

Chapter Thirty-six

POP STAR LIVE! *AND THE WINNER IS . . .*

It doesn't matter who wins. It doesn't matter who wins.

I say it, but I know I'm kidding myself. Twenty-four million votes say it matters. A big, fat contract at KCM Records to the winner—worth a million bucks, minimum—says it matters. Lurking backstage, I split my attention between the only two men who've seen me naked in the past two years. Well, with the lights on, anyway.

One onstage, one in the front row.

I'm as caught up in the drama as anyone else in the country. More, maybe. I'm part of it. Me. Jules Vernon. *People* magazine's Face Behind Reality TV.

What a joke.

"And, finally, the name we've waited all these long weeks to hear. America's new *POP STAR LIVE!* is—"

"STOP! HOLD EVERYTHING!!" Q leaps onstage. "I have an announcement to make."

We all groan. Everybody. The crew. Marshall. Joe and Norman. Roger and Nellie. The entire studio audience. I imagine millions of households across America, all groaning. The collective groan can probably be heard from space.

If aliens attack our planet, it will be Q's fault.

Roger stands up. "What's the damn announcement, already, you blathering idiot? If it's about your tour, we know and nobody cares. If it's that you're gay, just say it and get it over with. Frankly, most of couldn't care less who you're tossing in the sheets with. So just get on with it and get the hell off the bloody stage!"

Nellie stands up and leads the audience in a standing ovation. Then, in what may be the most shocking moment in the history of the show, Nellie's assistant yells at her boss.

"Sit down and shut up and let the man talk!"

Nellie is so blown away she actually does.

Go, girl!

Q says something, but nobody can hear it. So he starts yelling.

"SHUT UP! I'M NOT GAY, you moron. I'm not coming out of the closet. I'm coming out of this rap star idiocy. I'm coming out as A CLASSICAL PIANIST!!"

He pushes the host out of the way and strides over to the piano, still carrying the mike.

"I'm a classical pianist and I LOVE RACHMANI-NOFF. Now listen, you musical lackwits. This is Rachmaninoff's Piano Concerto No. 2 in C-Minor. Listen and weep."

And we do. Or at least I do.

I weep for the thundering majesty of the music as it soars through the hall.

And I weep with the love I feel so completely both for and from the wonderful man sitting in the front row, his dad on one side, mine on the other. I'll finally meet Sam's dad tonight, with his son's ring on my finger.

With thankfulness that my own father is healthy and

whole, and that he found a new love. And for my mother, so graciously sitting next to Amber. Mom, who supports me always.

I weep with gratitude for my friends, old and new. For Kirby and Jerry, in the second row of the audience, here to cheer for me on our big night.

And for Norman and Joe, standing next to me, shuffling their feet, no doubt wishing to be anywhere else.

And for—

"All right, already. Stop that damn sniveling. *Women!*"

Joe has a way of cutting right through sentimental nonsense.

I blow my nose, hugely, as Q brings his abbreviated version of the magnificent concerto to a close. Everybody takes a deep breath.

We cut to commercial.

Marshall is jumping up and down with glee. "That couldn't have gone better if I'd planned it. Did you see the faces of those network suits in the front row? They were eating it up. This is going to be all over the news tomorrow. Hell, tonight, even! Could my life get any better? *Could* it?" He chortles his way back to the monitors.

A sibilant hiss sounds in my ear. Actually, about shoulder level.

It's Nellie.

"Don't get too comfortable, Jules. Marshall and I took KC out to dinner last night, and I told him about your mother's pornography. I hope you enjoy tonight's show—it's going to be your last."

I stare at her as she rushes back to her seat before the cameras go live.

Fired. It can't be. It can't be. Not after everything. Not now.

I feel like I'm going to vomit, and shove my fist against my mouth. As I stand there, my brief career in television flashes in front of my eyes and I laugh bitterly.

Oh well. What the hell. It was fun while it lasted. Tonight is about Mary Ann and Carlos.

I take a deep breath and focus my attention on my final two contestants. *Here we go.*

The short commercial break is over, and our confused host tries again.

"And, finally, the name we've waited all these long weeks to hear. America's new *POP STAR LIVE!* is MARY ANN HAWKINS!!"

The crowd goes insane, and Carlos grabs Mary Ann in a huge hug. I search his face, and see nothing but happiness for her. She's crying and laughing, and Marshall runs up behind us and drags us all out onstage. Norman and I rush to hug Mary Ann and Carlos, and Joe walks to the other side of the stage to lead a man in a shiny neon-blue suit to the center of the stage.

Blue-suit Man takes the mike.

"Hello? Is this thing on? I have an announcement of my own."

The Texas twang in his voice gives him away. That's the President, CEO, and Chairman of the Board of KCM Records, here to award the million-dollar contract to Mary Ann. My heart is bursting with joy for her, even as it breaks for Carlos.

"We've been following the goings-on of this here show pretty closely, considering our stake in the outcome. I gotta tell you, at KCM Records, we don't love nothin' more than somebody with heart. Heck, I grew up on a dirt farm in south Texas and never had more'n one pair of shoes at a time. Anyway, what I'm trying to say is, we're going double or nothing here."

He throws an arm around Mary Ann and another around a confused Carlos.

"We're hereby awarding not one, but *two* million-dollar contracts tonight. One to each of these fine performers. And if you want to help me make these American dreams come true, you at home and you here tonight, you rush out and buy their CDs just as soon as they're in stores. Heck, buy a couple of them! Now, let's hear it for Mary Ann and Carlos, future platinum record holders!"

Understanding and joy break over Carlos's face like the sun over the white sands of his home state. He shakes Blue Suit's hand, pumping it up and down furiously until the man laughs and gently disengages his hand.

Mary Ann bursts into a fresh wave of tears and throws herself into Carlos's arms. "I'm so happy for you. I'm so happy for both of us."

As he hugs her and strokes her hair, I wonder. Mary Ann and Carlos? Maybe I could just . . .

Then Sam is leaping on stage and running up to swing me up into a huge hug.

"You did it, Hurricane Jules. You did it. You made Happily Ever After out of utter chaos. You're my hero." He kisses me, hard, and smiles down at my dazed face.

"Hey, snap out of it. You need to go congratulate your winners."

They *are*. My winners, that is.

And so I do.

As I rush past KC in his blue suit, I try not to look at him, afraid my bitterness will show on my face. I don't want to ruin a single moment for Carlos and Mary Ann.

A big hand reaches out to stop me. I look up into

the eyes of the man who splattered my future under his size-thirteen cowboy boots.

"Hey, Ms. Vernon. I wanted to talk to you."

I yank my arm out of his grasp.

"KC, or Mr. Records, or whatever you go by, I don't think we have anything to talk about. I don't work for the show anymore, thanks to you, so I don't have any obligation to listen to your puritanical drivel, do I?"

I can't believe my courage. No job, but finally a backbone. Hey, whaddaya know?

I sigh.

Mr. Big doesn't give up, though. "Um, er, Ms. Vernon. About that job . . . Well. My wife said she'd kick my heinie to Dallas and back, if I even thought about firing you. My little lady teaches feminist theory at UT and thinks your mom is about the most brilliant writer since . . . since . . . well, in a long time. Plus, Marshall gave me an earful about how talented you are. So, congratulations on a great job."

He grins at my obvious shock.

"KCM is in for the next season of *POP STAR LIVE!* if you are. What do you say, Jules? For nothin' else, how about just to piss Nellie off?" He winks at me, and I just can't help it. I have to hug him.

"Yes! Thanks so much! I'd love to. Please tell your wife that I'll try to get my mom to come down and talk to her class or autograph books or something. You're the best!"

I'm babbling again, but I don't care. I thank him again and turn to Carlos and Mary Ann and tackle them both in a flying leap. As we fall down the stage, arms and legs everywhere, I hear Sam laughing.

"Hurricane Jules strikes again."

Much, much later, when everyone has gone to their respective houses, hotel rooms, or wherever, Sam and

I lie side by side, hand in hand, in my bed at Contestant Mansion and stare at the ceiling.

"You know, Jules, champagne makes me horny."

"Sam, breathing makes you horny." I laugh.

"Only around you." He rolls over to face me.

"Jules, I have a proposition for you."

I start laughing harder, thinking of Roger's job offer in the conference room. "I hope *this* one is personal, at least."

"What?"

"Nothing. Just remembering another touchdown of Hurricane Jules. What's your proposition?"

"Blake and Sons are in the running to do set design on a movie in Hollywood in the spring. You'll be on hiatus from the show, and I wondered if you'd like to come to work with me. Or I bet you could get a job with the movie, now that you're so famous."

"That sounds wonderful, Sam," I say idly as I concentrate on unbuttoning his shirt.

"What's the movie?"

"I don't know. Some mystery about an archaeologist. Professor Maxwell does something or other. Sounds fun, though. Hey, don't stop now!"

I look at him, my hands frozen in place on his shirt. Then I start laughing again and keep unbuttoning. "You know, Sam, I bet I can get a job on that movie set, too."

Then there's a lot of kissing and touching, and more kissing, as Sam and I work on our very own version of the American dream.

Reality-TV style.